THE COLD DISH

D0531362

By Craig Johnson

Walt Longmire Mysteries

Craig Johnson is the author of eleven novels and a collection of short stories in the Walt Longmire mystery series, which has garnered popular and critical acclaim. Among other awards, *The Cold Dish* was a Dilys Award finalist and the French edition won Le Prix du Polar Nouvel Observateur/BibliObs; *The Dark Horse*, the fifth in the series, was a *Publishers Weekly* Best Book of the Year; *Junkyard Dogs* won the Watson Award for a mystery novel with the best sidekick, and *Hell Is Empty*, selected by *Library Journal* as the Best Mystery of the Year, was a *New York Times* bestseller, as was *As the Crow Flies*. The Walt Longmire series is the basis for the hit TV drama *Longmire*, shown on TCM in the UK and starring Robert Taylor, Lou Diamond Phillips and Katee Sackhoff. Craig Johnson lives in Ucross, Wyoming, population twenty-five.

CRAIG JOHNSON
THE
COLD DISH

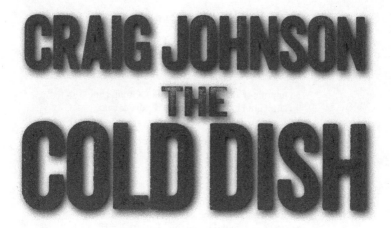

An Orion book

First published in the United States in 2006
by the Penguin Group USA (Inc.)
This paperback edition published in 2015
by Orion Books,
an imprint of The Orion Publishing Group Ltd,
Carmelite House, 50 Victoria Embankment,
London EC4Y 0DZ

An Hachette UK company

3 5 7 9 10 8 6 4 2

A CIP catalogue record for this book is
available from the British Library

ISBN 978 1 4091 5903 2

Printed and bound by CPI Group (UK) Ltd, Croydon, CR0 4YY

The Orion Publishing Group's Policy is to use papers that
are natural, renewable and recyclable products and
made from wood grown in sustainable forests. The logging
and manufacturing processes are expected to conform to
the environmental regulations of the country of origin.

www.orionbooks.co.uk

ACKNOWLEDGMENTS

A writer, like a sheriff, is the embodiment of a group of people and, without their support, both are in a tight spot. I have been fortunate to be blessed with a close order of friends and associates who have made this book possible. They know who they are and, as the tradition goes, you can never thank a good cast too much.

Thanks to Sheriff Larry Kirkpatrick for a quarter of a century of fighting the good fight, the Wyoming Division of Criminal Investigation's Sandy Mays and Harry's pizza, which isn't so bad. To Henry Standing Bear for the magic and more, Marcus Red Thunder for the sweat, Charles Little Old Man for the words, Dorothy Caldwell Kisling for the stimulation, Donna Dubrow for the motivation, and Gail Hochman for the belief. To Kathryn Court, Clare Farraro, Sarah Manges, and Ali Bothwell Mancini, my ferocious pride of lionesses at Viking Penguin.

Finally, to my wife and muse Judy all the love in the world for greeting my daily reappearance from Absaroka County with patience and good humor. I would be Walt without you.

For the dairy princess of Wayne County
and the crack shot of Cabell . . .

Revenge is a dish best served cold.
—Pierre Ambroise François
Choderlos de La Clos,
Les Liaisons Dangereuses

1

"Bob Barnes says they got a dead body out on BLM land. He's on line one."

She might have knocked, but I didn't hear it because I was watching the geese. I watch the geese a lot in the fall, when the days get shorter and the ice traces the rocky edges of Clear Creek. The sheriff's office in our county is an old Carnegie building that my department inherited when the Absaroka County Library got so many books they had to go live somewhere else. We've still got the painting of Andy out in the landing of the entryway. Every time the previous sheriff left the building he used to salute the old robber baron. I've got the large office in the south side bay, which allows me an unobstructed view of the Big Horn Mountains to my right and the Powder River Valley to my left. The geese fly down the valley south, with their backs to me, and I usually sit with my back to the window, but occasionally I get caught with my chair turned; this seems to be happening more and more, lately.

I looked at her, looking being one of my better law-enforcement techniques. Ruby's a tall woman, slim, with a direct manner and clear blue eyes that tend to make people nervous. I like that in a receptionist/dispatcher, keeps the riffraff out of the office. She leaned against the doorjamb and went to shorthand, "Bob Barnes, dead body, line one."

I looked at the blinking red light on my desk and wondered vaguely if there was a way I could get out of this. "Did he sound drunk?"

"I am not aware that I've ever heard him sound sober."

I flipped the file and pictures that I'd been studying onto my chest and punched line one and the speakerphone button. "Hey, Bob. What's up?"

"Hey, Walt. You ain't gonna believe this shit. . . ." He didn't sound particularly drunk, but Bob's a professional, so you never can tell. He was silent for a moment. "Hey, no shit, we got us a cool one out here."

I winked at Ruby. "Just one, huh?"

"Hey, I ain't shittin' you. Billy was movin' some of Tom Chatham's sheep down off the BLM section to winter pasture, and them little bastards clustered around somethin' in one of the draws. . . . We got a cool one."

"You didn't see it?"

"No. Billy did."

"Put him on."

There was a brief jostling of the phone, and a younger version of Bob's voice answered, "Hey, Shuuriff."

Slurred speech. Great. "Billy, you say you saw this body?"

"Yeah, I did."

"What'd it look like?"

Silence for a moment. "Looked like a body."

I thought about resting my head on my desk. "Anybody we know?"

"Oh, I didn't get that close."

Instead, I pushed my hat farther up on my head and sighed. "How close did you get?"

"Couple hundred yards. It gets steep in the draws where the water flow cuts through that little valley. The sheep stayed all clustered around whatever it is. I didn't want to take my truck up there 'cause I just got it washed."

I studied the little red light on the phone until I realized he was not going to go on. "No chance of this being a dead ewe or lamb?" Wouldn't be a coyote, with the other sheep milling around. "Where are you guys?"

" 'Bout a mile past the old Hudson Bridge on 137."

"All right, you hang on. I'll get somebody out there in a half hour or so."

"Yes sir. . . . Hey, Shuuriff?" I waited. "Dad says for you to bring beer, we're almost out."

2

"You bet." I punched the button and looked at Ruby. "Where's Vic?"

"Well, she's not sitting in her office looking at old reports."

"Where is she, please?" Her turn to sigh and, never looking at me directly, she walked over, took the worn manila folder from my chest, and returned it to the filing cabinet where she always returns it when she catches me studying it.

"Don't you think you should get out of the office sometime today?" She continued to look at the windows.

I thought about it. "I am not going out 137 to look at dead sheep."

"Vic's down the street, directing traffic."

"We've only got one street. What's she doing that for?"

"Electricals for the Christmas decorations."

"It's not even Thanksgiving."

"It's a city council thing."

I had put her on that yesterday and promptly forgot about it. I had a choice: I could either go out to 137, drink beer, and look at dead sheep with a drunk Bob Barnes and his half-wit son or go direct traffic and let Vic show me how displeased she was with me. "We got any beer in the refrigerator?"

"No."

I pulled my hat down straight and told Ruby that if anybody else called about dead bodies, we had already filled the quota for a Friday and they should call back next week. She stopped me by mentioning my daughter, who was my singular ray of sunshine. "Tell Cady I said hello and for her to call me."

This was suspicious. "Why?" She dismissed me with a wave of her hand. My finely honed detecting skills told me something was up, but I had neither the time nor the energy to pursue it.

I jumped in the Silver Bullet and rolled through the drive-through at Durant Liquor to pick up a sixer of Rainier. No sense having the county support Bob Barnes's bad habits with a full six-pack, so I screwed off one of the tops and took a swig. Ah, mountain fresh. I was going to have to drive by Vic and let her let me know how pissed off she was bound to be, so I pulled out onto Main Street, joined the three-car traffic jam, and looked into the outstretched palm of Deputy Victoria Moretti.

Vic was a career patrol person from an extended family of patrol people back in South Philadelphia. Her father was a cop, her uncles were cops, and her brothers were cops. The problem was that her husband was not a cop. He was a field engineer for Consolidated Coal and had gotten transferred to Wyoming to work at a mine about halfway between here and the Montana border. When he accepted the new position a little less than two years ago, she gave it all up and came out with him. She listened to the wind, played housewife for about two weeks, and then came into the office to apply for a job.

She didn't look like a cop, least not like the ones we have out here. I figured she was one of those artists who had received a grant from the Crossroads Foundation, the ones that lope up and down the county roads in their $150 running shoes and their New York Yankee ball caps. I'd lost one of my regular deputies, Lenny Rowell, to the Highway Patrol. I could have brought Turk up from Powder Junction but that had appealed to me as much as gargling razor blades. It wasn't that Turk was a bad deputy; it's just that all that rodeo-cowboy bullshit wore me out, and I didn't like his juvenile temper. Nobody else from in county had applied for the job, so I had done her a favor and let her fill out an application.

I read the *Durant Courant* while she sat out in the reception room scribbling on the front and back of the damn form for half an hour. Her writing fist began to shake and by the time she was done, her face had turned a lively shade of granite. She flipped the page onto Ruby's desk, hissed "Fuck this shit," and walked out. We called all her references, from field investigators in ballistics to the Philadelphia Chief of Police. Her credentials were hard to argue with: top 5 percent out of the academy, bachelor's in law enforcement from Temple University with nineteen credit hours toward her master's, a specialty in ballistics, two citations, and four years street duty. She was on the fast track, and next year she would've made detective. I'd have been pissed, too.

I had driven out to the address that she'd given me, a little house trailer near the intersection of both highways with nothing but bare dirt and scrub sage all around it. There was a Subaru with Pennsylvania plates and a GO OWLS bumper sticker, so I figured I was in the right place. When I got up to the steps, she already had the door open and was looking at me through the screen. "Yeah?"

I was married for a quarter century and I've got a lawyer for a daughter, so I knew how to deal with these situations: Stay close to the bone, nothing but the facts, ma'am. I crossed my arms, leaned on her railing, and listened to it squeal as the sheet metal screws tried to pull loose from the doublewide's aluminum skin. "You want this job?"

"No." She looked past me toward the highway. She didn't have any shoes on, and her toes were clutching the threadbare carpet like cat's claws in an attempt to keep her from spinning off into the ether. She was a little below average height and weight, olive complexion, with short black hair that kind of stood up in pure indignity. She'd been crying, and her eyes were the color of tarnished gold, and the only thing I could think of doing was to open the screen door and hold her. I had had a lot of problems of my own of late, and I figured we could both just stand there and cry for a while.

I looked down at my brown rough-outs and watched the dirt glide across the porch in underlining streaks. "Nice wind we've been having." She didn't say a word. "Hey, you want my job?"

She laughed. "Maybe."

We both smiled. "Well, you can have it in about four years, but right now I need a deputy." She looked out at the highway again. "But I need a deputy who isn't going to run off to Pittsburgh in two weeks." That got her attention.

"Philadelphia."

"Whatever." With that, I got all the tarnished gold I could handle.

"Do I have to wear one of those goofy cowboy hats like you?"

I glanced up at the brim of my hat and then back down to her for effect. "Not unless you want to."

She cocked her head past me, nodding to the Bullet. "Do I get a Batmobile like that to drive around in?"

"You bet."

That had been the first dissemblance of many to come.

I took a big swig and finished off the first Rainier beer and popped it back in the carton. I could see the muscles in her jaw flex like biceps. I made her knock on the window before I rolled it down. "What's the problem, officer?"

She looked pointedly at her watch. "It's 4:37, where the hell are you going?"

I relaxed back into the big bucket seat. "Close enough. I'm going home." She just stood there, waiting. It was one of her best talents, asking questions and just standing there, waiting for an answer. "Oh, Bob Barnes called, says they got a dead body out between Jim Keller's place and Bureau of Land Management."

She yanked her head back and showed me a canine tooth. "They saw a dead body. Yeah, and I'm a fucking Chinese fighter pilot."

"Uh huh, looks like the big sheepocide we've all been waiting for." It was the shank of the afternoon, and the one beer was already helping to improve my mood. The sky was still a VistaVision blue, but there was a large cloud bank to the northwest that was just beginning to obscure the mountains. The nearer clouds were fluffy and white, but the backdrop was a darker, bruised color that promised scattered snow at high altitudes.

"You look like hammered shit."

I gave her a look out of the side of my eye. "You wanna go out there?"

"It's on your way home."

"No, it's past there, out on 137."

"It's still a lot closer to you, and seeing as you're going home early . . ."

The wind was beginning to pick up. I was going to have to go long on this one. "Well, if you don't want to . . ."

6

She gave me another look. "You have done nothing but sit in your office, on your ass, all day."

"I'm not feeling real well, think I might be getting the flu or something."

"Maybe you should go out and get some exercise. How much do you weigh now? Two-sixty?"

"You have a mean streak." She continued to look at me. "Two-fifty-three." It sounded better than two-fifty-five.

She stared at my left shoulder in deep concentration, juggling the evening that she must have had planned. "Glen isn't coming home till late." She looked at herself in the side-view mirror and instantly looked away. "Where are they?"

"On 137, about a mile past the old Hudson Bridge." This was working out pretty well. "They're in Billy's truck." She started to push off and walk away. "They wanted you to pick up some beer on your way out."

She turned and tapped a finger on the passenger door. "If I was going to bring them beer, I would take that depleted six-pack in the seat beside you, mister. You know, we have an open container law in this state."

I watched her man-walk with the sixteen-shot automatic bouncing on her hip. "Hey, I try and have an open container with me no matter what state I'm in." She was smiling when she slammed the door of her five-year-old unit. It's good when you can bring unbridled happiness to your fellow workers. I nosed the three-quarter ton out to the west side of town, and Vic must've passed me doing an even eighty, sirens and lights all going full blast. She gave me the finger as she went by.

I had to smile. It was Friday, I had five beers in attendance, and my daughter was supposed to call this evening. I drove out through Wolf Valley and ignored the scattered, out-of-state vehicles parked illegally along the road. During the latter part of hunting season, my part of the high plains becomes a Disneyland for every overage boy with a high-powered toy. Instead, I watched the clouds slowly eat the

Bighorn Mountains. There was a little early snow up there, and the setting sun was fading it from a kind of frozen blue to a subtle glow of purple. I had lived here my entire life, except for college in California and a stint in the marines in Vietnam. I had thought about those mountains the entire time I was gone and swore that a day wouldn't go by when I got back that I wouldn't look at them. Most of the time, I remembered.

By the time I got out to Crossroads there was a fine silting of confectionery snow blowing across the road and falling through the sage and range grass. The shadows were long when I stopped at the mailbox. There was nothing but a Doctor Leonard's Healthcare sale catalog, which scared me it was so interesting. I navigated the irrigation ditch and drove up to the house.

Martha had grown up on her family ranch, some couple thousand-odd acres near Powder Junction, and had always hated being a townie. So, three years ago, we bought a little land off the Foundation, got one of those piles of logs they call a kit, drilled a well, and planted a septic tank. We sold the house in town, because Martha was in such a hurry to get out of it, and lived in a trailer I had borrowed from Henry Standing Bear, owner of the Red Pony and my oldest friend. By the fall, we had her all closed in and the heat on. Then Martha died.

I parked the truck on the gravel, pulled out the beer, and walked on the two-by-twelves over the mud that led up to the door. I'd been meaning to get some grass seed, but the snow kept putting an end to that. I pushed the door open and stepped up from the cinder block onto the plywood floor. The place still needed a little work. There were some interior walls but most were just studs and, when you turned the bare bulbs on, the light slipped through the wooden bars and made patterns on the floor. The electricals weren't done, so I had two four-ways plugged into the box and everything just ran into them. The plumbing was done, but I used a shower curtain as a bathroom door; consequently, I didn't get many visitors. There was a prewar, Henry F. Miller baby grand that had belonged to my mother-in-law, on which I had been known to pound out a little boogie-woogie, but I hadn't played it since Martha had died. I had my books all stacked in beer boxes near the back wall and, the Christmas before last in a fit of holiday optimism, Cady and I had gone out and bought a floor lamp, an easy chair, and a Sony Trinitron color television. The lamp and easy chair worked really well, whereas the TV did not. Without a dish, the only thing you could pick up was Channel 12 with snow for a picture and a soothing hiss for sound. I watched it religiously.

I had the phone set up on a cardboard box next to the chair so I wouldn't have to get up to answer it, and I had a cooler on the other side for the beer. I threw my coat and hat on the boxes, switched on my lamp, and sat down in my chair with Doctor Leonard in my lap. I flipped the catalog open to page three and pondered a genuine artificial sheepskin cover made for all standard recliners. I glanced up at the stacked log walls and tried to decide between the available ivory and the rich chestnut. Didn't really matter. After four years, I had yet to make any truly decisive steps in interior decor. Perhaps Doctor Leonard's machine-washable polyester acrylic fleece was my *Iliad*. This thought was unsettling enough to motivate the fourth beer, which was only slightly warmer than the first three. I screwed off the top, pinching it between thumb and forefinger, and tossed it into the drywall bucket that served as my only trash can. I thought about calling the Doc's 1-800 number but was afraid that I might block Cady's call. She had tried to get me to get call waiting, but I figured I got interrupted enough during the course of a day and didn't need to pay for the privilege at home. I hit the remote and surfed from automatic four to destination twelve: ghost TV. It was my favorite show, the one where the different-sized blobs moved around in a blizzard and didn't make too much noise. Gave me plenty of time to think.

I retraced the well-worn path of my thoughts to the report that had been lying on my chest when Ruby had come into the office. I didn't really need the actual file. I had every scrap of paper in it memorized. There is a black-and-white photograph that I had cropped down, the kind we use to attach a person to a particular brand of misery. Place photo here. The background is a vacant white, broken only by the shadow of an electric conduit, no proper venue for intimacy such as this. In another setting, the portrait might have been a Curtis or a Remington.

Melissa is Northern Cheyenne. In the photograph, she has dark stalks of healthy hair arching to her shoulders, but there are small discolorations there and at her throat, multiple bruises, and a contusion at the jawline. I hear noises when I summon up these wounds. To the trained eye, her features might appear a touch too small, like the petals on a bud not yet opened. Her almond-shaped eyes are unreadable. I keep remembering those eyes and the epicanthic folds at the inner corners. There are no tears. She could have been some half-Asian model in one of those ridiculously perfumed glamour magazines, but she is that poor Little Bird girl who was led into a basement and gang-raped by four teenage boys who didn't care that she had fetal alcohol syndrome.

Three years ago. After all the proceedings and counterproceedings, filings and counterfilings, the case went to court in May. I remember because the sage was blooming, and the smell hurt the inside of my nose. The girl in the photo had fidgeted and twisted in her seat, sighed, placed her hands over her eyes, then pulled her fingers through her hair. She crossed her legs and shifted her weight and laid her head, facedown, on the witness stand.

"Confused . . ." That's all she said, "Confused . . ."

There are other photographs in the file, color ones I'd clipped from the Durant High School yearbook. In a fit of comic relief, I had left the blurbs from their yearbook attached to the pictures: Cody Pritchard, football, track; Jacob and George Esper, fraternal twins in birth as well as football, tie-and-fly club, and Future Farmers of America; and Bryan Keller, football, golf, debate, student council, honor roll.

They had inserted a broomstick into her, a bottle, and a fungo bat.

I was the reluctant investigating officer, and I had known Mary Roebling since we were kids. Mary teaches English at Durant High School and is the girls' basketball coach. She said she had asked

Melissa Little Bird about the marks on her face and arms but couldn't seem to get a straight answer. Later, Melissa complained about abdominal pains and blood in her urine. When Mary demanded to know what had happened, Melissa said that she had sworn that she wouldn't tell. She was worried that she might hurt the boys' feelings.

Ruby says I get the file out about once a week since the trial. She says it's unhealthy.

At Mary Roebling's request, I went to the high school in the afternoon during basketball practice. While the girls ran laps, I took off my badge, cuffs, and gun and placed them in my hat behind her desk. I sat in the office and played with the pencils until I became aware of the two of them standing in the doorway. Mary was about six even and had told me quite frankly that the only reason she had gone to the junior prom with me was because I was one of the only boys in class who was taller than she. She towered over the Little Bird girl and kept her from backing though the door by placing her hands on Melissa's shoulders. The young Indian was coated in a youthful glean of sweat and, if not for the marks on her face and shoulders and the effects of fetal alcohol syndrome, looked like she had just been freshly minted. I held up one of the American Number Two pencils and said, "I can't figure out how they get the lead on the inside." To my surprise, her face became suddenly dark as she contemplated the issue. "I figure they got these trees that have the lead already in them." Her face brightened in the relief of having the riddle solved.

"You're the sheriff." Her voice was childlike and carried all the trust in the world. I was back twenty-five years with Cady in front of a Saturday morning *Sesame Street*, watching "Policemen Are Our Friends."

"Yep, that's me." Her eyes had traveled all the way from the rounded-toe boots to the matted silver hair that I'm sure was sticking out at undefined angles.

"Blue jeans."

We were the third county in Wyoming to adopt blue jeans as regular duty uniform, but it was one of the downfalls of our particular brand of vehicular law enforcement that the common populace rarely saw us from the waist down. "Yep, big around as they are long." Mary tried to stifle a laugh, and the girl looked to her, then back to me. Rarely do you get those glimmers of unadulterated love and, if you're smart, you pack them away for darker days. I started to get up but thought better of it.

"Melissa, is your uncle Henry Standing Bear?" I figured the best way to get started was to establish some kind of personal reference.

"Uncle Bear." Her smile was enormous. Henry was one of the most understated prophets I knew and one of the most personally interested individuals I had ever met.

I gestured for her to sit across from me and rolled up the left sleeve of my shirt to display the ghostly cross-hatchings that stretched back from my left hand. "I got hurt playing pool with your uncle Bear up in Jimtown, once . . ." The girl's eyes widened as she sat in the chair opposite me, and she instinctively reached to place a forefinger on the marbled flesh of my forearm. Her fingers were cool, and her palms were strangely devoid of any lines, as if her life was yet to be determined. I reached across the desk slowly, sliding a palm under her chin and lifting to accentuate an angry contusion at the jawline. "That's a good one, too." She nodded with a slight movement that freed her face, and she dropped her eyes to the desktop, which informed us of the potential for the president's physical fitness award. "How'd you get that?" She covered the offending jaw with a quick look to the side and a through-the-eyebrow glance at Mary.

"Melissa, I'm not here to hurt anybody, but I also want to make sure that nobody hurts you." She nodded and began gently rocking back and forth, hands firmly clasped between her legs. "Has anybody hurt you?" Her attention stayed with the glass-covered surface of Mary's desk.

"No."

I studied Melissa's reflection and tried to imagine her as she should have been. Her people were strong, clear-eyed Cheyenne from the Northern Reservation, with a little Crow from her maternal side. I tried to see a Melissa who hadn't had the spark of curiosity robbed from her by a mother who had ingested too many I-90 Cocktails—Lysol and rubbing alcohol—when she was pregnant. Melissa should have been a beautiful Indian maiden standing on the rolling, grassy hills of the Little Big Horn, arms outstretched to a future that held promise, security, and freedom. When I looked up, it was as if she had read my mind, that we had shared a vision. She had stopped rocking and was looking at the diamond snaps on my shirt.

"It was romantic." She said it flat, as if emotion would only rob her statement of its impact. Her eyes returned to the desk.

I leaned back in the office chair, allowing my fingertips to remain on the edge of the beveled glass. "What was romantic, Melissa?"

She spoke to the desk. "The walk."

I was out of beer, Cady still hadn't called, and I had given up on Doctor Leonard's sheepskin cover as the salvation of a future well-coordinated interior. I needed a Rainier and some company so I cranked my hat down hard, buttoned my sheepskin jacket up tight, and stepped into the horizontal snow flurries that were whipping around the corner of the house. I figured I'd drive the half mile down the paved road to the Red Pony. I stood there on the planks for a moment, listening to something above the wind, wings whirring only thirty feet off the ground as the geese honked their warning cries to each other in an attempt to get south. Maybe they had waited too long to leave. Maybe I had, too.

Off in the distance, I could make out the neon pony cantering in the darkness and a small number of peripheral trucks parked in the adjacent gravel lot. As I got closer, I could see that the inside lights of the bar were not on and felt a surge of panic at the thought of having to drive all the way back into town for a beer. I parked the truck and could make out a few figures moving in the darkened window of the carryout. Couldn't have been a blackout; the red neon pony shimmered across my hood and up the windshield. I pushed into the wind to open the bar's glass door and came within inches of running into the owner and operator of the Red Pony, Henry Standing Bear.

Henry and I had known each other since grade school when we had gotten into a fight at the water fountain, and he had loosened two of my teeth with a roundhouse left that had came from the Black Hills. We had played against each other in the trenches of interior line-manship from peewee through high school, whereupon I finished up at USC, lost my deferment, got drafted by the marines, and went to Vietnam. Henry had made a halfhearted attempt at the white man's educational system at Berkeley and had learned enough to protest against it before being rewarded for his efforts with an all-expense-paid, four-year vacation with the Special Forces SOG group at An Khe. It was here that Henry said he had learned of the white man's true vision and power, of his ability to kill the largest number of individuals in the most effective manner possible.

Upon his return to the States, Henry had reattempted college life but found that his ability for being lectured to had deteriorated. He returned to political activity in the seventies and had been a seminal member of every Native American movement for the next ten years. Sensing that revolution is the industry of young men, however, he returned to Absaroka County for the funeral of the grandmother who had raised him and somewhere came up with enough cash to finance a deal with the Foundation that would transform an old Sin-clair station, the only public building in Crossroads, into a kind of half-assed bar that he called the Red Pony. Henry had been known to read a great deal of Steinbeck. It was in the Foundation's interest to promote the bar, if for no other purpose than to keep the shit-caked rubber boots of the locals out of their oriental-carpeted meeting rooms.

We looked at each other, his expression carrying the quiet self-deprecation that usually held some hidden meaning. "Beer, Tonto?" he asked as he handed me an open Rainier and continued past with what appeared to be a tire iron in the other hand. I looked through the poolroom into the bar proper and could make out about eight people seated on stools, outlined by the fluorescent glow of the beer coolers. Big night. I took a sip and followed him to the far end of the room where he seemed to be preparing to tear apart the wall. Leaning against the offending structure he slipped the flat end of the tire iron behind the weenie-wood that made up the interior of the bar.

"You forget to pay your REA bill again?" He paused for a second to give me a dirty look and then put all 220 pounds into the tire iron and propelled the four-foot board from the wall, with nails still attached, to clatter at our feet. I bent from my vantage point to look at the ring-shanked holes in the plaster surface that lay underneath the removed board. Henry's face was, as always, impassive.

"Damn." Without another word, he slipped the tire iron beneath the next board and popped it to the floor. Same result. "Damn."

I figured it was time to ask, "Are we redecorating, or are we looking for something specific?" He gestured to the wall with a hand that pleaded and threatened at the same time.

"Fuse box."

"You covered it up with boards?"

Another sidelong glance. "At least I have walls."

Henry was one of the chosen few who had been to the cabin. His statement was hard to refute. "I've been thinking about getting an imitation sheepskin cover for my recliner." This got a long look.

"Are you drunk?"

I gave the question thought. "No, but I'm working on it." He grunted a little laugh and popped off another board, which added to the considerable pile that was collecting at our feet.

"Damn." He placed the tire iron in the next board. "Cady call you?"

"No, the brat."

"Huh . . . She called me." He popped the board loose to reveal the gray cover of an ancient fuse box. "Yes."

I turned to look at him. "What?"

He tapped the small, metal cover and glanced at me. "Fuse box."

"Cady called you?" His eyes were dark and clear, the far one split by the strong nose that I knew had been broken at least three times, once by me.

"Yes."

I tried to contain myself and sound casual, but he had me and he knew it. "When did she call?"

"Oh, a little while ago . . ." His casual was far more convincing than mine.

With a forefinger he pulled open the small metal box to reveal four fuses that looked as if they hadn't been changed since Edison was a child. The box itself was rusted out in the back, victim of some age-old roof leak. The conduits surrounding it were rotten and peeled back, revealing frayed tendrils of green and black corroded wire. The four fuses were covered in a thick coat of dust and were surrounded by sockets, which held a strange patina of white and green crystals. They looked like two sets of angry eyes embedded in the wall, just waiting to unleash 220 volts into anything that came close.

He placed a hand on the uneven surface of the plaster where he had taken most of the wall apart and leaned all his weight against it. His other hand brushed back the crow-black hair, smattered with touches of silver, in an arch over his shoulder and down the small of his back. "One in four, I like the odds."

"Did she say anything about calling me?"

"No. Hey . . ." He bristled with mock indignation and gestured to the fuse box. "I have a situation here."

I tried to be helpful. "They've got little windows in them so you can see which one is blown." He lowered his head and squinted into the box.

"It is not that I do not trust your home-improvement skills, even though I know you do not have any." He carefully wiped the dust from the surface of the four fuses. "They are all black."

"Do you have any extras?"

"Of course not." He held up the roll of pennies that had been hidden in his front shirt pocket. "I have these." He smiled the coyote smile, the one that had made offensive linemen part their hair in the middle, NVA officers sweat between their shoulder blades, and otherwise intelligent women occupy bar stools in his immediate vicinity. Henry was the dog that wouldn't stay on the porch.

I watched with great apprehension as his fingers began twisting one of the rusted fuses from its corroded green outlet. The muscles on his forearm writhed like snakes rolling under sun-baked earth. To my knowledge, Henry had never lifted a weight in his life, but he still carried with him the tone of the warrior and was betrayed only by a very small amount of baggage at the middle. As the applied pressure began to take its toll, the glass knob turned and the remainder of the building went black. "Damn."

Hoots and laughter came from the darkness as we stood there trying to see each other. "I don't think that was it." I listened to him sigh and replace the fuse, and the lights from the beer coolers once again lit up the far room. There was a smattering of applause from the patrons.

"She did not say anything about calling you." He was still staring into the metal box, his odds having improved dramatically.

"So, what'd she have to say?"

"Nothing much. We talked about you."

"What about me?" Throughout the entire conversation, he studied the fuse box with the half-smile that told me he didn't take either the electrical crisis or my familial life all that seriously. Cady and Henry had a symbiotic, avuncular relationship that had led her into a quasi-bohemian lifestyle. She was professionally adept at billiards and darts, had majored in Native American Studies at Berkeley, his almost alma mater, had continued on to law school at the University of Washington, and was now an attorney in Philadelphia. When together, they spent the majority of their time whispering to each other, pointing toward me, and giggling. The thought of the two of them conspiring at long distance was enough to worry me but, with Ruby's involvement, something was definitely up.

Deciding on the fuse diagonally opposite the first, Henry reached in and boldly twisted. The red neon horses that had stampeded across the parked vehicles outside flickered off to more cheers from the peanut gallery. From his lack of response, I wasn't sure if Henry had noticed. "The pony . . ."

"Damn."

He screwed the fuse back in. The neon roan paused and then leapt across the hood of the Bullet. The flurries were letting up; the bad weather had decided to whistle on down the Bozeman trail to the rail-heads. The bar held a kind of conspiratorial coziness what with the subdued light of the beer coolers filtering through the cracks in the dividing wall. The soft murmur of small talk provided a buffer against the landscape that was now scrubbed with snowflakes.

"So, what about me?"

He tapped one of the remaining fuses accusingly with an index finger. "She is worried that you are still depressed."

"About what?" He looked at me, decided better of it, and looked back at the fuse box. I pushed off the wall and stepped carefully over the nail-laden boards that covered the floor. "I need another beer."

"You know where they are." I started to turn, but he caught me by tapping on one of the last two fuses. "The suspense is killing you, right?" I made a quick face, placed the empty beer bottle on the edge of the pool table, and bent over to pick up one of the boards. I spread my feet in a good, open stance and held the bark-covered board on my shoulder with both hands. This got a look. "You are going to knock me loose from this if I get electrocuted?"

I shrugged. "It's what friends are for. Besides, I want to see if anybody in this county has worse luck than me."

"Not yet." He twisted the next to last fuse and, to our amazement, absolutely nothing happened. We both looked for any absence of light, strained to listen for any lack of humming from the assorted coolers, heaters, and fans. Henry looked to the ceiling in deep concentration.

"Well, at least I didn't have to hit you with the board."

"Yes, but now we have to do the penny part." He nudged one of the coins from the paper roll and held it up for me to view.

"Where do you get this 'we' shit, Kemosabe?"

"Have you not ever done this before?"

I lowered my board, careful to avoid the nails. "No." We had reached the conceptual stage of the project, so Henry joined me in leaning against the pool table. "Have you?" He crossed his arms and considered the single lowest common denominator of legal tender.

"No, but I have heard that you can."

"From who?"

"Old people like you."

"I'm less than a year older than you."

He shrugged and read the inscription, "IN GOD WE TRUST. I was going to use a buffalo-head nickel, but it has to be copper to conduct, that much I know."

I dropped my board with a clatter. "Well, all I know about this stuff is enough to be scared shitless of it. Is there any reason why this has to be done tonight?" He made a face. "I mean your beer coolers are running, the heat's on, even the horse out front is working . . ."

"Pony."

"Whatever."

He sighed and looked around the bar. "Only if somebody wants to play pool."

I nudged him with my shoulder. "Is your life worth a game of pool?" He thought for a moment.

"Seems like it has been." He placed the penny on his cocked thumbnail. "Heads we go for it, tails we go sit in the dark with everybody else." I nodded, and he flipped the coin to me, whereupon I promptly dropped it in the pile of boards. We looked at each other.

"I didn't know I was supposed to catch it." He peeled another penny from the paper roll.

"Do not worry, I have got forty-nine more. You ought to be able to catch one of them." He flipped the second penny, and I snatched it from midair and slapped it on the back of my other hand. I left my palm covering the penny for a few moments, building my own little tension.

"Is the suspense killing you?"

"Not really, next we flip to see who puts the penny in the fuse." I uncovered the coin and thanked the God we trust it was tails.

"C'mon, I'll buy you a Coke."

19

* * *

I ambled along behind Henry as we joined the others at the bar itself. The walls were covered with the works of different artists who had received residencies with the Foundation. It was a mixed lot, but each piece reminded me of the individual who had occupied the adjacent barstool, and artists are always good for conversation, so long as you want to talk about their art.

The small group was clustered in the bar's corner, only slightly illuminated by the dim glow of available light. There were a couple of stray hunters, still dressed in their camouflage and optical-orange vests; evidently the deer were wearing blue this year. I could make out Buck Morris, one of the local cowboys who took care of the Foundation's nominal cattle herd. He was easy to spot because of his hat; a weather-worn Resistol that some oil executive had offered to buy for $250. General opinion was that Buck had missed the boat. The young man next to him wore a frayed jean jacket and had strong Cheyenne features. He must've been from out of county, because I didn't know him.

Next was Roger Russell, an electrician out of Powder Junction in the southern part of the county who had come up here to expand his business. Turk said that he was kind of the black sheep of the family and that he had little bastards scattered all up and down the Basin: "Powder River, let'r buck, a mile wide and an inch deep." I wondered mildly why Henry and I had just been gambling with our lives while an expert nursed a C and C in the next room.

Sitting next to him was probably the reason why Roger happened to be here. Vonnie Hayes was old school Wyoming; her grandfather had had a spread of thirty thousand acres of good land. Vonnie and I had kind of known each other when we were children but, after her father had committed suicide, she was sent to boarding school and her art life had taken her east for a number of years, where she had become an accomplished sculptress. Much later, she returned to take care of her aging mother. Vonnie and Martha had worked together on the library board and a number of other community projects in the county, and my daughter had worked for Vonnie as a housekeeper one summer. After Martha died, Cady tried to fix us up, an endeavor that Vonnie and I both viewed with equal parts humor and open-handed flirtation. Even in the dim light I could make out Vonnie's features, strong, with a lupine slant to the eyes, sandy hair pulled back in a casual bun.

I leaned against the bar beside her, bumping into Roger and giving him my substantial rear. "Jeez, Rog." I looked around in the darkness. "Don't you know we've got an electrical emergency on our hands here?"

He carefully placed his drink back and nudged it with his fingers. "I am . . . retired."

Henry appeared on the other side of the bar, slid a Rainier to me, and leaned into Roger. "What about this penny thing?"

Roger looked at him, attempting to gather himself for an answer. As he did, I looked over to Vonnie. "Boy, the things you find in the dark."

She took a sip of her chenin blanc. Henry kept a special bottle of the white wine in the cooler for her. I had always wanted to ask her for a sip but had never gotten up the nerve. Her eyes glowed softly, and the corner of her lips curved into a warm, sad smile. "Hello, Walter."

Undaunted by conversing with drunks, Henry continued. "Those old fuses, the big ones, you put pennies in them to get them to work?"

Roger laughed. "Yes you can, and you can also fuse every bit of the substandard wiring in this shit-hole and burn us all up alive." I kind of leaned Roger against the bar, stabilizing the listing that had begun as he spoke, and pulled a loose stool from the far side, placing it and myself, between Roger and Vonnie.

"Vonnie . . ." Her eyes had a way of opening a little wider when you spoke to her, then closing a little like they were capturing what you were saying and holding on to it. I was starting to remember why I had had a crush on her and continued. "You see this heathen, devil red man across the bar here?" Her eyes glanced at Henry for a moment, then returned to mine. "He and Cady are plotting some sort of intrigue against me."

Her eyes widened again, and she returned her gaze to Henry. "Is that true, Bear?" It irritated me that every woman I knew was on a cuddly first-name basis with the man.

Henry nodded toward me. "White man full of shit."

We were on a Technicolor roll now. I was Randolph Scott to his . . . I don't know, one of those bigger than life Indians that either got beat up or killed by the end of the third reel. "It's true, he's government trained to be involved in these kinds of covert operations." I pointed to the framed boxes on the wall behind the bar that contained a burnt map of North and South Vietnam, Laos, and Cambodia. On this map were Henry's Special Forces pin, Purple Heart, Army Distinguished Service Cross, Vietnamese Cross of Gallantry, and assorted campaign medals. There were also black-and-white photographs of Henry with his infantry platoon leaders, and one with his friend and team member Lo Chi, whom he had brought back and relocated in Los Angeles. There was even a picture of Henry and me, wearing the two ugliest Hawaiian shirts in Saigon, on a three-day leave in 1968. "You see all that stuff on the wall? He was trained in the war to be the gravest irritation to all those around him. There is no way a common soldier, such as myself, could possibly compete with a hand-picked, combat-hardened pain in the ass like him." Few people knew the shadowy history of the Special Operations Group that had operated out of Laos, but the numbers said it all: For every American Special Forces soldier that was lost, the North Vietnamese lost between 100 and 150 troops. The Bear had been a part of one of the most effective killing machines on either side of the war.

Henry's face pushed up and curved to the side as the weight of his head held steady in the palm of his supporting hand. "Common soldier? The closest he came to any real fighting was when he agreed to meet me for a three-day in Saigon." Under his breath he continued, but I'm pretty sure I was the only one that heard it, "Except for Tet . . ."

I left Henry to leverage Roger into doing some free electrical consulting work and turned my attention back to Vonnie. She was staring

into the glass eyes of one of the mounted antelope behind the bar.
"Pretty animals." Her eyes remained steady on the pronghorn. "Do
you think they feel pain like we do?"

"Nope."

She turned to look at me, seemingly irritated. "Really?"

"Really."

She stayed with me for a second, and then, fading into disappoint-
ment, glanced at her wine glass. "So, you don't think they feel pain."

"No, I said I don't think they feel pain like us."

"Oh." The smile slowly returned. "For a minute there I thought
you had become a jerk."

"No, a blacksmith's son."

She continued to smile and then nodded. "You used to come out to
our place with your father . . . Lloyd."

I watched her. "Nobody remembers his name."

"I think my mother had a little crush on him."

"Just another Longmire, plying his wiles. When I was real little, I
used to make the shoeing rounds with him. It looked painful to me, so
I asked him."

"What did he say?"

"Pop used to speak in biblical terms, but what he said was that the
brutes of the field don't feel pain like humans. That that's the price we
pay for thinking."

She took another sip of her wine. "Comforting to know that we're
the species that feels the most pain."

I half-closed an eye and looked at her for a second. "Is that East
Coast sarcasm I'm hearing?"

"No, that's East Coast self-pity."

"Oh." I was getting in way over my head. I can do the bull about as
well as it can be done, but that edgy buzz-talk makes me weary in a
heartbeat. I try and keep up, but after a while I start to drag.

She placed a hand on mine, and I think it was the hottest hand I
had ever felt. "Walter, are you all right?"

It always started like this, a touch and a kind word. I used to feel

23

heat behind my eyes and a shortness of breath, but now I just feel the emptiness. The fuses of desire are blown black windows, and I'm gone with no pennies to save me. "Oh, you mean you really want to talk?"

Her eyes were so sad, so honest. "Yeah, I figured since we didn't have anything else to do."

So I leaned in and told her the truth. "I just . . . I'm just numb most of the time."

She blinked. "Me too."

I felt like one of those guys in the movies, there in the foxhole asking how much ammo your buddy's got. I got two more clips, how 'bout you? "I know the things I'm supposed to do, but I just don't seem to have the energy. I mean, I've been thinking about turning over my pillow for three weeks."

"I know . . ." She looked away. "How's Cady?"

Here I was floating in the white-capped Pacific of self-pity, and Vonnie threw me a lifeline to keep me from embarrassing myself. Three fingers, bartender . . . "She's great." I looked at Vonnie to see if she was really interested. She was. "She's doing so well in Philadelphia."

"She always has been special."

"Yes, she is." We sat there for a moment, allowing the crackle and roar of my parental self-satisfaction to fade into the soft glow of friendly conversation. Her hand was still on my arm when the phone rang.

"Looks like she's tracked you down." The hand went away.

I watched as Henry allowed it to ring the second time, his tele-signature, then snatched it from the cradle. "It is another beautiful evening here at the Red Pony bar and continual soirée, how can I help you?" His face pulled up on one side as if the receiver had just smacked him. "Yes, he is here." He stretched the cord across the expanse of the bar and handed me the phone. His eyes stayed on mine.

I nudged it between my chin and shoulder with one hand, took a sip of beer with the other, and swallowed. "Hello, Sugar Blossom . . ."

"Hello, shithead," the voice on the other end said. "It's not a dead sheep."

I stood there, letting the world shift at quarter points and then got a bearing and dropped my voice. "What've we got?" Every eye in the bar was on me.

Vic's voice held an edge that I had never heard before, approaching an excitement under the grave suppression of businesslike boredom. "Male, Caucasian, approximately twenty-one years of age . . . one entry wound characteristic of, maybe, a .30-06."

I started to rub my eyes, noticed that my hand was shaking, and put it in my pocket. "All right . . . call the Store and tell them to send the Little Lady."

There was a brief pause, and I listened to the static from a radio on 137 patched through to a landline in Durant. "You don't want any Cashiers?"

"No, just the Bag Boys. I've got a highly dependable staff."

She laughed. "Wait till you get out here. These fucking sheep have been marching around on everything; I think the little bastards actually ate some of his clothes. And they shit on him."

"Great . . . Past the Hudson Bridge; you got your lights on?"

"Yep." She paused for a moment, and I listened to the static. "Walt?"

I had started to hang up the phone. "Yeah?"

"You better bring some beer to quiet Bob and Billy down."

This was a first. "You bet." I started to hang up again.

"Walt?"

"Yep?"

"It's Cody Pritchard."

2

There's nothing like a dead body to make you feel, well, removed. I guess the big city boys, cataloguing forty or fifty homicides a year, get used to it, but I never have. I've been around enough wildlife and stock that it's pretty commonplace, the mechanics of death. There's a religion worthy of this right of passage, of taking that final step from being a vertical creature to a horizontal one. Yesterday you were just some nobody, today you're the honored dead with bread bags rubber-banded over your hands. I secure what's left of my dwindling humanity with the false confidence of the living, the deceitful wit of the eight-foot tall and bulletproof. Yea, verily, though I walk through the valley of the shadow of death, I will live forever. If I don't, I sure as hell won't become an unattended death in the state of Wyoming with sheep shit all over me.

We had pretty much done our work, secured the area, lit it up, and finished taking pictures. There's a kind of cocksure attitude that overtakes a man in the presence of the dearly departed, a you're-dead-and-I'm-not kind of perspective. There's something about a carcass of an animal like oneself, the post-shuffled, mortal coil that brings out the worst in me, and I start thinking that I'm funny.

"I've been thinking about a search-and-rescue sheep squad." I picked some of the dried shit from my pants and flicked it from my fingernails. "The way I figure it, the sheep would work up a damn storm and never raise any hell about working conditions. Might even get rid of some of this leafy spurge." I looked around at the frosted milky-yellow plants that had been half eaten by the baahing attending witnesses we had corralled at the base of the hill. I had been here for

26

nine hours, and the sun was beginning to scatter the gray blocks that made up the eastern horizon. The crime scene was a slight depression at the middle of a wreath-shaped ridge. "What do you think?"

T.J. raised an eyebrow from her clipboard. "Cody Allen Pritchard." She returned the eyebrow to the hunting license and wallet that were clipped to the official forms. "DOB, 8/1/81. Kind of has a ring to it."

Cody had looked better. Whoever had dispatched the young man had done so with a smooth and consistent pull-off as center shot. From the back, it looked as though someone had drilled a perfectly round hole between Cody's shoulder blades; from the front, it looked as though someone had driven a stagecoach through him. The body was lying facedown, all the limbs arranged in a normal fashion, arms at the sides with palms turned to the lemon-colored sky. I was tempted to see if Cody's lifeline was abnormally short, but his hands had already been bagged. A green John Deere hat with an adjustable strap in the back had been carted off with the unfired Model 94 Winchester 30-30 that had been found at his side. His clothes were in bad shape, even for a person who had had more than ten cc's of lead pushed through him at approximately twenty-five hundred feet per second. The sheep had done a number on him. The orange vest was torn where they had tried to eat it, the sleeves of his flannel shirt were shredded, and even his work boots looked as though they had been nibbled on. They had slept on him, gleaning the last energies of the late Cody Pritchard as his body cooled. Finally, much to the dissatisfaction of the crime lab people, they had shit on him.

I gestured to the sheep down the hill. "I'm assuming that you're going to want to question all the witnesses."

T.J. Sherwin had been the director of the Division of Criminal Investigation's lab unit for seventeen odd years. I had always called her the Little Lady, as opposed to many of the other nicknames that periodically circulated through Wyoming's law enforcement community: Bitch on Wheels, the Wicked Witch of the West, and Bag Lady. The last referred to the Division of Criminal Investigation's home away from home, a converted grocery in Cheyenne, commonly tagged as the Store. Hence, DCI lab personnel were routinely called Bag Boys, and criminal investigators were Cashiers.

When I first met T.J., she had informed me that I was just the kind of dinosaur she was going to make a personal career of eradicating. As the years passed and we worked numerous cases together, I remained a dinosaur, but I was her favorite dinosaur. "So, what do you think?" She had finally lowered the clipboard.

"He doesn't look like a deer." I gave Cody another study.

"Walt, let's drop the aw shucks bullshit. This is one of the boys that was involved in that rape case two years ago." T.J. had held my hand through the Little Bird rape investigation, introducing me to the world of secretors, medical swabs, and gynecological exams.

"Yeah, well, I'll follow up on the home front; he wasn't any angel. We'll go through the licensees, and, hopefully, find some poor, dumb bastard from Minnesota that got a little trigger happy."

"You don't think it was an accident?"

I thought about it. "Like I said, he wasn't an altar boy."

"You have a feeling about this?"

I started to give her the old Colonel-Mustard-in-the-library-with-the-candlestick routine, but thought better of it. "No, I don't."

When we got back, the Bag Boys had already zipped Cody up and loaded him onto a gurney; some of the others were still processing evidence into freezer bags. One of the boys was dropping a tattered eagle feather into a plastic envelope. He looked up as we approached. "Looks like everything out here's been making a meal of this poor guy."

T.J. turned to me. "Walt, are you going to be the primary on this one?"

"Do you mean am I going to be riding in one of those Conestoga wagons of yours for five hours down to Cheyenne?"

"Yes."

"No." I pointed to the group of vehicles where Vic was busy putting away the photography equipment. "At the bottom of this hill, you will find my somewhat agitated, but highly skilled, primary investigator."

T.J. smiled. She liked Vic. "She have any cases pending?"

"Well, she's been hanging Christmas lights in town, but I figure we can let her go for a few days."

"It's not even Thanksgiving."

"It's a city council thing."

We followed the body down to where the rest of our little task force had congregated. Someone had brought a number of Thermoses full of hot coffee and a few boxes of donuts. I got a cup of coffee; I don't eat donuts. I spotted Jim Ferguson, one of my deputies and head of Search and Rescue, across the bed of the truck and asked him if they had turned anything up on their walk around. His mouth was full of cream-filled, but the gist was no. I told him I was going to replace his staff with the sheep.

"We did a three-hundred-yard perimeter, but the light wasn't so good. We'll do another soon as everybody gets a donut and some coffee. You think this guy left brass?"

"I hope."

I took my coffee and moved over to where T.J. and Vic were seated on a tailgate. They were looking at some of the evidence; hopefully, they were discussing something I could understand.

"Single shot, center, didn't get too much of the sternum." Vic held a bag up to the rising sun and looked at the metal fragment inside. "Fuck, I don't know." T.J. patted the spot beside her with the palm of her hand, and I sat. Vic continued, "It looks like a slug. I'm thinking 12 gauge or something just a little bigger."

"Bazooka?"

She lowered the bag, and her eyes met mine. "You're getting rid of me?"

I nodded my head. "Yep."

"Why?"

"Because you're a big pain in the butt."

"Fuck you."

"And you talk dirty."

She handed the bagged bullet to T.J. "You're going to be stuck up here with Turk."

"Yeah, well, maybe we'll get the Christmas lights put up together." Vic snorted and readjusted her gun belt. "Besides, you've forgotten more about this space-age stuff than I'll ever know. You can relay information back to me." The tarnished gold stared at me, unblinking. "You'll only be down there for two days. It will take us that long to round up all the usual suspects." I was the old dog who had learned his fill of new tricks, and it was only logical that I work the county and the people.

She poked me in the belly. Her finger remained in one of my fat rolls, and she poked each word for emphasis, "If Search and Rescue don't find anything, you gonna call Omar?"

"That's another reason for you to leave, you don't like Omar."

She poked me again. "You be careful, all right?"

This all sounded very strange coming from Vic's mouth, but I took it as affection and punched her on the shoulder. "I'm always . . ." She knocked my hand away.

"I mean it." She didn't have kind eyes, they rarely looked away, and they always told the truth. I could use eyes like that. "I've got a funny feeling about all of this."

I gazed back up to the patch of sage and scrub weed and watched the sun free itself from the red hills. "Yeah, well you got five hours to talk to T.J. about this woman's intuition thing." The next poke hurt.

I hung around the scene until Search and Rescue had finished their second sweep; I sat in the Bullet and filled out the reports. Ferg strolled up with a cup of coffee and another cream-filled. "Anything?" Fortunately, I caught him between bites.

"Nothing. We got a lot of sheep shit and tracks."

"Any suspicious sheep tracks?"

"Nope, no suspicious sheep shit, either. It's like the Denver stock-yards up there."

I thought about how you could kill a victim only once, but how a crime scene could die a thousand deaths. I hoped that whatever useful information could be deducted from this patch of God's little acre was traveling safely in plastic bags toward Cheyenne. Motives are all fine and good, but if we could find out the how, we'd have a shooting's match chance of finding out the who. I had the niggling feeling I was going to have to call Omar.

On the drive over to the Pritchards' place I thought about the last time I had seen Cody alive. He was a heavyset kid, built like a linebacker, curly blond hair and pale blue eyes. He had his mother's looks, his father's temper, and nobody's brains. I had pulled him out on three occasions, the last being the rape case. Cody had endeared himself to the local Native American community by being quoted in the Sheridan paper as saying, "Yeah, she was a retard redskin, but she was asking for it."

The Pritchards had a place on the outskirts of Durant and, by the time I got there, there must have been eight or nine cars and trucks in the drive. Word carries fast in open spaces. As I cut off the engine, the full impact of what I was going to have to do hit me like a Burlington Northern. How do you tell parents that their child is dead? Sure, they'd heard it through the grapevine, but I was the official word. I allowed myself a long sigh.

There were field swallows swooping near the Bullet. I was probably disturbing their family, too. Seemed to be my day for it. It had been longer than twenty-four hours since sleep. It's easy to work all night because the sun doesn't come up, but when it does, my eyes start to sting and the rest of me gets a little shaky. I've always been this way. I was focusing my eyes when I heard the screen door slam and saw John Pritchard walking down the drive. I never cared too much for John; he was one of those guys who always had to be in control. The conversation wasn't as bad as it could have been. The pertinent information from him was that Cody had left the house twenty-seven hours ago with an extra doe license. The pertinent information from me was that he wasn't coming home.

* * *

I did the best I could, drove the seven miles back to my place, and sat on the porch—well, the front doorway—but not for very long, because it was cold. I had the presence of mind to fall into the house instead of out of it. I drifted in and out of consciousness until the phone rang, and the answering machine my daughter made me buy picked up. "You've reached the Longmire residence. No one is available to answer your call right now, 'cause we're out chasing bad guys or trying on white hats. If you leave a message after the tone, we'll get back to you as quickly as we can. Happy trails!" She had taken a great deal of joy in recording the message printed in the instructions, with a few minor alterations. I smiled every time I heard it.

"It's Pancake Day!" The voice resonated through the lines from fourteen miles away. Jim Ferguson was not only head of Search and Rescue and my longest standing part-time deputy, but he was also the man in charge of driving around Durant once a year at dawn in the fire department's truck, proclaiming through a bullhorn, "It's Pancake Day, Pancake Day!"

There are only three major vote-getting days in Absaroka County, and I can't remember the other two. "Oh God, no. It's Pancake Day." I thought about shooting myself. I could see the headline: SHERIFF SHOOTS SELF, UNABLE TO FACE PANCAKES.

"It's Pancake Day!" Ferg really enjoyed his work. "I've been trying to get a hold of you for the last hour, just thought somebody ought to call and remind you. But if you really are gonna retire next year, then who gives a shit?"

I stumbled to the phone beside the recliner. "Is it really today?"

"If I'm lyin' I'm dyin'." There was a pause. "Hey, Walt, if you want, I can just tell 'em we were up all night." Ferg was slightly in the Turk camp for future sheriff, but I had other plans. If Vic was going to be the first female sheriff in Wyoming, I only had a year to pull in all my political markers. I could last an hour of Pancake Day with the Elks, the Eagles, the Lions, the Jaycees, the Daughters of the American Revolution, and, of course, the AARPs.

"I'll be there in a half hour."

"Remember, it's at the Catholic church this year."

"You bet." I plugged in the coffeemaker and dumped enough coffee for eight cups into the filter with only enough water for four. I took a shower while it was perking. The plumbing was somewhat makeshift, but the water that came from above went away below. It went away below through a bathtub that Henry had found for me for twenty dollars. Somebody on the Rez had used it for target practice with a .22 but had only chipped the porcelain. Then there was the shower curtain. I don't know what the exact physical dynamics are that cause a shower curtain to attach itself to your body when you turn on the water but, since my shower was surrounded on all sides by curtains, I turned on the water and became a vinyl, vacuum-sealed sheriff burrito.

I slid behind the wheel of the Bullet and started driving the fourteen miles to town. Durant is situated along the Bighorn Mountains and, because there is abundant fish and game, it's become the retiree capitol of Wyoming. In Absaroka County, to ignore the octogenarian vote is to pump gas at the Sinclair station for a living. Service jobs are about all there are in Durant, somewhat stunting the younger generation and forcing the majority out by age nineteen; but the retirees keep coming from Minnesota, Wisconsin, Illinois, and Iowa, with the odd Texan and Californian thrown in for spice. They come looking for the romance of the west that they had paid shiny quarters to view on Saturday afternoons in flickering black and white. They waited half a century of stamping out automobile bumpers to get their western dream; they paid for it and, by God, they were going to have it. Most ended up picking up and moving out, headed for Florida, Arizona, or wherever the weather was easier. I liked the ones who stayed. You'd see them out after the blizzards, shoveling away, and waving at the Bullet like it was the circus come to town. Hell, I'd stop and talk to them. Sheriffs have to get elected in Wyoming, so we have to be liked. I imagine that, if you had to elect the average police force, the turnover rate would spin your Rolodex.

When I first started out, it was the part of the job that I enjoyed the least, courting the public. But as time wore on, it got to be the part that I enjoyed the most. Martha was right when she said that I needed a bumper sticker that said BORN TO BULLSHIT. The debates were the best part. In '81, old Sheriff Connally planned a peaceful takeover. He ran against me so no one else could and had lofted softballs to me so that I felt like Harmon Killabrew by the time the debate was over. I was elected. Lucian retired and was now living the high life in room 32 at the Durant Home for Assisted Living. I still went over on Tuesday nights to play chess, and he still kicked my ass, to his unending delight.

I looked at the inch of snow that dappled the sagebrush. It looked like a Morse code of white dots and dashes leading down the road. If I could read the message, would it tell me the story I wanted to hear? The truth still stood that I was a sheriff who had survived by the cult of personality, and that, if the trend were to continue, my heir-apparent would not be elected. Was I just trying to force Vic down the throats of the county because I could? No, she was the best person for the job and that was the reason I was going to have to keep pushing. Pancake Day, Pancake Day.

I idled down into second gear at the corner of Main and Big Horn and looked down the street to see Turk's Trans Am parked at the office. Just seeing his car made my ass hurt. I didn't feel like facing him on an empty stomach. I hoped he would have already contacted Lavanda Running Horse over at Game and Fish for any information we could get about last night's incident. I circled quickly around the courthouse to avoid being seen and made a beeline for the Catholic church. The place was mobbed, and there was no parking. I wheeled the Bullet onto the concrete pad beside the HVAC unit and cut the engine. I figured the Pope wasn't coming today.

"Well, if it isn't the long arm of the law." It was an old joke, but one I didn't mind. "Longmire, pull up a chair and sit yourself down." Steve Brandt was the mayor of Durant and the de facto president of the Business Associates Committee, a loosely affiliated group of warring tribes that made up the commercial facet of the downtown. He also owned the screen-printing place on Main and had done the T-shirts for the annual Sheriff's Department *vs.* Fire Department softball game, but the less said about this the better. Next to him was David Fielding of the Sportshop, Elaine Gearey who had the Art Gallery, Joe of Joe Benham's Hardware and Lumber, Dan Crawford from the IGA, and Ruby.

"What are you doing here?" Ruby's chin rested on her palm, fingers trailing into the hollow below her cheekbones. I figured cheekbones were one of those things you gained from speed walking five miles a day.

I slipped off my coat and sat on it. "Well, I'm here to support the courageous Durant Volunteer Fire Department's men in nonflamma-ble nylon . . . Do you think their hats are cooler than ours?"

"Shouldn't you be home, in bed?"

I took my hat and perched it on her head. It looked jaunty. I turned to the others at the table. "This is the problem I have with all the women I know, they're always trying to get me into bed." There was a derisive chuckle around the table, and Ruby took my hat off, sitting it on the table brim up—good Wyoming girl. "It's 'cause I look so much like Gary Cooper." General opinion at the table projected their cine-matic consensus to more like Hoot Gibson, whereupon I changed the subject. "So, how are the pancakes?"

"We don't know. We been here for twenty minutes and ain't seen a damn pancake yet." Joe Benham was in a lean and hungry mood.

"Might be for the best. They aren't letting the firemen cook again, are they?"

"You think they'd learn to not trust 'em with fire." David's com-ment referred to the infamous Stove Oil Incident wherein the firemen had set fire to the old wood-burning stove at the Future Farmers of America hall, resulting in that year's pancakes tasting roughly like roofing shingles.

"The best was when they almost burned their truck up at that grass fire out near you." Elaine, being a patron of the arts, always appreciated spectacle.

Ruby placed a steaming Styrofoam cup of coffee in front of me. I hadn't even seen her get up. "Thank you, ma'am." I took a sip and listened to the rumble as it joined the other four cups in my stomach. I was hungry and that was not a good thing on Pancake Day.

"We were just discussing the city Christmas decorations, Walt. Do you think they're the ugliest in Wyoming?" Elaine had a twinkle in her eye. As part of the city council, she had been lobbying for new decorations for about six years now. The problem was that Joe's father had designed and executed the offending artistry of Santa, elves, reindeer, bells, wreaths, candles, trees, mistletoe, holly, stars, and toys twenty-five years ago. Say what you want about three-quarter inch exterior ply, it holds ugly for a long time.

"Gillette's are uglier," I ventured.

"We heard you had a busy night." Dan Crawford picked up his coffee and blew into it, watching the swirls of cream separate at the riptide on the other side of his cup. It got quiet.

This was going to be the prime topic of conversation for the morning, so I might as well develop an official line. "Nothing big. We had a hunting accident out near 137 on BLM land." I tried to make it sound like the end of the story.

"We heard there was a boy dead." Dan continued to look at his coffee.

"Well, what else have you heard?" It got even quieter. "No offense, Dan, but I'm not gonna sit here and play guessing games with you. Why don't you just tell me what you know, and I'll either confirm or deny it or not." His face reddened, which was not what I was after.

"I didn't mean anything, Walt. Just curious."

He meant it. I rubbed my face with my hands and looked at all of them. "I hope you'll all excuse me, but it's been a long night." I sighed. "With all due respect to the ongoing investigation, it would appear that, on the night past, one Cody Pritchard departed for the far country from which no traveler born returns."

The allusion was not lost on Elaine. "Have you narrowed it down to a couple of hundred thousand suspects, as in something rotten in the state of Denmark or Iowa?"

Joe nodded. "Well, I don't figure there'll be any public outcries of mourning . . ." Elaine ventured that there might be a parade, then saved me by asking if I was willing to play the Ghost of Christmas Future in the civic theatre's upcoming production of *A Christmas Carol*. I was pretty sure that she wanted me for my height and not my dramatic skills. This was confirmed when she assured me that I wouldn't have to learn any lines and that all I had to do was point.

I excused myself to see a man about a horse and made for the boy's room at the far end of the hall. On the way, I got a peek through the kitchen service opening and was startled to see Vonnie Hayes sliding a stacked platter of pancakes to a waiting fireman. She looked much as she did last evening, which seemed like another life. Her hand came up and swiped back a stray wisp of hair that had escaped from the loose bun. It's funny how the little movements that a woman makes seem so individualized, like a signature. It was the rotation of the wrist with a two-finger pull. I gave it a ten and was aroused. I waved and thought she had seen me, but maybe I was wrong. She smiled at the young fireman and disappeared into the kitchen. Those firemen, they make out like bandits.

In the boy's room, I attended to business, washed my hands, hit the button on the hand dryer, and wiped my hands off on my pants to the quiet hum of modern technology. It was then that I realized I was wearing my weapon. I don't wear my gun to community functions, and I don't wear it on weekends. I was actually famous for taking it off and leaving it places. Periodically, Vic would bring it back to me from the bathroom in the office or out of the seat of the Bullet. She liked to make fun of my antique armament by calling it the blunderbuss. Heavy, hard to aim, slow rate of fire, it was the weapon I had used in Vietnam for four years, and I'd gotten used to it.

The Colt 1911A1 had a grisly but effective past. During the Philippine campaigns, the islanders took to getting doped up and wrapping themselves in sugarcane. United States servicemen had the glorious experience of shooting these natives numerous times with no result before being hacked to death by their machetes. Obviously, something with a little more hitting power than the standard issue .38 was needed. John Browning's auto-loading, single-action child graduated to .45 caliber, and the Filipinos began flying back out of the trenches they had hurled themselves into. Unaccurized, the weapon was about as precise as a regulation basketball but, if you hit something with it, chances were good the fight was over.

I thumbed the standard duty holster open and took the weapon out to check it; an old habit. The matte finish was rubbed off at the sights and the ridges along the barrel's slide action. Fully loaded, which it was, it regularly weighed 38.6 ounces, but today it seemed to weigh about three tons. What the hell was it doing on? Was I responding to some unconscious threat? Did I know more than I thought I knew? It was about this time that I became aware of the bathroom door being opened, and a fully dressed fireman looked at me and my gun.

"I didn't think the pancakes were that bad."

"Hello, Ray." He was the young one I had seen talking to Vonnie at the kitchen window. "You need in here?" It took him a moment to respond.

"Ms. Hayes sent me over, you got a phone call in the kitchen."

It was probably the first time he had ever used the title *Ms.* in his life. He still didn't move. "Anything else?"

He smiled, embarrassed. "You gonna shoot somebody?"

I thought for a moment and sighed. "Anybody need shooting?"

"Not that I know of." He looked away for a second. "Sounds like the only one that needed it got it last night." He was roughly Cody Pritchard's age, and they probably had gone to school together. I nodded and started to squeeze by him. "What's the um . . . story on Cody?"

I stopped, and we were lodged in the doorway. I looked down at him. "Well"—I paused for effect—"he's dead." I watched him to see if there was anything else. There wasn't, so I smiled. "You better get some pancakes over to the mayor at the Business Associates Committee table before you guys are putting out fires with a bucket brigade."

"You bet." Always good to know on which side your pancake is buttered.

As I made my way toward the kitchen, I mused on the thought of being caught in the bathroom playing with my gun. Great, as if everybody in the county didn't already think I was loony as a waltzing pissant. When I got to the kitchen door, Vonnie already had it open.

"No rest for the wicked?"

"I wish." God, she looked good with that little bit of sweat in the hollow at the base of her throat.

"The phone's over by the sink, back hallway."

I breezed by, trying to exude competent professionalism as I picked up the receiver from the drain board. "Longmire."

"Jesus, are you eating again?" The long distance whine from Cheyenne was no surprise; in my experience most things from Cheyenne whined.

"I am motivating the constituency and have yet to eat any pancakes. What are you still doing awake?"

"The state medical examiner just finished his preliminary."

"Let me guess. Lead poisoning?"

"Yeah, the rig/liv says it was about six-thirty when he got it. Gives some credibility to the hunting accident scenario, changing light and all, but . . ."

This must be good. "But?"

"Massive cavitations with a lot of radiopague snowstorm."

My mind immediately summoned up a visual X-ray with the usual fragments of civilian hunting ammunition. Obviously, this was not the case. "Nonmilitary?"

"Maybe semijacketed, maybe not. It's a really strange caliber, and it's big."

"What?"

"We don't know yet."

This was something. With Vic's specialty in ballistics back in Philadelphia, I had assumed her initial assessment that it was a .30-06 was gospel. "What do you think?" There was silence for a moment.

"I don't think it's a deer gun."

I raised an eyebrow. "Really?"

"I know what a fucking high-powered slug looks like, all right?" I let it set for a moment, and so did she.

"Why don't you get some sleep?" It was fun saying it to someone else. Silence.

"He had a cheeseburger with jalapeño peppers."

"I'll go by the Busy Bee and talk to Dorothy. Anything else?" Silence.

"Go talk to Omar. He's a crazy motherfucker, but he knows his shit." Silence. "So, do you miss me?"

I laughed. When I hung up the phone, Vonnie was holding a plate where a steaming stack of pancakes lay waiting. "I figured this was the only way you were going to get to eat." She relaxed and leaned her back against the wall. With the apron on and her hair up she looked like an Amish centerfold. "You have a lot of women in your life."

"You think that's a good thing or a bad thing?" I said between bites.

She peered over her coffee cup. Her eyes were enormous. "Depends on the women." I nodded and chewed. "It's just got to be difficult. I don't know how you do it."

"Well, it's not my usual routine, running ten miles at dawn, three hundred sit-ups . . ." She let go with this snorty laugh and apologized, holding her hand to her face.

"How are your pancakes?"

I took a breath. "They're great, thank you."

"I heard you used to make animal shapes with pancakes." She smiled mischievously.

"You've been talking to one of the women in my life."

"I have, it's true. I learned all kinds of little secrets about you when she was working for me."

I nodded, thought about little secrets, and took my last bite. "The deal was this, if she went to church on Sunday mornings with her mother, she didn't have to eat her heathen father's breakfast. It's a wonder she didn't turn into a devout Methodist."

"That's not what she told me. She said she liked having you all to herself."

"And now she does." It was out before I knew I had said it. I had gotten so used to joking about Martha's death, but here it just seemed wrong. "Sorry."

"Do you ever get lonely, Walter?"

"Oh, sure." I tried to think of something else to say, but nothing seemed honest enough. All I could think of was how soft and inviting she looked. I had this unfocused image of her, my bed back at the ranch, and all my worldly needs being gratified at once. This didn't seem appropriate either.

"Maybe we should get together sometime."

Maybe it was appropriate. "Why, Ms. Hayes, are you making a pass at me?" I emphasized the *Ms.*

Her eyes sparked. "Maybe, Mr. Longmire, though I must admit your indifference and the gauntlet of women I may have to face seem daunting."

"Well, they're a pretty tough bunch, so I can understand."

"The term a *pride* comes to mind." She took a sip of coffee. "Maybe we should start with lunch?"

It was a short drive back to the office where I parked behind the jukebox Turk called his car. It was some kind of Trans Am, at least that's what it said all over it. That wasn't all it said, since it looked as if every available surface was covered with some sort of sticker. It had stickers on the bumper to proclaim every ill-considered political opinion that had ever crossed Turk's apolitical mind. Advice on the ex-president, his family, gun control, ProRodeo, state nativism, and honking if you were horny. On the back window, it had little cartoon characters peeing on each other and on the emblems of other vehicles. It seemed to me that there wasn't anyone that could look at this car and not be offended. It was a lot like Turk.

When I pushed open the door, no one was in the reception area. I stood there with the doorknob in my hand and listened. There was a shuffling noise in my office, and I heard one of my file cabinets shut. A moment later he turned through the doorway in full saunter. His eyes stayed steady as I shut the door behind me.

"Man, it's about time. I been sittin' around here for hours." I wasn't sure if he considered being offensive to be the best defense or if it was just his natural state. "Running Horse called. She said they had some hunters that asked about the BLM land out on the Powder River near 137, section 23. They're still here, stayin' at the Log Cabin Motel. Wanna go talk to 'em?"

I let it set for a few seconds. "What are you doing in my office?" He was a handsome kid with what the romance novels would call smoldering good looks. Dark coloring with wavy black hair and a Van Dyke goatee accenting the Basque on his mother's side. Just shy of six and a half feet, most of it shoulder, he was a handy thing to have crossing his arms and looking menacing behind me in a domestic disturbance but, other than that, I had found little use for him. I had taken him on as a favor to Lucian. He didn't like him either, but Turk was his nephew, and I felt obliged.

"I was just checkin' things out."

"In my office?" His face darkened a little past smoldering.

"Hey, might be my office some day." He looked toward Vic's windowless little room across the hall from mine. There were no pictures on her walls. There were just books, shelves and shelves of books. You had to reach through the blue binders of Wyoming Criminal Procedure on the third shelf next to the door to turn the light on and off.

"Turk, I've been up for two days and I'm getting a little edgy. You get my meaning?"

He straightened. "Yes, sir."

I was liking him better. "Now there are a few things you can do to endear yourself to me in the next few days. Starting with doing what I tell you to do, keeping your mouth shut as much as possible, and staying out of my office. Got it?"

"Yes, sir."

"Now what I want you to do is run over to the Busy Bee and ask Dorothy Caldwell when she saw Cody last."

"You want me to get a statement from her?"

I lowered my head. "She's not a suspect, so don't treat her like one or she's liable to kick your ass. Just go over and ask her when she last saw Cody Pritchard, okay?"

"Yes, sir."

"You don't have to keep calling me sir."

"Hell, I'll call you anything you want, 'long as it gets me on your good side for once." I tried not to, but the smile played on my face for an instant. "You sure you don't want me to go with you to talk to the hunters?" I sighed as he pulled out a small, black vinyl notebook and a section map of the state. "I went by earlier and got the plate numbers, Michigan, with no wants or warrants. Willis at the office said there were four of 'em." He paused for a moment. "They're going to be armed."

"Well, I'll put on an orange vest before I go over." I reached out and tore the page from his notebook and took the map. He didn't like me taking his evidence but followed me out the door anyway. I pointed over to Vic's unit. "Take that one."

"That's all right, mine's warmed up."

We paused beside his car. "I am proud to say that this vehicle does not accurately represent the Absaroka County Sheriff's Department." I guess it hurt his feelings.

"This car will do a hundred and sixty."

"I doubt that and, if it does, it better not do it in this county. Anyway, I don't think Dorothy's gonna run for it, so you're safe." I nodded toward the office. "Hanging by the door with the Phillies key chain." Whiz kids.

He slumped and started back, stopping to ask, "We meet back here?"

"Sure, we'll synchronize watches."

It was six blocks to the Log Cabin Motel on 16 leading toward the mountains. It's an old style place with twelve-by-twelve log structures and faded red neon. I pulled the Bullet up to the office and went in to talk to Willis, who informed me that the Michigan men had been up late celebrating their last night in town. This didn't sound like men who had shot somebody, but you never knew. Willis asked who whacked Cody Pritchard, and I asked him why it was that when somebody died in town everybody started talking like John Garfield.

They were in cabins 7 and 8, so I walked down the row beside the imprint of Turk's 50-series tire tracks. Topflight detective work. I'm sure with the glass-pack mufflers he had been as inconspicuous as the Daytona 500. There was a brand new Suburban parked between the two cabins, Michigan plates. I couldn't believe he had called them in. I knocked at the door of the nearest cabin and heard a muffled groan. I knocked again.

"Oh God . . ."

I knocked again. "Sheriff's Department. Could you open the door, please?"

"Randy, this is not funny . . ." I leaned against the glossy, green doorjamb and knocked once again. After a few seconds, a young man in his underwear and a camo T-shirt snatched open the door. "Do you know what time it is?!" He was short and kind of round with light brown hair and a two-week beard. It did not take long for him to figure out I wasn't Randy.

"Good morning. I'm Sheriff Longmire, and I'd like a word with you." At first he didn't move, and I could see the wheels turning as he tried to figure out what it was that he had done to bring himself in contact with me. These few moments in the beginning can often tell me what I need to know. You hear about eye movement, nose touching, all that crap but, when you get right down to it, it's just a feeling. The little voice in the back of your head just says, "Yeah, this is the guy." My little voice had taken the fifth, and I figured this was not the guy. Besides, I was probably looking for a perpetrator who had acted alone. I told him he could put his pants on.

I waited out by their SUV and watched the cars go by. The air was brisk, and I was starting to regret not bringing my coat from the Bullet. The aspen trees around the cabins and adjacent campground were a bright butter and shimmered in the light wind. They had been tenacious in the face of the small snowstorm of the evening before, trying to hold onto fall. Only a few loose leaves tumbled across the gravel toward the alley behind the motel. But the sun was shining this morning, and the whole place just seemed to glow.

He remembered his jacket. After he closed the door to the cabin, the curtain flipped back just a touch and then hung slack as it had before. "You want the other guys, too?"

I introduced my most ingratiating smile. "No, I figure you'll do." He didn't seem happy with this turn of events. "I'm afraid you have me at a disadvantage, mister?"

"Anderson, Mike Anderson." He was quick with it, and the name matched the registration of the vehicle.

"Mr. Anderson, do you mind taking a little walk with me here?" I gestured toward the office, where the Bullet was parked and, more importantly, where my jacket lay on the seat. He started, and I figured this guy's never had any dealings with law enforcement in his life other than traffic violations. I figured to start easy. "Why don't you tell me about last night?"

He bit his lip, nodding his head in agreement. "I am really sorry about all that noise."

"Um-hmm." *Um-hmm* was one of my secret weapons. I could give out with a noncommittal *um-hmm* with the best of them.

"We didn't tear anything up . . . I mean we made a lot of noise?"

"Willis did mention it . . . But that's not why I'm here." Now he looked really worried. "I just need to ask you about the areas that you might have hunted in your visit here." We had arrived at the Bullet, where I opened the door, fished out my coat, and pulled it on. "Sorry, it's getting a little cool. The areas? Sections for your hunting permits?"

His eyes stayed in the truck, taking in the radio, radar, and especially the Remington 870 that was locked to the dash. After a moment he spoke. "You mean the numbers?"

"Yep, that would be helpful." I waited. "You're not sure what the numbers are?"

"No, but they're in the truck."

As we started back, the tone became a little more conversational. I commented on the weather, and he related how he and his friends had been surprised by the little storm last night, how the roads had been slick with snow coming off the mountain. "You fellows were hunting on the mountain?"

"Yes, sir." He unlocked the Chevy and dug into the center console where I caught a glimpse of a red box indicating Federal brand ammunition. After a moment, he produced four bright and shining bow-hunting permits.

Bow hunting permits. I pursed my lips and blew out. "You fellows are bow hunters?

"Yes, sir." I checked the permits; they were all mountain, 24, 166, 25. "Look, is there something we're being charged with? Should I be getting a lawyer or something?

"I'm hoping that won't be necessary, Mr. Anderson. Do you or any of your party have any firearms?"

"No."

Maybe he was just nervous. "You're sure?"

"Yes. Well . . ." Moment of truth. "Randy has a .38 in the glove box."

"Is it loaded?"

"It might be."

"Are you aware that a loaded, vehicularly concealed weapon constitutes a misdemeanor offense in this state?" Vehicularly—was that a word? Where did I get this stuff? I smiled again to let him know I didn't think he was Al Capone. "So, let's say you and I make a deal? I won't examine the legendary Randy's pistol to see if it's loaded and you answer a few more of my questions." He figured it was a good deal. I pulled the section map out of my coat pocket, spread it out, and, with Mike's help, held it on their hood. He said they had asked at the Game and Fish about sections 23 and 26 because Anderson's father had hunted there years ago, claiming the deer on the Powder River draw were much larger than those on the mountain. Anderson's father was right, but I didn't share that with Mike; my ranch was in that section. They had driven out there Friday at noon and circled up along the Powder River coming back past Arvada, Clearmont, and Crossroads.

"Did you get off the main road at any point?"

"Um, three times. Once to watch some antelope just at the top of the hill after that little town at the main road?"

"Arvada."

"Once where there was an old bridge headed south."

Maybe something. "An old kings-bridge structure?" His face was blank. "A trestle system of steel girders that goes over the road with an old car stuffed into the bank on the far side?"

"Yes, sir. Now that you mention it."

"Did you see anyone, or anything else, out there?" He paused to think. I was going to have to talk to all of them. Was I ever going to get to sleep?

"No."

"You're sure?"

"Yes, sir."

"Did anybody see you?"

"No. I mean there were some cars and trucks that went by . . ." He was thinking hard but wasn't coming up with anything.

"But you didn't speak to anyone?"

"No."

"What about the third stop?" His face brightened. I guess he figured the governor had called with the reprieve.

"We had lunch at a little place about twenty miles out."

"The Red Pony?"

He pointed a finger at me, and I started figuring that Anderson sold something for a living. "That was it."

I asked him what they had, and he said cheeseburgers. I asked how they were, and he said they were okay.

"Just okay?"

"Yes, sir. Why? Is that important?"

A gust of wind fluttered the map. "No, I just want to give the chief-cook-and-bottle-washer some flak. You ate at this place on the way back to town? About what time was that?

"Right after noon, maybe one." I took out my pen and made some notes on the map. "Your picture is on the wall. Out there at the bar with all the medals, maps, and stuff, isn't it?" I continued to scribble away. "You two were in the war together? You and the Indian guy?"

"Yep, the war to start all wars." I don't think he got it.

"I mean the food wasn't that bad . . ." He started sounding apologetic. I couldn't wait to give Henry an earful. "It took him a little while to get it out to us, but I think he had just opened. You sure get your money's worth. He cut the fries out of potatoes right there on the bar, and I got this cheeseburger that had about a half pound of jalapeños on it."

I stopped scribbling.

3

There was a clattering as someone tried to pull what sounded like pots and pans from one of the many boxes that lined the kitchen wall. My head slumped against my pillow; almost fourteen hours of sleep and I still felt like shit. It looked like a nice day though. From my perspective near the floor, I had a clear view of brilliant blue skies without a cloud in sight. There was more noise from the kitchen, and whistling. Unless I missed my guess, it was Prokofiev's Symphony Number One, sometimes in D, and it was being butchered. I dragged myself to a sloped sitting position and stretched my back, allowing the little muscle just left of my spine and halfway down to decide how it was going to let me live today. The prognosis was fair.

I looked through the opaque plastic coating that still clung to the glass door between the bedroom and kitchen, pushed to my feet, and stumbled. I turned the glass knob, stolen almost a decade ago from our rented house in town, and confronted the Cheyenne Nation who was resplendent in his old Kansas City Chiefs jersey, complete with YOUR NAME printed on the back. "Hey, people are trying to sleep in here."

"After fourteen hours you have constituted clinical death." He was popping open a can of biscuits on the particle board edge of the counter and lining an old pie pan with them.

"Did you wash that?"

He paused. "Should I have?"

"Well, there's mouse shit on most of that stuff."

His shoulders sagged as he pulled the biscuits out of the pan and inspected the underside of each one. "How do you live like this?" He turned to look at me. "Will you please go put some clothes on?" I retreated into the bedroom, retrieved my bathrobe from the nail in the stud wall, and ambled back to the kitchen.

I took a seat on the stool by the counter and poured a cup of coffee into a Denver Broncos mug. I figured it was my job to do everything possible to irritate him this afternoon. I was feeling better. "What's for brunch?"

"You mean besides mouse shit?" He had dropped about two pounds of pork sausage into a frying pan that I couldn't recall ever having seen before. I took a sip of the French roast; it seemed like all I did was drink the stuff. Cady sent me fancy, whole-bean coffee from Philadelphia in trendy little resealable bags, but I hadn't gotten around to getting a grinder.

"Game Day." It was a tradition. Twice a year we found ourselves locked in the death struggle of the AFC Western Division: Broncos vs. Chiefs. Pancake Day and Game Day on the same weekend.

"Yes, I know. You are going to get your ass kicked today."

"Oh, please . . ." I tried the coffee again; it wasn't so bad. "Where did you find a grinder?" He ignored me and continued to look through the Folgers can that held my meager selection of utensils, so I asked, "Spatula?"

"Yes."

I looked at the scattered containers resting haphazardly against the wall, at the strata of Rainier beer crates that were stacked in every available space. It was daunting, but he had found a frying pan. "Box."

"Jesus." The pork sausage began to sizzle. He approached the boxes and began going through them in a methodical fashion, top row first, left to right. "Walt, we need to go over a few things." This had an ominous tone to it. "There was a time when this particular lifestyle had its place, the grieving widower valiantly sallying forth through a sea of depression and cardboard. This gave way to the eccentric lawman era, but now, Walt my friend, you are just a slob."

I hugged my coffee cup a little closer and straightened my robe. "I'm a lovable slob."

He had made it through the top row and was now working the collapsed fringe toward the backdoor. "At the risk of sending you into a tailspin, Martha has been dead for four years."

"Three." He stopped and leaned against the door facing, the other hand at his side.

The sausage popped, sending a small splatter to the plywood floor. I looked at the splatter mark; it was relatively contained, with a few scalloped edges due to the height of trajectory, ray-emitting tendrils reaching for the center of the room. If the object emitting the splatter is in motion, the drops will be oval and have little tails, which will project in the horizontal direction that the drop was moving. As the top of the teardrop lands last, splatters on a wall can tell you if the assailant is left- or right-handed. I knew a lot about splatters. I wondered how Vic was doing. I looked at the unopened manila envelope sitting in my chair, a priority set of pictures illustrating the next-to-final resting place of Cody Pritchard. I had been so tired by the time I had gotten home that I had thrown them on the recliner, too exhausted to concentrate. Ruby's handwriting looked personal and out of place: Scene Investigation Photographs, 9/29/2:07 A.M.

"Four." His eyes were level, and his voice carried a tired resignation to the battle joined. "Walt, it is time to get on with your life . . . I mean college kids live better than this." I didn't know what to say; I had had a kid in college and then in law school, and she had lived better than this. "But I have a four-fold plan for your redemption."

I sipped some more coffee and stared at the floor. "Does this involve getting me a woman?" He pulled the spatula out of the nearest box. I advised him to wash it, which he did after making a face, then set about breaking up the brick of meat in the pan.

"Getting you a woman is the third part."

"I like this plan, but I think we should move the third part up."

"We have to get you to the point where you are worthy of a woman."

"Why do I get the feeling that I'm not going to like the other parts of this plan?"

"Walt, your life is a mess, your house is a mess, and you are a mess.

It is about time we did some cleaning up." He looked around the cabin, I'm sure for dramatic effect. "Let us start with the easy stuff. This was a nice little house when you first got started, but that was five years ago." I thought it was four. "You have got to get some gutters so the run-off stops cutting a moat around the house. You are going to have to use a bleach solution to cut the gray off the things and then put some UV protection on them. You need a porch, and a deck out back would not be such a horrible thing . . ."

My head hurt. "I don't have the time for all that, let alone the energy."

He found the opener on the counter and began opening a number of small cans. "We are not talking time, energy, or money, which will be your next argument. We are talking inclination. Now, I know these two young men . . ."

"Oh, no. I'm not going to have a bunch of thieving redskins roaming around my place while I'm not here."

He choked laughing, his arms spread wide to encompass the entirety of the room. "What would they steal?" He had a point. "These boys just started up their own contracting firm; they are hungry, cheap, and they are good. I can have them over here tomorrow morning at eight." I looked around the room at the stud walls, exposed wiring, and dirt-encrusted plywood floors.

I sighed. "Okay, what's part two?"

"We get you in shape."

I took another sip of coffee; it was getting cold. "Oh, I'm past that shit."

"I want you to think about part three." He smiled. "I want you to think about part three while we're going through parts one and two." He bumped me in the shoulder, and I spilled a little coffee. More splatters. He turned and dumped a small can of green chilies into the pan.

"I don't suppose any of this might stem from conversations you may or may not have had with Cady, Ruby, or Vic."

He was working the meat around, and the smell of the green peppers was intoxicating. "I talk with a lot of people about a lot of things."

"How come you didn't talk to me about Cody Pritchard eating his last meal at the Pony?"

He placed the metal stem of the spatula on the edge of the frying pan so that the plastic handle wouldn't melt and leaned against the counter. I listened to him breathe and realized how much he had aged in the last twenty years, or the last two seconds. After a moment he reached across the counter with a steady hand and poured me another cup. "I did not think it was that important. You ran out of the place Friday night and did not say a word to anybody, and I knew I was going to see you this morning. I guess I thought I had more important things to talk to you about." He poured himself a cup and placed the pot back on the burner. He looked me in the eye just to clear the air. "Well, officer . . . It was the night of November second at approximately 6:02 P.M. that the aforementioned, one Pritchard, Cody, entered the establishment known as the Red Pony. Witnesses to this fact are Mssrs. Charlie Small Horse, Clel Phillips, and the attesting Henry Standing Bear. The condition of Mr. Pritchard at that time was one of profound intoxication, whereupon he was refused alcoholic beverage and served one Mexican cheeseburger deluxe, including fries and a Coke. Twenty-five minutes later there was a verbal altercation between Mr. Pritchard and Mr. Small Horse, which resulted in Mr. Pritchard being escorted to the door of the establishment and asked to leave. The last I saw of Cody, he wheeled that piece of shit palomino-primer truck of his around in my parking lot, sprayed gravel, and headed east to a far better place than he had ever been before. So, do you want to book me, or you want to go take a shower?" He sipped his coffee.

"You seem a little defensive."

"No shit? I just want to keep my proficiency and conduct reports up to snuff." He smiled a tight little smile. "Anything else?"

"No, you pretty well covered it. I think I'll go take a shower." I stood up and walked past him toward the bathroom. I picked up the coffee since it was growing on me. I was hoping he'd say something, anything that would give me the excuse to turn around.

"Do not get me wrong, Walt, I did not like the kid, but then I do not know anybody who did. If you are looking for a suspect, just open the phone book." He was watching the sausage as it burbled. "Are there any leads?"

I sighed and leaned against the refrigerator. "Toxicology at DCI said a high content of brewed barley malt, cereal grains, hops, and yeast . . ."

"Known in the trade as Busch Lite."

"Ground beef, jalapeños, and American cheese."

"Mexican cheeseburger. Anything else?"

"Nothing from toxicology. Ballistics says no lands or grooves, and the deformity of impact with the sternum makes identification that much more difficult."

His curiosity sharpened. "Smoothbore?"

I shrugged. "Who knows, but if it is, it narrows the search to ten yards or less."

"Which means it was somebody the little shit knew." He smiled the tight smile again. "At least well enough to let them get close with a shotgun." He pushed down on the frying pan handle, allowing the grease to puddle at the end of the skillet closest to him. "That is pretty close."

"Yep."

"No companions, no tracks?"

"Nope."

"Any cover?"

My turn to smile. "That Powder River country, there's a good-lookin' woman behind every tree . . ." He joined me for the rest. "There just ain't any trees."

"Back to square one. Wadding or contact dispersal?"

"Nope. No powder tattooing, either."

"Any hope of brass?"

"Ferg and that bunch didn't come up with anything."

"Hmmm . . ." He grunted. "I will withhold comment on whether Ferg and his bunch could slap their ass with both hands." He frowned at the frying pan, spooned the pooled grease into a measuring cup that he must have used to apportion tomato paste, and flipped the majority of the contents. "Meteorite?"

I had to smile. "The more people I talk to, the more I am convinced that this may have been an act of God."

"Hate to see the Supreme Being take the fall for this one."

"He sees even the smallest sparrow fall."

"That would pretty much describe the decedent, but would this not be stretching the jurisdiction thing?"

"Maybe." The mood had lightened, and it was an opportunity that I couldn't pass up. "Hey?"

"Hmm?" He looked at me, and the expression his face carried was one of open concern for a friend who had all but accused him of impeding a murder investigation. My heart wasn't in the question, but I had to ask. "You know the scuttlebutt on the Rez?"

"What, you worried about the Indian vote?" He smiled to let me in on the joke, but it still hurt. "What?"

"The Little Bird rape case . . ."

"Melissa."

"Melissa." I was feeling lower and lower. "What's the general feeling on the Rez about the job I did?" There was a brief look of irritation as he flipped his hair back and trapped what would have been a fine tail on a good cutting horse in a leather strip he had pulled from the back pocket of his jeans.

"General feeling"—he pointed up the phrase as silly white-man talk—"is that you could have done better."

"And what is the basis of my failure?"

He turned his head and looked into the distance at the log wall only two feet away. "Two years suspended sentence, two years parole."

"People don't think Vern Selby and a jury had something to do with that?"

"These people do not have any bond with that judge or jury, none of whom were . . . Indian, and they do with you." He paused. "You should take that as a grave compliment." He opened a ziplocked bag of preshredded cheese and offered me some. I took a pinch and stuffed it in my mouth. Pepper jack. "Anyway, the goodwill of these people is not going to have much effect on your condition. There is only one person who can offer you absolution in this case, and he is a difficult individual with whom to deal . . . he forgives everyone but himself, and he never forgets." We stood looking at each other, chewing. "You should go take a shower. Part three said she would be here for kickoff at two." He pulled open the door of the oven and checked on his biscuits. The smell was marvelous.

"Part three?"

"Vonnie Hayes expressed a desire to participate in the bonding ritual this afternoon. I thought it might lead to a more desirable ritual between the two of you later this evening."

I took a moment to reply. "I just saw her yesterday morning. She didn't say anything."

"Women seem to enjoy surprising you, perhaps because it is so easy."

I looked around the house at the piles of books and accumulated dirt on the floors, the walls, and the ceiling. "Oh, shit . . ."

He followed my eyes and shook his head. "Yes, it is very bad, but we will tell her you are under construction. Red Road Contracting, the young men I told you about, will be here tomorrow morning." He pulled the biscuits from the oven and placed them on one of the front burners. "Go take a shower."

I started, but turned. "What's part four?"

"Spirituality, but that may have to come from somebody else."

I turned the water on in the shower and spent the time waiting for it to heat up by inspecting my bullet holes. I had four: one in the left arm, one in the right leg, and two in the chest. I looked at the one in my left arm since it was the closest. It was 357/100ths of an inch with two clean, marbled white dots on either side. The one on the inside had well-defined edges and was about the size of a dime. On the other side it was blurred, had a tail like a tadpole that had drifted back to my elbow, and was about the size of a silver dollar. The water temperature was acceptable, so I stepped in and grabbed a bar of oatmeal soap that Cady had sent me. I liked it because it didn't smell. I kicked at the slow contraction of the vinyl curtains.

It was a monkey-shit brown Olds Delta 88 with two hubcaps and a peeling, blond vinyl top. I could see they were kids and just flipped the lights on for a second so they would pull over. It took what seemed like a little too long for them to do it. The driver threw open the door and started back toward the car I was using at the time; I figured he was upset because I had pulled him over for what seemed like nothing. I was wrong. He was upset because he and his friend had robbed a liquor store in Casper and had gotten away with $943 when I stopped them en route to Canada.

I lathered up, rinsed off, and felt like I had new skin. I reached for the shampoo and, feeling how light the bottle was, made a mental note to get some more. I had enough unattended mental notes to fill up the Sears wish book.

Near as we could figure, the bullet must have ricocheted off the window facing of the car and passed through my left arm. People always ask what it's like, and the only answer I can come up with is that it's like having a red-hot poker shoved into your flesh. It burns, and it hurts like hell, but only after. I wondered mildly if Vonnie would think that bullet holes are sexy. Martha didn't; she hated them. A beautiful woman in my house; a woman who looked you over from head to toe, was confident and interested. I felt complicated and dreary.

I wiped off the mirror to look into the eyes of Dorian Gray. What I saw did not inspire me with confidence. My hair, wet or dry, has a tendency to stand on end. I fought with it for a while and decided that it was a good thing I was able to wear a hat in my chosen profession. I have large, deep-set gray eyes, a gift from my mother, and a larger than normal chin, a gift from my father. The older I get, the more I think I look like a Muppet. Cady vehemently disagrees with this assessment, but she's fighting her own battle with this particular gene puddle.

It was with a great deal of panic that I heard a mixture of laughter resonate through the spaces at the top of the bathroom drywall and through the shower-curtained doorway. It was a quick right to the bedroom, maybe four feet, but I didn't figure I could make it without being seen. I pulled the old black-watch pattern around my waist, slipped on my worn, moose-hide moccasins, and stepped into the cool, fresh dawn of interpersonal abuse.

As usual, she looked magnificent. Long fingers were wrapped around one of my Denver Broncos mugs, the old one with the white horse snorting through the orange *D*. She wore a plain, khaki ball cap with her ponytail neatly tucked through the adjustable strap in the back, a gray sweatshirt that read VASSAR, blue jeans, and a pair of neon running shoes. She exuded health, sparkling intelligence, and sex, though the last might have just been my read on things. She sat on my foldout step stool and laughed as Henry tried vainly to adjust the reception on my television.

"All right, I give up. What the hell do you have to do to get a decent picture on this thing?"

We had always watched the game at the bar on Henry's satellite-assisted television but, for today's game, he had thought it best to view it within the comfortable confines of my house. He was kneeling by the set, adjusting the fine tuning with the same finesse he had shown with the fuse box two nights ago. "That is decent."

He turned to regard the screen as the usual blobs moved about in indiscriminate patterns. "You have got to be kidding."

I crossed the room and leaned against a six-by-six. "Vonnie, welcome to Château Tyvek."

"Is this the uniform of the day?"

Henry was right; I was going to have to make some changes. "Oh, this was just a little something I threw on." I looked at the Cheyenne Nation. "What's the score?"

He stood with his hands on his hips as two vague football helmets collided and exploded into a million pieces on the screen amid triumphant musical accompaniment. "It hasn't started yet. Is it me or has football gotten more and more like wrestling these days?"

She squeezed my hand. "Bear says he doesn't mind Native American mascots for athletic teams." I noticed he didn't correct her use of the term Native American.

"I don't have a problem with native accoutrements. If they wish to use the tools of our trade to strike fear into their enemies' hearts, who am I to deny them?"

This from the man who had worn a horse-head amulet around his neck for four years in Southeast Asia. Chinese Nung Recon teams and Montagnards believed it had been carved from the sternum of an unfortunate NVA colonel. Henry had done nothing to dissuade them from this thought, and only he and I knew the bone had come from the leg of his mother's old, dry dairy cow that they had had to put down. "How's lunch coming?"

"Who am I, Hop-Sing here?" He opened the oven door and peered in. "Almost there. Plenty of time for you to go put some clothes on."

Her hand trailed after mine as I started for the bedroom. "Don't go to any trouble on my part."

I continued into the bedroom so she wouldn't see how red my face was growing. I looked around the room and saw my life as it was. The edges of the mattress were threadbare and dirty, the sheets an uninviting gray. A battered gooseneck lamp sat on the floor beside the bed with a copy of *Doctor Dogbody's Leg* opened to page seventy-three, where I had left it a while ago. The ever-present beer boxes loomed at the far wall, and the naked light bulbs allowed none of the low-rent squalor to escape. It was like living in an archeological dig. I thought about the woman in the other room and felt like climbing out the window. Instead, I went over to the crate that stood as my bedside table and punched the button just below the flashing red light on the answering machine. Evidently, I hadn't heard it ring.

"Okay, so, after forty-eight hours of intensive ballistic study, we're no fucking closer than we were at the beginning of the weekend." She sounded ragged and edgy, and I was glad I was five hours away. "The cast content on the ballistics is fairly soft; 30 to 1, lead to tin." She took a breath. "Here's the kicker. There's some kind of strange chemical compound . . . You remember those old Glaser Safety Slugs? The GSS's? If that's the case, Cody was SOL."

Shit out of luck.

"So, can you imagine somebody tracking that kid down with Teflon slugs?"

No.

"Yeah, well me neither." There was a pause. "Anyway, I've done all that I can do here, and the pizza at Larry's sucks. So, I'll be home tomorrow. Any questions?"

I stared at the phone machine and shook my head side to side.

"Good. I'm taking tomorrow off. Any problem with that?"

I continued to shake my head.

"Good." Pause. "Maybe I'll see you tomorrow anyway."

When I entered the kitchen, Henry was holding the photographs that had been in the envelope at arms length.

"You need new reading glasses or longer arms?"

"Both."

Vonnie was glancing at the television and questioning him. "Twenty-five percent of all domestic murders go unsolved each year?" She shifted on the stool and smiled at me.

I poured myself another cup of coffee and extended the pot toward her. She shook her head and waited to capture my next words with those eyes. "About five thousand cases go unsolved." Her eyes widened. "About sixty-two percent of homicides in the United States involve firearms, which means me and my compadres have failed to identify some thirty-one hundred killers and their weapons every year."

"Seems like the guys on TV and in the movies always get their man; you real cops must be falling down on the job." He lowered the photographs, and I noticed Vonnie made no effort to look at them.

"Personally, I never miss an episode of *Dragnet*."

She cocked her head, and the eyes narrowed. "It seems like a lot. It was Sheriff Connally here before you, wasn't it?" She grinned and looked off toward the front door.

"You know Lucian?"

"Oh, I had a few run-ins with him back in my bad old days." She laughed, flashing that canine tooth that sparkled like a Pepsodent commercial. "Some of my posse and I had absconded with a fifth of my father's Irish whiskey and high-tailed it to the Skyline Drive-In in Durant."

Henry perked up. "I think I heard about that. Didn't you and Susan Miller dance naked on the hood of that '65 Mustang during *Doctor Zhivago*?"

She was turning just a little pink at the throat. "I was of a young and impressionable age."

"Hell, I would have been impressed too." He stuffed the photographs back into the envelope and handed them to me. "Good luck."

Her smile went away. "You don't think it was an accident?"

"Not really." Henry crossed behind me and opened the refrigerator door to pull out a pitcher I had never seen before, filled with a murky maroon liquid, ice cubes, and lemon and orange slices. I sat the envelope down on the counter and stared at it. "I'm hoping real hard that it is, but evidence is mounting that such is not the case."

"Why?"

"Short-range weapon did the deed, no way you could sneak up on somebody out there. I'd hazard to guess that there aren't many hunters looking to shoot pronghorn or mule deer with a 12 gauge. And there are some things that just don't make sense."

He stirred the contents of the pitcher. "Powder burns."

She was following, but I figured I should explain the details. "When you shoot a shotgun at any range . . ." I paused and weighed the next question. "You know what a shotgun is?"

Her eyes stayed steady to show no offense. "My father used to shoot skeet."

"Right. Well, this is looking like a rifled slug."

"Slug. Doesn't sound pleasant."

"It's not. Slugs basically convert shotguns into oversize rifles with enough power to crack automobile engine blocks."

"Why would somebody want to shoot somebody with something like that?"

"Emphasis."

It rumbled in his chest, and I wondered about all the people who would consider it a good thing that the world was shed of Cody Pritchard. "Cody wasn't exactly beloved by the . . ." I gave him a side-long glance. "Indian community."

She placed a hand on the counter to get his attention. "It's not Indian anymore, it's Native American. Right, Bear?" She nodded for confirmation.

He looked up and pursed his lips sagely. "That is right." He turned his head toward me ever so slightly. "You must learn to be more responsive to Native American sensibilities."

Bastard. "The problem is the slug decreases the range of an already relatively short-range weapon."

"But wasn't he shot in the back?"

"Yep, but you'd still have to get close."

"Could he have been drunk or asleep?"

"Drunk, certainly." Henry wandered over to look at the blobs moving in the television. I had forgotten about the game. "Even with the complications of extensive tissue damage, his posture was likely erect. And since Henry was the last to serve him food and see him alive, I can take his word that Cody was at least capable of driving his truck and walking."

She turned her stool. "You saw him last?"

He stared at the television screen, his arms crossed. "Do not ask me how I can tell, Walt, but I think your team is winning."

She turned back to look at me, then back to him again. "Bear, have I said something wrong?"

"No, you did not say anything wrong . . . We will just say that I was the next to last person to see Mr. Pritchard alive." He smiled to himself and crossed back to the counter. "Sangria, anybody?" He poured the liquid into three tall glasses and handed one to each of us. "How about a toast?" He raised his glass. "Here is to the three thousand one hundred that get away."

"Uneasy lies the head that wears the crown."

I looked into the big, brown eyes with wisps of butterscotch slipping by. "To Doctor Zhivago."

The game was uneventful and, as near as we could tell, the Broncos won by two field goals. By six-thirty we had dispatched the casserole, and Henry had made excuses that he had to go check on the bar. At the moment, I was massaging Vonnie's foot from the opposite stool, with the gentle warmth of what remained of the sangria seeping into every relaxing muscle in my body. It had been one of those spectacular Wyoming sunsets, the ones everybody thinks only happen in an *Arizona Highways* magazine. Broiling waves of small bonfires leapt on top of one another as far as the horizon with injured purples drifting in multilayered, frozen sheets back to the skyline.

"So, I didn't hurt his feelings?"

"No, I can guarantee that wasn't it." Her toenails were burgundy; the color matched the sangria, and I figured she had them done in Denver on a regular basis.

"You must know him best?"

I thought about what knowing Henry Standing Bear best meant and that that opened up a lot of country. "I don't know about best." I paused for a moment, but it wasn't enough for her. "About ten years ago we were over in Sturgis for that motorcycle fiasco that they have every year. They put out this desperate plea for assistance and, if you're an off-duty police officer, you can make a lot of money in one weekend. I was saving for Cady, to get her a car, and figured an extra thousand wouldn't hurt. Henry hadn't ever been over for the big wingding, so he decided to tag along. So, we're sitting there at this little greasy spoon near the motorcycle museum the morning after, and I'm telling Henry that if I ever get this bright idea again to just slap me in the back of the head with a stilson wrench. That's when this Indian fellow . . ."

"Native American."

". . . This Native American walks over to our table and just stands there. He's a big guy like Henry, and I'm quickly running through the faces I've locked up for DUI, public indecency, aggravated assault, reckless endangerment, and jaywalking that weekend alone. I'm not making any connections, but the longer I look at this guy's face, the more I'm sure that I've seen him somewhere before. That's when Henry stops chewing his bacon, still looking at his plate, and says, 'How have you been?' I'm looking at this guy like never before, but damned if I can make the reach. He's good-looking, maybe thirty, but he's got a lot of miles on him. The guy says, 'Good. You?' I look at Henry and all he says is, 'Cannot complain.' You know how he never uses contractions. Well, the fellow just stands there for another minute, pulls out a cigarette, and lights it. Then he says, 'Who'd listen?' And with this he just kind of turns and glides out of the place. I'm watching him walk out, and it hits me. He walks just like Henry. I turn to look at him and start to speak, but he cuts me off. 'Half-brother.' And that's all he says. Come to find out, he hasn't talked to the guy in fifteen years. As far as I know, he hasn't talked to him since."

She looked puzzled. "Big falling out?"

"Who the hell knows?" I squeezed her foot and leaned back on my stool. "I don't think you hurt his feelings. I think it's just a lack of windmills." She laughed. "That, and probably there's a part of Henry that wishes he had done it."

"You're joking?"

I wished mildly I hadn't brought it up, because it was going to be hard to explain. "Nope."

"You really think he's capable of something like that?"

"I think under certain circumstances, everybody's capable of doing something like that."

She exchanged feet, tucking the other one under her, and thought for a moment. "I guess I don't, but then I haven't seen all the things you've seen." Her eyes held steady as they met mine. "Is there part of you that wishes you'd done it?"

I thought for a moment, but she had me. "Yep, I guess there is a vicious little part of me that does."

I looked out the front window and watched the big cottonwood at the end of my road sway in the breeze that had just come up. It wasn't bone cold, but it would be by the end of the night. Probably in the teens, and I could see the frost on the windows even though it wasn't there. Winter was almost here, and I had to start remembering to look for the fall.

She seemed lost in thought too, staring at my hands that were wrapped around her foot; but as long as I didn't give it back, she had to stay. "Well, since we're sort of telling our deepest, darkest secrets . . ." She trapped her lower lip in her teeth, let it slide out slowly, and continued, "When Cady was trying to fix us up a few years ago?" I waited. "I think a little part of me really was kind of hoping that it would work out." She paused. "I'm telling you this because I don't want to be sending mixed signals."

I was getting a sinking feeling, but I still held on to the foot.

"I just don't want to get moving too fast. The last relationship I was in was not a good one, and I think a lot of it had to do with the fact that I was in too much of a hurry." Her eyes dulled and the angles on her face flattened and grew sad. "I think there was an awful lot about him that I thought I knew, but the truth was I was just coloring in the missing parts with colors I liked." Her eyes sharpened again when she looked at me. "I can't afford that with you; I like you too much."

"Thank you." I still wasn't giving up the foot. "What if you don't like the way I look when I sleep with my mouth open?"

We both laughed. "I'm willing to take that chance."

I sniffed and bit my own lip. "Vonnie . . ."

She did her best Gene Tierney. "Walter?" We laughed again.

"Don't let this lusty, youthful appearance fool you. I'm not seventeen anymore, and I don't have the expectations of a seventeen-year-old." I took the last sip of my sangria. "I, uh . . ." I cleared my throat and forged ahead. "At least you had a last relationship . . ." I cleared my throat again. "I haven't had any relationships since Martha died. Talk about pushing a virtue to vice . . ."

And to my absolute shock, her eyes welled and a single tear streaked like lightning across her face. I fought back the sudden burning in my own eyes and squeezed her foot. It was a fine foot, long and narrow with toes that looked like fingers. Aristocratic, as feet go. My mother used to say it was a sign of royalty; that, and eating one thing on your plate at a time. I'm not sure how much royalty my mother ever met and whether she ever got to break bread with them or examine their feet, but she felt strongly about things. It's a family trait.

I took one of my calloused paws and drew the soft part on the back across her cheek, smearing the seawater to her hairline. She sobbed a broken sob and pulled at a loose strand of hair, tucking it behind an ear, and then caught my hand. She placed it on her knee. She wasn't a small woman, but it took both hands to conceal my one. She pushed my knuckles apart, stretching the fingers around her calf and securing them there. She seemed like a child, satisfied with her work. Pulling back, her fingers spread to examine her creation, she smiled through the contractions of her diaphragm. I wanted her more than anything in the world. I set my jaw and just looked. It was more than enough.

I drove her home through the fog that crept off Piney Creek, which was desperate to find its way through to the Clear and, in turn, the Powder. One stream started in the high reaches of the Bighorn Wilderness Area, at the very top of Cloud Peak, dropping a couple of thousand feet to shoot past Lake Desmet through the valley of the Lower Piney and making a left at Vonnie's house. The other flexed its hydraulic muscles from Powder River Pass to the south, widening like a river at the flats through Durant till it met its lover about a half mile from my place. The small patches of snow were melting in the last warmth of the day's heat before the night could get a firm grasp, and the low-lying fog was like riding on clouds.

I shifted gears, making the turn at Crossroads, and looked down 16 toward the Red Pony. The lights were on, and I thought about my friend, patiently listening to another drunk telling another drunken story about getting drunk. Vonnie moaned a little and then readjusted her head. I put my hand on her shoulder, and she snuggled under my sheepskin coat, her legs curled up in the passenger seat. I listened to the heat blowing through the vents, the hum of the big V-10, and thought back.

She argued at first, but the sangria and the emotional impact had layered her with fatigue. She was surprisingly light, and I was surprisingly smart enough to open the truck door before I carried her out. I figured she could get a ride back over the next day to get her little red Jeep or send somebody over.

It took about ten minutes to get to her place, and I didn't pass another vehicle the whole way. I had the feeling I was involved in some sort of clandestine operation as I pulled through the wrought-iron gates. Tucked in a hillside in Portugee Gulch, I was impressed by the size of the place. Cady had told me all about Vonnie's house, about the indoor pool, spiral staircases, massive stone fireplaces, and statuary everywhere you looked. It wasn't the usual big box log house; instead, it looked like it had started out at a reasonable size and geometrically evolved as Vonnie's lifestyle had developed. As a reflection, I wondered where her lifestyle was headed.

I pulled the Bullet up to the front door of the largest part. A number of movement-activated halogen lamps came on, but there were no lights in any other part of the house. I climbed out and went to the door; roughly four thousand dollars for a highly intricate, electric home-defense system, and it was unlocked. It was a large Spanish-style one that clicked solidly and opened to reveal an expansive living room with numerous leather sofas. I figured she could sleep on one of them for the night. I went back outside and got her, carefully easing her through the doorway and down the three steps that led to the larger part of the room. The walls were an oversanded plaster that looked like they had been done and redone by numerous old-world crafts-men. Three archways led toward an elevated dining room that over-looked a pool in the back, and the Saltillo tile gleamed with the luster of polished mahogany. There were paintings on all the walls, mostly abstracts, and I felt like I lived in one of my cardboard boxes.

I placed her onto the largest of the sofas and arranged her head on one of the Indian-blanket pillows. I was at a loss as to what to do next, thinking I should leave a note or something, finally deciding that my coat was enough. I pulled the scruffy, sheepskin monstrosity up around her chin and kneeled there, looking at her. She truly was an exquisite female and a remarkable thing to take in, even with the little furrows that now crowded the bridge of her nose; it was probably the smell of the coat. I stood and backed toward the door, sad to see the evening come to a close. I was feeling very tender, and I didn't know how long it would be before I felt that way again. Then I saw him.

About halfway across the elevated dining room in the archway to the left, he stood looking at me. He hadn't made a sound as we pulled up, hadn't made a sound when I opened the door, not even when I brought her in and laid her on the sofa. That's what worried me. Here, at Portugee Gulch amid the fog of Piney Creek, stood the Hound of the Baskervilles. She hadn't said anything about having a dog. He must have weighed close to 155 pounds, most of it chest and head. The yellow reflection in his eyes blinked once, and then he slowly walked to the edge of the stairs. The better to see you with, my dear.

There was German shepherd or wolf in there somewhere and cer-tainly some Saint Bernard. The muzzle and ears were dark, dappling into a reddish color, with a white blaze at his chest. His right lip lifted to free a canine tooth out of the Paleozoic period, and he rumbled so low it sounded like thunder rolling down the valley. I glanced over at Vonnie, who was sleeping soundly, and figured she'd wake up when she heard the strangling sound of my last scream. I have to admit that my hand drifted down to where my sidearm usually was and then rested not so casually on my empty leg. He didn't move any farther, and I heard this strained version of my voice saying, "Good dog, good doggy . . . Easy, boy."

I fought the urge to run, knowing that such an enticement to wolves and to the Cheyenne was impossible to resist. Backing toward the door, I tripped at the bottom step and his head bobbed at the opportunity. We locked eyes, and I think there was an understanding. He might kill me, he might eat me, but I didn't have to taste good. There was an umbrella and a loose assemblage of three golf clubs in the umbrella stand at the door. I figured that I could hold him off with the one iron, but then I'd most certainly need divine intervention, because everyone knows that God's the only one who can hit a one iron. "Easy boy, easy . . ."

He didn't move, just watched. I backed the rest of the way out the door and slowly shut it in front of me. For a moment, I thought about opening it again and locking it, then figured the hell with it. Whoever went in there next would get what he deserved. I quietly walked across the red-slate gravel as the halogen lights came on again. The place was like a disco. I wheeled the truck around the compound and headed out through the gate from whence I came. Absentmindedly, I turned on the radio, suddenly feeling the urge to hear voices, voices I didn't necessarily have to respond to. Then I had a rotten thought. I keyed the mic. "Absaroka County Sheriff's Department, this is Unit One, come in Base."

His voice was sleepy. I didn't blame him; I would have been asleep, too. "Jesus, yeah. This is Base, yeah, go ahead."

I suppressed a laugh. "Are you okay?"

Static. "Yeah, I'm okay, are you okay?"

"Yep . . . I'm okay." I looked out the windshield and navigated my way through the fog. "I'll talk to you in the morning."

"Roger that, okay." And with that, he was gone.

And I really was okay. It wasn't exactly the evening I had planned. To tell the truth, I was probably relieved. The untold expectations of my first date in four, not three, years had kind of hammered me. When I made the turn at Crossroads, the lights were off at the bar, and I was glad there was nobody there to share war stories with. It was time to go to my little cabin with its stud walls, plywood floors, and UV-unprotected logs. Henry was right. It was time I got around to a few changes.

When I got home, the red light was once again blinking on my phone machine, so I punched the button. "Hi, Pops . . ."

4

"You are not dying."

"How do you know, you've never died." I pushed my spine into the depression in the mile-marker post and eased my weight against its scaly green-painted surface.

"I have died many times."

"Oh, shit."

"Get up."

I picked a piece of cheat grass from the red shale roadbed, and it came out in one whole stalk, roots and all. It was cold, too. The frost clung to every surface, encasing the poor little fellow like those dragonflies you see trapped in thousand-year-old amber. If I was going to keep doing this every other morning, I had to get a pair of gloves. I raised my head and looked at him as he positioned himself in front of the rising sun like some fighter pilot moving in for the kill. He nudged me with his foot. "Get up."

I took a large swipe at his legs, but he nimbly jumped back out of the way, gravitating to the balls of his feet and rolling up on another set of wheels. The tendons and veins popped out of his naked ankles like those of some skinned cat, and I looked away, colder than when I hadn't noticed he wasn't wearing any socks. He came back and nudged me with the same foot as I resettled against my post. "If you don't stop kicking me, you really are going to find out about dying."

"This is something I did not know about you, grumpy in the mornings." He looked into the little breaths of wind, which clattered the dried leaves that had refused to release their grip on the black cottonwoods along the Piney. Under Tiepolo skies, shrouded with banks of

71

gray, rolled back at the lavender and cream edges like waves receding from a high shore, the sun was just starting to hit the tops of the hills in the Wolf Valley. I wouldn't die, so I was feeling better.

"What are you smiling at?"

"Leave me alone, I'm having a moment of grace."

He stared at me. "Well, we would not want to interrupt that."

I tossed a piece of shale at him, missing by a good two feet. "If you can have multiple lives, I can have moments of grace."

He grunted. "How was your moment of grace last night?"

"Not bad, as moments of grace go." I thought for a while. "More like a moment of truth."

He nodded. "That is good, they are harder to come by." He winced as he stretched the tendons in his right knee; maybe he wasn't indestructible. "So, she left the Jeep?"

"Yep."

"You drive her home?"

"Yep."

He stretched for a minute more, leaned against the mile-marker post I was sitting against, and sighed. "Okay . . ."

"Okay, what?"

"We do not have to talk about it."

"We are talking about it."

"No, I am talking about it, and all you are doing is saying 'yep.' "

I put on my best faraway smile and looked at the glowing hills down the valley. "Yep . . ."

He kicked me again.

A battered black and maroon three-quarter-ton diesel with a roll feeder, signature MCKAY RANCH, was coming down the road; it slowed as it got to the bridge and rolled to a stop beside us. Clel Phillips was the head ramrod for Bill McKay and was probably wondering what the Indian was doing beside the road with the sheriff laying alongside the barrow ditch. He rolled the window down on the feed truck and rested his shoulder against the door. "Hey."

Clel poured himself coffee from an aged Stanley Thermos and

offered Henry a sip, which was gratefully declined, so he motioned toward me, and I left grace behind for a steaming cup full of drip-dry Folgers. My legs were about to kill me. "Hey."

The coffee tasted good, and I used my other hand to pull the sopping sweatpants from between my legs. Clel filled the cup up again. "What're you fellas up to?"

"Running."

He looked up and back down the road. "From what?" He took the insulated cap back and took a sip. "Hey, Sheriff . . ." Business call. I never ceased to be charmed by the cowboy way of priming the pump. They were like cattle, constantly looking into your eyes to see if there was danger or if there needed to be. It was the best part of the cowboys' character, the animal husbandry part. They stayed up through many nights in frozen calving sheds, running their hands over and into expectant mothers, comforting them, soliciting them. The cows' lives depended on them, and their lives depended on the cows. It wasn't an easy way to live, but it had its rewards. "I'm havin' a little trouble with Jeff Tory."

"What kind of trouble?"

"You know that stretch of bottom land between his place and McKay's? Well, he's been lettin' bird hunters on his place, and they seem to be havin' a little trouble figurin' out where Tory's place ends and ours begins."

Escaped pheasant, Hungarian partridges, and chuckers were prevalent up and down the valley as they fled from the two local bird farms and from the eastern Remington Wingmasters that pursued them. We had the best bird hunting in the state, and every once in a while somebody else found out about it. I hadn't hunted since Vietnam; somehow, it had lost its appeal. Clel was finishing up his saga by the time I got interested in his problem, ". . . and Bill says he's gonna give 'em a load of rock salt for their trouble."

"Well . . ." Henry was bobbing up and down, but I paused for a moment to collect my thoughts. In sheriffing, shooting people with anything was bad business, and Bill McKay was just the kind of ornery

73

cuss that would go after double-ought buck hunters with rock salt just to call it even. "Does Bill have signs up along that stretch of fence?"

This is not what Clel wanted to hear, another chore to add to his ever-growing list. "No, we ain't got no signs. You'd think the fence would be enough."

"Well, I guess it's not." The state law was fence to keep out, which meant that if you didn't want anything on your land, you were responsible for the fences, but evidently it took stronger measures for the two-legged variety. "Why don't you run into Shipton's and get some of those yellow metal no hunting signs and just wire 'em to the fence?"

"Then what?"

"Then you call me."

He mulled that one over. "Sheriff Connally woulda let us shoot 'em."

I reached over and took his coffee away from him. "Yep, Lucian probably would have done the job himself, but we're living in more enlightened times." I drained his cup and handed it back with a smile. "Ain't it grand?"

I pushed off the truck and casually thundered the entirety of my 255 pounds, shoulder first, into Henry's chest, emptying his lungs and sending him sliding backwards into the frosty grass below. I turned to smile and wave at Clel as I cut behind his truck and ran for my life. Past the county line, another hundred yards to my driveway, and another hundred to the cabin. I would never make it. I started listening to the rhythm of my breathing as I pushed with every muscle I didn't have. Maybe this was all I needed every morning, somebody angry to chase after me. I figured it could be easily arranged. This was not the first time a white man in this part of the country had found himself in this particular situation. I must have pushed him farther than I had thought, because I could just make out the scratching of his shoes as they fought the shale bed at the side of the road.

Tell them Standing Bear is coming.

My head started feeling gorged with blood, whereas my legs began feeling as if they'd been left out overnight. To make things worse, my clammy sweatpants were now riding up the crack of my ass. I wondered if the Seventh Cavalry had had this problem as I ran for all I was worth, listening to the growing pat of his cushioned running shoes. I thought about turning to meet him, but the sound seemed to be coming from a distance yet, and I figured I'd play it out till the end.

The sun was shining on the driveway when I got there, and I was careful not to slip on the thawing frost as I cut the corner and headed into the final furlough. The receding wind was enough to flip the dried leaves up in salute as I passed, and I started thinking about making it: mistake. It didn't take much, just a little nudge that forced my left foot in front of my right just before we got to the Big Bonanza irrigation channel. The results were cataclysmic as my already top-heavy momentum carried me into the only partly empty ditch.

By the time I got to the cabin, Henry was standing with two young men at the southeastern corner about ten feet from the front log wall. One of them was the young man with the strong features I had seen at the bar the other night. I walked past the '69 half ton sitting in my drive and glanced at the hand-lettered writing on the door. Hopefully, Red Road Contracting's carpentry skills were better than their sign painting ones.

"Well, if you do the porch at ten feet, then you can use dimensional twelves for the roof overhang." He turned to look at me. "Run the porch all the way across the front."

"Porch?" They were looking me over, but I guess they figured I was covered with mud every day.

"Yes, most people have areas outside their houses so that they can keep the majority of the outdoors outside." Henry folded his arms and looked at me. "Charlie Small Horse, Danny Pretty on Top, this is Sheriff Walter Longmire."

Pretty on Top was Crow, so it was a two-tribe deal. "How much is this going to cost?" I had to do this quickly; my pants were already starting to harden.

"I am glad you asked that question, because I like to be real up front with people on the cost of things. That way there isn't any problem later on." He looked down the front of the house and imagined the porch that would be the first step forward in home improvement I had taken in years. "About fifteen hundred in materials if you use rough-cut, not including the tin. Then labor." Charlie Small Horse and I were going to get along.

After my shower, using soap as shampoo, I passed them on the way to the Bullet. They had already placed stakes and run string lines to give the general dimensions of the structure, and Charlie Small Horse was using a digging bar to break away the frozen topsoil. He paused to look up and smile as I carefully stepped over the bright green twine.

His head tilted a little as he looked at me. "You really a sheriff?"

I looked down at my uniform shirt and opened my coat to show him the badge. "Duly, at least until the next election." I stuffed my hands in my pockets. "Mind if I ask you a question?"

He smiled. "Hey, you're the sheriff."

"I understand you had a little argument with Cody Pritchard the other day?"

He looked at the digging bar. "Who?"

I waited a second. "Cody Pritchard, the fella we found over near the Hudson Bridge Friday night?"

"Oh, him . . ."

"Yep, him. You had a little argument with him at the bar?"

"Yeah."

"What was that about?"

He shifted his wide hands on the digging bar. "He didn't like Indians."

"How could you tell?"

He poked at the hole. "The usual. He sat there and gave me hard looks till he worked up his nerve."

"He said something?"

"Yeah."

"What?"

"The usual shit."

"You say something?"

"Yeah."

"What?"

He grinned with bad teeth. "The usual shit."

It felt strange to have somebody working on my house. It felt strange just to have anybody there. I looked over at the little red Jeep and figured I'd give her a call later.

It was one of those beautiful, high-plains days, where the sky just blinks blue at the earth and you have to remind yourself to take it in. The second cuttings were all up and tarped, and the perfectly round shadows of the bales looked surreal stretching across the disc-turned fields toward Clear Creek like stubble fields at harvest home. I didn't pass a single car on the way into Durant. It was a little before eight when I got to the office, and Ruby already had five Post-its plastered on the doorjamb of my office. I spotted them when I came through the front door. "It's a five Post-it day already?"

"Vic's been here."

I sat on the corner of her desk. "I thought she wasn't coming in today."

"She's not, but she dropped some stuff off for you." She looked up, and her hand went to her mouth. "What happened to your face?"

I didn't think the scratches were that bad, but there were a lot of tumbleweeds in the ditch. "It's a long story. Turk head back for Powder Junction?"

"After he decided how he was going to arrange the furniture when he got to be sheriff next year."

I rolled my eyes as I got off her desk, headed for my office, and snatched all the little yellow Post-its as I went in. This was the system she had devised to get me to do all the things I was supposed to do during the course of my workday. On the top of my desk was a Tyvek envelope from the Federal Bureau of Investigation via FedEx. It still gave me a cheap thrill to get stuff from the Bureau, kind of reassuring me that I was on epistolary terms with the big guys: my pen pal, Elliot Ness. Vic must've brought it in. She wasn't as impressed by the fed-erales; considered them a case of dumb-asses-with-degrees. I broke open the nylon-reinforced filament tape and pulled out the mummy-wrapped container as an envelope fell to my desk. It was from the General Chemical Analysis Division, file number 95 A-HQ 7 777 777. Hell, with all those sevens we were bound to get lucky. And we were. The FBI laboratory said the foreign chemical compound on the ballistics samples had been identified as Lubricant SPG or Lyman's Black Powder Gold.

Son of a bitch, that narrowed the field. That meant that whoever shot Cody Pritchard had done it with a black-powder shotgun. That didn't make sense, though. I wasn't even sure if you could shoot solid slugs out of antique shotguns without having them blow up in your face. And why use an antique shotgun? As the ultimate in nostalgia, at least thirteen American firms produced black-powder muskets, rifles, pistols, and shotguns, including flintlock and percussion designs. Traditional muzzleloaders are occasionally used for hunting, but black-powder arms turn up more frequently at pioneer celebrations, traditional turkey shoots, and in the hands of Civil War reenactment groups. They come with the original drawbacks of slow reloading, inconvenient ammunition, and lots of smoke. On the other hand, as certified antiques, their sale and ownership is generally not regulated under current firearm legislation. Two sides of the coin and neither one any help. Who had antique shotguns in this part of the country? The answer to that came roaring back: everybody. Even I had an old double-barrel Parker that had belonged to my grandfather and an old Ithaca 10 gauge coach gun. Okay, so it didn't narrow the field. I looked up and found Ruby leaning against the doorjamb. "Yep?"

"I just wanted to see your response."

I held up the letter. "To this?"

She smiled. "Underneath that."

I slid the envelopes aside and picked up a pair of what looked like sweatpants. In blue screen printing it said CHUGWATER ATHLETIC DEPARTMENT XXXXL. "Very funny." Chugwater was a little town about two-thirds of the way down to Cheyenne and is known for its chili mix and Hoover's Hut, a gas station/gift shop. I held the pants up for inspection. "You could fit three of me in here."

"Maybe she thinks you'll grow into them."

"Everybody's a wise guy." I tossed them over my chair. "Do you think you can track down Omar?"

"It's hunting season."

"I know."

Her shoulders slumped a little. "If we had infrared satellite capabilities, I would say yes."

I eased my sore legs into a sitting position. "I guess what I'm asking is if you could make a few phone calls and see if he's around and not in Rwanda?"

"Sure, but I'm not making any promises." She started to leave but not without a parting shot. "Read your Post-its, you have a busy day ahead of you."

I tossed the letter from the FBI onto my desk and picked up the little pile of notes. The first was a vehicle inspection that needed to be done down on Swayback Road, south of town. No one had done it yet because it was a twenty-mile loop, and there was nothing else down there. How was I supposed to keep Gotham safe when I was out in the hinterlands reading VIN numbers? The next was from Kyle Straub, the prosecuting attorney for the county; he probably wanted to know why it was that I had released a crime scene without consulting with him. Another one was from Vern Selby, the circuit court judge, about my trial date on Wednesday, and Ernie Brown, Man About Town, had called and wanted a statement for the *Durant Courant*. The final one simply said WE HAVE AN OCCUPANT. Hell. I yelled after her, "Who is it?"

"Jules Belden."

Shit. "PI or D and D?"

"Both; and assaulting an officer. I've got the report in here."

I got up, walked out, and sat on her desk again. Before I could get settled, the file was under my nose. I flipped through quickly enough to let Turk's childlike scrawl piss me off and stuck it under my arm. "Anybody feed Jules?"

"Not that I am aware of."

"Do you want to go down to the Bee and get him something?"

"Do you want to finish these reports?"

I stood up. "I'll be back."

"I'll alert the press."

As I made my way out the back door, I mused on the little bed and breakfast that we had behind our offices, two holding cells upstairs and the regular jail downstairs. Not too many people understand the differences between jails and prisons. Jails are county or municipal facilities; prisons are state facilities. Jails usually hold two types of lodgers: those awaiting trial for both felonies and misdemeanors and those who have been convicted of misdemeanors punishable by a sentence of one year or less. Prisons, on the other hand, only hold those convicted of felonies punishable by sentences of one year or more. Hence, in my opinion, the major difference between a felony and a misdemeanor was that you either got to stay out back and eat Dorothy's cooking or share an eight-by-eight room with Bubba the Sheep Squeezer in Rawlins.

The downside of sheriffing a jail was we had to provide three squares a day. The upside was that the Busy Bee Café was only three hundred yards away, past the Owen Wister Hotel and the Uptown Barber Shop, down a pair of crumbling, old steps behind the courthouse. The only time things got lean was on Sundays when Dorothy was closed and we fell back on the varied selection of potpies in the minifreezer in the back.

As I slipped behind the building, I looked up into the windows of the courthouse and hoped that neither Kyle Straub nor Vern Selby would see me. I spotted their cars in the parking lot and made a mental note to deal with the powers that be later in the day, possibly with the charm of a personal visit. By the time I got past the barbershop, the thought of biscuits and sausage gravy quickened my aching step considerably. The Bee was perched next to the bridge alongside Clear Creek and, with its definite slant toward the water, was vintage Alistair MacLean. The little bell on the door announced my entrance, and a couple of hunters looked up; nobody I knew. I sat at one of the end stools by the cash register and picked up the paper. There was a picture of Ferg and the Search and Rescue team standing around eating donuts and drinking coffee near the Hudson Bridge. I was glad to see the *Courant* had captured the spirit of the thing. Above the picture, in medium print, was the headline LOCAL YOUTH DIES IN SHOOTING INCIDENT. Incident, that was good; at least everybody in town wasn't referring to it as a gangland-style slaying. I guess I owed Ernie Brown a cup of tea and an interview. I folded the paper back and laid it on the counter for a quick read, as a steaming cup of coffee slid in front of me. "Somebody took the funnies."

"I usually find the whole paper funny."

Seemed like this country was loaded with good-looking older females, even if the pioneers deemed it hard on horses and women. Dorothy Caldwell was about sixty-five as near as I could figure and had run the Bee as far back as I could remember. The place had gotten its name from Dorothy's claimed spiritual attachment to Napoleon and from the impressive bee collection that resulted from this fondness and that rested on the shelves above the cutting board. There were wooden bees, ceramic bees, stuffed bees, glass bees, every kind of bee imaginable. It was a small town crusade to provide Dorothy with bees from every corner of the globe, and I noted with satisfaction the little porcelain one on the end that had come all the way from Tokyo via Vietnam. The name was also due to the fact that Dorothy knew every piece of gossip circulating about the entire county. If I really wanted to know what the hell was going on around here, I would talk to her. Hell, she probably knew who killed Cody Pritchard. So I tossed it out. "Who killed Cody Pritchard?"

Her face was immobile. "As opposed to Cock Robin?"

"He's missing too?"

She rested her knuckles on the counter and leaned into me. "This is the second time this week you guys have been in here questioning me about this. Should I consider myself a suspect?"

I bit my lip and thought about it. "As much as everybody else."

"Good. Things were getting boring around here, and I rather like having an air of mystery and danger." She looked at my armpit; it was not the first file I had brought to the Bee. "Who's that?"

"Jules Belden."

She sighed. "Oh, God." She looked up. "Do you want the usual?"

"I didn't even know I had a usual."

"Everybody's got a usual."

"I'll have the usual."

I took a sip of my coffee, sat the folder on the counter, and began reading the newspaper. "In the cold, gray dawn of September the twenty-eighth . . ." Dickens. ". . . The slippery bank where the life of Cody Pritchard came to an ignominious end . . ." Faulkner. "Questioning society with the simple query, why?" Steinbeck. "Dead." Hemingway.

Ernie had been an English Literature major at University of Wyoming before landing the job of lone employee and chief editor for the *Durant Courant* in 1951. I had two favorite parts of the paper: the Man About Town on the editorial page, which was Ernie; and the Roundup, which was Ruby's contribution to the fourth estate. The dispatcher's log was transcribed and documented under police reports in a rather surrealistic style. This resulted in profound statements, such as "A pig was reported on Crow Street, officer dispatched. No pig was found." I considered them my moment of Zen on a daily basis.

A heaping mound of biscuits and spicy gravy slid over top of the paper, quickly followed by a napkin-rolled set of flatware. The usual. She reached over and grabbed the pot of coffee from the burner and poured me a fresh cup. "So, I'm assuming Jules Belden did it."

"Only if it had been alcohol poisoning." I cleaved off a section of biscuit dripping with gravy the consistency of wallpaper paste. It was the only place in the state where you could get spicy sausage gravy, and it tasted wonderful.

A lacquered fingernail tapped on the folder. "Do you mind?"

"Go right ahead." She flipped the file open and began reading Turk's report.

After a moment, "What does the little pissant mean by . . . ?"

"Please . . . I haven't read it yet. Don't ruin the ending." She propped her elbows on the pebbled Formica and rested her chin on her fists, cool, hazel eyes directly over me. "What . . . I'm chewing too loud? What?"

"I just like watching you eat."

"Why?"

"You enjoy it so much. You're very appreciative."

I rubbed my stomach. "Yeah, a little too appreciative."

"Oh, Walt. All the women in town chase around after you now. Can you imagine what it would be like if you were good-looking to boot?"

I chewed for a moment. "All right, I'm not sure which part of that statement I'm going to take umbrage with first."

A modicum of silence passed. "I hear Vonnie Hayes is sparkin' around after you now."

I looked up into the twinkling mischief in her eyes. "I'm supposed to be eating my breakfast."

"Oh, excuse me." She went off in mock indignation to recoffee the hunters, and I shook my head in amazement at the speed in which information could be transmitted in this damn place. I spun the folder around and started decoding Turk's scrawl.

The Jules Belden Incident, as it shall hereafter be known, began at the Euskadi Bar in downtown Durant at approximately nine-twenty last night. At least that's where the altercation took place, in the alley out back. Finding the men's room occupied, Jules had decided to avail himself of the great outdoors and relieve himself in the fashion most convenient. It must have been a grand relieving, because it lasted long enough for Turk to pull up, get out of the Thunder Chicken, walk around, have a short discussion with Jules, and be irrigated. Damn, I'd have paid money to see Turk assaulted with urine.

I put down the folder and started thinking about the other boys involved with the Little Bird rape case: Bryan Keller and George and

Jacob Esper. I would have to give them a call; see if they'd had any contact with Cody Pritchard. Did I think there was some kind of connection? Did I want there to be? I just had to keep a lid on the situation long enough to find some pieces. I did my best work when I wasn't thinking, sometimes considering my mind to be a body of water that worked best once things had settled to the bottom. The trick was not getting mired in the mud.

I carried the to-go container of biscuits and gravy back to the holding cells. Jules was getting the usual, too. I walked past the partition wall between the male and female accommodations, a remnant of the unecumenical fifties, and pulled up for a second. Careful not to spill the paper cup of coffee and the usual, I leaned in and gave a hard look to the identification Polaroid that was posted on the bulletin board. It was a standard way of keeping track of people in the cells. Jules stood there smiling, holding up a number with his name scrawled by Turk on the paper below. None of this was what caught my eye.

I took the keys, turned the corner, and flipped the light on in the small hallway. The mound under the blanket on the cot moved. I used the softest voice I could muster, "Hey, Jules. Breakfast time." The mound moved again and rolled over as I unlocked the door and swung it wide. I went in and sat on the bunk opposite, placing the food on the floor between us. He was lying facing me but still covered over with the blanket. "C'mon, Bud. It's biscuits and gravy, and it don't age well." With an exaggerated groan, he listed to one side, the thin arm barely supporting him. I reached over and set him up straight, as the Property of Absaroka County Jail blanket slid away from his face.

I winced. Dried blood had scabbed over the right eye, and his prominent cheekbone and nose were skinned back, revealing a sickly yellow underneath. His nose had been bleeding, and he had applied some rolled toilet tissue into the left nostril. It had soaked through, hardened, and gave his voice an even higher whine than usual. "Mornin', Walt."

"Jules . . ."—about fourteen dozen things were bursting out as I picked up the usual and handed it to him—"eat your breakfast." I opened his coffee as he cannonballed into the biscuits and gravy. I watched the steam roll off of the fresh cup Dorothy had made for him and handed it over when he looked like he was having trouble swallowing.

"Thank ye . . ." After a few sips and a little wincing on his own part, he cleared his throat. "I guess I look kinda shitty, huh?"

His gums were bleeding as he smiled, but it was difficult to tell if that was from the beating or from alcoholism, which was his chosen profession. Jules Belden had been a hardworking cowboy and a carpenter of considerable repute. I remembered him being around town ever since I was a kid; he used to give me a quarter and candy every time I saw him. The only crime he was guilty of was having too big a heart. He was a small man, wiry, with skin that looked like it had been applied and set on fire. The eye that I could see was a ferocious blue.

"Who did this to you?"

He took another sip of the coffee. "I don't wanna cause no trouble."

"You want to press charges?" It rumbled out of my chest like an avalanche, and the force of it pushed Jules back just a little before he shrugged it off and looked at his food.

"Good gravy." I waited as he handed me the coffee cup and took another bite. "I just don't want to cause no trouble."

"We're talkin' legal trouble, and that ain't nothin' compared to the trouble that piece of shit's gonna have when I lay hands on him next."

His eyes stayed steady, and his voice took on a patriarchal tone. "Now, Walt . . . don't you hurt that boy." I straightened up in indignation. Here was a battered man lying in my jail who hadn't even been allowed to clean himself up after having been beaten. I was about as angry as I could remember being. "Hell, I peed all over him . . ." His smile broadened at the thought of it. "Then I peed all over the back of his fancy car."

I tried to keep a straight face, but the thought of anybody peeing all over the back of the Thunder Chicken brought joy to my heart. I thought of all the decals with little characters pissing on each other in Turk's back window. It seemed like he should have a better sense of humor about such things. I chuckled along with Jules, in spite of myself.

"I think I got'm again before he put me in here."

"The floor did seem a little sticky on the way in, Jules." We laughed some more. "But I think you ought to press charges." Between bites, he reached for his coffee and replied.

"Stop it, yer ruinin' my breakfast."

By the time I got down the hallway from the jail, my anger had subsided into a calculated ember. As I attempted to storm into my office, Ruby called out, "Vern Selby on line one."

I was at her desk before we both knew it. "What?"

She stiffened a little, and her eyes widened. "Vern Selby . . ."

Before she could say anything else, I slapped the receiver from her phone as she fumbled and punched line one, and I yelled at the circuit court judge on the other end, "What?"

After a pause, "Walt, it's Vern."

"Yep?"

"I just called to remind you about the court appearance you've got Wednesday and see if you wanted to have lunch?"

"Yep."

Another pause. "Yep yep or yep no?"

"Yep. I'll have lunch, goddamn it."

Yet another pause. "Well, I know Kyle Straub is looking for you. He was wondering if you had come up with anything on that Cody Pritchard thing?"

I vented out a low burst of steam. "No, I haven't interviewed all the butlers."

The longest pause yet. "Well, I know Kyle wanted to catch up with you, but I think I'll tell him to go find something else to do today."

"That'd be wise." Ruby was not looking at me as I slammed the phone down on her desk. "Omar?"

"The airport at four o'clock; he's picking up hunters." The thank-you was all I could get out. "At the risk of having my head bit off, is there anything I can do?" She was one in a million.

"Get the big first-aid kit and give it to Jules so he can get himself cleaned up. If he wants to sleep, let him. The door's open back there. If he wants lunch, get it for him. I'll be back later to give him a ride home . . . Do me a favor?" She smiled, and I was starting to feel better. "Call up the Espers . . ." The smile soured a little.

"As in Jacob and George?"

"Yes, and the Kellers at the 3K."

"Something I should know about?"

"I hope not. I'm just checking to see if they had any contact with Cody before he bought the proverbial farm." This thank-you was easier.

I took the drive down to Swayback Road to cool off. Along with my better judgment, I took the exit and drove up toward Crazy Woman Canyon past the two fishing reservoirs, Muddy Guard One and Muddy Guard Two. Ah, the colorful contrasts of the Wild West. I spent twenty minutes crawling all over a patched-together '48 Studebaker pickup trying to find a vehicle identification number that matched any of the ones on paper. After the third number, Mr. Fletcher and I were losing interest, and we settled on the first one, as it was the most legible.

When I got back to town, Ruby informed me that Jules had wandered off. She had spoken with Jim Keller and asked him to bring in Bryan. She had left a message on the answering machine at the Espers and, as of yet, had received no reply. "What time do you want them in here?"

I thought about Omar and the airport, Ernie Brown and the newspaper, and Vern Selby and the courthouse. "Oh, how about five? And call the Espers again; I'd just as soon get this all over with in one shot."

"Bad choice of words." She reached for the phone and hit redial.

I walked over to the courthouse and in the back door by the public library. Our courthouse was one of the first built in the territory, which gave the exterior a look of steadfast permanence. The inside, on the other hand, was steadfastly seedy after suffering the indignities of numerous remodelings. Cheap interior paneling, acoustic-tile ceilings, and threadbare green carpeting stretched as far as the fluorescent-lit eye could see. I called it the outhouse of sighs. Vern's office was on the second floor and, as I swung around the missing newel post and trudged up the steps, I waved at the blue-haired ladies in the assessor's office down the hall.

I sat on one of Vern's chairs and waited for him to get off the phone. He was a precise older man, about seventy, who had wispy locks of silver hair that looked like Cecil B. DeMille had stirred them. He was just the kind of person you wanted to look up in the courtroom and see: patrician, calm, and even noble. The fact that he made life and death decisions on peoples' lives was only slightly diminished by the fact that he never knew what day of the week it was. "Isn't it Tuesday?"

"Monday, Vern."

"I guess I lost a day in there somewhere."

I wondered where, between Sunday and Monday, he had lost it.

He rested his elbows on the desk and carefully placed his chin on his clasped fists. "This Pritchard boy . . ."

I leaned back in the chair. "Haven't you heard? That's not a problem anymore."

The Norwegian eyes blinked. "I'm thinking that the problems are just beginning."

I spread my hands. "You know something I don't?"

No blink. "I'm simply thinking that this unfortunate occurrence may exacerbate some of the hard feelings that resulted from the Little Bird rape case."

"Exacerbate. Is that a double-word score?" I yawned and relaxed farther into the chair. "And what would you like me to do about this exacerbation?"

Still steady. "Is there any chance of a quick resolution to this situation?"

"I could plead guilty and arrest myself."

He leaned back in his own chair, and I listened to the soft hiss as the air escaped from the leather padding. My chair didn't have any padding. I was exacerbated. "Walter, I am sure I do not have to warn you that this case has all the earmarks of blowing up in our faces." He rested his fingertips on the edge of the desk and sighed. "It was a high-profile case, and there are still a lot of tender feelings both on and off the reservation." He paused a moment. "Why are you making this difficult for me?"

I slumped a little farther in my chair. "I'm having a bad day."

"I gathered as much. Does it have to do with the case?"

I shook my head. "Not really."

"Well, perhaps we should tackle one problem at a time. You've talked to the girl's family?"

I leveled a good look at him. "You aren't telling me how to do my job, are you Vern?" He raised his hands in surrender. We looked at each other for a while. "Lonnie Little Bird is a diabetic and had both legs amputated. I figure that moves him pretty far down the list of suspects." We looked at each other some more. "He was the one that sat in the aisle in the wheelchair during the rape trial."

He shook his head slightly and dismissed me with a wave. "We'll talk on Wednesday."

As I left, I cleared the air. "That'd be the Wednesday after tomorrow, Vern?"

It was getting close to four, so I drove up to the airport. I figured Omar would be early; he always was. The local airport was famous for the Jet Festival, which celebrated an event that had taken place back in the early eighties when a Western Airlines 737 had mistaken our airport for Sheridan's and had slid that big son of a gun to a record-breaking stop in only forty-five hundred feet. The town celebrated the avionic miracle by throwing a big party. They invited the pilot, Edger Lowell, every year. Every year, he declined. We never were made a hub, but we still got our share of polo players, dudes, wealthy executives, and big game hunters. The polo players come because of the Equestrian Center; the dudes come to play cowboy for a couple of thousand a week; the executives, to escape a world they had helped create; and the big game hunters, they come for Omar. So far, none of them had gotten him, but it wasn't for a lack of trying.

Omar was a local enigma, the big dog of outfitters along the Big-horns. You could run the entire length of the range along the mountains and ownership would concede seven names, one of which was Omar Rhoades. His ranch followed the north fork of Rock Creek at the top of the county, stretched from I-90 to the Cloud Peak Wilderness Area, and was about half the size of Rhode Island. He was originally from Indiana and had inherited the place from a rich uncle who had despised the rest of the family. Omar knew everything there was to know about hunting and firearms. His personal collection was known worldwide, and the number of international hunters he wooed as a clientele was legion. He had his own airport on the ranch, but after the FAA had curtailed the size of his landing strip, the hunters that arrived in larger aircraft landed here.

I pulled through the chain-link fence and parked alongside the control tower. Old concrete pads patched with asphalt stretched across the flat surface of the bluff, and a frayed windsock popped in the strong breeze. I walked past the white cinder block building, which proclaimed DURANT, WYOMING, ELEVATION 4954; I guess they felt compelled to put the state on there just in case somebody really got lost. I had a great affinity for the few old Lockheed PV-2s parked along the end of the runway that dwarfed the three Cessna 150s chained to the tarmac in front of the building. There were no contracts for the naked aluminum birds, and they sat there with their cowlings and nose cones becoming a flatter and flatter red. The Pratt and Whitney engines slowly seeped aviation grade oil on the concrete, and the Bureau of Forestry decals had begun to peel away. At the end of the building, I looked down the flight way and saw what I was looking for: George Armstrong Custer leaning against a custom crew cab.

To say that he looked like the General was partly slighting to Omar; Omar was better looking and, I'm sure, a head taller than Ol' Goldilocks. A carefully battered silver-belly Stetson sloped off his head, and his arms were folded into a full-length Hudson blanket coat with a silver-coyote collar. The locals considered him to be quite the dandy, but I figured he just had style. We had gotten to know each other through a lengthy series of domestic disturbances. Omar and his wife Myra had attempted to kill each other in an escalating process of more than eight years that had started out with kitchen utensils and ended, as far as I was concerned, with a matching set of .308s that had been a wedding gift from the uncle. They were both crack shots and incredibly lucky that they had missed; they could live neither with nor without each other. At the moment, they were living without, and things had become considerably quieter on Rock Creek. He always looked like he was asleep, and he never was.

"So, if a man wanted to kill an innocent animal around here, what would he do?"

"Move. There isn't any such thing as an innocent animal, especially around here."

I leaned against the shiny surface of the Chevrolet and wondered how he kept all his vehicles so clean. He probably had about twelve guys on the job. "Didn't you watch the *Walt Disney Hour* on television?"

"I was more partial to Mutual of Omaha's *Wild Kingdom*." He yawned and tipped his hat back. His cobalt eyes squeezed the distance to the mountains, and you could almost hear the clicking of his internal scopes as they measured the yards and calculated the trajectory. "Anyway, the animal you're looking for is about as far from innocent as you can get."

I pulled the plastic bag from my coat and held it up in front of him. It looked like a Rorschach test in lead. "Which brings me to the point at hand." His eyes shifted to the Ziploc, and he looked more like a lion than anything else.

He yawned again. "Somebody meant business."

He held out a hand, and I dropped into it the most important piece of evidence in our case. He palmed it for a moment, bouncing it between the band of his gold-trimmed Rolex and the three turquoise rings on his right hand. Omar was ambidextrous. Style. "Soft?"

"30 to 1, lead to tin."

"Anything else?"

"Some sort of foreign substance, SPG or Lyman's Black Powder Gold."

"Lubricant made specifically for black-powder cartridge shooting."

"Black-powder cartridge?"

It was the first time he looked at me. "How many people have seen this?"

"Vic, T.J. Sherwin at DCI, Chemical Analysis at Justice, and Henry."

He blinked and continued to look at me. "The Bear didn't know what this was?"

I paused. "We figured it was an antique shotgun slug, black powder?"

"Hmm . . ." He could noncommittal *hmm* almost as good as me.

"Something?"

He handed me back the baggie and stuffed his hands in his pockets. "I could tell you, but I'd rather show you."

"You're that sure?"

He looked at the pointed toes of his handmade, belly-cut, alligator-skin Paul Bond boots. "I'm that sure."

I ran through the rest of my day. "After 5:30?"

He looked again to the sky above Cloud Peak. "Tomorrow morning would be better, Sheriff. I've got a business to run."

"What time?"

"Doesn't matter, I'm always up."

By the time I got back to the office, a green Dodge with a flat bed and fifth wheel was pulled up to the building, and the woman in the front seat made a point of not seeing me as I went in. Barbara Keller did not believe her child was guilty and never would. I went in the office and motioned for the two men to follow me. "Get you fellas some coffee?" Jim Keller shook his head, and Bryan studied his hands. "You sure? It's been brewing since about eight this morning. Should be about right."

"How can we help you, Walt?" Of all the young men in the group, I had found it the hardest to believe that Bryan had been involved with the rape. I wasn't sure if he had always looked so sad or if the look had just intensified since the trial. "Jim, you own that land out next to the BLM where Bob Barnes runs Mike Chatham's sheep?"

"Yes."

"That's where we found Cody Pritchard." I glanced at Bryan. "You didn't have any contact with him in the last couple of weeks, did you?"

"He has not." I turned to look at Jim. Jim in turn looked at Bryan, who in turn looked at his hands. "Have you?"

Bryan found his hands even more interesting. "No, sir."

"Jim, your wife is looking a little upset out there in your outfit, maybe you ought to go check on her?"

He gave Bryan another look. "You tell this man anything he wants to know, and you better damn well tell him the truth."

I let the directive settle till the front door quietly shut. Bryan Keller was a handsome kid with wide cheekbones, a strong chin, and a small, hooked scar at the jawline. He had taken life on, and life had kicked his ass. I looked at the young wreck and felt sad too. "Bryan?" The jolt was two staged, and his eyes briefly met with mine. "Did you have any contact with Cody?"

"No, sir."

"None at all?"

"No, sir."

I believed him. Shells don't lie, mostly. I stretched and laced my fingers behind my head. "Have you had anything to do with him since the trial?"

"No, sir."

"Are you aware of any threats that might have been made toward him? Any enemies he might have had?" This got a brief exhale. "Other than the obvious?"

"I'd liked to have killed the son of a bitch."

I couldn't help but raise my eyebrows. "Really?"

His eyes darted back to his hands. "Is sayin' that gonna get me into trouble?"

"No more than the rest of us." I went out into the reception area and poured myself a cup of coffee. "You sure you won't have some? It really isn't that bad." He said okay, probably because I asked him twice and he had been taught that if somebody asks you something twice you say yes, no matter what it is. It looked like a heated conversation going on in the truck out front, and I thought about my child. I don't know how you get them to make right choices, how you keep them from ending up like the two-parent pileup that was sitting in my office.

I brought Bryan his coffee and sat down in the chair beside him, taking off my hat and tossing it onto the desk. My gun belt was digging into my side, but I was ignoring it. We were both ignoring it. I sipped my coffee. "Bryan . . . Just for the record, I don't think you killed Cody Pritchard . . . As I recall, your statements and testimony indicated that you didn't participate in the rape."

"I didn't." His eyes welled up, and I wished I washed cars for a living.

"You were only convicted as an accessory, with suspended sentence."

"Yes, sir."

"Well, that's a good thing."

He took a sip of his coffee and made a face. "There are days when I just can't stand it." He was crying openly, and I watched the tears stripe his face and drip onto his shirt.

"Stand what?"

He wiped his face with the sleeve of his Carhartt. "People . . . the way they look at me . . . like I'm not worth shit."

"Well, at the risk of sounding trite, I guess it's up to you to prove them wrong."

"Yes, sir."

"Stop yes-sirring me."

"Yes, sir."

I bought shampoo on the way home. When I got there, the substructure of a porch ran the entire distance of the cabin. Six six-by-sixes stood unflinching in the growing wind, and the little red Jeep was gone.

5

I left the house around 5:30 in the morning and succeeded in avoiding
Red Road Contracting and Henry. I wasn't sure if he was going to
make me run two days in a row, but I didn't want to risk it. It was
partly cloudy, but the sun was making a valiant attempt at clearing the
sky, and it promised to be warmer than it had been in the last few days.
I sometimes thought about moving south, following the geese, shooting through the pass at Raton, and seeing if there were any sheriff
openings in New Mexico. Good Mexican food was hard to come by
north of Denver. I liked Taos, but Hatch was probably my speed.

I took 14 to Lower Piney and cut across 267 to Rock Creek, slowly
tacking my way up the foothills. I thought about Vonnie and missed her
a little bit. It was probably way too early for that. I was going through
that little bit of worry that I had said or done something wrong and that
she might not want to see me again. I saw me every day, and I wasn't so
sure I was that fond of my company. I promised myself that I would call
her up and make a real date, maybe a lunch of lessening expectations.

As far as I knew, Ruby hadn't gotten any response from the Espers.
I was going to have to swing out to their place and square things up on
the way back from Omar's unless I radioed in and got Vic to do it.
With Turk back in Powder, I was shorthanded. I thought about Turk
and forced my train of thought elsewhere. It was a big train. I waited
till I got to the top of one of the ridges to tell Ruby to send Ferg out to
the Esper place. She reminded me that I hadn't taken my sweatpants
and that Vic's feelings were probably going to be hurt.

"Is she there?"

"Talking on the phone with Cheyenne."

95

"This early? Well, tell her that the evidence stuff is on my desk from . . ."

"She's already got that."

"Oh." I waited for a moment, but she didn't continue. "Anything you need from me?"

"Like where you are?"

"Yep, like that."

"No, we don't care." I thought I heard someone laughing in the background, but I wasn't sure.

Palace Omar was made of logs, same as mine, but that was where the likeness ended. Unlike Vonnie's, you had to park in a circular holding area after being buzzed through the gate, which was about a mile back down the asphalt road. No one said anything, but the gate had slowly risen, and I smiled and waved at the little black video camera. I looked up at the house and wondered how many cameras were on me now. The place was impressive, as multimillion-dollar mansions go. The architects from Montana had used a combination of massive hand-hewn logs and architectural salvage to produce a combination of old and new and all expensive.

I knocked and made faces at the security camera at the door, but no one answered. Entering Omar's house unannounced was less than appealing, but I could hear a television blaring in the depths of the structure and decided to risk it. I pushed open the doors, listened to the satisfied thump as the metal cores closed, and walked into the two-story atrium that made up the entryway. I counted the mounted heads that were hung down the great hallway to the kitchen in the back. There were twenty-three. I knew the inside of the house pretty well; I had followed Omar and Myra through the majority of it while listening to their running, psychosis-ridden monologues on how they were going to kill each other.

As I made my way toward the kitchen, the sound from the TV became more distinct, and I was pretty sure some pretty dramatic lovemaking was going on. Obviously Omar got a lot better reception than I did. When I got there, Jay Scherle, Omar's head wrangler, was standing at the counter and watching a watered-down version of *Lady Chatterley's Lover*, which I gathered was taking place in a hayloft somewhere. Every time the leading lady became overcome with passion, the camera would drift to the casually billowing curtains at a window. Jay was dressed for work, complete with chaps and spurs. I asked if Omar was up. His eyes didn't leave the screen. "I've worked here for seven years, and I've never seen the son of a bitch sleep."

I nodded and watched Jay watch the flip-down flat screen that was hung under the kitchen cabinets. I wasn't sure if D. H. Lawrence would have recognized his work, but the plastic surgeon specializing in breast enhancement would have recognized his.

"Where is he?"

"Out back, getting set up."

I looked at the screen, a curtain again. "Set up for what?"

"Hell if I know . . . took a pumpkin with him." After a moment, he spoke again. "You ever seen a barn with so many damn curtains?"

I walked through the french doors Jay had indicated with his chin, across an expansive deck, and down a stone walkway to a courtyard walled in by four feet of moss rock topped with Colorado red granite, but I didn't see Omar. I was about to go back in when I noticed a couple of sand bags, shooter's glasses, and a spotting scope laying on the picnic table at the other side of the wall. My eyes continued up, and I saw Omar at the foot of a hill about a quarter mile away. He had been watching me and slowly raised his hand. I wasn't sure if it was an invitation, but I started walking, my breath still blowing clouds of mist into the warming, easterly breeze.

When I got there, he was putting the finishing touches on the vegetable by adjusting it in the lawn chair just so and placing a thick piece of rubber behind it. Beside him on the ground lay a Sioux rifle scabbard, which was completely beaded with eagle feathers leading from the edge all the way to the butt. If the Game and Fish knew Omar had real eagle feathers, they'd come take them away and slap Omar with a $250 fine. I figured Omar probably lost that much in the daily wash. It was brain-tanned leather, as soft as a horse's nose, and the color of butter melting in the sun. The minute glass trading beads were Maundy yellow, a faded mustard tint I recognized as over a hundred years old. He picked up the scabbard, and we started back for the house.

"How far have we gone?" He was wearing a black, ripstop down jacket and now favored Ted Nugent over Custer.

"I have no idea."

"Use the range finder."

I aimed the little scope gadget he had given me at the pumpkin that was sitting in the aged lawn chair. The distance did nothing to diminish the ludicrous image, especially with the little green indicator numbers jumping back and forth in the lower-right-hand corner. I lowered the scope and looked at him. "You tell me, Great White Hunter."

He looked back across the slight grade at the squash luxuriating at the base of the hillside. "Three hundred and one yards."

I smiled. "Close. Three hundred."

"Step back here where I am." He continued walking as I stood in his spot and looked back. The range finder read 301, and the small hairs on the back of my neck stirred. He stopped and looked back at me and then unbuttoned three Indian-head nickels from the scabbard and slowly slid the rifle from its protective covering. The sheath looked like the skin of a snake coming off and what glistened in the early morning sun looked twice as deadly as any rattler I had ever seen.

The eighth-century pacifist Li Ch'uan branded the use of gunpowder weapons as tools of ill omen. "Eighteen-seventy-four?"

"Yep."

".45–70?"

"Yep." He handed me the rifle and crossed his arms. "You ever seen one up close?"

"Not a real one."

It was heavy, and it seemed to me that if you missed what you were shooting at, you could simply run it down and beat it to death, whatever it was. The barrel was just shy of three feet long. I gently lowered the lever and dropped the block, looking through thirty-two inches of six groove, one in eighteen-inch, right-hand twist. From this vantage point, the world looked very small indeed. The action was smooth and precise, and I marveled at the workmanship that was more than 125 years old. The design on the aged monster was a falling block, breech-loading single shot. The old-timers used to take a great deal of pride in the fact that a single shot was all it took. The trigger was a double set, and the sights were an aperture rear with a globe-style front. I pulled the weapon from my shoulder and read the top of the barrel: Business Special.

What kind of special business had Christian Sharps intended? In 1874 the rifle had been adopted by the military because it could kill a horse dead as a stone at six hundred yards—six football fields. Congregational minister Henry Ward Beecher pledged his Plymouth church to furnish twenty-five Sharps rifles for use in bloody Kansas. Redoubtably, the preacher may have done more for the cause of abolitionism with his Beecher's bibles than did his sister Harriet with her *Uncle Tom's Cabin*. But it was John Brown who brought the Sharps to a bloody birth at Harpers Ferry, and a nation's innocence was lost at Gettysburg. After the Civil War, free ammunition had been handed out to privateer hunters to usher the vast, uncontrollable buffalo herds into extinction. Then there were the Indians. Good and bad, these actions had earned the Sharps buffalo rifle the title of one of the most significant weapons in history and in language. Sharps shooter: sharpshooter. "What makes you think . . . ?"

"The amount of lead, cartridge lubricant, no powder burns . . . A feeling." He turned and walked toward the house, the rifle scabbard thrown over his shoulder. After a moment, he stopped. "Three hundred and seventy." Big deal.

I was sitting at the picnic table and contemplated muzzle velocity and trajectory sightings at 440 yards. The Sharps was now wedged between three small sand bags, and a much larger spotting scope sat atop a three-pronged pedestal at my elbow. Omar returned with two cups of coffee, at my request. The cups were thick buffalo china with his brand on them, and it was really good coffee.

"Jay still enjoying the matinee?"

"You know, I've seen men ruined by drink, drugs, and Dodge pickup trucks, but this is the first time I've ever seen one ruined by soft-core porn." He nudged his mug a little farther over and leaned his elbows on the table. "You'd think he'd never seen a set of tits before."

"Amazing what they can do with special effects these days." I looked down the three-foot barrel. "Trajectory?"

"Like a rainbow, and it hits like a twelve-pound sledgehammer at fourteen hundred feet per second."

"Sounds slow and painful."

The noise he made was not kind. "Like my marriage."

I looked across the range and unbuttoned the top button of my uniform coat. The sun was getting higher, and the warmth felt good on my back. "You think this is what did it, huh?"

"Reasonably sure."

"We need to broaden our search grid."

"By a wide margin." He pushed the mug even farther away; maybe he didn't drink coffee. "If you want, I'll go up there and do a walk around. Might be less intrusive than Search and Rescue."

I wondered why he was being so helpful. "You curious about this case?"

"A little."

"I'd have to send somebody with you."

He laughed. "Does this mean I've made the list?"

"Don't feel so honored, everybody with two ears and a trigger finger has made it so far."

"Maybe I can help you to shorten it." He looked out at the doomed pumpkin. "Well . . ."

"Well, what?"

He nudged the butt of the rifle toward me with his fingertips. "I've shot it before. Your turn."

By the time I got back to the paved county road we were in a full-blown Chinook, and the temperature had risen above sixty-five degrees. I regretted not taking off my jacket before I'd gotten in the Bullet and flipped the heater over to vent. The Esper place was out near the junkyard south of town, so I hopped on the interstate and blew by Durant. I was about a mile past the exit when I remembered that I had told Ruby to send Jim. I figured I'd just keep going and radioed in to tell Ruby to tell Ferg I'd just take care of it myself.

"I left a message at his place and on his cell. It's before noon, so he's probably out fishing." Static. "When are you going to get a mobile phone?"

"Then we wouldn't be able to say cool things like 'roger that.' "

More static. "I'm willing to make the sacrifice." Static. "You better get back here and let the Ferg go round up the Espers, Vic says she's got news from DCI."

I was already looking for a turnaround and spotted one at the top of the next rise. "Nothing she wants to tell me over the radio?"

Silence for a moment. "She says she'd tell you over a mobile phone."

"I'll be there in a few minutes." I whipped through the official vehicle crossover, checked my speed, and automatically looked around for the HPs; they love to give tickets to sheriffs.

I parked the Bullet and reached over onto the passenger seat to get the small satchel Omar had given me. Vic was seated across from Ruby in one of our plastic civilian chairs with her feet propped up on Ruby's desk. Her legs were barely long enough to make the reach. It didn't look comfortable, but it was Vic.

Big smile. "How you doin', faddass?"

"I'm sorrowed to see the time spent in the echoing halls of criminal investigation have done nothing to curb your native vulgarity."

They looked at each other, and Vic raised her eyebrow. "He are a college graduate."

I slapped her small feet and continued on to my office. She followed after me and watched as I eased into my chair. "What's the matter with you?"

"I've been running." I was watching, but her expression didn't change.

"Bullshit."

"Honest." I didn't have to tell her how far.

"How far?" I smiled at her. "I mean from the Bullet into the office doesn't really count."

"Sure it does."

"Or up to the drive-through to get more beer."

"It's a cumulative effect, right?" She tossed another registered packet onto my desk; this one was from the Store. "And this is?"

"You're king of the big words this morning, you tell me." She turned and swaggered out of the office. "I'm getting another cup of coffee. Should I get you one, or do you want to run out here and get your own?"

I was reading the cover letter when she put my coffee in front of me. She sat in the chair opposite and now propped her feet up on my desk. I looked at the Browning tactical boots laced up past her ankles. I followed them up to her big, tarnished gold eyes, one of which winked at me over the Philadelphia Police mug. "Glad to have me back, aren'tcha?"

I grunted and turned the letter around for her to see. "We have a state ornithologist?"

She sipped her coffee. "Makes you proud, huh?"

"*Haliaeetus leucocephalus?*"

"Sounds dirty, doesn't it?

I shook my head. "Boy, are you in a mood."

"I actually got some sleep; you ought to try it sometime." She continued to look at me over the lip of her mug.

"Are you going to help me out with this gobbledygook, or do I really have to read this?"

"*Haliaeetus leucocephalus,* the national bird of los estados unidos."

I read a little farther. "*Meleagris gallopavo?*"

The gold rolled to the ceiling. "Think Thanksgiving."

"Turkey?"

"The feather they found on scene with Cody Pritchard."

"So, they're saying that it wasn't an eagle feather, that it was a wild turkey?" I let that sit awhile. "I wasn't aware that eagles or turkeys were suspect; I thought we had all agreed that the gunshot wound might have had something to do with the cause of death."

She uncrossed her legs, put her feet on the floor, and sat her cup on the edge of my desk. "Wait, it gets better."

"If you bring Cock Robin into this, I'm going to send you back to Cheyenne."

"It was a turkey disguised as an eagle." She reached across the desk and reopened the extended envelope, plucking out the feather, and handing it to me in its cellophane wrapper. "It's a fake."

I turned on my desk lamp and examined it under the light. It looked real enough to me.

"They sell 'em all over the place, even got 'em down at the pawn shop with all the shells and beads and shit." I thought about the eagle feathers hanging from Omar's rifle sheath. "They use them for crafts and such. You can fit your thumbnail into the spline of a turkey feather, but not a bird of prey like an eagle."

Sure enough, my thumbnail fit in the spline ridge. "What was Cody Pritchard doing with fake eagle feathers?" She sat back in her chair. "You don't think . . . ?"

"I do."

I looked at the feather again; it was about a foot long and the quill was about a quarter inch thick. It was dark about three-quarters of the way up, then solid white where it had been bleached. "A calling card."

"Knowing Cody's predilection for all things Native American, I would say that's a safe bet."

I continued to look at the faux feather. "Damn, I don't like the direction this is taking."

Her eyes dropped; she didn't like it either. "I confiscated some samples from the pawn shop and FedExed them down to Cheyenne to check the dye lots, but they said not to hold our breath. They said the majority of Native Americans just dip them in Clorox themselves." She laced her fingers together and leaned forward. "I could get some more samples from over in Sheridan. Bucking Buffalo Supply Company over on Main Street carries them, too. I don't know about Gillette."

I held up the feather and looked at it. "Working on the supposition that this is a calling card, who should we say is calling?"

"Good question. I guess this means we can keep our shingle out."

"Yep, business is good." I turned the feather in my hand. "All right, bearing this in mind, we're looking at a murder."

"Yeah." She looked resigned.

"But we're going to have to go back and check the feather thing with Cody's family, friends, and such."

"Let me guess who's gonna have to do that."

"I can stick the Ferg on it. His fishing career is about to get cramped." I held the feather up between us. "This immediately points to Indian involvement." I looked at the feather some more. "Well, on the surface of it."

"And a fake eagle feather?"

I shrugged. "Fake Indians?"

"I'm getting confused. Running with the supposition that this is real Indian mojo . . ."

"Doesn't make sense. I don't know everything about Indian medicine, but I don't think they tolerate this fake stuff. Not when it's this big."

"What is the significance of the feather?"

"Not a clue, but I know this guy . . ." I punched up automatic dial number two, and Henry's number at the Pony began ringing. "How was Cheyenne?"

She took another sip of her coffee. "The wind blows, along with everything else." Nobody answered. He was probably waiting at my house to make me run. "Nobody?"

"Otherwise engaged. I'll get him later." I handed the feather over to her.

"Fuck."

"Yep. Looks like we're gonna have to go talk to some Indians."

"Fuck."

"Yep."

"What's in the bag?"

I reached over and opened the flap of the canvas bag and tossed her a cartridge. It was as long as her index finger and about as big around. Her eyes shot to mine and then returned to the shell.

"Fuck."

"Yep."

I put Vic on tracking down all the Sharps buffalo rifles registered in Wyoming under curio and antique registration. It wasn't required, but maybe they would be registered for insurance purposes. Then she was going to check all the gun shops in the area and call up the replica companies that might have sold such a weapon or ammo. I thought we might have a better shot at the ammunition but that was balanced out by the possibility that the shells were loaded by the shooter. That meant tracking down reloading dies and paraphernalia for big calibers. It was going to be a lot of work, but she smiled when I gave her the slug shot from Omar's gun to have compared with the original. The smile faded when I told her she was going to have to go out with him for a quick spiral search of the site this afternoon. "How's Myra these days?"

"Last word from her was that Paris, half of Omar's money, and none of him was suiting her just fine."

She took her empty coffee cup and started for her office. "I wish Glen was rich."

I thought about Vic being rich. She already had the fuck-you attitude; fuck-you money might be too much. I trailed after her and asked Ruby if she'd heard anything from Ferg. "Nothing; they must still be biting."

"I'm gonna have to drive down to the Espers."

She paused to look at me. "Not really. I think Ferg was fishing down on the north fork of Crazy Woman; as soon as he gets on the highway he'll get the message and head over there. It's on the way."

"Any Post-its?"

"Vic got them all."

I stood there. "Any pencils need sharpening?"

"Why don't you go talk to Ernie Brown, Man About Town? He's called here about six times since yesterday." She went back to her keyboard and began typing. "Maybe he's afraid of being scooped." I gave her a hard look as I shambled out of the office with my tail between my legs. "Should I call and tell him the great man is on his way over, seeing as how you have nothing else to do?"

I didn't slam the door; it would have been undignified. It was still gorgeous outside, so I decided to walk over to the *Durant Courant's* office, a block down and over. That would show them.

Omar and I had had a brief conversation on the more practical aspects of what I had still hoped wasn't a murder case. Who could do it? What were the logistics of shooting an almost .50 caliber rifle more than five hundred yards? Omar had his own theories. "I can narrow it down to almost a dozen men who could make a shot like that on a consistent basis."

"In county?"

"In county." He stroked his goatee and pulled on the long hairs at the end. "Me, you, Roger Russell from down on Powder, Mike Rubin, Carroll Cooper, Dwight Johnston in Durant, Phil La Vante, Stanley Fogel, Artie Small Song out on the Rez, your pal Henry Standing Bear and . . ." He shrugged.

"Let's go with the 'and' first?"

"A sleeper. Somebody who does this stuff, is very good at it, and who nobody knows about."

"Let's move on to you."

He looked back at the pumpkin without smiling. "I'd either be a liar or a fool to tell you anything different. I've got the talent and the weapon, just no motive."

"You mind if I check the ballistics on your rifle?"

"I'd be offended if you didn't."

"Me."

"Yep."

"Roger Russell's a shooter?"

"Yes, he is. You know that turkey shoot they have out Tipperary Road, near the Wallows?" I nodded. "He won that three years in a row."

The last time I'd seen Roger Russell was at the Red Pony the evening of the shooting. I'd have to ask Henry if he was a regular. "Mike Rubin?"

"Best gunsmith in the state; he could do it."

"Carroll Cooper?"

"Same as Roger, one of those reenactment crazies. Does a lot with the Little Big Horn people."

"Dwight Johnston?"

"Drinks, but he used to be a damn good shot. He was on the NRA National Shooting Team back in the late seventies."

"Phil La Vante is seventy-two years old."

"That old Basquo can still shoot."

"Stanley Fogel? The dentist?"

"He's a shooter."

"Artie Small Song?"

"I don't know a lot about those guys out on the Rez, but him and Henry immediately come to mind. I like Artie, and I've used him to guide for me. He's good, and the dollar dogs love Indians."

I set my jaw. "Henry?"

"I knew that was one you didn't want to hear, but he could most definitely do it. Jesus, Walt, the son of a bitch used to jump behind enemy lines in Laos, air extract NVA officers for interrogation. You ever stop to think how many he didn't bring back?"

It had crossed my mind about the NVAs. "Out of this list, how many do you figure are capable of killing a man?"

He didn't pause for a second. "Half."

"Are we in that half?"

He looked at me. "One of us is."

I turned the corner at the bridge, resisted the temptation of an early lunch at the Bee, and crossed the street down the hill to the little red brick building that had served the *Courant* since before the turn of the last century. The bell tinkled as I pushed open the antique beveled-glass door. "I wanna speak to the editor of this so-called newspaper!" He looked over his trifocals and smiled. I walked over to Ernie's train set. The train was legendary around these parts in that it passed through an exact replica of our town, proceeded into the mountains, where it disappeared into a maze of tunnels only to reappear on the plains east, followed the flow of the Powder River, and returned to town. I leaned over Durant, past my office with me getting out of the Bullet, and looked at the mountainside to the little logging operation that had begun about a third of the way up. "That's new."

He got up and codgered his way over. "I'm not sure about it."

I looked at the trucks, miniature sawmill, and diminutive little loggers. "Looks like a responsible operator, 'long as he doesn't overwork the tree line."

"I suppose so . . ." He still didn't sound sure, but his eyes met mine. "I'm sorry to bother you, Walter. I know how busy you must be these days." He smiled. "Would you like to sit down?"

"Thanks, Ernie, but if it's not going to take long . . . ?"

He made a gentle waving gesture with his hand. "Just a few statements." He drifted over to his desk and came back with a small, spiral-ring notebook and a pencil that had probably been sharpened since yesterday morning. I had to smile at the importance of being Ernest. "Just a few general questions." He pursed his lips and poised the pencil over the pad. "How is the investigation progressing?"

I flipped a switch and went into publicspeak: "We're very satisfied with the cooperation we've received from the Division of Criminal Investigation in Cheyenne and the Federal Bureau of Investigation in Washington." Where the hell else would it be, Peoria? "We've been able to make significant progress on the case with the help of some of the top-flight ballistics labs in the country."

"That's wonderful. People will sleep better knowing the scope of response to this incident."

I looked at him, just to make sure facetious sarcasm hadn't entered the office when I wasn't looking. "We've put a substantial amount of our force on this case and are making every attempt to bring this particular incident to a quick conclusion." What else was I going to say? That there were only three and a half of us and that we were going to drag the case out as long as we could, just so we could have something to do? I dreaded the running monologue that accompanied these public statements and lived in fear that my mouth would someday open and I'd accidentally speak the truth. So far, it hadn't happened; that worried me too. When I looked back up, Ernie had stopped talking. "I'm sorry, Ernie."

"It's perfectly all right. I can't even imagine all the things that must be going on in your head right now." I was at least glad of that. "Any breakthroughs in the case?"

"Nothing that I can relate, as the investigation is ongoing at the moment."

"Certainly."

"Anybody else said anything that might be of any use to me?"

He blinked; it's possible I derailed him by asking him a question. I watched as he stared at the little train tracks. "There have been a number of unfortunate statements concerning the young man. It is still an accidental situation, isn't it?"

I thought about it. "Yes. Nothing strong enough to lead me to believe otherwise, at this time."

It was close enough to publicspeak to get me through. I half turned toward the door. "Anything else?"

"Oh, no." Lost in thought, he tapped the notebook with the pink, oversized eraser pushed onto the end of his pencil. "Do you ever get the feeling that the world is tired, Walter?" I stood there, not quite sure of what to say next. He looked embarrassed. "I'm sorry. I sometimes forget myself and wax philosophic in the afternoons."

I walked over to the door and pushed it open, pausing to lean against the frame. "I don't know about the world, but I sure as hell get that way." He smiled, I smiled, and I left. It was only eleven forty-five.

I climbed the hill and turned the corner on Main and became

untired. The jaunty, little red Jeep sat at the curb just outside the Crazy Woman Bookstore. I went over and sat against the fender. It was a long walk back to the office, and I needed a rest. After about three minutes, she came out.

"Hey, you." She was wearing a black cashmere sweater, a fancy western jacket all of fringe, vintage jeans, and a pair of high-heel boots. Her hair was loose and kind of rumpled. She looked great. "What, am I parked illegally?" She opened the door and tossed her paper bag of books onto the front seat. She did not come back around the door.

I continued to smile, but I was worried. "How's your dog?" That at least got a partial smile.

"He scare you?"

"Yep."

She smiled at a young couple walking up the street. "He has that effect on people." She pulled her keys from her purse and then tossed it on the same seat as the books. Her eyes came up, steady. "Do you really want to talk about my dog?" I wanted to talk about anything. I wanted to run for my life. "Look . . ." I dreaded female statements that started with "look." In my limited experience, there was nowhere to hide after they were made. "You've probably been pretty busy lately . . ."

"That seems to be the consensus."

She flipped the butterscotch hair back and laid those frank, lupine eyes on me again. "I've been thinking that this is probably a really bad time for both of us to think of starting a relationship."

I nodded and pushed off the fender and thought about sweeping her into my arms and giving her a big wet one right on Main Street. Fortunately, I always check my shots, just buried my fists deeper in my jacket pockets, and stood with my legs apart on the other side of the door so that I could absorb the impact. "I thought we already had this conversation."

It was the wrong thing to say, I could tell that right away. Her eyes sharpened along with her voice. "Maybe we weren't clear." I looked around to see if anybody was around to watch the sheriff get gunned down at what I'm sure was approaching high noon. "Walt . . ."

"Before you say anything else, let me get this out, because I might not get a chance later, or I may not want to . . ." I drove ahead, looking for light. "That measly, little, pathetic attempt at the beginnings of a romance, I refuse to use that word relationship, are all I've had to go on for the last three years. It may not seem like much to you, but for me it was giant steps, and if you think that you're going to take it away from me with a few curt words here on the sidewalk, then you've got another think coming." In my limited experience, women dreaded male statements that ended with "then you've got another think coming." It usually meant there was a lot more coming, but in this case there wasn't. It had taken everything for me to get that out; so, I just stood there, watching the tired world fall apart around me.

I'm not sure what I had hoped to accomplish with this particular outburst. I was just being honest and, to my utter surprise, she placed her hand under my chin, leaned over the door on tiptoes, and kissed me on the mouth, slowly and gently. As our faces parted, and my eyes were once again able to open and focus, she whispered, "You should call me, very soon." As the little red Jeep skimmed away, I felt the thought of a mobile phone growing on me.

On the way back to the office, I picked up three chicken dinners from the Bee and fended off Dorothy's questions about what had just taken place on Main Street across from her restaurant. She reminded me that hers was a family establishment and that such overt demonstrations of lust might be better served in a more private setting, by getting a room.

Ruby took one Styrofoam container and one iced tea out of my hands. "You keep this up and I might vote for you myself."

I continued on my way to the door of Vic's office. She was sitting with her feet up on her own desk for a change; folders and clipboards with legal pads ran the distance from her hips to her ankles. She was writing on one of the tablets with the phone cradled between her chin and shoulder. I carefully placed her tea and lunch on the desk. She nodded thanks, and I sat down to open mine. It was when I realized I hadn't gotten any napkins that Ruby appeared in the doorway and handed me a roll of paper towels from the kitchenette in back: fine dining at its best. The steam rolled out as I opened the container and prepared to eat Dorothy's famous Brookville, Kansas, recipe chicken. It was a religious experience.

Vic nodded and grunted a few agreements before she hung up. "This is a really fun job you've got me doing here." She looked at me again. "Do you have lipstick on your face?"

I wiped it off with a paper towel and picked up a thigh. "Don't be silly, what've you got?"

She looked at me for a moment longer, then continued. "Guess where the majority of these replicas are made?"

I momentarily paused on the batter-covered thigh. "New Jersey."

She began placing the folders, clipboards, and paraphernalia on the desk. She fanned the information she'd gathered across the surface and placed her chicken container on her lap, taking the lid off and sipping her iced tea. She never used a straw. "Italy. The damn things are made in northern Italy by some firm called Pedersoli."

"Sounds dirty." That got a look. I continued to eat.

She picked up a breast. "What?"

"Only thing I know about Italian war rifles is you can buy 'em cheap, never fired, only dropped once." She cocked an eyebrow and bit into her own chicken. "Sorry, old World War II joke." She stuck a hand out, and I tore off a paper towel. "It's chess night with Lucian; got me thinking about it." I nodded toward the desk. "What've you got, other than a nation of origin?"

She got that predatory look on her face, unimpeded by the way she was dismembering the poor chicken. "There are a few made in this country, the most famous being the Shiloh Sharps made up in Big Timber."

"New Jersey?"

"Montana." Her eyes flattened. "Are you going to behave so we can get through this in a reasonable amount of time?"

"What happened to your good mood?"

She wiped her fingers off on her pants and picked up one of the clipboards. "My boss gave me this shitty job to do." She took another sip of her tea. "The Shiloh version is the top of the line, with a waiting list of about four years. The only one sold in our area as far back as registration goes is one to a Roger Russell, about two years ago." I stopped chewing. "Bingo?"

"He's on Omar's short list, and he was in the bar the night you called."

"Really? Who else is on the list?"

"I think me, but I'm not sure."

She looked back at the clipboard. "Well, your name didn't come up."

"And Roger Russell?"

"Special ordered his from the Sportshop here in town, .45-70 caliber. Mean anything?"

"I'll go talk to David Fielding; I was going to anyway." Dave would be a better source of information concerning a particular caliber in the area than the FBI and ATF combined.

"Then Roger Russell?"

"Among others."

She turned the plastic spork in her mouth, pulling it out to speak. "Sounds like Omar's list is bothering you."

I took a deep breath and was amazed at how quickly the weight of my chest forced the air out. "A little."

"Who else is on it?" I told her as she worked on another piece of chicken. "Considering our earlier conversation, the Indian suspects worry me the most." I agreed. "You're going to have to get a federal search warrant to go out there."

"You know, Balzac once described bureaucracy as a giant mechanism operated by pygmies."

"What'd your buddy Balzac have to say about inadmissible evidence?"

"Not a lot. I think he considered the subject beneath him." She shook her head as I continued to smile at her. "What else you got?"

"We've got a few registered bona fides."

"Antiques and curio weapons?"

"Do you believe Omar has his registered?"

"That would be the insurance thing we talked about."

"Mike Rubin was one."

"Well that's two on our list." I put my chicken down and wiped my hands. "It's really going to piss me off if Omar turns out to be right."

"At least you don't have to go on a fucking picnic with the prick this afternoon. What time am I supposed to be out there?"

I looked at my pocket watch. "Three."

I didn't catch the look, because by the time I got back to her she had returned to the clipboard; the coleslaw spork jutted from the corner of her mouth like a fishing lure. "You really did miss me."

It was true. I had.

I parked the Bullet in front of the Sportshop. I was damned if I was going to be caught walking on Main Street again, it was too emotionally dangerous. I passed the fishing department, went through the acres of fleece wear, and stopped in front of the center counter. There was a skinny, redheaded kid reading the *Courant,* and it took a while for him to notice me. I was the only other person in the place. "Can I help you?"

"Dave around?"

"He's in the back." I waited. "Do you want me to go get him?"

"If you would." He looked uncertain. "Don't worry, I won't steal anything." He rounded the corner and hightailed it for the stock room.

I looked over at the gun rack along the right-hand wall and thought about the statement that guns made this country what it is today and wondered if that was good or bad. We were a combative breed. I was not hard on us, though; I didn't need to be, history was. Ten major wars and countless skirmishes over the last two hundred years pretty much told the tale. But that was political history, not personal. I was brought up on a ranch but, because of my father, the romance of guns had somehow escaped me. In his eyes, a gun was a tool, not some half-assed deity. Guys who named their guns worried him and me.

I walked down the aisle and looked at the shining walnut stocks, the glistening blue barrels. There were beautiful hand-engraved, over-and-under fowling pieces next to ugly Armalite AR-15s that looked and felt like a Mattel toy. Small chains wound their way through the trigger guards with little bronze locks at the end of each row. It was like a chain gang for weapons. Some of them might be good, some of them might be bad, but there was no way to tell until somebody picked them up. By the time I got back to the front of the aisle, Dave was waiting for me.

Dave had a studious quality framed in the metal-edged glasses, which emphasized his pale eyes. He looked like a basketball-playing owl in an unbuttoned shirt. He was originally from Missouri and had a matter-of-fact quality to his speech that I had always found entertaining. He also knew how to keep his mouth shut. "You're looking for a gun?"

"Naw, I got plenty." I looked past him to the kid, who was hovering at the counter.

"Matt, why don't you go help them unload the truck, okay?" He disappeared. "Something important?"

"Maybe." I explained the situation without giving out any names, motives, or qualified information.

"Sharps?"

"Or anything pertaining to . . . ?"

He held his chin in his hand and looked down the row of rifles and shotguns. "We've got a few of the replicas."

"Italian?"

"Yeah."

"Pedersoli?" I was showing off.

He released his chin and pushed the glasses farther up on his nose. "As a matter of fact, they are." We walked down the aisle, and he unlocked the end chain. I expected them all to make a run for it. "These are early Pedersolis, not long after they bought out Garrett." I nodded sagely. "I don't believe they changed the production line much." I nodded sagely some more. It was fun being an expert on Italian buffalo rifles, having a specialty. He handed the rifle to me. It was similar to Omar's in size and weight, but that was where the similarities ended. The metal on this one had an antiqued, cloudy-blue appearance, and the wood stock seemed hard and plastic. Comparing it to the museum piece I had fired this morning was inevitable but not fair.

I set the hammer to the safety/loading notch before opening the action just as if there were a fired case in the chamber, preventing any unnecessary stress on the firing pin. Amazing the things you learned hanging around with Omar. It was smooth but nothing like the one from this morning.

"What's the accuracy on these things?"

"Actually, pretty good."

I placed the narrow butt plate against the deep bruise on my shoulder. It fit my wound perfectly. I raised the barrel toward Main Street and envisioned Italian buffalo sitting at a street-side café, drinking Chianti. "Five hundred yards?"

"Oh, God no."

I let the buffalo go. "Won't get there?"

"It'll get there but not with much accuracy. Not with these repros."

I handed the rifle back to him. "Sell many of 'em?"

"A few; here and there."

"Mind telling me who bought them?"

He slowly exhaled, blowing out his lips. "I could go off the top of my head, but I can get it out of the computer and you'd have an exact list."

"Great." He locked the guns back, and I followed him to the counter and the computer. "You ever sell any of the real ones?"

"No."

"How much is one worth, a really good .45-70?"

The exhale again. "As much as a vacation in Tuscany."

"How about ammunition . . . do you sell much for these?"

"Who knows?"

"Can you get that for me?"

"It'll take longer."

I was asking a lot, and I knew it. "It would be a great help."

"Can I get it to you tomorrow?" He reached over and turned on the printer.

"That'd be fine." He watched the paper roll through the printer for a moment, and then tore loose the list and handed it to me without looking at it. "You don't want to see?" I asked him.

"None of my business."

I folded the sheet in half and stuck out my hand. "Thank you, Dave."

Ruby had said there was a cold front on the way and, by tomorrow morning, there was supposed to be more than four inches of the white stuff. I tossed my jacket onto the passenger seat. If the warm weather wasn't going to last long, I was going to enjoy it while it was here. I fired her up, rolling down the window and resting my arm on the door. It felt good to have the extra elbow room.

You couldn't blame the computer; it probably did the list of three names in alphabetical order. The first name on the list was Brian Connally—Turk.

6

In 1939, Lucian Connally had been told by his mother to sweep the front porch of their dry and dusty ranch house. He had refused and, when asked what it was that he intended to do, he had replied, "Go to China." Which he did.

Lucian didn't like family.

After finishing Army Air Corps flight school in California, he immediately joined the American Volunteer Group, a collection of a hundred U.S. military pilots released from enlistment so that they might serve as mercenaries in the lend-lease born, fledgling Chinese Nationalist Air Force. Lucian's political zeal was reinforced by the $750 a month salary and by the $500 a head bonus promised by the Chinese for every Japanese plane shot down. Lucian found he had a knack for such activities and, by the time he left China on August 6, 1941, he had accumulated quite a little nest egg. A little over a year later he returned to the Pacific on the aircraft carrier *Hornet* and, in a cumbersome B-25, bombed Tokyo, crashed into the Yellow Sea, and was captured by the Japanese and sentenced to life imprisonment.

Lucian didn't like Japs.

There was a sun-yellowed, decomposing circular in an intricate gold frame on the wall of private suite number 32 at the Durant Home of Assisted Living. Below the grainy photograph of five men in flight jackets and the exotic print was the translation, "The cruel, inhuman, and beastlike American pilots who, in a bold intrusion of the holy territory of the Empire on April 18, 1942, dropped incendiaries and bombs on nonmilitary hospitals, schools, and private houses, and even dive-strafed playing school children, were captured, court-martialed, and severely punished according to military law." Two of the men had been ushered outside immediately following the mock trial and summarily executed; the remaining three survived forty months of torture and starvation. Lucian was the short one in the middle with the cocky look on his face, who was smiling like hell.

After the war, Lucian had drifted back to Wyoming and then back to Absaroka County. He then drifted into being sheriff on the strength of his being the toughest piece of gristle in four states. This had been tested when Lucian had had his right leg almost blown off by Basque bootleggers back in the midfifties.

Lucian didn't like Basquos.

He had tied the strap from an 03 Springfield he carried in the backseat of his Nash Ambassador around the exploded leg and drove himself back to Durant from Jim Creek Hill, thirty-two miles. They took the leg.

Lucian didn't like sawbones.

They say the subzero temperatures that night saved his life, but I knew better. His more than a quarter century of sheriffing had been nothing short of epic, and his reputation in the Equality State was ferocious. Simply stated, he was the most highly decorated, retired law enforcement official in the country. "How's them big titties on that Eye-talian deputy of yours?"

He was also a colossal pervert.

I kept my finger on the bishop and looked up at him. "Lucian . . ."

"Just askin'." It was one of his favorite tactics, shocking me out of any sense of concentration. This might be why I had not won a chess game since the spring of 1998. I slid the bishop against the border as he looked at me through his bushy eyebrows. "What's goin' on?"

I settled back in the horsehide wing chair and took in the site of the losing battle. Lucian had been allowed to bring his own furnishings to the "old folks home" as he called it, and the jarring effect of the genuine western antiques in the sterile environment was unsettling. I had been coming here and playing chess with Lucian since he had moved in eight years ago. I never missed a Tuesday for fear that Lucian might lose some of his faculties and, in the eight years, he had not lost one iota. I, on the other hand, was sinking fast. "Nothing, why do you ask?"

He moved. "You ain't said shit since you got here."

I looked at the board. "I'm trying to concentrate."

"Ain't gonna do you no good, I'm jus' gonna spank yer ass again, anyway." He dug a finger in his ear, examined the wax on his pinkie, and wiped it on the faded blue-jean flap at the end of his stump. "I can't believe you didn't bring any beer."

I couldn't believe it either. For almost a decade I had been sneaking beer and Bryer's blackberry brandy in to Lucian on Tuesday nights. "I need to talk to you about some stuff."

"I figured as much, I'm just waitin' for you to start." He moved. "Important stuff?"

"Sheriff stuff."

"Oh, that shit." He watched me move a knight out to the slaughter and slowly shook his head. "Well, let's talk it out and get it over with so I can get at least one decent game tonight."

"It's about your great-nephew."

He looked up. "What'd he do now?"

"Beat on Jules Belden."

His hands stayed still. "How bad?"

"Bad enough."

He leaned back in his own chair, readjusting his weight and looking at his reflection in the dark surface of the sliding glass door behind me. He was a handsome old booger, movie starish like the judge, but in a more rugged way. The spiderweb wrinkles spread out from the corners of his eyes to his unreceding hairline and the trim landing strip of platinum white hair. He lacked the aesthetic of the judge; everything on him was square, even his flattop haircut, which I'm sure hadn't changed since Roosevelt had been in office. His eyes were the darkest brown I had ever seen, the black of the pupils seemed to blend into the mahogany surrounding them. I'm sure they were swallowing the darkness outside and in. Lucian didn't have any children of his own, and the responsibility of carrying the line into perpetuity rested solely with Turk. He was not completely satisfied with this turn of events, and the set of his jaw made that fact clear. "You wanna drink?"

"In case you've forgotten, after reminding me all these times, I didn't bring anything."

He scratched the slight stubble on his jaw with fingernails that had been cut down to the cuticles. "Well, thank Christ I don't depend on you for much." He pointed to the corner cupboard. "There's a bottle of bourbon behind the star quilt on the bottom shelf."

I got up and retrieved the bottle, Pappy Van Winkle's Family Reserve, nothing but the finest at the Durant Home of Assisted Living. I brought the three-quarters of a bottle over. "You got any glasses?"

"What, you too good to drink out 'a the bottle?" I handed it to him and watched as he took a slug and then with a great deal of animation wiped off the mouth of the bottle with a flannel shirtsleeve I was sure hadn't been changed in a week.

"Thanks." I didn't like bourbon, as a general rule, but I sure liked this. I couldn't even describe the number of smooth buttery tastes in my mouth, but I felt like I should chew. The fire in my throat felt cleansing, like part of a scorched-earth policy.

"Jules in custody at the time?"

"Yep."

"Gonna press charges?" I took another sip and handed the bottle back to him, unwiped.

"Mighty damn liberal with my bourbon, for a man that didn't bring me a thing to drink this week." I sat, and he returned to looking out the glass doors. I wondered at the vitality of the man. Aristotle said that some minds are not vases to be filled, but fires to be lit. Excluding the bourbon, Lucian had been lit for a long time, and the flying tiger's eyes still burned very bright. "If I had two good legs, I'd go out and kick that little son of a bitch's ass myself." The finger pointed at me this time. "You gonna handle this yourself?"

"I suppose so."

He settled farther back in his chair. It was starting to sound like a contract hit. He sniffed, worked his jaw a little, and took another slug. "What you want from me?"

"Formal absolution."

He took another slug and handed the bottle back. "Damn, that stuff's addicting. Better have another pull and put it back in there where it came from." He burped. "Fore we get drunk as a couple 'a hooty-owls. Bastards around here'll steal anything that ain't nailed down . . . What?"

"Sheriff stuff."

"More?"

He watched me look out the glass doors for a change. "I don't know how much of this you want to hear about . . ."

"Oh, hell, I got important crafts to make out 'a tongue depressors tomorrow morning. I'm not sure if I wanna cloud my mind with a murder case."

I turned around. "What makes you think it's a murder case?"

"What makes you think it's not?" I stood there looking at him. "Sit down, you're puttin' a crick in my neck." I did as ordered. "Don't look so surprised, I read the damn newspaper."

"It could be a hunting accident, Lucian."

He crossed his arms, concentrating. "Bullshit. Near as I can figure, there's an awful lot of folks out there that would just as soon see that kid dead, one of 'em just decided to take the law into his own hands." I told him about the ballistics. "Goddamn, was there anything left of the little bastard?"

"Extremities."

"Where'd it hit him?"

"Center shot."

"Front or back?"

"Back."

"Not much of the front left, I suppose?"

"Nope."

"Lead?"

"Yep. It's pretty scattered, but everything seems to support the theory that it's a big caliber breechloader."

"Sharps."

"Well, there are others . . ."

"Sharps." He rested his chin in the palm of his hand, the stubby fingers wrapped around his jaw like a knuckleball. The gnarled old fingers looked like they could crack walnuts. Lucian's grip was legendary and, if you were ever unfortunate enough to have him lay hands on you, you suddenly paid very close attention. It was fun to watch the mechanisms start up, to see Lucian's eyes flying over Absaroka County, sweeping down from the mountains, through the gulleys, over the foothills, and into every attic, cedar chest, closet, and gun case in a hundred square miles. He added five more names to the list, none of which were Indians. I told him about the feather. "Shit. Anything else?"

"Nope." He chewed on the inside of his mouth but, other than that, he was still. After a while, I asked, "What are you thinking about?"

"I'm thinkin' about gettin' that bottle 'a bourbon back out." I carefully put the little kingdoms back into their storage place in the compartment within the board. I figured we were done with chess for the night. "You still runnin' with that Indian buddy of yours, Ladies Wear?"

"Standing Bear."

"Yeah, him." Lucian did things to Indian names that were nothing short of criminal. He called the Big Crows the Big Blows, and the Red Arrows were Dead Sparrows. The list was endless and, no matter how many times you corrected him, he would just smile a little smile and keep on talking. Even with all this, the Indians loved him. They respected him for his toughness and his sense of fair play. On the bridge where I had recuperated yesterday, Lucian had waged a campaign against public intoxication when he stopped his overturned bathtub of a Nash and demanded the bottle from which two middle-aged braves were drinking. They took one last sip and then tossed the container into Piney Creek. "What bottle?"

Lucian unstrapped his wooden leg at the bank, took off his hat, jumped into the creek, and a minute later came up. "This goddamned bottle." They helped him with his leg and his hat and then cheerfully jumped in the back of the squad car for the ride into town. The Cheyenne elders were careful when they spoke his name, Nedon Nes Stigo, He Who Sheds His Leg.

Lucian knew who Henry was, and he knew his name. "He can probably help you figure out who did the feather and where on the Rez it came from. Gawd, all my contacts out there are dried up dead and traveling on the wings of the wind. But you gotta start with that girl's family."

"Henry is her family."

He shook his head. "How's Ladies Wear tied into the Thunderbirds?"

"Little Birds. Melissa's father is Henry's cousin."

"So, the daughter'd be his second cousin."

"Yep, but with the age discrepancy they just call her his niece."

"Her father the one that lost his legs, Lonnie?"

"Diabetes."

"Damn, that's rough." I looked at the one-legged man before me. "The mother was a drunk, and the kid turning out feebleminded the way she did . . ." The hand went back to his face, and the air that came from his lungs rattled like a snake. "Well, go talk to ol' Ladies Wear."

"You don't think he's a suspect?"

His eyes quickly looked like the muzzle of a double-barreled shotgun. "Do you?"

"No."

He continued to look at me. "He's your best friend, seems like it's something you'd know."

"Yep."

He leaned his head to one side and half-closed the nearest eye, sighting me in. "You don't sound so sure."

"I am." He watched me as I reached over to the sofa and got my coat. "Anybody else I should put on the list?"

He shrugged. "How the hell should I know. I'm retired."

It was still nice when I got outside. I always used the emergency exit by the commissary at the end of the hallway. I never looked down into the sliding glass windows as I crossed the parking lot; it seemed demeaning to Lucian. In my peripheral view, I could see the lights were still on, and I was sure he still sat there watching me, waiting for next Tuesday. I turned around.

"What the hell do you want now?"

It hadn't taken long to get back to his room. I leaned on the doorway, pretty much filling the opening and pushed the brim of my hat back. "Have you thought about that dispatcher's job we talked about a while ago?"

He had unbuttoned his shirt and hopped to the dividing wall, his hand steadying him. "Two years ago?"

"Yep." He stared at me through the eyebrows. "Things are awful busy, and I could use some help."

"Two days a week?"

"Weekends, yeah."

"I'll have to think about it." He didn't move, embarrassed at being caught hopping through his suite and heading for bed.

"You were going after that bourbon, weren't you?" He didn't smile very often but, when he did, he had great teeth. I wondered idly if they were his.

I started back to the office with the windows down. If it was going to snow, it wasn't giving any indication of it. The moon glowed a clear white, slipping through the slender arms of the willows along Clear Creek. Late at night you could hear the water, and most of the summer I would leave the windows in my office open so I could listen. It was only about eight-thirty, but the town had already put itself to bed.

There was a note from Ruby saying that Ferg had swung by the Espers but that nobody had been home. He would telephone them himself and stop by again tomorrow. There was an addendum Post-it, in which she related that she had informed him that he was being drafted to full time. She said his response hadn't been enthusiastic, but he hadn't been spiteful enough not to leave four dressed brown trout in the refrigerator for me. I wandered past Vic's office and looked in at the explosion of legal pads. The display was daunting, and I would be cursed at if I messed up any of what I'm sure was a carefully detailed arrangement. We were little but we were mighty. I thought of Don Quixote, being far too powerful to war with mere mortals and pleading for giants.

I sat at my desk and looked at the phone as the windmills loomed overhead. Vonnie would still be up, but my courage had curdled. There was a sheet of paper from one of Vic's legal pads with her angry scrawl spreading across the top quarter. I picked it up, turned on my desk lamp, and read . . . "Where the hell are you? Spiral searched the site with a fine-tooth comb. Full six hundred yards, and do you have any idea how fucking long that took? Numb-nuts thought there might have been some grass blowdown on one of the rises about five hundred yards away, so we had to stake and cover it. Guess how fucking long that took? He's an expert with a camera, too. Go figure. Asked me out for a drink. Guess how fucking long that took?" It was signed, VIC. With an addendum, "PS: More grist for the investigative ballistics' mill tomorrow, nothing worth hampering your extensive social life with." And another. "PPS: I took the film over to the drugstore, and they said they would drop it off tomorrow morning, first thing. Read: noon."

I had never received a note from Vic that had less than two PSs. I continued to hold up the yellow legal sheet and noticed the little pinholes of light shining through everywhere she had made a period. I laid the sheet of paper down and looked at the phone again. The feather caught my attention, and I picked it up, turning it in my fingers as it had turned in my mind all day. I picked up the phone, but it just hovered in my hand, a foot away. I could hear the dial tone, so it was working. I gently sat it back on the cradle and looked out the windows; as I suspected, the clouds were starting to haze out the mountains. I hoped that whatever Vic had found with Omar this afternoon was safely tucked away or covered with a staked plastic drop cloth.

I picked up the phone again, dialed, and listened to it ring. On the fourth ring there was the mechanical fumbling of the answering machine, and I left the daily message I had been leaving since last week, "This is your father, I just want to know if you've escaped, or do we have to pay the ransom?" Nothing, so I hung up.

My attempts at reviving my mood were failing, so I went back to the refrigerator in the jail to retrieve my trout dinner, and there, proudly standing at the front of the top shelf among the potpies and Reynolds-wrapped fish, was a mountain fresh, twelve-ounce bottle of Rainier beer. There was a yellow Post-it stuck to the bottleneck with Ruby's careful handwriting, "In honor of your getting in shape." That Ruby.

I twisted off the top and tossed it into the trash can, headed back into my office, and sat back down. I took a swig of the beer and felt a lot better. I picked up the phone yet again, and then remembered I was going to have to look up her number. I finally found my battered phonebook in the bottom drawer of my desk and sat about working my way through the Hs. Michael Hayes. I dialed, and she picked it up on the second ring. "Yes?"

The yes surprised me, but I got back on my feet quick. "Hey, I haven't even asked you yet."

The response was soft. "Hello, Walter."

I could see her curled up on one of those leather couches by the fire with the phone pulled in close. It had been so long and I was so out of my depths, I was always feeling dizzy when I spoke with her. "I can take that yes as a blanket response?"

"Is a sheriff supposed to be making these kinds of phone calls?"

I sat the bottle down and began working on the label with my thumbnail. "Sheriff who?"

"I was thinking about inviting you over for dinner." There was a pause. "How about tomorrow night?"

"Perfect. What can I bring?"

"How about a bottle of fine wine and your fine self."

"I can do that. Tomorrow's a court day, but then I'll just be running around like a chicken with its head cut off, standard operating procedure." She laughed, and it was warm and melodic. I should have pushed for tonight. She advised me to take care of my head till then and bid me farewell till light through yonder window break. It was hard to describe, but courting Vonnie seemed to elevate me onto another plane. Without trying to sound like some lovesick teenager, the world just seemed better, like the air I was breathing had a little something extra.

I finished off the beer, gathered up the feather and fish, and headed for the Bullet. I looked at the smear of clouds reflected by the moon. It looked cold on the mountain. We were in the fifth year of a drought cycle, and the ranchers would be glad of the moisture collecting up there. In the spring, the life-giving water would trickle down from the precipices, growing the grass, feeding the cows, making the hamburgers, and paying the sheriff's wages. It was all in the natural order of things, or so the ranchers told me . . . and told me.

I fired the truck up and let her run, rolling up the windows and looking at my right eye in the rearview mirror. It was a handsome right eye, roguish yet debonair. The right ear was also evident, a handsome ear as ears go, well formed with a disattached lobe. A sideburn had a little gray, just enough for seasoning, and it blended well with the silver-belly hat. A damn fine figure of a man or a man's eye and ear. I avoided the temptation of ruining the effect by readjusting the mirror for a fuller view.

I had a date. My first date in . . . since before I was married. Wine, I had to remember wine. The only place that would be open was the Sinclair station's liquor annex. Somehow, I didn't think they would have the vintage I was looking for. If I could catch Henry at the bar, he could supply me. I backed out and headed for the Wolf Valley.

When I got to the bar my mood deflated a little; the lights were all off, and there wasn't a vehicle in sight. Henry often closed up if no one was around. I suppose he figured that nursing the drunks through the nights when they were there was one thing, but anticipating them was another. I swung around and headed back home. I thought about continuing on out to his place but figured I would just call him at the Pony tomorrow. I looked over at the lovely fish resting on the passenger-side floor mat and tried to think of how to cook them without messing them up. I relaxed a little when I caught a flash of reflected taillight as

I pulled up the drive to my little cabin. I looked in at the powder blue Thunderbird convertible with its top down and at the pristine white interior as I gathered my assortment of things.

Henry's father had bought the car new in Rapid City back in 1959, about three months before he was diagnosed with "the" cancer. That's what they called it back then, "the" cancer, like "the" winter, or "the" Black Death. I leaned over the door and read the odometer: 33,432 miles. When the old man passed over, there had been a great deal of controversy in the family as to who would get the T-bird. Henry ended the debate by fishing the keys out of the old man's last pair of pants that lay crumpled beside his deathbed. Henry started the Thunderbird, drove the old girl forty miles, and parked her in an undisclosed garage somewhere in Sheridan. None of them ever asked him about it again, ever. He called the car Lola.

"Hey, get away from that car." The deep voice had come from the darkness, somewhere under the new porch roof. I walked up the slight grade to the front of my newly transformed log cabin. The porch ran the entire length of the house, and the smell of the freshly cut redwood was enchanting. The roof consisted of two-by-six tongue and groove; the green tin surrounded the edges and joined seamlessly with the already existing roof. It was a really good job, even I could see that. The rough-cut six-by-sixes gave the place a look of permanence, the look of a home. There were a couple of concrete blocks stacked on the ground at the center, which allowed access between the railings.

I stood beside the blocks and leaned against one of the upright timbers. "Damn."

"Not bad, huh?" He sat by the front door and leaned against the wall with his legs crossed and stretched out in front of him. His worn moccasins translated the print of his feet through the moosehide. He reached down and plucked out a bottle of beer from the holder and tossed it to me; it almost slipped, but I caught it. "You were going to be able to have three, but then it got late. Now, you only get two."

I opened the beer and took a sip. "They do good work."

"They are going to be back tomorrow to finish the railings and put some steps in."

"They know it's going to snow tonight?"

He shrugged and straightened his shoulders against the log wall. "Not until after midnight." I looked out at the convertible and hoped he was right.

I took another sip, wandered down the porch, and nodded toward the car. "Special occasion?"

"Last hurrah. I do not suppose I will get a chance to drive her anymore this year." His eyes stayed on the car and, in the flat moonlight, it looked very pale; another ghost pony for Henry.

"Slow night at the bar?"

"Yes. What is in the tinfoil?"

"Couple 'a browns." I stuck out a hand and pulled him up. "You want help putting her top up?"

He looked past me to the hills across the valley. "I told you, it is not going to snow until after midnight." I laid the fish on the counter by the sink and tossed the feather packet over toward the edge. He went to the refrigerator and pulled out a carton of milk and eggs he must have brought Sunday. He opened the carton and sniffed. "Do you still have the cornmeal?"

I went over to the lower cabinet by the door and retrieved the cardboard container; the corner was already eaten through. I shrugged as I handed it to him. "Sorry." He shook his head and cracked two eggs in a bowl, whisking them with a fork and adding some milk. He retrieved the frying pan from earlier in the week, checked it for mouse shit, turned on a front burner, and dropped a dollop of butter onto the slowly warming iron. He was fun to watch in the kitchen, his movements easy and smooth. It dawned on me that I should ask, "Anything I can do?"

"No, I prefer my trout meuniere sans poopi." He opened the tinfoil and admired the fish. "Beautiful. Where did you get them?"

"What makes you think I didn't catch them?"

He didn't honor this statement with a response but dumped out a bed of cornmeal in a dish and whisked the batter some more. Finishing this, he picked up his beer and started to take a sip. "I don't suppose you have any peanut oil, parsley, or white wine?"

"No, but I have a date tomorrow night."

He nodded, extended his arm, and poured part of his beer in the batter. He coated the fish, layered them in the cornmeal, then took a dish towel hanging from the drawer pull under the sink and tilted the handle of the frying pan. "Good."

"I need some help."

He watched the butter slide down the inside of the pan, added a little more, and rested it back on the burner. "Yes?"

"Wine?"

"Yes, wine is a good thing."

He didn't see the sarcastic look I was giving him. "I need help picking one out."

He stared at the fish. "Dinner is in her home?"

"Yes."

"What is she serving?"

"I don't know." He slowly shook his head and took a sip of his beer; I was driving him to drink. I took a swig of my own and smiled, putting a good face on things. "She didn't say."

He nodded, spreading his hands over the repast. "Red with beef, white with fish, or cheap beer with everything." He leaned against the counter and braced his weight on one arm. "Is this to be a gift or to accompany dinner?"

"Does it matter?"

"Yes. If it is to accompany dinner and it is white, then it must arrive chilled. If it is a gift, then it should not."

"What if I just don't let her touch the bottle?"

He nodded sagely. "Are you going to let her drink any?"

"Oh, there is that." He finished off the abbreviated beer and pulled the last one from the cardboard carrier. "I thought that was mine?"

"You do not deserve it." He opened it and took a swig before I could grab it away. "Then there is chicken."

"What about chicken?"

"It can go either way."

"I've heard that about chickens."

He shook his head some more. "According to how it is prepared, it can go with either red or white. The whole idea of wine is to complement the meal. There are dry wines, moderately dry wines, dessert wines, aperitifs, sparkling wines, fortified wines, sherries, and ports . . ."

"Mad Dog 20-20?" I was trying to be helpful.

"There are an infinite number of both white and red wines: sauternes, chardonnays, pinot grigios, sauvignon blancs on the white side; bordeaux, burgundy, beaujolais, pinot noir, zinfandel, shiraz, merlot, syrah on the red side; never mind the vineyards themselves and the vintners. The wine of the year is a cabernet blend from the coastal region of Bolgheri. Antinori planted sixty percent to cabernet sauvignon, thirty-five percent to merlot, and five percent to cabernet franc. Then there are the appellations—St. Emilion, Margaux, Barolo, Barbera, and Chianti . . ."

"Which ones come in cartons?"

He nudged the empty carrier with the punt of his bottle. "How about a nice six-pack?"

"I'm trying to change my image."

"Yes, I am trying to change it, too, but it does not seem to be working." He took two of the fish and plopped them in their reflective image in melted butter; they sizzled and settled in as he returned the skillet to the stovetop. There was only room for two of the fillets at a time.

"What about the chenin blanc she drinks at the bar?"

"That is a good choice, along with a merlot. Just in case."

"You can hook me up?" A term I had picked up from Vic.

"Yes."

I went ahead and ate while thinking about which subject I wanted to raise first as he prepared the next brace of trout. "Things really that slow at the bar?"

He flipped his own dinner onto a plate and joined me at the counter. "Slow enough that I could get out of there this evening."

"Ever get tired of it?"

"Every day, but then I look at my bank account and get over it." He started on his dinner, and I let him eat for a while before I disturbed him with another question. I knew why he owned the bar, why he had gravitated to it. A sense of community. In a way, it was why we both did what we did. It was a way of looking after things, making sure everything was all right. "How is your fish?"

I guess that meant he was ready to talk. "Great, thanks."

"Hey, they were your fish."

"Jim Ferguson's, to be exact." He was like that, always making an attempt to put everyone at ease. "Roger Russell come out to the bar a lot?"

He thought about it. "No."

"That time the other night, the only time he's been in?"

"Yes." His head rolled to one side, and he leaned back a little to keep his hair out of his food.

"He's on Omar's short list of shooters."

He continued eating. "Who else is on the list?"

I told him, and his face carried nothing. "Comment?"

He grunted. "I am not sayin' nothin', shamus, till I talk to my mouthpiece." We talked about the list for a while, his assumptions riding alongside mine. He didn't spend enough time in town to make any real connections to the group. The only one he was interested in, for obvious reasons, was Artie Small Song. "He has worked for Omar."

"Yep, Omar said."

I watched the air fill his lungs and admired the way the weight of his chest didn't force it out. I would never be built like Henry, capable of fight or flee. I was stuck with fight, but maybe I could be a little better at it. I could still feel the dull ache in my legs, and somewhere, down deep, I could feel a slight twinge at my stomach where most people had abdominal muscles. I readjusted my weight on the stool, and his eyes came up. "Artie was in the bar the day Cody Pritchard was shot."

Shit. "At the same time, before, after?"

He nodded his head ever so slightly. "Before."

"How much before?"

"About an hour before, left when Cody came in."

I sat my fork and knife down, as I rapidly lost my appetite. "You see which way he went?"

"No."

We sat for a few moments more. "I need you to tell me what you're thinking." He got up and walked over to the window with his hands on his hips and looked out at the wind picking up and at his car with the top down. "You want me to help you put the top up on the T-bird?"

He didn't turn, and his voice sounded far away. "I told you, it is not going to snow until after midnight." I waited for what seemed like a very long time. "You must understand that this puts me in a very uncomfortable position."

"How about I just call Billings or Hardin?"

"How about you just put your questions in a bottle and float them up the Powder River? Same result." I waited some more, watching him breathe.

"I'm perfectly willing to be turned down."

"Yes, you are, and that is one of many reasons I would do it."

"Think he'll be cooperative?"

"No. Not if he has any suspicions." I didn't like using Henry like this, but I convinced myself it was for a greater good. I was sure that the same thought was going through the back of the head at which I was looking.

"Know him very well?"

"Well enough."

I changed the subject in my usual subtle fashion. "Know of any Sharps out on the Rez?"

There was no pause. "Lonnie Little Bird has one."

"What?"

He half turned and smiled. "Lonnie has one."

I leaned back on my stool and crossed my arms. "You know, for a relatively rare firearm, the damn things are popping up all over the place."

His hands gravitated forward and into his pockets. "It was given to him by my great uncle, many years ago."

"Where'd he get it?"

"From his father, who got it from a white man."

"Dead white man?"

"Eventually." He was still looking at me from the side of his face.

".45-70?"

"Yes." He looked back out the window, and I turned back to the counter. He could see me plain as day in the reflection of the glass. I was getting tired of looking at people's reflections, and I was damn sure I was tired of them looking at me. "You are going to have to talk to Melissa Little Bird's family. I will go with you."

"I've got something else to show you." I picked up the envelope from DCI, tossing it to his side of the counter. He turned and looked at me. "Yet another reason I have to go onto the reservation." He came back and sat down, opened the cardboard envelope, and pulled out the cellophane-wrapped feather. His eyes narrowed a little, but that was all.

"Turkey."

"How the hell could you tell that so fast?"

He laughed and looked down the length of the feather like the sight on a gun. "Bend." He held it up straight between us. "Turkey feathers have a wicked bend to them, this one has been straightened, over-bent, then flipped over, and bent again."

"How?"

"Household iron, light bulb, or steam, but steam is more difficult."

"Why bother?"

"Eagle feathers are straight." I thought about the feathers on Omar's rifle scabbard; they were straight. "There's also a deeper ridge on the spline. Can I open the plastic?"

135

"Sure, there are no fingerprints."

He smiled again. "You are not going to use this against me later, are you?"

"Nah, I was going to get your prints off the beer bottle."

He opened the cellophane by loosening the Scotch tape at one side. He was one of those guys who saved Christmas wrapping. He held the feather by the stem and ran his fingers up the side, the delicate quills tracing the movement between his index finger and thumb. He was looking at something, but I didn't know what it was. "Some artisans use Minwax to get the right color. It is a much richer tint than the turkey's. Mahogany furniture stain, with a sponge. Do you mind if I ask where it came from?"

"Cody Pritchard."

His eyes stayed with mine. "On the body?"

"Yep, we thought it was just a leftover from one of the local critters, but . . ."

"Yes." He reconsidered the feather. "Yes . . ."

"He didn't have anything like this on him at the bar, did he?"

"No." He turned the feather in his fingers, much like I had all day. "This is a good one. There are only a few individuals who could have made this."

I nodded. "Can you get me a list?"

"I can check them myself." He sighed and sat the feather down between us.

"You think someone is counting coup?"

He shrugged. "I am not sure if you understand the spirit of the thing. When we used to fight battles against other tribes and the army, no deed was more honored than counting coup. It means to touch an armed enemy who is still in full possession of his powers. The touch is not a blow and only serves to show the enemy your prowess—an act considered greater than any other, a display of absolute courage, conveying a sense of playfulness."

"Well, that lets this out." I watched him. He studied the feather again, his eyes running the length, back and forth. "For many reasons, this does not make sense."

I took the last swig of my beer and sat the bottle aside. "Like?"

"It is the owl feathers that are the sign of death, the messengers from the other world. The eagle feather is a sign of life, attached to all the activities of the living: making rain, planting and harvesting crops, success in fishing, protecting homes, and curing illness. The feather is considered the breath of life, processing the power and spirit of the bird of which it was once a living part."

I sometimes forgot about how spiritual Henry was. I had been raised as a Methodist where the highest sacrament was the bake sale. "The eagle is big medicine. It symbolizes life, boldness, freedom, and the unity of all. In the Nations, the eagle feather must be blessed. The eagle feather must be pure, so that the recipient does not catch the evil that might be in the unblessed feather. A medicine man must bless the feather, and then it can be passed on to someone else."

It didn't seem like we were getting anywhere. "That doesn't make sense in our particular situation."

He took the plates away and sat them in the sink, then leaned against the counter and crossed his arms. "That is not a real eagle feather."

"So, what does that mean?"

"I am not sure. It could be an Indian sending mixed signals, or . . . ?"

"Or what?"

"A white attempting to make it look like an Indian." I thought of that. "Or back to square one; not all Indians would be able to tell the difference between this feather and a real one." He shrugged.

"You're a lot of help."

"This is going to be tougher than the wine. It means we have to go ask some questions." He looked around at the makings of dinner. "Do you want me to clean up?"

"I think I can handle it. You're leaving?"

"I have an early morning tomorrow."

A slow but steady panic was starting to set in, and the pain in my legs began to grow. "We're not going running again, are we?"

He didn't say anything, just turned and walked out the door.

I went over to the window and watched him start up the Thunderbird and carefully back it around my truck. The two taillights bobbed and weaved down the gravel driveway and faded into the night like red turbines. It still looked nice out, so I took the remainder of his beer onto the new porch and leaned against one of the supporting timbers. They were rough-cuts, and the splinters felt like fur being brushed the wrong way. I lifted up the bottle and took a swig. It was almost full, and I smiled. Small gifts.

I looked up at all the little pinpricks in the heavens and thought about Vic's handwriting, the tiny holes in the paper. I thought about my daughter for a while and Vonnie, but then my mind settled on Melissa Little Bird. I was going to have to see Melissa again. I hadn't really had any interaction with the young woman since the trial, only seeing her once at the reenactment at Little Big Horn and that was more than a year ago.

She had been sitting in her aunt Arbutus's car and was waiting to leave one of the roped-off grass parking lots that caught the overflow of the yearly event. It was the end of June, and the waves of heat and the reflection of the afternoon sun made it hard to see, but I saw her. I had raised my head and laughed at something Henry had said, trudging along in the late-afternoon sun, thinking about the individuals who had died there, wondering if their ghosts hovered near. They must have because, when we came up over the rise, my eyes came to rest on Melissa Little Bird, and everything happened in slow motion.

She was wearing the Cheyenne jingle-bob dance headgear, with a band of beaded sunbursts and feathers. It was different than any I had ever seen before; it had three loops of beads that draped below Melissa's eyes. Trade beads flowed down past her ears to the mussel-shell choker at her throat and onto the elk-bone breastplate. There was also a cardboard number, printed in red, hanging from around her neck, and it read 383. Instantly, I wondered at the number of hours that her family must have taken to prepare her for the dance competitions. I hoped she had won. Her head turned from the direction in which the car was then slowly traveling. Her eyes were soft, yet animated, but they froze when they saw me. Her hand crept up against the glass, flattening against the surface with the pressure she applied. Her lips parted, just enough for me to glimpse the perfect white of her teeth, and she was gone.

Somewhere in all this musing, I noticed a fat little snowflake drift across my field of vision and settle against one of the concrete blocks and disappear. There were others, now that I noticed, gently floating through the cooling night air. Scientists say there is a noise that snowflakes make when they land on water, like the wail of a coyote; the sound reaches a climax and then fades away, all in about one ten-thousandth of a second. They noticed it when they were using sonar to track migrating salmon in Alaska. The snowflakes made so much noise that it masked the signals of the fish, and the experiment had to be aborted. The flake floats on the water, and there is little sound below; but, as soon as it starts to melt, water is sucked up by capillary action. They figure that air bubbles are released from the snowflake or are trapped by the rising water. Each of these bubbles vibrates as it struggles to reach equilibrium with its surroundings and sends out sound waves, a cry so small and so high that it's undetectable by the human ear.

I looked up at the few remaining stars. It seemed that an awful lot of the voices in my life were so small and high as to be undetectable by the human ear.

I pulled out my pocket watch and read, 12:01.

7

We all have a list of the vehicles we forever despise. Mine began with the dull yellow '50 Studebaker in which I learned to drive. It had the finely honed suspension and thrilling acceleration of a large rock. Another on the list was the M-151A1 Willys Jeep that the Corps made me drive in Vietnam, which flipped over a lot and which had the torturous habit of kneecapping me every time I went for third. But the one that has been the continual thorn in my vehicular side has always been Henry's '63 three-quarter-ton pickup truck. I was with him the day he bought it. We were in Denver for Game Day, sitting in a small Mexican restaurant behind old Mile High, the football stadium that didn't look like a shopping mall. I read the *Post*'s sports section, and he read the classifieds.

Three-quarter ton, V-8, four-speed, Warn lock-in/lock-out hubs, grill guard, headache rack, saddle tanks, and the heaviest suspension ever forged by man. The thousand-dollar price tag seemed too good to believe, and it was. They said it had been used to get Christmas trees from a farm they had over in Grand Junction; they didn't say it had also been used to harvest them. It looked like it had come out of the ugly forest and had hit every one of the ugly trees. If there was a straight piece of metal on it, I was unaware of where it might be. It looked like it had been painted with crayons and poorly. The truck was mostly green, while the grill guard and headache bar were phosphorescent orange. He called it Rezdawg, and I called it misery. We had never taken a trip in it where it had not either broken down, run out, gone flat, overheated, or spontaneously burst into flames. "Get in."

"No." Henry had made me run, in the snow.

"Get in."

"No." He wanted to go to the Rez early, so I had to get a continuance on court day and cancel lunch with the judge.

"Get in."

"No." He had made me change my clothes, twice.

"Look . . ." His hands were wrapped around the steering wheel, and the majority of his face was hidden behind the hair. "We are undercover here." I looked longingly at my comparatively brand-new truck, with a motor, suspension, and heater that worked; but my truck also had very large golden stars on the doors. They were handsome stars with the snow-capped Bighorn Mountains rising from an open book in their center, but incognito they weren't.

He had opened the passenger-side door, and I was looking through the holes in the floorboards at the melting snow. Part of the dashboard was turquoise, part of it was white, and the large mic of an antiquated citizens' band radio was bolted to the front edge over the shift lever. There was a shifter; a transfer-case lever; a worn, white steering wheel; and an unending number of chrome handles and knobs guaranteed to dislocate, jab, or stove anything that might come in contact. Most of the windows were cracked, and there were no seat belts. At the top of the antenna, even though there was no radio, perched a little, dirty-white Styrofoam ball that read CAPTAIN AMERICA. "It's gonna break down."

"It is not going to break down. Get in, I am getting cold."

His breath was clouding the inside of the glass, and I looked down at the heater box, which was taped together with duct tape. "As I recall, the heater in this thing, among other things, doesn't work."

"I fixed it." He really was undercover, dressed in a gray hooded sweatshirt, army field jacket, and a khaki ball cap that read FORT SMITH, MONTANA, BIG LIP INVITATIONAL CARP TOURNAMENT. "Come on, get in." I gave up and crawled onto the multilayered seat, repaired most recently with small bungee cords and a used Pamida shower curtain.

The truck had always been an enigma in Henry's carefully ordered life, but it was something primal and important to him. He could have had it fixed, I mean really fixed, but he didn't. Somehow, in all its ugly glory, it signified something about the thin-chested kid whose glittering eyes knew something I didn't and never would. No matter how far he went, no matter what he did, he would always be from what we were going to today.

The truck wasn't turning over. I saw his hand in his fingerless gloves holding the key to the right and two urgent red lights in the instrument panel that said GEN and OIL. He nodded knowingly like he knew what it was saying. "Do you have any jumper cables?"

After we pulled my truck over and got the Rezdawg started, we headed out slowly, because that was as fast as Rezdawg would go. We rolled like a Conestoga wagon across the bridge that divided the county from the reservation, and in a blink of an eye we were in a foreign country, a sovereign nation unto itself. The topography didn't change all that much. The sun was up, and the light glowed from right angles highlighting the ridges and peaks in greeting-card warmth. The sharp edges of the turned pastureland pointed out the work ethic of the passing owners, some prepared for the arriving winter, some not.

Numbers always come to mind when I'm on the Rez, social numbers, government numbers, and life expectancy numbers: The average Indian dies eleven years before his white brother. I spent a lot of time ignoring these numbers when I was with Henry; they got in the way of seeing the people, and I had learned a long time ago that seeing these people was important.

"Are you armed?"

I felt a little guilt along with the pressure of the pancake holster at the small of my back. "Yep, why?"

He shrugged. "I just like to know." We drove on for a while. "Do not shoot anybody, okay?"

"Okay."

I watched the passing cottonwoods and scrub sage. "Where to first?" he asked.

"You tell me."

"Oh, no. I am just the scout on this expedition."

"I thought you guys left that stuff to the Crow." He hunched over the wheel a little more and grunted. This was the response to the Crow in general; most of the Cheyenne I knew still hadn't forgiven Kick in the Belly for scouting for Custer; most of the Indian Nations I knew about hadn't forgiven each other much of anything. This had not been lost on the federal government, since they had put reservations of warring tribes alongside each other with regularity. "Where can we get some coffee?"

"White Buffalo."

I nodded and listened to the heater motor begin to squeal as a few drops of antifreeze dripped from the core onto the brittle, rubber floor mat and trickled a sickly green toward my boot. "Is the heat on?"

"Yes."

"Well, I don't want to start with the Little Birds. You wanna try and dig up Artie Small Song first?"

The White Buffalo Sinclair station was located diagonally across from the Lame Deer Community Center and next to it was Baker's IGA. I wondered if we were taking our chances by going by the Community Center, since it was an outpost for Indian Affairs, a thought that was solidified by the green Jeep Cherokee that sat parked diagonally at the corner of the building. The IA is really into gadgets, and the sleek little Jeep conveyed that in spades. Their units bristled with antennae, roll cages, push bars, divider screens, radar, laser, radios, and an assortment of firearms that were locked in place all over the inside of the vehicle. There were eagles on the side, with feather tips at the quarter panels that seemed to swirl in the wind even though the thing was parked. No stars, though. I didn't question as Henry carefully guided his rattletrap of a truck past the Center and pulled up alongside the White Buffalo Sinclair, but then couldn't resist the temptation. "Problem?"

He threw open the door and slid out. "No, I just do not like cops."

When I looked behind the counter at Brandon White Buffalo, I started feeling good about my own cholesterol intake. I never worked at the carnival, but I'm guessing he was about 375 pounds if he was an ounce. He was a lot taller than either of us, and he seemed twice as

143

wide and thick. His head was as big as the pumpkin I had been shooting at yesterday, and he even looked like a jack-o'-lantern. It was the smile. I don't think I've ever seen a smile that big in my life, with or without the gold. Like the rest of him, the smile seemed to fill the room; against it, the fluorescent lighting of the White Buffalo's world didn't stand much of a chance. The hairnet that held copious amounts of the blue-black hair in place as he came around the counter in his bright green apron didn't diminish his image. I noticed the clear plastic gloves on his massive hands, and forearms as big as Easter hams. Brandon White Buffalo had been making breakfast sandwiches, and he carried two with him as he came. Standing there, as he walked by, was like watching a passing train. His voice was like Henry's, halting in a charming way, but as deep as the bass in a three-piece combo.

"Little Brother, where have you been?" I watched as the Buffalo wrapped up the Bear and easily lifted him from his feet. Henry didn't squirm or make noise; it would have been useless against such overwhelming warmth. He just hung there, his feet dangling about six inches from the ground. "You have been up to no good?"

Henry started to respond, but it was halfhearted. I watched as the Buffalo's arms began to close, the plastic-covered hands crossed at the small of Henry's back still gently holding the sandwiches. I watched as Brandon's tendons and muscles slowly became more pronounced, but how his eyes remained flat and mischievous. The Bear's face was just starting to show tinges of red, but he dare not let any of the saved air in his lungs escape. If he exhaled, his ribs would collapse like a fragile structure of wooden dowels. Henry's face was slightly higher than Brandon's, his chin about two inches from the Buffalo's forehead. Henry could easily head-butt him, but I guess that wasn't the point. I wondered if this was an everyday thing, if Henry had to run this gauntlet every time he came into the White Buffalo Sinclair. I would get my gas somewhere else.

I knew a story about Brandon White Buffalo; it happened a number of years ago and had to do with his mother's house up near the Montana border. It was a dry camp, and the old girl didn't have the money to drill a well, so Brandon dutifully made the trek into Durant's public park every Saturday morning to the municipal water station where they had a machine that dispensed public water. A teenaged Turk had been there with a couple of his buddies when Brandon had rolled the fifty-five gallon drum off the back of his truck and began filling the barrel with the hose. They were boys and nudged each other and began giggling as the steel barrel grew fuller and fuller. Brandon heard the giggling and looked up with that beatific smile of his. The hose got loose and sprayed the crotch of his pants, and Turk and his friends laughed even louder. Brandon joined them, shaking his head. Calmly, Brandon White Buffalo squatted, grabbed the barrel, and lifted it onto the tailgate of the crouching pickup. In one swift push, the barrel slid into the back of the truck, and Brandon closed the tailgate. He smiled, danced a little dance to help dry off his pants, and waved at the townies as he drove away. At this point, Turk told me, no one was laughing.

There really wasn't much I could do for Henry, other than pull out my gun and shoot Brandon. I figured the Buffalo would just eat the bullet like he ate life. "Brandon, do you think you might be hurting him?"

The Buffalo glanced at me and then looked back at the Bear. "No, he is very tough. He deflowered my sister, and you have to be tough for that."

"You . . . should . . . know . . ." It was a tortured reply through gritted teeth, shot out in bursts, but it was enough. I watched the seismic tremors begin at the base of Brandon's huge back, building and filling his lungs, exploding in short blasts that blew Henry's hair back until they overtook the Buffalo and he dropped the Bear, laughing with a joy that shook the racks. When he regained his breath, he stood over Henry with his arms apart. "Little Brother, I have lovely sandwiches!"

We sat on the plastic window seat, Henry and I on one side, Brandon taking up the entire bench seat on the other. We ate our sandwiches and drank our coffee from hot cups that read ALWAYS FRESH. I watched Henry catch up on the last month. "Anything new with Lonnie?"

The Buffalo shifted his weight and laid an arm along the seatback. "It is a sad story of the Little Birds, with Margie drinking as much as she did an awful lot of the life went out of the family, but perhaps it is better that she passed?" His eyes turned to me. "You lost a wife too, Lawman?"

I was surprised. "Yes, I did."

"It is a horrible thing to lose, a wife?"

His conversation was made up of questions, giving it a philosophical bent; I wasn't sure which ones I should answer, so I just answered them all, "Yep."

"They say it's like losing part of yourself, but it's worse than that?"

"How so?" Two could play this game.

"When they are gone, we are left with who we are after we were with them, and sometimes we don't recognize that person?" He patted the table between us to show that no harm had been meant. "You will be all right, Lawman. He's a good man, this man you are left with?" He turned back to Henry before I could reply. "You should go see Lonnie, he asks about you. You are bad about your family?"

The Bear ignored the chastisement and smiled into his coffee. "I will. Is he home today?"

"He has no legs, so where would he go? He's home everyday; he watches television? He watches everything. It is as if he thinks the things on the television aren't happening if he's not there to watch?"

"He might be right."

"Mm-hmm, yes. It is so . . ." At which they both began snickering slyly and not looking at each other. I waited for a moment, then the Buffalo turned to me. "Have you met Lonnie?" I admitted I had. Years before the trial, I had been forced to convince Lonnie that just because a vehicle in town had been left running didn't mean that you could take it for a little spin. "Mm-hmm, yes, it is so." They burst out laughing again. If Lonnie had been there, he would have been laughing, too.

The conversation switched to Cheyenne and, through Henry, I discerned that Melissa was not living with her father and had been spirited off by one of the many aunts that lived closer to town. In a while, they switched back to English. "So, he might be living with his mother?" They were talking about Artie Small Song now.

"Yes, that girl he was going out with from Crow Agency? She decided she did not like his drinking?"

"He is drinking again?"

The big, netted head bobbed slightly. "Yes." He glanced at me and nodded some more, ever smiling. "You like your sandwich, Lawman?"

I took another bite and chewed; it really was good. "Best on the Rez."

His fists bounced off the surface of the table and our coffee cups hopped with little ringlets emanating from the centers of the dark liquid. "Best in the world!" I nodded my head in agreement and smiled back as Henry's attention was drawn out the window.

"Does his mother still live out near Rabbit Town?"

The big arms crossed over the green apron, but the smile held. "Little Brother, I'm beginning to think that you didn't come here today because of my beautiful sandwiches or because you love me?"

Henry's eyes rolled to the ceiling but then quickly rested on the Buffalo. I had seen that look before. It wasn't a look you could stand for long; it burned. It burned because he cared. I watched the Buffalo to see what kind of effect it had on him, but the only thing that happened was that I heard drums, far in the distance. I'm sure they were just in my head but, as I thought this, I could see the Buffalo's head nod ever so slightly keeping time with my drums. His eyes stayed locked with Henry's, and I'm sure he heard them, too.

When we got outside, one of the tires was flat, so I loaned Henry a quarter and we pumped it back up. He said it would hold, and I cursed the day the truck was built. As we pulled out of the parking lot, I noticed that the Cherokee was gone. We couldn't afford tricked-out Jeeps with the measly budget we had. I had a truck that was two years old, but the rest of the force either had five-year-old vehicles or, like Jim Ferguson, drove their own and got reimbursed for mileage. I had meant to call in to the office while at the Buffalo's place, but it had slipped my mind; some way to run a murder investigation.

* * *

The Little Bird case had gone to the jury at 2:50 on the afternoon of September 16, Yom Kippur, the Day of Atonement. I'm pretty sure I was the only one in the county who noticed it on the calendar that hung on the bulletin board behind the witness stand. The trial and all its paraphernalia seemed to take on the lessening expectations of some television movie of the week. I had to remind myself that it was real.

The jury was charged with reaching a decision on nine counts: one charge of conspiracy; four counts of aggravated assault, involving the use of the broom and bat and the act of oral sex; and four counts of sexual contact, in which the defendants were charged with fondling Melissa's breasts and forcing her to masturbate them. They were also given a list of fifteen lesser charges. I remembered Vern Selby leaning over his desk and clasping his hands into a joined fist. He instructed the jury to ponder two main questions: Was force or coercion used against Melissa Little Bird; and was the Cheyenne girl mentally defective; and, as an auxiliary, did Cody, George, Jacob, and Bryan know that, or should they have known that?

The judge had explained that coercion was not simply the use of brute force but that it could be a subtler process; that the jury would have to decide if Melissa had been conned into going into the basement; whether she had been vulnerable because of her psychological condition; whether the size and configuration of the basement intimidated her; or whether the number of boys and what they had told her before she left had pressured her into submitting.

Vern didn't look up when he changed gears; he just kept looking at his collective fist and talking like one of those auctioneers at an auction where nobody's buying anything. He told them that the legal term mentally defective did not mean that someone was slow or retarded. It meant that a person did not understand that she had a right to refuse sex or was incapable of refusing; and, that to convict on this charge, the jury would have to agree that the defendants knew or should have known that Melissa Little Bird was defective.

Lucian and I had had a long conversation about it after the trial; he said you had to do what you could do, and you did it the best you could; that if things turned or didn't turn out the way you wanted, you let it go. If you did anything else, you were opening yourself up to very bad things. I hadn't let it go, so was that where I was now, in the land of very bad things? Was I there alone, or was Melissa there with me, dragging our red rowboat across the teepee rings of the high plains? And who else was there with us, under those black and blue skies, carrying a very large caliber buffalo rifle?

"What are you thinking about, badass?" I didn't respond, just sat there looking out the windshield at things to come. "You know, I think I will start calling that the Little Bird Look."

I stared at the decrepit chrome antenna shivering in the velocity of roughly forty-five miles an hour. Captain America was hanging in there. Yea, verily, though I walked through the valley of very bad things . . . I was going to have to bring Turk back up from Powder Junction, and there was a dark little part of my soul that was looking forward to it. I told that dark little part to shut up and go curl up in a corner, and it did, but not completely. It never did, not completely.

"It is the one where the eyes bug out a little, and those two little lines dig in at the corners of your mouth." He turned back to the road. "It is very manly." I continued to look through the glass and attempted to un-bug my eyes. "I wish I had a look like that . . ."

I needed a change of subject. "You still have your horses?"

A little breath of air came out as he responded, "My uncle's horses, yes." Henry never claimed the horses, even though they had been his for more than ten years. It was because they were Appaloosas. He felt about Appaloosas the way I felt about his truck; they were here just to piss him off. Henry figured that the reason the Cheyenne had always ridden Appaloosas into battle was because by the time the men got there, they were so angry with the horses they were ready to kill everything.

"We should go out and ride sometime."

He turned to look at me again, his eyes bugged a little this time. "You hate horses."

I didn't hate horses, I just didn't like them. I didn't really want to go riding; I was just hoping the shock value of the statement would change the subject. "The founding fathers used to say that riding was good for the digestion."

"Whose founding fathers?"

"Mine. Your guys didn't even have horses until you stole them from the Spanish . . . We headed over to the Mission?"

He smiled and nodded. "Yes."

Like most of the houses on the reservation, the St. Labre Mission had a basketball court out back. It was a rough looking place, with large chunks of the asphalt crumbling off at the edges in pieces as big as softballs. What little paint there had been to signify the out-of-bounds, foul, and three-point areas had long since faded into the dark gray of the asphalt's aggregate. It had a steel backboard painted to depict a war shield in faded and chipped reds, blacks, yellows, and whites. There was a hoop with no net, and despite the cold there were four young men playing a game of pickup in their shirtsleeves; one of the T-shirts read MY HEROES HAVE ALWAYS KILLED COWBOYS and another read FIGHTIN' WHITIES in fifties script. The boys were classic Cheyenne, tall and lean, with a touch of casualness that betrayed their age. I wondered why they were here and not in school, but I figured I had enough on my plate without being a truant officer. He cut the motor and started to get out. "Do me a favor and stay in the truck."

I looked back at him, concern in my eyes. "Even if they don't hit the open man on the give and go?"

He closed the door, and I watched him saunter toward the court. The word insouciance was invented for Henry and, against it, the teenage version suffered. The Bear was doing vintage James Dean, and it made the boys look like a bunch of basketball-playing Pat Boones. I wondered if they knew Henry. Everybody out here was related in a complex order of extended family. I wondered how many the Bear helped. I had been with him when he made the numerous deposits into the various accounts, a hundred dollars here and a hundred dollars there. I also knew that all the groceries he bought in town didn't end up at the bar. All of these actions made up an intricate network that provided for the individual without exacting the cost of self-respect.

Henry stopped at the edge of the pavement and leaned against the opening in the sagging chain-link fence, his thumbs hooked in his jeans. They looked at him, sneaking glances, figuring that whatever he wanted was his problem. It would be interesting to see how quickly he could make his problem theirs; it didn't take long. After a fade away from the far corner, the ball deflected off the hoop and bounced right over to him. He didn't move, just lodged the ball to a stop with his boot.

They fanned out as they came, like coyotes approaching their first wolf. One of them, the tallest one, said something, and Henry nodded by throwing his head back a bit and inviting them closer. The tall one started to stoop for the ball but pulled up short. The Bear must have said something. Nobody moved, then I saw the back of Henry's head shift slightly, and the teenagers started laughing, all of them except the tall one. He cocked his head to one side and said something back, and I would bet it wasn't pleasant. A brief moment passed, and Henry bent over and came up with the ball, spinning it in both hands. From the movement of his head, I could tell he was talking trash. The tall kid nodded, turned, and started walking back toward the court as Henry took one step after him, lined up, and shot. It wasn't anything all that miraculous, about a twenty-five foot jumper that bounced off the rim twice and fell through, but for a guy who hadn't held one of the things in ten years, it wasn't bad. The tall kid turned and looked at him. Henry spread his hands out in an apologetic gesture and walked over to the young man. Throwing a paw around his shoulders, he steered him back over to the group. They were all talking and laughing now, with a few gestures from the boys indicating the road behind the Mission's Indian School and beyond. They tossed Henry the ball again as he turned and started back for the truck. I saw him stop, look at the much greater distance to the basket, then shrug and throw the ball back to the tall one. It would have been showing off. The boys helped push start the Rezdawg, and we got going again. "You know, I remember a time when you would have made that shot, nothing but net."

Artie Small Song's mother lived up a dirt road off 566 going toward Custer National Forest. It looked like a cliff dwelling with the parted-out vehicles and abandoned, lesser trailer homes wedged into the rock walls of the little canyon. It was a grand location, if a little cluttered, and the farther you went back into the place, the older the vehicles got. By the time we climbed our way to the trailer that had a little stovepipe with a trail of smoke coming out, I was looking for the original wheel. I asked him to park the truck headed down the hill, which he did after a little grumbling. Once again, I waited and wondered why it was I was even here.

I rolled down the window as far as it would go, about halfway, and breathed. The sharp contrast of the canyon air mingled with the musty warmth of the truck. There was one thing I liked about Henry's truck, even if I never told him: its comfortable smell of old steel, earth, and leather. I had grown up in old trucks like these, and there was a security there, a sense memory that transcended brand names and badge loyalties. I looked around at the assembled vehicular dreams and thought about the mobility of western longings. None of the wheels around me would likely ever roll again, but were there any deep-seeded passions still harbored in the sun-dried interiors and slowly rusting bodies? It was doubtful, but hope does tend to roll eternal.

He was on the makeshift porch, talking to an older woman through a closed screen door. His hands hung loose to his sides; after a while the inside door closed, and he returned. He grinded the starter a few times, then quietly turned the wheel and coasted down the hill, hopes dashed.

"Well?"

Once the truck lurched to a start, he mumbled, "A different girl-friend."

We followed 566 to 39, took a right, and headed north. "Would the gun be there or with his mother?"

The response was a little ominous. "Artie always keeps his guns with him."

Artie Small Song's latest hit didn't live too far from the cutoff that headed back to Lame Deer. Alice Shoulder Blade was a dental hygiene student at the college in Sheridan but spent her weekends back on the Rez with Artie. Henry said that chances were she wasn't there, it being a Wednesday, but you never knew when Artie might pop up. It was a smallish, white house with wooden clapboard sides and a bare dirt yard that had a number of dogs asleep alongside the foundation and under the porch. When we drove up they roiled out at us from all directions and made a great show of attacking the truck and raising a general Cain. There was one blue-heeler/border collie mix; the rest were anybody's guess. Henry rolled down his own window as he parked and growled very loudly, "Wahampi!" The dogs slid to a stop, yelped, and ran back under the porch, so far back I couldn't see them. As he opened his door, he paused and looked at me. "Lakota for stew. Those dogs are Sioux from Pine Ridge."

"How can you tell?"

Henry knocked. "Cheyenne dogs would wait quietly, till you got out of the truck." Nobody answered, so he knocked again. This time, the force of his knocking jarred the door open about two inches, and we looked at each other. "On the reservation, this constitutes an invitation."

I thought about the numerous laws, both federal and local, that I was breaking as I crept in after him. There wasn't a whole lot there, only a few pieces of furniture and a framed picture of Alice at what I'm sure was her senior prom. There were lots of boxes scattered around the living room, filled with hunting clothes, old lace-up boots, videotapes, and reloading equipment. It was difficult to discern whether Artie was moving in or out. "Maybe Alice doesn't live here anymore." This to the roll of the eyes and a turn of the back as he checked the small kitchen.

I kneeled by the box containing the reloading equipment and took a look at the dies; the ones that were in the machine read .223. Henry came back through and wandered farther down a short hallway, checking each room as he went. I carefully rummaged through the loading box and came up with a small wooden container of dies in separate cardboard; the third one I pulled out was old and didn't have any markings. Automatically, I reached to the pancake holster at the small of my back. By the time I had popped the safety strap and pulled the .45 out, Henry had returned from the hallway. When he saw the gun, he stopped and quickly looked around the little house, finally returning his look to me. "What?"

"What?"

"The gun?"

"Checking the caliber on his dies."

He stretched his shoulder muscles. "Jesus, you scared the shit out of me."

I smiled and unlocked the safety, pressing the side of my thumb against the button, allowing the magazine to slide into my other hand. I rested the die on the closed wooden box and thumbed a shell from the Colt, setting the bullet next to the die. The circumference was identical. Artie Small Song could reload Sharps .45–70s. "Okay, if I were a gun in this house, where would I be?"

We both said it at the same time, "Closet."

I carefully repacked the dies, placing everything back in the box as it had been. Then I popped the bullet back in the magazine, reloaded my weapon, and replaced it in the holster. I followed Henry down the hallway to the only bedroom at the end, turned the corner, and saw him standing with his hands on his hips. "You better come look at this."

I walked over to the open door of the closet and looked in. There were enough weapons in there to arm a small platoon. There were FAL .308s, AK-47s, MAC-10s, and the M-16s leaned against the inside wall. There was even an Armalite M-50 and a collection of Mossberg 12 gauge, short barrel, and tactical shotguns. Even sitting on the wooden cases of ammunition, in a dental hygienist's closet, they looked deadly. Some of the guns were civilian versions, but others were fully automatic and fully functional. I leaned against the door-jamb and crossed my arms. "Wow."

"Yes." He looked sad. "I am guessing Artie does not have a federal license for all this automatic stuff."

"Maybe he's gonna open a store?"

"Yes. Guns-R-Us." He leaned in for a closer look. "Is that an M-50?"

"Looks like to me." I poked my head in and looked in the other corners. "I bet if we dig in those crates down there we'll find ourselves a couple of .45 ACPs that match the dies in the other room." I looked around. "Maybe this is a conversation we should have in the truck?"

He followed me out after closing the closet door, and I felt a lot better when we were standing on the porch. I think I heard a few low growls as we walked off the steps, but the mad rush for our heels didn't come. We leaned against the front of the truck's grill guard and talked. It had turned out to be a beautiful day, and the temperature was rapidly approaching forty-five. I unbuttoned my jacket and put an arm up. "Well, I'll tell you what I didn't see in there . . ."

"Yes. Artie's taste in weapons seems to run au courant."

I turned to look at him. "I'm pleased to see that some of that high school French took."

He continued to look at the house. "Oui."

"What do you know about Artie, other than his momma don't love him no more?"

I waited while he composed himself. I don't know if not knowing Artie was a full-fledged militia-ist or if weighing the odds on his being guilty of murdering Cody Pritchard embarrassed him, but his jaw set and the eyes hardened.

"Artie is an angry young man." He paused. "What do you know about him?"

I had looked Artie up and came clean. "He's got two cases of aggravated assault, one pending. He did a domestic for spousal abuse over in South Dakota and has two unpaid speeding tickets here in Wyoming." I waited a moment. "You seem to be taking this personally."

He shook his head. "I am reacting to the lost potential."

"Yep, I know you wouldn't know anything about that angry young man stuff."

We both shook our heads. "No."

I had to push the truck this time, twice. The first time, it jumped when he let out the clutch and barked all the skin off my right shin. The second time, with my arm locked straight with the effort of moving the two-ton beast, it stoved my shoulder and blew a sooty cloud of smoke and unburnt gas in my face. I climbed in and shut the door. "I hate this truck." We drove back toward Lame Deer on 39, and I peeled off my jacket and laid it on the seat between us. I thought about where we were headed, about Lonnie.

I wondered how long it would take for the Little Bird look to come back.

Jim Ferguson wore a gun at the trial; that alone was enough to make me laugh, but the context robbed me of my sense of humor. It was before Vic, so my two deputies were Lenny Rowell and Jim. Jim kept fussing with his belt, and Lenny was trying to catch a nap as he leaned against the bookcases of burgundy leather-covered Shepard's Wyoming Citations. I told Jim to get his belt adjusted because fidgeting deputies with guns made the common populace nervous and excused myself to go to the bathroom. When I got there, Lonnie Little Bird was trying to get his wheelchair into one of the stalls. The county hadn't gotten around to putting in handicapped facilities, and Lonnie wasn't fitting. He looked up through his coke-bottle glasses and smiled. "Mm, hmm. Yes, I am having troubles. It is so."

I looked around. I hadn't noticed anybody on the way in. "Lonnie, is there anybody to help you?"

"Mm, hmm . . . Mm, hmm." He continued to smile. "You."

He was a small man, even counting the two missing legs, and it was relatively easy to lift him up and hold him as he unbuttoned his pants. I sat him on the toilet. The grin never left his face. He had a large head with prominent ears. The nose was flat and looked like it had been broken numerous times. There was a rumor that the old guy had played professional baseball for one of the teams in the Midwest but, as far as I knew, it was only a rumor. He spoke as I started to close the stall door. "Mm, Sheriff?"

I paused. "Yep, Lonnie?"

"You know how old I am, Sheriff?"

I figured about sixty-five. "No, Lonnie. I can't say that I do."

"Mm, fifty-three years old. Yes, it is so."

Jesus. "Lonnie, that's pretty young." There was silence for a while, and I was afraid I had said something wrong. "Lonnie?"

"Mm, sometimes I think it's very old." Another pause, and I zipped up and moved over to the sink to wash my hands. "Sometimes I feel like I've been here a very long time."

I pulled out a paper towel and dried my hands. "Yep, I feel like that sometimes too, Lonnie."

"These boys, the ones that have done this thing to my daughter?" My breath caught in my throat. "It's a bad thing they've done, yes?"

I leaned against the counter and looked at the stall door. "Yes, it is a bad thing that they have done." There was a long silence, and I was glad no one could see my eyes well in anger and frustration. "Very bad."

The voice that came back was soft. "Mm, I get confused sometimes, and I just wanted to ask you."

When I got back to the courtroom, the jury light was glowing red.

There was a small dish attached to Lonnie's house that brought in the world, and I'm pretty sure who had ordered and paid for it. Henry's eyes were beginning to glaze over as Lonnie gave us his version of what was happening on this particular daytime drama, but I did my best to pay attention. "The problems started at the health clinic, that's where Dirk begged Catalina to not go through with the abortion. Cat agreed and said she was looking forward to having a family, mm-hmmm, mm-hmmm . . . But I'm not so sure. After they left the clinic, there were complications, but the doctors said she would be all right, so Dirk dropped her off at the mansion and went over to see Latisha.

But when he got there, Latisha told him that he needed to be with Catalina now that she is pregnant, so he left, but that's okay 'cause now Latisha is with Ben, and he seems to be a good fellow. Mm, hmm. Yes, it is so."

Lonnie watched soap operas because there was no baseball in November. The rumors of Lonnie's playing pro ball turned out to be true. There was baseball paraphernalia scattered in a few spots around the place, baseball bats tucked into corners, old gloves stacked up on shelves. There were pictures of Lonnie standing around with Cubs, Billy Williams and Ferguson Jenkins; Cardinals, Lou Brock and Joe Torre; Reds, Tony Perez and Johnny Bench, whom he blamed for ending his career. "After I saw him coming up, I just didn't see any reason to go on playing. He's part Indian too, you know. Choctaw. Mm, hmm . . . Yes, it is so."

The only thing that outnumbered the baseball pictures were photographs of Melissa. The only photographs I had of Melissa were not good ones. I stopped before an especially wonderful one of her in full dancing regalia, seated on a Palomino in front of a painted teepee. Its frame had started out as gold but was now rusted and tarnished at the edges. It was likely it was taken down and handled a great deal. I thought about defects, about the rape, the trial, and the Little Big Horn reenactment where I had seen her last. Lonnie probably thought about those things a lot, too.

It was nearing one o'clock, and Lonnie had wheeled himself into the kitchen to instruct Henry how to make the pickle-loaf, yellow American sliced cheese, and Kraft-spread sandwiches on Wonder Bread that would be our lunch. This was my kind of food, but Henry's gourmet sensibilities were having a hard time of it. "Lonnie, I buy you good food, why don't you eat it?"

"Your good food is complicated and takes too long to make. Mm . . . There are Vlassic pickle stackers in the door there."

With a sigh, Henry returned to the refrigerator, retrieved the jar of sliced pickles, and got ice from the freezer side of the appliance. "Lonnie, are you buying all that frozen food off the Schwan's truck again?"

He looked over at me through those thick, metal-frame glasses, needing an ally. And if Lonnie had said that little green men had deposited the eight boxes of Hot Pockets in his freezer, I was going to agree. "I feel sorry for him when he drives all the way up the driveway." I nodded as he continued. "We have good talks; he is from Kentucky." I nodded some more.

It was a little single-level ranch house that must have been built in the fifties, and the only things that kept me from thinking I was on one of those family sitcoms from the period was the amount of Indian art and craft that decorated it and the concrete ramps that led up to the doors of the spotless house. Lonnie Little Bird was on a campaign to get his daughter back from that gaggle of aunts in closer to town. This campaign meant Lonnie didn't drink, Lonnie didn't smoke, and Lonnie didn't use the Lord's name in vain, at least when any of the aunts were in earshot. There was Barq's root beer in the refrigerator beside the pickled pig's feet, and that's what we were drinking. I finished off the end of my two sandwiches. "When did Artie sell that rifle, Lonnie?"

"Mm, hmm. About a year ago. He sold that gun to that Buffalo Bill Museum over in Cody. Yes. It was winter, and he needed the money." He took a swig of his root beer and studied the Formica for a moment. "Not everybody has a nice house like mine . . ." His eyes glanced furtively at Henry. I got the feeling Lonnie liked secrets. A moment passed. "Sheriff?"

"Yep, Lonnie."

"Do you think that Artie did this thing to this boy?"

I picked up the root beer can and looked at it; as near as I could figure it had been about twenty years since I had tasted the stuff. "Well, I'm just checking everything out, everything and everybody."

He smiled. "Mm, hmm. Am I being checked out also?"

I looked at the little spark behind the glasses and wasn't going to be the one to tell him that without any legs he was kind of low on our list of suspects. "Just following up on all the leads, Lonnie."

He continued to smile but looked over to Henry and said a few short words in Cheyenne. Henry glanced at me, then back to his cousin, and then got up and walked out, turning the corner at the hallway. My eyes returned to Lonnie with a question, but he only sat there looking back through glasses so thick you could see little rainbows at the edges. After a moment or two I heard Henry returning down the hallway, his boots padding softly on the wall-to-wall carpeting. When he turned the corner again, he was carrying an old leather rifle scabbard with the straps you attach to a saddle hanging down, unbuckled. Due to my recent course of study, I recognized the Sharps butt plate that stuck out the end. When he got to the counter, he handed the weapon to me. I looked up at Lonnie, who gestured for me to take out the buffalo gun.

I carefully slid the rifle from its wool-lined sheath and rested the butt on my knee, and it was the most beautiful gun I had ever seen. It wasn't in as good shape as Omar's, there were scratches along the stock and the part of the foregrip that was wood, but each scar had been lovingly poulticed with oil and polished to a gleaming sheen. The metal had not been so lucky. Someone had taken steel wool to it at some point, and the ruddy sepia tone of its original color only showed in small creases; the rest was ghostly silver. There was a simple cross of brass tacks in the stock, the pattern a great deal like the one on the side of Red Road Contracting's truck, and ten distinct notches along the top ridge of the stock. The foregrip had three red-wool trading-cloth wraps ornamented with quillwork and with smaller feathers than I had seen on the scabbard of Omar's gun or, lately, in plastic bags. I touched the feathers and looked at Henry. "Owl." Messenger from the world of the dead indeed.

I turned the rifle around and looked at the magnificent pattern beaded underneath. Lonnie looked at me through the magnifying glasses. "Mm, hmm. The pattern is called Dead Man's Body. Yes, it is so."

On the afternoon of June 25, 1876, as the heat waves rolled from the buffalo grass, giving the impression of a breeze that did not exist, Colonel George Armstrong Custer and five companies of the Seventh Cavalry rode into the valley of the Little Big Horn. Also that afternoon, Davey Force, a pitcher for the Philadelphia Athletics, went six for six against Chicago, who scored four runs in the ninth to pull out a 14 to 13 victory. Custer was not so lucky.

The report of the Secretary of War states that the five companies had 405 Springfield carbines caliber .45, along with their single action 396 Colt revolvers caliber .45. What the Seventh Cavalry contingency did not carry were any Sharps. When the fight began, only about half the Indians had guns, and they were a varied sort: muzzleloaders, Spencer carbines, old-fashioned Henry rifles, and an unspecified number of Sharps. The army didn't stand much of a chance, trapped on that beautiful hillside, with no reinforcements coming. I thought about how those gentle slopes smelled and sounded on a glorious summer day, about how they might have smelled and sounded that June day in 1876. I also thought about the pumpkin that had exploded from a very long distance in Omar's back pasture.

When Little Wolf led a straggling band of thirty-three Northern Cheyenne warriors into surrender two and a half years later on March 25, 1879, they handed in twenty assorted rifles and carbines, of which the majority were Sharps, numbering nine. I held in my hands the tenth. "So, your great-great-grandfather didn't surrender his?"

He continued to look out the windshield as he drove. "I guess he did not completely trust the white man. Go figure."

161

I looked down at the rifle, the butt resting on the toe of my boot; I didn't want the truck to touch it. "Do these ten little notches along the ridge here mean what I think they mean?"

"Another potato digger bites the dust." He slowed as a mule deer darted across the road a couple of hundred yards ahead and, sure as anything, another followed. "No, it stands for the tenth rifle. It was so they could tell them apart." He saw me looking at all the beads, feathers, and silver tacks. "All that was put on later."

The Cheyenne got their weapons by trading or capture; I didn't ask how they got this lot of ten. "Okay, so your great great grandfather surrenders in 1879 but hides this ol' boy out on the range?"

"Wrapped up in two inches of bear grease."

"When did they get out?"

"As near as I can tell, we never have."

I raised an eyebrow. "When did the soldiers let him go?"

"About six months later; winter was coming on, and they did not want to have to feed them."

"He went back and got it six months later?"

"Yes." He smiled to himself. "We were tough, in the day."

I looked at the gun again. "Any idea when it was last shot?"

The smile played out thinly on his lips. "Friday of last week?"

"Very funny. How come your cousin has it?"

"It is in the family; that is all that matters. No one in the family has personal ownership, but I doubt anybody would argue if I claimed it."

I thought of the T-bird. "Like Lola?"

"Like Lola." He smiled to himself some more. "Anyway, it is haunted."

As it grew darker, the soft Wyoming sky drifted into night. I pulled out my watch to see what time it was: 5:30. I still had time to go home and take a shower and get the truck off of me. I was looking forward to being with Vonnie, with somebody who didn't have any connection with the case.

* * *

When we picked up the wine at the Pony, he left the truck running. Dena Many Camps came out to talk with me while Henry rummaged through the wine coolers. She tended bar for Henry when he wasn't there, was one of Henry's protégés in billiards, and was a good friend of Cady's, although she was about four years older. You would be hard pressed to find a better-looking woman. She walked with a wicked grace, like a panther with a pool cue. "What're you doing, Trouble?" She always called me Trouble, even though I'm sure she had caused more than I ever would.

"Well, if it isn't what makes the Badlands look good." She wrote poetry and had been offered a scholarship to Dartmouth but had decided to pursue billiards instead. She probably made more money at pool, but I wondered if she ever regretted not going to college. "What're you up to other than luring men to their financial doom a quarter at a time?"

She rested her arms on the scaly sill of the truck, fingers drumming lightly on her exposed elbows. "I like torturing them slowly. Anyway, a girl's gotta make a living, and I can't do it on what this guy pays me." She pulled her lips back into a broad smile, just to show me there was no malice. "There's a pool tournament down in Vegas, and I'm leaving next week."

I looked at the white fringe on the silk yoke of the western shirt-dress she wore. She always had on flamboyant western clothes when she competed in the tournaments. Somehow, it didn't seem fair. She looked back toward the bar. "What's he doing in there?"

"Getting some wine for me."

"Wine . . . for you?"

"What, I don't look like a wine guy to you?"

She reached in and felt the feathers on the rifle with her fingertips. "Owl." She looked closer and her hand froze. "Ohohyaa . . ."

"That mean owl?"

"No." She shook her head. "No, it means . . . terrible. Sehan . . ." Her eyes narrowed, and her hand came away from the gun as though the rifle might bite. "This is a weapon from the Camp of the Dead."

"Actually, it's from Lonnie Little Bird." Her hands went to her hair, and I could tell she was unbraiding it for a reason. "It's for a ballistics test."

Her eyes met mine, and she continued to undo her long braid. "This is a ghost weapon, a weapon sent from the dead to retrieve."

"Retrieve what?"

"Not what . . . who."

"What, they need a fourth for bridge?"

Her eyes sharpened to slits of flint. "This is not funny. It's big medicine."

"Big medicine." I started to make another smart-aleck remark but thought better of it. "I was just . . ."

"Lonnie Little Bird gave this to you?"

"For ballistics, we've got to check it against the one that killed Cody Pritchard."

She finished unbraiding and shook her head, the dark hair falling loose over her shoulders. "Give it back to him."

"I will, after we shoot it." I reached out to touch her arm, but she shifted away. "What's the story with the hair?"

"It is a sign of respect and protection. There are spirits that linger near that weapon, and they can easily take away the soul of someone still living for the enjoyment of their society."

The hand that held the rifle suddenly felt cold, so I shifted to the other one. "I'll get it right back to him, just as soon as we get a test fire." Henry had exited the bar with the two bottles of wine and opened the door of the truck, his eyes meeting Dena's.

"What is up, Toots?" He climbed in, but her eyes stayed on him as he concerned himself with the shifter and with shutting the door. Finally, he cocked his head and looked at her again. "What?"

"You let Lonnie give him this?"

His voice growled, low and steady. "It is his job." A full fifteen seconds passed before she exhaled, turned, and walked into the Red Pony without looking back; the fringe on her dress matched the sway of her hair. I turned to look at him. "Women." He put the truck in gear and backed away from the bar, hitting the tired brakes, shifting into first, and pulling out toward my place. I continued to look at him. "What?"

"What? I've got 'the' Cheyenne death rifle here?"

He shook his head. "So to speak." He glanced over. "Bother you?"

"Only if ghosts are going to fly out of the barrel and carry me off to the Camp of the Dead." He laughed a hearty, honest laugh. "What?"

He laughed some more. "Your company is not that good."

The rifle, Henry, the ghosts, and me drove up the road and deposited me at my cabin. The rifle and I went in, Henry went back down the road, and where the ghosts went was anybody's guess. I carefully sat the rifle on the arms of my easy chair and looked at it.

Retriever of the Dead. The thing was worth a million dollars—was priceless probably—and leaving it lying around my little house that had no locks didn't seem like a good idea. I was going to have to take it with me over to Vonnie's, but I could always leave it in the Bullet. I wrestled a shower out of the bathroom and put on clean clothes. The phone machine in my bedroom was blinking, but I ignored it. The rifle was still there when I got back to the living room, so I looked around the place for any apparitions and was a little disappointed when none appeared. Maybe Henry was right; maybe I was lousy company, even at a dead man's party. I walked back into my bedroom and stared at the answering machine. I hoped that Cady had called, but the little blinking red light was looking angry. Maybe the ghosts had left a message, so I pushed the button.

"Okay, we had three mailboxes at Rock Creek reportedly hit, got a call on some kid chasing horses with his snow machine, turns out the kid owned the horses and there's no law saying you can't herd livestock with a snow machine . . . that from the eleven-year-old perpetrator. Earl Walters slid off the road at Klondike and Upper Clear Creek and took out a yield sign; I always knew the ancient fucker couldn't read. And our crime of the day, Old Lady Grossman reported somebody stealing the snowman out of her yard and driving off with it. Ferg stopped the suspect, who turned out to be her nephew who had taken it as a joke."

We weren't likely to make America's Most Wanted with a selection of crimes such as these, but it was premium Roundup material.

"So, out of our list, the only ones that have reloading equipment are Mike Rubin and Stanley Fogel."

The dentist.

"The dentist." There was a pause, as the machine recorded her thinking. "Wouldn't it be a pisser if it turned out to be the dentist? I know it doesn't have the ring that the butler does, but wouldn't people be surprised?"

I nodded my head in agreement.

"Anyway, I went over and checked on him. He's cute. I think I'm going to change dentists."

Jesus. There was a rustling of papers, and she continued.

"I also went out to Mike Rubin's shop while you were out joyriding on the Rez. Is that fucker goofy or what?"

I nodded.

"I don't know if he was more rattled by having a sheriff's deputy there or a woman. He doesn't get out much, does he?"

I shook my head this time.

"I got samples from both, and neither match up with what we think we've got. The Ferg finally got around to checking on the Esper place, and he says that there weren't any tracks in the snow leading up to the house. I called the post office and, sure enough, they put a hold on their mail that goes off tomorrow. I called the mine and asked them. They said he was down in Colorado, visiting his sister, no number left. The sister is married, and nobody here seems to know the name or where in Colorado they live, so here we are at the beginning. I'll swing around there tonight and see if they've gotten back from the other square state."

There was a pause, then the machine beeped, and she spoke again,

"Okay, so I swung by the Espers and left a note behind the storm door telling them to contact us as soon as they get in. Ferg's right, there hasn't been anybody there for days. If they call, I'll call you. I'll be here tonight, if you need me. All night. Glen and I are fighting, so I'm sleeping here."

I stared at the machine.

"Don't worry, it's nothing big, just the usual shit. Don't call to check on me and don't come in here. I'm fine. Oh, and by the way, Phil La Vante died about three months ago, so should I take him off our short list?"

I nodded, and the machine clicked off. I hated marital discord; I hated it when I was married. I often wondered about Vic's marriage. There were times when she and Glen appeared to get along, but most of the time it seemed like they led separate but unequal lives. This wasn't the first night she'd spent at the jail. She wasn't the frequent lodger I was but, only a month ago, I'd been in my office one night catching up on paperwork when I heard somebody open the front door. As she walked into her office opposite mine, all she said was "Don't ask" and slammed her door behind her. After a few moments though, she reappeared with her Philadelphia Police mug and a bottle of tequila, had sat down in the chair by my door, threw her feet up on my desk, poured herself a drink and hissed, "All men are assholes, right?" I nodded vigorously, quietly finished my reports as she drank, and then crept out, my back to the wall.

I fought the urge to call her and went back to the front of the house to collect the two bottles of wine and the rifle; it weighed enough to be haunted. The emotional toll of the day was having an effect on me, and I wondered if I wasn't already in the Camp of the Dead. I wondered if I hadn't been for the last four years. I sat the bottles down and pulled the old girl from the scabbard, looking at the rubbed spots. The barrel was round, the heavy military model rather than the expected octagonal like Omar's. I looked at the beads attached to the hide covering on the foregrip.

Dead Man's Body was an intricate design of triangles, points, and geometric figures showing not only the body itself, but the wounds and the spears that had done the deed. Henry had explained that it was more of a Sioux pattern, but that that might have been the reason for using it, to warn the Lakota that they should not take their alliance with the Cheyenne lightly. They were the small Venetian seed beads that had become more predominant around 1840 and had a richer color than the earlier pony style. The stitching was overlay, not the usual lazy stitch you saw nowadays, and when you held the rifle up to the light there was no space between the rows. I thought about all those little strings of beads sailing across the Atlantic from Italy. Maybe Vic's ancestors had supplied the ornamentation for Henry's in six degrees of beaded separation.

I smiled and made a conscious effort to be better company for the Old Cheyenne and, to prove it, I raised the rifle high over my head and gave out with the most blood-curdling war cry I could manage. I'm pretty sure I could do it better when I was seven, but the shout rattled around my little house and made me feel better, so I did it four or five more times. The last one hurt but was the best. I felt like an extra in a fifties B movie, so I put the rifle back in its scabbard, picked up my wine, and headed for the truck.

The temperature was dropping, and it was starting to look like we might get more snow. I hit the NOAA band on my radio and listened to the little computer-generated Norwegian tell me that two to four inches was expected on the mountain but only an inch down here. So far, not a flake had fallen, but I figured I could always call Henry; he could tell me exactly when it was going to begin.

I started digesting Vic's oral report; the Espers worried me. If Reggie Esper and his wife had taken off for Colorado, and I believe his sister lived in Longmont, had the two boys gone with them? It didn't seem likely that two college-aged boys would go with their parents to visit an aunt for a week. I had honestly believed that Cody's death had been an accident, at least mostly, until the feather. I was getting that fretful, nagging feeling that this case might end with all the loose strands that I had picked free. The old police adage says, when you're done and there's nothing there, go back to the beginning and start over. So, here I was, staring at the beginning and trying to figure out what it was I'd missed the first time.

I turned into Vonnie's drive, pulled through the opening gate, and parked in front of the house. All the motion-detecting lights came on again, and I gathered up the stuff and started for the house. By the time I got to the porch, she had the door open. "You still look tired."

"That bad, huh?" The light from the entryway was warm and tawny, reflecting the reddish highlights of her hair as she stood in the doorway.

"Your voice is hoarse. Are you all right?"

"Yep, I just had to do some shouting today. Sorry."

She took my arm as I got there. "No, I like it. It's sexy."

I was feeling better and gave her the two bottles of wine after she shut the door. "Here, I brought wine. I picked it out myself."

She looked at me for a moment, then her eyes dropped to the scabbard. "What's that?"

I raised the rifle and shrugged. "This is a very long story . . ."

"Is it a gun?"

"Yep . . ."

"Not in my house."

I looked at her face for the contention I expected to find, but there wasn't any. It was a simple statement of fact, and her eyes still held the warmth that had invited me in. I felt the need to explain. "It's an expensive piece, it doesn't belong to me, and I thought it would be safer in here." She looked down at the rifle again but didn't say anything. "I'll put it back in the truck." I started to turn, but she caught my arm.

"No."

There was a moment as she tried to weigh the options open to both of us. "It's okay, I'll just lock it up in the truck."

"No. I'm sorry." Her face came up, and the smile was a little sad, but generous. "Is it okay here, by the door?"

I smiled too. "Yep, that'll be fine." I propped the rifle in the corner and for the first time noticed my sheepskin coat draped across the chair that was also there. I turned and looked at her. "You gonna send me packing?"

She cocked her head and was instantly delicious. "No, I like the way it smells, and if you don't take it with you tonight you're not likely to get it back." With this, she turned and started down the hallway and through the living room where I had left her the last time I was here. She was wearing low-heeled ropers, buckskin leather-laced pants, and an off-white silk blouse with western accents. The effect from the rear was breathtaking. I left the Cheyenne Rifle of the Dead to commune with the smell of my coat and pursued some preferred company myself.

The elevated area between the arches was a dining room and on the other side of it was the kitchen. The smell of something wonderful was drifting through the doorway, a delicate smell, tangy, but with an underlying sea scent that spoke softly to the base of my stomach. The olive loaf sandwiches had worn thin.

The kitchen was a study in contrasts. The floors were Mexican tile, and the walls were the same reworked plaster as in the other parts of the house, only these were differing shades of red. Massive hand-hewn beams straddled the room overhead, and the cabinets looked like they had been salvaged from somebody's line shack. The actual appliances were huge stainless-steel brutes that reminded me of the DCI coroner's lab in Cheyenne. A number of things seemed to be simmering on the eight-burner stove, but my attention was drawn to the center island where a small glass vase of tulips sat between festively painted plates and silverware that looked stately enough to have been used at the Queen's coronation. There were linen napkins in brass-and-silver rings, and I was getting that diminishing feeling that I was there to read the meter.

"I hope you don't mind if we eat in the kitchen?" She went to the stove, lifted the lid on something, and stirred it with a long wooden spoon that came from a crock full of implements that was tucked into the corner of the counter. The steam rose and separated as it drifted past the shining adzed surface of the beams. I was willing to bet she didn't have to worry about mouse poop. She had turned and was looking at me. "It just seemed cozier. If we eat in the dining room with just the two of us, it will be like that scene from *Citizen Kane*." I nodded, trying to think of the scene from *Citizen Kane*, only able to come up with the one with the screaming cockatoo. "In anticipation of the snow, I've made hot buttered rum, or would you rather we start with some of this wonderful wine you've brought?"

"I think it's only supposed to snow an inch." Henry had his magic; I had the little computerized Norwegian. "But the hot buttered rum sounds great."

She sprinkled sugar, cloves, and nutmeg into two thick-faceted glass tumblers, poured rum on top, added a couple of sticks of cinnamon and hot water, and finished it off with a large dollop of what read on the wrapper as IRISH COUNTRY BUTTER.

"We'll save the wine for later. This'll do your throat some good." She leaned on the counter and raised her own glass. "Here's to our first official date." We touched glasses, and I felt the warmth in my chest before I even took a sip.

"So, he was clinically depressed?"

"Undiagnosed."

Dinner was everything my stomach had hoped it would be: pasta with a cioppino of spinach, tomato, clams and mussels, and homemade country bread with which we both sopped up the leftover sauce. She followed this up with a homemade apple pie, topped with vanilla bean ice cream, and continued with the hot buttered rum, in spite of the wine. My mood was so warm and tranquil that I was beginning to fear that I might fall right off the little Italian stools and onto the floor. "I remember coming out here with Dad when I was a kid. He shod your father's horses, and I tagged along."

"Yes. I was trying to remember if I was here."

"Yep, you were."

She looked into her glass. "Was I a little snot?"

"Yep, you were."

She laughed a soft laugh. "One chance and I blew it, huh?"

"It was summer, and you were gone all the other times. Didn't you used to go somewhere?"

"Maine."

"Maine. Doesn't seem fair; summer is the payoff in Wyoming." She stirred her drink with one of the thin sticks of cinnamon.

"I didn't get much of a choice at the time."

I tried to steer the conversation without appearing boorish. "Richest man in three counties, what'd he have to be depressed about?" She smiled, allowing the tiny bit of boorishness to pass.

"I don't think he cared for himself too much."

"How about you?"

"Did I care for him?" She paused, genuinely considering the question. "I suppose not, but the further down the road I go, the more I see my relationship with him having had an effect on every single choice in my life . . . in a negative or positive way." She stared at the candles that had melted into the holders and blew them out. "That would have made him happy." She stretched a hand across the table, and I stuck a paw out to meet her. She took my hand and turned it over, examining the creases on the sides of my fingers. I could feel an electric charge racing up my forearms as she traced the folds with a fingernail. "I like your hands, big and powerful, but they move very carefully, like an artist."

"Piano lessons."

"Really?"

"Very early on, I developed a love for boogie-woogie."

"Oh my. I guess that's what they call full-octave hands." A moment went by. "That explains the piano at your house. You'll have to play for me."

172

"I'm kinda out of practice, which is kind of the theme for my life as of late."

There was a long pause. "One of the cowboys found him in the tack shed. I guess he didn't want to make a mess in the house." She continued looking at my hand, and for a moment I thought she was going to cry, but instead she laughed a short laugh and smiled as she looked up at me. "Daddy's little girl; not exactly the most compelling of psychological profiles, huh?"

"How could he leave something like you?" It was out before I could analyze how corny it was going to sound, but she didn't laugh. Instead, it was a short, broken sob that forced her to wipe her nose and run the side of her thumb past the corner of her eye in an attempt to keep her mascara from running. I handed her my napkin but held on to the other hand. She laughed this time and straightened slightly. "Where's your dog?"

She sniffed and then laughed again. "He's in the mudroom out back, sulking."

"Maybe I should meet him?"

She straightened an imagined run at the corner of her eye with the napkin. "I didn't think you liked dogs."

"I like dogs fine. Does he like people?"

She wiped her nose. "He hasn't met that many."

"Great, let me go get the rifle." This time the laugh was wholehearted. "Your father is why you don't allow guns in the house?"

"I just don't like them. It seems to me that no matter what they always lead to bad things. My opinion is that produced for their specific purpose, they are inherently bad." We stared at each other for a moment, then she continued, "I know that they are a necessary evil in your line of work, but I don't allow necessary evils in my home."

I cleared my throat and nodded. "How about your life?" Her eyes stayed with mine.

"I'll have to think about that."

"Okay." I released her hand. "Speaking of necessary evils, where's the mudroom?"

She stood and patted the table the same way Brandon White Buffalo had earlier in the day. "Maybe I better introduce the two of you."

I waited with my hot buttered rum and killed off the last bit of crust. For pies like this, a man could hang up the old star and gun and slowly become as large as a minivan in stretch jeans. I sat the fork down and listened to the clatter as very large claws attempted to gain purchase on the Mexican tiles. I heard mild protests and a few thumps, and I would have been alarmed but for the continued giggling that accompanied the general commotion.

He was bigger than I remembered, and I remembered him being very big. He was caught by surprise at seeing somebody besides her in the house, and the disconcerted quality was evident in the head that was as big as a five-gallon gas can and quizzically turned to the side. She still had a hold on the leather collar; if she hadn't, I'm sure he would have gone straight for me. I heard the throaty warning start deep in his chest as I desperately tried to remember the word for stew and hoped he understood Lakota.

She slapped him on the head and growled herself. "Stop that. Now!" The change was instantaneous; the eyebrows shifted, and his head dropped. He looked like a scolded Kodiak. He began panting and looked at me with his head rising to a comfortable interest, ears forward, and with the inquisitive slant once again visible. She shook his head a little with the collar but didn't release it. "There, you can come over and say hi."

I stood, and his eyes traveled up with me, but he still seemed calm. I thought about what Henry had said about dogs and hoped this one wasn't Cheyenne. As I came around the center island his tail began to wag. I knew the drill and approached, standing with my hand out, palm down and fingers in. His big head stretched forward, sniffing, then a tongue as wide as my hand lapped my knuckles. I stroked the big, furry head and scratched behind his ears as a hind paw as big as my foot thumped on the ceramic surface. "He's a big baby."

We took our drinks into the living room, and she brought the phone from the kitchen; she said she was expecting a call from Scottsdale. She waited on the sofa as I began making a fire in the moss-rock fireplace. The dog dutifully groaned and stretched out on the Navajo rug in front of the hearth. Periodically, his eyes would glance toward the rifle tucked into the corner by the door. He did it more than once, and I was sure he was seeing something over there that I couldn't.

I was thinking about the Espers and Artie Small Song when I noticed her looking at me. "How's it going?"

"I beg your pardon?"

"The case. I'm betting that's what you're thinking about." She took a sip of her drink and continued as I tried to think up a harmless subject to distract her with. "It's okay. If I were you, it's all I would think about."

I smiled, nodded, and looked at my lap. "On the way over here, I was looking forward to spending the evening with someone who had no connection with it."

She looked over the rim of her glass. "Great expectations."

I took a sip of my own drink and reassessed. "I spent the day out on the reservation with Henry."

The phone rang, and she picked it up and talked to some real estate broker in Arizona about some property she wanted to buy in the White Mountains. I listened to the one-sided conversation as they discussed an investment property that was going to cost more than our county's yearly fiscal budget. When she hung up, I asked, "Get it?"

"She's going to call me back. They're being cranky about the mineral rights." She paused for a moment. "I'm sorry, it's incredibly rude, but if I don't act on this now, I'm not likely to get it."

"It's okay." I smiled. "You're quite the wheeler dealer?"

"I keep my hand in. I'm acquiring a lot of property on the southern portion of the Powder River right now. I even bought some land from the family of one of those boys."

"The Espers?"

"There's talk of a power plant out there . . ." I smiled some more. "What?"

"You're just not what I picture as a robber baron."

"Robber baroness." She looked at the fire.

"Something wrong?"

She took a moment to answer. "No, I was just thinking about that girl."

"Melissa?"

"Yes." She turned back to me. "She cleaned out here for a summer with her aunt, but it just didn't work out." She looked sad and changed the subject. "Walter, how in the world did you ever end up in law enforcement?"

"In the marines, during Vietnam." I looked at her for a good while, taking in all the details. Her hair was down, and I noticed how thick and luxurious it was, held back from her face on one side by a single etched silver barrette that draped the reddish curtain behind one ear. It was like a box seat to a command performance. The earring that showed was a roweled spur studded with little turquoise and coral stones and dangling jingle bobs. She had great ears, even better than mine. Up close, I could see the wrinkles around her eyes, and it was nice. They softened the lupine slant, and the soft brown in her eyes looked inviting, like the mud on the banks of streams that beg you to take off your shoes and wade through them.

I squirmed a little and started in. "I graduated in '66, lost my deferment and got drafted by the marines. I got the letter, and it scared the shit out of me. Hell, I didn't even know the marines could draft you. I got through Paris Island, officer's training, and because I was big got shuffled into the marine military police, which meant that I got to do exciting things like man checkpoints at traffic control areas, provide convoy security, investigate motor vehicle accidents, and patrol off-limit areas. And then there was the traditional task of maintaining good order and discipline within the battalion." I turned to look at her, stiffening my back for effect.

"I guess you don't forget that stuff."

I laughed and looked over at the fire. "No, you don't. Now,

granted, I was just some dumb kid from Wyoming, but it was all pretty confusing."

"The war?"

"The war, the military, a foreign country; hell, I was just getting used to California. So, I decided to devote myself to the police side of my job. It was the only part that seemed to make sense. It wasn't easy, because the marine police were not a formalized occupational specialty. We were only cops on a rotational basis, operating under a skeleton force of navy officers. I was lucky, and after a while I gained some experience and credibility as an investigator."

"How did you do that?"

"A couple of cases."

"You don't want to talk about it?"

I went back to looking at the fire. "They're not good stories."

"Good?"

"Happy."

"Oh." She shifted and warmed up both of our drinks with straight rum. "Do I seem like the kind of person who only wants to hear happy stories?"

"Maybe not, but I'm not sure I want to be the one to tell you the sad ones." She held on to my glass and wouldn't let me have it. I laughed. "All right, you've broken me." I took a sip of the almost straight rum and thought back, remembering the heat. "In January of '68, I was assigned as a liaison to the 379th Air Police Squadron, 379th Combat Support Group, NCOIC Air Police Investigations. A number of Corps personnel were shuttled in and out of Tan Son Nhut Air Force Base, and a lot of them were turning up self-medicated."

"So the air force called in the marines?"

"Oh, no, not at all. They didn't want me there, but the Marine Corps Provost Marshall's office did. They saw it as a wonderful opportunity for me to get some on-the-job training from the investigative operations officer there who was career air force and who consequently hated my guts because I was a marine."

"Nobody told him we were fighting the North Vietnamese?"

"Only as a secondary front." I laughed a little at the absurdity of the situation long passed. "I was assigned to him, but I wasn't particularly one of his. I broke up a lot of fights, patrolled a lot of outlying areas, like Laos and Cambodia . . ."

"You're joking?"

"Yep, but I did get to meet Martha Raye." This time she laughed, hard. "Don't get me wrong, a lot of the air police I worked with were the best, but they were overworked, and sometimes it helps to have a new set of eyes come in from outside. The Vietnamese were selling it right on the base in exchange for black market items from the PX. There were an awful lot of Vietnamese military police involved as ring leaders. I tracked the problem back to air force personnel."

"They must have really loved you for that."

"Semper Fi."

"What else? You said there were a couple of cases?"

"Yep, I did." I took another hit from my drink and rested it on my knee; the plain rum with the sugar remnants and cinnamon sticks was surprisingly good. "There was this prostitute that was killed off base. We really didn't have any jurisdiction, but I made a personal campaign out of it."

She put her hand out and rested it along the back of the sofa near my shoulder. "How have you survived, doing this for so long? I mean, you still care." Her eyes closed a little like they did. "Do most guys still care after thirty years in this line of work?"

I thought for a moment. "No, I don't think they can afford it. Nobody makes an emotional bulletproof vest, so you just have to carry the shrapnel around with you."

It took her a long time to respond. "You must be tough."

I turned and looked at her. "No, I'm not. It's one of my secret weapons." She smiled. "There was this prostitute in the village up near Hotel California, this old French fort where they housed an RVAN company at the northernmost tip of Tan Son Nhut Air Base. It looked like something out of *Beau Geste*. It had twenty-foot walls that were three-feet thick, whitewashed concrete that formed a perfect rec-tangle. It had solid iron gates that shut the arched doorways into this huge courtyard with all these smaller cubicles. There was a small vil-lage out past the fence line, a civilian mortuary, and a cemetery with thousands of little white headstones . . ."

I thought back as I told the story, and it was amazing how all the details were still there, like some carefully packed footlocker that had withstood the consistent inspection of time. "Her name was Mai-Kim, and I met her over Tiger beers in the village at the Boy-Howdy Beau-Coups Good Times Lounge. They told us not to drink the water, so I didn't . . . habitually."

"Were you a customer?"

"No, they told us not to do that either, and I was a young marine and did what I was told." She laughed some more. "She was cute, though. Had good teeth, a rarity in that place. She was tiny, and she loved to talk about America. She took a great deal of pride in the fact that she had lots of American friends."

"As many as money could buy?"

"Yep, but she was better than that."

"I'm sorry, I didn't mean . . ."

"No, I know that." I rushed ahead, so she would know that no feel-ings were hurt. "They had an old upright piano in the bar, and I know I single-handedly overdosed all of Vietnam with Fats Waller and Pete Johnson." I thought for a moment. "She would read *Stars and Stripes* at the bar between clients, and I would help her with the pronunciations and meanings of words she didn't understand. After the drug thing, none of the air force guys would talk to me and neither would the Vietnamese police, so I talked to her." I paused a moment, remember-ing. "She had a great voice, husky like yours. Like she had just gotten out of bed." I nodded. "In retrospect, she probably had." Another laugh.

"She died?"

"Yes. Badly."

I looked back at the fire and listened to the dog breathe. "Her body was found in one of our abandoned forward bunkers. She'd been raped and strangled. I still remember the crime scene. The killer had pulled down a number of the sandbags to make a bed, and it all looked so normal, until you saw her eyes or the marks on her neck." I started to take another sip of my rum but stopped a little ways away from my mouth to just smell it. "Nobody was talking, nobody. So there I was, at the last outpost of the last war, investigating a murder that nobody cared about." I exhaled a short breath, laughing at myself. "It was my way of introducing a little order into the chaos."

She waited a moment, but she had to ask, "Did you get him?"

The dog yawned loudly and rolled over on his back. I watched as his huge fan of a tail slowly dropped. "War stories; I'm even boring the dog to death."

"Who did it?"

I took another sip of my rum and got cagey. "Can't tell you all my stories, then you wouldn't have a second date with me." She punched my shoulder, and I continued to lighten my tone. "She wanted to live in Tennessee. One of her customers must have sold her on it, telling her how it was the greatest place in the world. The Volunteer State, where Elvis was from; she knew everything there was to know about Tennessee." I looked at the pineapple upside-down dog and waited, but she didn't say anything. "Okay, let's talk about you."

"Oh, no."

"Yep, fair's fair; it's your turn."

"I don't have interesting stories like you."

I gave her my most disbelieving look. "Tell me about New York. Isn't that where you were for all those years?"

She laughed. "I had a gallery on the Upper East Side, near Eighty-sixth Street."

"What'd you sell?"

"Really shitty expensive art."

"You seem defensive."

"I'm an artist." She swirled the sugar from the bottom of her glass.

"We're always defensive about shitty art; afraid we might be producing it."

"Are you still sculpting?"

She was talking into her glass, her eyes avoiding mine, so I placed my arm across the back of the sofa and gently touched her hair when the phone rang again. She looked at me with a sad smile and brushed her cheek against my hand before leaning over and answering it.

I listened for a while, then got up and went over to the fire. The dog's eye opened, and his head looked even bigger with the ears trailing up, but he didn't move. I reached down, patted his stomach, and the eye closed. I guess he liked me, or at least he trusted me. I sat on the elevated hearth, pulled the poker from the stand at the right, and jostled the logs into a more active position. The glowing red embers made a checkerboard across the burning wood, and small sparks disappeared up into the darkness of the chimney.

The wind continued to howl in the flume, and I thought about getting home. Tomorrow was the back-to-zero day. I figured I'd start with the Cody scene; if it was a murder, that was where the killer had started. I would reexamine all the evidence: the feather, the guns, and the ballistics sample. Then I would start reinterviewing. I was going to have to circle the wagons and bring Turk back. I looked at the dog, and he was looking at the rifle beside the door again.

A little over two years, two years since the suspended sentences for all four boys. Why now? It just didn't make sense. Why single out Cody Pritchard? He had been the most repugnant during the trial, but why kill him now? The feather was a real twist, and somehow I had to get some answers from it.

I looked back at the Cheyenne Rifle of the Dead. Was it speaking in tongues? Could the dog hear it? I was dealing in a subject matter in which it was expert. I wished I had a war party of Old Cheyenne to follow me around and whisper things in my ear about life and death. Would old Little Bird or Standing Bear help me find the killer of the boy that had raped their great-great-great-granddaughter? I don't know precisely why, but I believed they would. Lucian had told me stories about them, about their honor, their grace, and their pursuit of the Cheyenne virtues.

There was this incident back in '49 where Lucian did this routine pullover of an older Indian couple who were driving just outside of Durant and were headed for the reservation. He said it was one of those wonderful winter nights when the wind had died down and the snow looked like scalloped icing on a vanilla cake. The moon was full and bright, bright enough for him to spot this old Dodge slide through a stop sign, make a right, and head for the Rez with no taillights. Lucian wheeled the old Nash around and pulled in behind their car to just give them a warning about the lack of illumination aft. He said it took two miles for them to pull over, and they were only doing about twenty miles an hour.

I could just see that little bandy rooster straightening his belt and buttoning up his old Eisenhower jacket as he got out and walked on two then solid legs up to the ancient, black-primer Dodge. I could see him pushing his old campaign hat back with a thumb, like he used to do, and leaning on the back of the Dodge's windowsill as the window rolled down. "Hey, Chief." He wasn't joking; Frank Red Shield was a chief of the Northern Cheyenne. "I pulled you over 'cause you've got a couple 'a taillights out back here."

He said the old chief's eyes twinkled, and he patted Lucian's arm that rested on the car. "Oh, that's okay. I thought you were pulling me over 'cause I didn't have no license."

Lucian said he nearly bit his lip to bleeding trying to not laugh until Mrs. Red Shield slapped her husband across the chest and said, "Don't pay no attention to him, Sheriff. He don't know what he's sayin' when he's been drinkin'."

I smiled and laughed to myself. Maybe the old guys in the rifle were already helping me. I was aware of some movement from the sofa and looked up to find Vonnie holding the phone out to me. I had been so wrapped up in my musings that I hadn't even heard it ring again. Her face was immobile, and her shoulders shook like she was cold. "It's for you."

I looked at the phone, back to her, and then reached over and took it from her. She looked scared, and I suddenly felt very tired. I heard my voice say, "Sheriff."

I listened to the static of the mobile phone and the pitched battle the wind was having with her, wherever she was. Her voice was tight, and she was straining to be heard over the howl that seemed to match its brother in the fireplace perfectly. "Well . . . we found one of the Espers."

9

"Welcome to Hooverville." It was creeping up on midnight, and she was trying not to look like a turtle with her head ducked down in the artificial brown fur of her duty jacket.

"Where is he?" She turned into the steady wind, with her hands buried in the depths of her coat pockets, and led me over to where all the headlights were shining. The pulse of the blue and red lights reflected off the frozen gravel of the impromptu parking lot that had been set up along the barbed-wire fence.

Hooverville referred to the assortment of little shacks that surrounded Dull Knife Lake at the southern part of the Bighorn Mountains and was known by the locals as the South End. Outside the jurisdiction of the Cloud Peak Wilderness Area and the federal government, numerous lots had been bought and sold and built upon until the surrounding shoreline resembled a collection of chicken coops. Some of the little cabins weren't bad, but the majority were hunting trailers with little annexes attached that had been towed in a long time ago. The fishing was good all around the lake, but the view was better at the northern part where the shore got steeper and the water disappeared into the thick forest. I thought about the original Hooverville in Washington, D.C., where WWI veterans had been chased out of town and figured it would take a young Patton and MacArthur to clean this one out, too.

I shined the beam of my flashlight in the path and saw that the single set of tracks leading to the body were slowly filling in. I gave Vic my keys and asked her to repark my truck so that it would form a snow fence that would knock down the wayward flakes that were impeding the crime scene investigation.

184

It was Jacob Esper all right, sitting with one foot folded underneath him and the other sticking straight out. He was leaning against the rear wheel of his truck and had a quizzical look on his face. There was a small torn spot at the center of his Carhartt jacket, and he was surrounded by a frozen liquid with brown shading. Dried blood, discounting the temperature, thirty minutes to two hours. I didn't have to worry about his back, since most of it was a frozen smear on the side of the dirty truck. It started with the explosion behind the door and trailed to where he now sat. His eyes were open, but tache noire had already set in. Three hours. I reached out and tugged at his boot; the body was stiff with fully developed rigor. Six to twenty-four hours. We needed a body core temperature, and we weren't going to get it for another seven hours.

One of the footprints behind Vic's yellow nylon barrier was close to me, so I blew into it and examined the impression: about a size nine, medium width. At the arch was a registered trademark, SKYWALK, with a medallion print of some kind with words around the edges and a diminutive mountain range. The headlights subsided in shadow for a moment. "Where are they?"

"Over there in the Hummer. They're about to run out of gas from operating the heater, so they're in a hurry."

"Oh, really?"

"I told them you'd be real concerned." She stamped her feet, trying to get some feeling back in them. "I wasn't sure about how to secure the sight, but Ferg and I thought we could zip-tie the tarp to the top of the truck and then tie it off to another vehicle. It's probably going to flap like a Windjammer cruise, but . . ."

"Yep." I looked around me, trying to absorb it all because in another hour it might look like Stalingrad. There were trailing wisps of snow dunes arching away from the higher points of Jacob's body already. "Tire tracks?"

She kneeled down beside me. "Only those guys, pulling in once, circling back out, and then pulling in again."

"How did they call?"

"Cell phone."

"Why did they pull out?"

"Bad reception."

"You look at the boot prints?"

"Yeah, Vasques. So's the dearly departed and one of the execs."

"Popular boot."

"Popular size."

We both shrugged and looked at Jacob. "No sheep?"

She pursed her lips and shook her head. "No sheep. Preliminary triangulation indicates an area across the lake, maybe even over where those really shitty-looking cabins are."

I turned in the opposite direction from the truck and peered through the darkness and the snow. The headlights of Vic's unit weren't helping. We stood up to escape them and strained our eyes into the darkness. "Where would you shoot from?"

"Top of that ridge, along the tree line."

I turned to look at her. "Any local activity?"

"They say they heard somebody shouting over on the other side about the time they pulled in, around nine."

"What're they doing pulling in here at nine o'clock at night?"

"Supposed to borrow a cabin from Dave McClure; drove up from Casper after work. Now they're not sure if they have the right day."

"It's Tuesday."

She nodded. "That fact's been established and corroborated. Ferg is checking with Dave about their plans."

I thought about the next move. "Get the tarp tied down as soon as Ferg gets off the radio."

She stomped her feet again. "DCI in Wheatland by now?"

"Weather permitting."

She was looking at the side of my face as I looked at Jacob. "We're not going to be able to keep them out." I continued to look at Jacob. "Walt?"

"Get Ferg to help you get the tarp done. Then tell him to get that metal detector he has at home and check that hillside over there when he gets back . . ."

"Gets back?"

"Then get in your truck, put on your winter gear, and warm up." She stopped stomping, looked at me for a while longer, and then went off to check on Ferg.

She was right. We had gone from a sleepy little death by misadventure to a multiple homicide, and the Division of Criminal Investigation was going to want their pound of postmortem flesh. The nagging voice of reason kept reminding me that their experience and technical capabilities gave them a much better chance of breaking the case, but then a stronger voice came in and stated flatly that this was my case and my county. Along the way, it had gotten personal. The first thing I had to do was get the two remaining boys out of county, out of state, out of the country if I had to. Lucian would say there was a fox in the henhouse, and I would say it was time to get the chickens on down the road. I turned back to Jacob. He hadn't changed much. Dead men don't tell tales, but I always expect them to pop up and tell me it had all been a big joke. In thirty years of law enforcement, I had been deeply disappointed.

The interior light of Jacob's truck was on, but very dimly. The door was ajar, key chain hanging from the ignition. I looked under the truck at the exhaust where a few drips of condensate were frozen at the bottom of the tailpipe. There was a shallower impression in the snow where the exhaust would have blown out and a large slick of ice under the engine. I glanced down the fender for insignia and, sure enough, it said diesel. Jacob had started his truck to let it warm up, and whatever had happened had happened when he was exiting or reentering the vehicle. With the orientation of the body, I would think that he was getting out. I'm pretty sure he had been sitting here, like this, and the truck had run out of fuel.

There were no fishing rods lying about, and he wasn't wearing a vest, waders, or any of the other accoutrement that fisherman usually wore. I stood up and walked around the truck to get a look inside. The passenger-side door was locked; hardly anybody ever does that in Wyoming. There was frost on the inside of the windows, but I could still make out a couple of aluminum fly-rod cases lying along the seat, two vests, and a small cooler. The cooler was a battered old thing with a bumper sticker on it that read CHARLTON HESTON IS MY PRESIDENT.

Working with the preliminary observations, without checking for discoloration of the right and left sides of the abdomen, the victim had been dead approximately, and I was guessing, fourteen to sixteen hours, which placed the TOD at the earliest at five o'clock this morning. If there were trout in the cooler, I could reasonably assume that Jacob had been fishing early. Before dawn? I looked around the rest of the truck for a tent, sleeping bag, or any other evidence that he might have spent more than one day. There were the cabins, but we were going to have to do a sweep of them anyway.

I walked back around the truck and looked at the spot where the gore of his heart and part of a lung had sprayed against the edge of the bed. That meant there was lead in the hillside adjacent to the gravel lot, or in the truck, or in Jacob. Maybe. Something moved under the truck, and I lowered my perspective to see what it was. Jacob's black cowboy hat had blown under the transfer case and had lodged against one of the front wheels. There was a small collection of feathers stuck in the side of the headband. I looked back at the boy's dull eyes, shining my flashlight along his body, and got to wondering. I stood, leaning over the body, and extended the flashlight to the open section of his jacket and pushed it back, just enough to reveal the pristine tip of a bleached, straightened, Minwaxed turkey feather.

"What the hell is going on over here!"

I'm pretty sure I stood up and turned around faster than I ever had before. He was a little older than me, well below medium height but nowhere near medium build. He had a face like an old prizefighter, bulbed and knobby wherever it protruded. It was like life was bound to come out even if circumstance was bound to pound it in, and circumstance was standing over him at the moment. Circumstance also noted the broken blood vessels and the flaccidness of the rest of his face; this was not an amateur drinker but a full-blown alcoholic. As my eyes traveled down the open, olive drab parka, past the polyester fur around the hood and the red-and-white–striped tank shirt to the bulging stomach, I noticed the floral print swimming trunks and the thin, birdlike legs that extended into a pair of unlaced arctic boots. I also noticed the drink in his hand, in a martini glass, complete with a sour apple slice and a little green paper parasol. "Who are you?"

He wasn't paying any attention to me but had leaned to one side to get a better look at the crime scene. "Holy shit!"

I moved over a little, blocking his view. "Excuse me?"

He looked back at me and actually saluted. "Sorry, General. What's up?" I sighed and repeated the question. "Al Monroe, I got one of them cabins over by the lake." He listed farther to the side. "Jesus, he's deader than hell."

"Mr. Monroe, have you been up here long?"

"Last three days, had a hell of a drunk goin' till I saw all these damn lights over here; thought somebody'd died." He took a sip of his martini and looked at me thoughtfully. "Looks like somebody fuckin' did."

As I stared at the spectacle of Al Monroe, a thought occurred to me. "Al, can you make coffee over at your cabin?"

"Oh, hell yeah. Best coffee on the mountain."

"Would you mind going over and making us a big pot? It looks like we're going to be here for a while."

"You damn well bet!" He saluted again and traipsed off toward the lake.

"Al"—he turned as Vic came up beside me—"which one of the cabins is yours?" He pointed in the vague direction of one of the dilapidated shacks across the water. He saluted again before he climbed onto an enormous mule with only a rope lead and disappeared into the darkness without spilling a drop of his martini.

Vic looked after the departing vision. "Who the fuck was that?"

I looked sidelong at her. "You two are going to get along."

The two execs in the Hummer calmed down when I explained that they wouldn't have to worry about a place to stay and that the Sheriff of Absaroka County always had a few extra beds he could share with the primary witnesses to a homicide. I told them that I would be happy to put them up for three to six weeks, meals included. They said no thanks. Maybe they'd heard about the potpies on weekends but, either way, they got a lot more cooperative and that was all I was really after.

They had arrived from Casper after dark and had seen the truck when they drove by the first time. They were supposed to meet Dave McClure but weren't sure which cabin was his; they had seen the truck and circled around to ask directions. By the time they had, the truck had stopped running. They pulled into the parking lot, and one of them got out to check on the guy who looked like he was resting on the ground. They hadn't touched anything and said the only reason they had driven halfway back to Muddy Guard Ranger Station was so that they could get reasonable reception on their cell phone. 911 had routed them through to us, Vic had responded, and here we were standing in the wind and snow.

I asked them about the yelling, and they said that someone had hollered at them from across the lake when they first pulled up to the scene. From the direction and colorful and varied usage of language, it could only have been the now infamous Al Monroe. He had wanted to know if he could interest them in a sour apple martini or twelve.

Ferg had gotten through to a sleepy Dave McClure, who not only backed up the men's story but also told us the location of his place and about the key that was hidden on the top shelf of his grill. I released them to go warm up in Dave's cabin and joined Vic and Ferg as they set up work lights and began taking photographs of the scene. Vic lowered the camera and set her shoulders. "Is that what I think it is, sticking out of the deceased's jacket?"

"Yep." I folded my arms and started in. "Ferg?" He joined me after adjusting the work lights, and the warmth of the halogen felt good along my shoulders. "You're going to have to make the run." He said he didn't mind. Ferg was my mule, and I wouldn't trade him for all the thoroughbreds in the world. "Get Ruby to throw us together some supplies, sandwiches, and coffee. Tell her to arrange with Lucian to pull an early watch on dispatch and to bring Turk up from Powder."

"Lucian?"

I nodded. "Yes, Lucian. Also, bring Bryan Keller and George Esper in under protective custody."

"To the jail?"

Vic half snarled, "No, the fucking Motel 6."

We were all under a lot of pressure and, having maximized our manpower to burgeoning, I ushered Ferg to his truck. "Call the Espers and then go by there if you have to. If they're still not there, Reggie Esper's sister lives in Longmont, Colorado. Call the Longmont city police and tell them that we're looking for whatever it is that the Espers have registered with the DMV other than this maroon diesel."

"Then what?"

"Get back up here." I watched as he jumped in his little navy Toyota. I knocked on the window. "Ferg?" He rolled it down and leaned out. "Do you have one of those little digital Breathalyzers?" He handed it to me with a questioning look. "Don't forget that metal detector. And, thanks." I stuffed the device in my pocket and walked back to where Vic was still taking photographs. "When you get through, get in your truck and warm up some more. It's going to be a long night. I'm going to walk over and get a statement from Al Monroe."

She nodded, lining up for the next shot. "Good luck."

It turned out to be a half mile around the east bank of the lake. No wonder Al had ridden his mule. Al's cabin was homemade; it didn't have the singularity of purpose of those that had started out as campers. The original structure was a sixteen-by-sixteen shack, complete with T-111 siding and a multicolored tin roof. The rest of the cabin was made of lean-tos, which leaned to with such ambition that the outer perimeter of the cabin lay on the ground. I wasn't sure what Al did for a living, but it was a safe bet it wasn't carpentry. The mule was in one of the upright lean-tos directly beside the cabin, and I had to take care not to step into her leavings. There were a good three cords of wood stacked alongside the door. The harsh glow of propane lighting illuminated the windows and the two-inch crack under the door on which I had just knocked. After a moment, I knocked again.

"Hold yer goddamned horses!" I listened to more stumbling, crashing, and profanity. He yanked open the door and waves of heat rolled from the interior of the cabin, along with the smell. "C'mon in, General. Coffee's ready."

The interior of Al's cabin was far worse than the outside, kind of like Fibber McGee's closet gone bad. There was a dilapidated sofa of indiscriminate color and shape along the wall, a La-Z-Boy of approximately the same vintage, and a gray Formica kitchen table surrounded by three folding chairs—two brown, one off-brown. At the center of the room was one of those homemade stoves that you put together with two 55-gallon drums; the underside of the bottom drum glowed orange, and I was sure it was close to a hundred and ten degrees in there. There was a halfhearted attempt at a Tiki theme, with native paintings of naked women and carved wooden sculptures as decoration. The most amazing stacks of magazines and catalogs towered against the walls; *National Geographic* and *American Rifleman* made up the visible majority. It was like being in the dead letter office on Fiji.

I followed him in and reluctantly closed the door behind me as he threaded his way back to the kitchen area. He wasn't wearing a shirt, and his entire upper body was covered in tattoos. When he returned with a steaming cup of coffee, I expected to see an albatross hanging from his neck. He seated himself on the La-Z-Boy and gestured for me to sit on the sofa. I pushed back my hat and looked at him. "Merchant marine?"

He scooped up his martini from a convenient stack. "Goddamned Eleventh Engineers, you?"

"First Division."

"I'll be damned." He leaned forward and extended his hand, and we shook like old friends. "Semper Fi. I bet you seen some shit."

"Al, I need you to do something for me."

He did his best to look serious. "Name it."

I pulled the digital Breathalyzer out of my jacket pocket and handed it to him as I took off my coat and laid it beside me. "Need you to blow into this."

His eyes looked at the device and then back at me; then he shrugged. "No law against driving a mule drunk."

"Only way you'd catch me on one."

He blew into the device and handed it back to me. "How'd I do, General?"

I tapped the Breathalyzer, but it remained at 4.2. "Rapidly approaching alcoholic coma." He toasted with his martini glass and added to the percentage of complex sugars already racing through his bloodstream. "Al, how come I don't know you?"

He shrugged again; it seemed to be his favorite form of communication. "I don't know. Hell, how come I don't know you?"

I looked down at my civilian clothes, my sheepskin coat, and the brim of my unadorned silver-belly hat. "Al, I'm the sheriff of Absaroka County."

"Really?" He processed the information for a moment. "Where's that?"

"You're in it."

He looked around as if there might be a sign. "I thought we were in Big Horn County."

I studied him for a moment. "You a bartender, Al?"

"Thirty-two fuckin' years."

"How'd you get here?"

"Buddy'n me partnered up and bought it off some asshole in Kemmerer."

"That where you live the rest of the year?"

"Lander." He took another sip of his martini, and I took the first sip of my coffee; it wasn't bad, and it was hot. "I need to ask you some questions." I tried not to concentrate on the fact that my primary witness had been drunk for the last three days. "Hear any loud noises early this morning?"

"Like that goddamned howitzer that went off just before dawn?"

Our eyes met. "Hear that, did you?"

"Well, hell, it's hunting season, so it's been soundin' like a small arms war ever since I got here. Had to tie ribbons all over Sally, so the simple-minded bastards wouldn't shoot her." He paused for a second, remembering. "But this was different, closer; and it was early, real early."

"I don't suppose you noticed what time it was?"

He sniffed. "Oh-five-twelve."

My eyes widened after making the translation. "You're sure of that?"

"Oh, hell yeah." He gestured to the large windup alarm clock that sat on the table. "Looked at my clock."

"Then what?"

He gestured. "Went over here to the door and shouted for 'em to knock that shit off."

"Why did you go to this door?"

"S'where the shot came from."

"East or west?"

He shook his head. "Directly up the hill." I nodded as he sipped his martini. "That what killed that boy?"

"Maybe." I leaned forward and rested the coffee cup on my knee; it was still very hot. "When you went over to the door, did you open it and look out?"

"Yeah."

"Did you see anything?"

"Saw somebody walkin' back up through the tree line with their back to me." My expression was probably easy to misinterpret. "This any help?"

"I never had it so good. What'd they look like?"

"Pretty big, near as I could tell. It was early, and there wasn't much light."

"Any distinguishing features? Hair?"

He shook his head no. "Wait." I could feel my heart beating. "It was long."

I'm pretty sure I skipped a beat. "Long hair . . ."

"Yeah, now that I think about it. Yeah."

"You're sure about that?"

"Yeah, long hair."

"How long?"

"To the shoulders, at least."

"Color?"

"Dark?" But then he shook his head. "Not enough light to tell, but dark, I think."

"Hat?"

"Nope."

"Could you tell what kind of clothing?"

He nodded slowly. "Overalls, one of those insulated jobs." He waited for a minute. "You okay?"

It took me a moment to think of a word and get some moisture in my mouth. "Yep. This individual was carrying a weapon?"

"Yeah, a big one."

"Type?"

"Couldn't tell you. I mean, I could see 'im carryin' something, and from the way he carried it . . ."

"Both hands?"

"Nope, one. Hanging down to the side."

"Why do you say big?"

He sat his martini glass down and spread his hands apart by more than four feet. "Long."

"Anything else? Wooden stock?" He shook his head and shrugged. "Anything hanging off the rifle?"

He continued to shake his head. "Sorry."

"Anything else? Anything at all?" He stared at the arm of his chair and shook his head. "You want to revise or amplify anything in these statements?"

He looked confused. "Wha'? I'm under arrest or somethin'?"

I shook my head and smiled. "No, you just made a very important statement in a homicide investigation. I want to make sure there isn't anything you might have left out."

He looked around for the invisible signs that were supposed to tell him where he was, what he was doing, and when he should do it. I was starting to understand Al's relationship with the clock. "Something might come to me?"

"That's fine. When did you notice the truck over there that was running?"

"Didn't."

"You didn't. All day?"

"Nope, went back over to the sofa there and went back to sleep." He stopped and then looked around at the painted concrete floor for the thought he had lost. "Did notice it around lunchtime. Got up and heated some stew." He started to get up now. "You want some?"

I stopped him with a hand. "Maybe later. What time was that?"

"Twelve hundred forty-seven."

I glanced over at the kitchen table at the two-handed face that told me it was now one. "You look at the clock a lot, Al."

"Thirty-two fuckin' years of waitin' for closin' time."

He confirmed the fact that he had yelled at the two guys in the Hummer at exactly twenty-one hundred twelve. As I went off to check the ridge, I asked Al if he would hitch up the one-mule team and take my ardent deputy a cup of coffee and some stew. He said he would be fucking happy to.

The hill was steep, and the fact that I was wearing cowboy boots didn't help. The snow had tapered off, but the wind remained persistent, and by the time I got to the top I had worked up a decent sweat. I stood there, catching my breath and looking down at the lights of Al's cabin and at the red-and-blue emergency lights revolving from our vehicles in the parking lot. The only consistent sounds were the wind, Sally munching, and the revolving click of our lights. It was a beautiful place, peaceful, terminally peaceful for Jacob Esper.

It was a four-hundred-yard shot if it was an inch. It was colder this morning, probably with a slight to negligible headwind and an approximate scale of elevation would be eighty at four hundred yards.

I sighed a full breath and watched the steam blow back in my face. It was quite a shot, even with a scope.

I started at the first few trees at the ridge's edge, shining my flashlight down along the partially covered ground. Al had said that the shooter was big, but Al is short, so I was beginning to wonder how big *big* meant. There were no telltale signs in the stiffening grass, so I began using this trail as my pathway as I searched the surrounding area on both sides. If I were shooting someone, would I use the trail? Probably not. I kneeled by the end of the opening that faced the lake and went over each blade of grass. If I were shooting someone from four hundred yards, would I lie down? Probably. There was something funny about the slight depression in the grass to my right, so I walked out of my safe area and looked back where the grass seemed to lay in an odd pattern. I kneeled down and looked back into the hypotenuse of a thin triangle: All the blades bowed in my direction.

Blowdown. This is where it had all started, all .45 caliber seventy grains of it. There was a weak swipe where someone had scuffed a foot across the area in an attempt to hide the marks, but Al Monroe's appearance must have curtailed such activity. I extended my view and looked straight back through the trees. I suppose somebody my size could make it through, but their ability to limbo would have to be considerably better than mine. I went back to my path and began working my way deeper into the woods, searching the narrow area for footprints but finding none. If they were big, they were light on their feet. I transferred my search to above ground, looking for any disturbance in the thick foliage of the pines. Nothing.

I thought about Henry and took my first full breath since Al had made his partial identification. I stood there with my hands in my pockets and tried to convince myself that a man with 4.2 blood alcohol content would be lucky if he could properly identify his own mule. It wouldn't wash; he had been too precise about all the other points. Al might be a professional alcoholic, but he was an observant one.

Why would Henry do it? There was the immediate connection with the family; the oldest of motivations, revenge. If somebody had done this to my niece, how would I react? I kept thinking about Omar's remarks about Henry; was it productive to look at those who had killed when looking for a killer? It wasn't easy to do, take a life. Henry had killed men, but so had I. Try as I might, I couldn't develop Omar's line of thought and went back to the one I liked best, the rationalization of why it didn't have to be Henry.

With Al's partial physical description, we were looking for a largish person, probably male and possibly Indian. Sticking with motivation, it had to be someone connected to the victims' victim, Melissa Little Bird. And that meant Artie Small Song or Henry Standing Bear. I was going to have to have a conversation with Artie Small Song.

Did long hair necessarily mean Indian? Omar had long hair and half my staff had longish hair. Vic and Turk both had hair at least to their shoulders. Vic had been growing hers for the last two years, and Turk's hockey hair was perennial. I always tried to keep an open mind when lining up the suspects. Law enforcement personnel were people, too, which meant they could commit murder just like the rest of us. If I was going to play the game, everybody got a piece.

Why would Vic do it? She was a pretty militant female, a master in ballistics, and she was also the first on both crime scenes. I had talked her into joining up about two years ago, when these boys had been handed down their suspended sentences. I looked down at the revolving lights, at the flickering shadows cast on the sides of the vehicles, and at Jacob's shadow-smear that didn't move. Her sense of justice just didn't seem to fit. She didn't have any reason to do it, and she wasn't big, even if she had the hair.

Why would Turk do it? Just being a prick wasn't enough, and the fact that I was looking forward to our next meeting like Grant did Gettysburg shouldn't interfere with my abilities to investigate. Did he want my job bad enough to try and make me look this bad? None of it seemed likely, but he was big, his name was on Dave's list, and he had the hair.

Why would Omar do it? Omar could make this shot, but what

could his motivations be? I started thinking about which grade B actor would play Omar in the television movie of the week and quickly dropped it. But he was big enough, had the hair, had a Sharps, and knew how to shoot.

Why would Artie Small Song do it? And why wouldn't he have used a rocket launcher or a bazooka? This spoke to the violent-death side of the case, and his family connections loomed large. Basic investigative technique was jumping up and down and screaming it was Artie. He was large, might have the weapon, and he had the hair.

Why would Henry do it? I didn't believe he did, and that was all there was to it. But . . . he had been late running yesterday morning; he hadn't gotten to my house until after eight. I thought back and tried to think of what time it had been when he arrived, but I didn't have Al's gift for chronographic pinpointing. If the Cheyenne Death Rifle was the one he used, how did he get it back to Lonnie in time? Two men could keep a secret if one of them is dead, or so the old saying goes, but I didn't think it was possible to get from here to the Rez and back to my place in three hours.

I took one last look around, satisfied that I had done as much as I could, and started down the hill. By the time I got to the path, Al was making the return journey to his cabin. "Al, how long are you going to be here?" He truly was a vision atop his mule with his floral print trunks in full display.

"I was thinkin' about getting the hell outta here tomorrow, but with all this stuff happenin' I might just stick around."

"Well, if you do decide to head back, would you mind checking in at my office? It's down in Durant, behind the courthouse, or you can just give me a call." I handed him a card. "This's got my home phone on it, along with all the office numbers. If you think of anything else, anything at all, be sure to call me. There'll probably be somebody over later to ask you the same questions and get your personal information. Do you want me to tell them to wait till the morning?"

"What time is it?"

I started to laugh, then pulled out my pocket watch. "Oh-two-hundred."

"Aw, hell, it's the shank of the evenin'. Send 'em on over."

I got out of the mule's way and started the long slog around the lake. When I got to the scene, Vic was warming up in her unit. I walked over and kneeled beside Jacob Esper. Something was bothering me, something had been niggling at me for the last few hours. I looked at the body and back over my shoulder. It was a clear shot and had planted the young man squarely against the side of the truck. How did the perpetrator get the feather onto the body? Granted, there seemed to have been long periods of Al's drunkenness where somebody could've planted an entire aviary on Jacob, but it did add to the time that it would've taken Henry to complete the journey to my place. It was another reason my buddy couldn't have done it, and I was feeling a little better. Even if I was feeling better, the niggling thought remained like an itch at the middle of my back. There was something here, something I'd seen that was out of my reach. I stared at Jacob Esper, just like I'd stared at Cody Pritchard, and I hoped like hell that I came up with better answers.

"Unlock the door." She reached across with a yawn and flipped the small knob up. I must have woken her. It was like a nest, with little pieces of paper and equipment scattered and stuffed into every available spot. I pulled a collection of duty notebooks from under my ass, sat them on the floor beside my wet boots, and thought how much her truck reminded me of Al's oasis across the lake. Two Thermoses rested against the four-wheel-drive shifter; evidently she hadn't saved me any coffee. I got settled and looked over at my deputy, whose face was resting against her door. She appeared to have fallen back to sleep.

Vic didn't look like a killer. Her fine Italian skin contrasted with the dark luster of her hair and, even in sleep, an eyebrow was arched in disbelief. At this angle, you could just make out the little upturned point at the end of her nose that always made me want to pick her up and squeeze her. I hadn't ever done it, figuring she'd likely kick me in crucial areas. Not for the first time did I notice my deputy was a very good-looking woman. "So, you get to home plate or what?"

Just as I'd suspected, everything else could stop moving, but not the mouth. "Sorry?"

"Oh, you're one of those kiss-but-don't-tell guys. Fine, I'll just go back to sleep." I looked at the clouds of vapor on the window beside where she had spoken.

"Home plate?"

"Yeah, I was trying to cater to your delicate sensibilities. Did you fuck her?"

"I don't think this was the conversation I had in mind when I climbed in here."

"Too bad . . . put out or get out." She repositioned herself and smiled, satisfied with her wit.

"The truth would be pretty boring."

"I was afraid of that." I watched as the condensation on the side window grew and subsided with her breath. "I suspect that nobody's having sex in this county."

I waited a moment for her to continue, but she didn't. "That the problem with you and Glen?"

"What, the fact that we haven't had sex for three months? What would make you think that?" She still hadn't moved, and I was considering getting out and going for a walk. "Do you find me unattractive?"

"You?" That got an eye. It wouldn't hurt anything to level with her, and she was being vulnerable, which only happened on leap years. "I was just sitting here, a moment ago, thinking what a handsome woman you are."

"Handsome?"

I caught my breath. "Wrong word choice?"

"Sounds masculine." The eye again. "You think I'm too butch?"

"No, I don't, and I really was thinking what a good-looking woman you are."

The eye closed, but the smile returned. "Good."

"Then you opened your mouth . . ."

She tried to kick me but only glanced off the accelerator and gunned the motor. She glared at the dash. "Shut up." Her eyes shifted to me. "How often did you have sex when you were married?"

"In the beginning or the end?"

"Forget I asked that question." She settled back against the door and fluffed the rolled-up blanket she was using as a pillow. "How come you have never made a play for me?"

I couldn't help but laugh; life in general was just so much more interesting with women around. "I um . . . considered it a dereliction of the sheriff-deputy relationship."

"No, dereliction would be what Glen is doing to me."

"Well, that's another issue. You're married, and I'm not into hypotheticals at three in the morning."

"In six weeks it's not going to be a hypothetical." I sat there, letting that one settle in. "He got some bullshit job up in Alaska, and I'm not going. I did this drill once, and I'm not doing it again." She lay there, not moving. "You still going to want me around as a deputy if I'm single?"

"I'm not sure the county can take it." I reached over and squeezed her shoulder. "Hey, you don't know you're my heir-apparent?"

She snuggled a little more, and the smile broadened. "Yeah, I just like to hear you say it." The smile held, but her eyes remained shut. "So, you wanna fuck, or do I owe you an apology?"

I laughed what seemed like the first good laugh I'd had in a very long time and leaned against my own door, covered my face with my hat, and quickly fell into a deep and dreamless sleep.

Ferg showed back up at six-thirty with his metal detector. He liked gadgets, which was good, because I didn't. The wind had died down some, and what snow had fallen last night was piled up against the east side of everything, trailing away in long tails of white with edges as crisp as the blade on a knife. It was still relatively cold, but the promise of warmth had started and, if you weren't careful, you always found your face directed east.

As Ferg unloaded the equipment and supplies, I took the opportunity to get out of my dating clothes and put on the winter gear I always kept behind the seat of my truck. Mine were the same as Al had described as having been on the shooter last night: arctic weight coveralls and a hooded jacket that matched. The medium brown had faded to a light khaki and the seams were starting to look a little threadbare, but the little star was still holding fast, and it had my name on it. Everybody else in the department had these clothes, too; theirs just looked better. I was sitting on the tailgate of my unit, changing into my Sorels, when he came over with the metal detector. "Espers?"

He had the metal detector taken apart and was checking the charger pack on the thing. "I called DMV and got the registration numbers and descriptions of all their vehicles and put out an APB with the Longmont police, letting them know this was somethin' to do with a homicide case."

"That get their attention?"

"Oh, yeah."

I propped a boot against the side of the truck and started lacing; my foot felt immediately warmer. I should have done this last night, but I suppose I had been caught up in the moment. I dropped my foot off the tailgate and turned to face him. "Nothing at the house?"

"No."

"The 3K?"

"I got Bryan and brought him in." His face looked like he didn't want to talk about it.

"Rest of the family?"

"Mrs. Keller was there, but not Jim."

"I bet that was a warm welcome." I searched for my gloves in the pockets of my jacket and pulled the stiff leather onto my fingers, flexing them. "Where is he at four o'clock in the morning?"

"Hunting."

Jim Keller hunting, that was interesting. "Where?"

"She didn't say."

I let it go. "You bring supplies?"

"In the cooler. I also made arrangements with South Pass Lodge to bring in warm food."

"What about Turk?"

"Didn't talk to him, but I left a message."

"And where is he at five o'clock in the morning?"

"Some buckle bunny's bed, I suppose." He closed the little plastic door, turned the device over, and flipped a switch. The little LED display lit up.

I smiled, which was hard when it came to Turk. "Jealous?"

His eyes came up and met mine. "Yeah, a little."

"Me, too." I slid off the back of the Bullet and stood, stretching the stiff muscles that had bunched at my shoulders and neck. It felt good, and my feet were warm for the first time in twelve hours. I indicated the metal detector. "That thing going to work, or am I going to be forced to make a highly dramatic and emotional display by throwing it in the lake?"

"I think it'll work."

Vic joined us as I peered over the edge of Jacob's truck bed and turned to look at the snow-covered hillside behind us. "Well, it's not in the truck and from the looks of Jacob, I'd say it's not in him." I extended a finger in the direction a straight trajectory would have taken. "Detect."

I wandered over toward the lake to get out of the way and didn't see any lights on in Al's cabin; I figured he was still asleep. I was wrong. After a moment, I could hear the door open, and the familiar figure stepped around one of the lean-tos and hollered across the lake, "Hey, you want any goddamned coffee?!"

I laughed. "Love some!" The echo of my response sounded around the little bowl of the lake, and my voice sounded good, like I was capable. The niggling thought hadn't gone away though, and a little less than four hours of sleep hadn't been enough to make it surface. I comforted myself with the thought that I was doing what it took to solve cases like these: knocking on one more door, looking at the crime scene photographs one more time, making one more phone call, making one last try. I went back over to Jacob's body and ducked under the tarp for another look-see. Obviously, something had been bothering Vic, too. A small Tupperware stepstool was there, so I pulled it over and sat down facing Jacob again. I sat on the top, pulled a foot up on the first step, and rested my elbow on my knee, placing my chin in the palm of my hand. I was finally comfortable, which was more than could be said for Jacob. Here we were, Jacob and I, staring at each other, only one of us seeing. Something wasn't right, and I'd be damned if I could figure out what it was.

I listened as Vic and Ferg conferred on the other side of the truck. "I think we've got something."

He didn't sound sure. "In the trajectory of the reference points?"

"We're getting a strong reading off to the right."

"Dig there."

A moment passed. "Don't you want to wait for DCI?"

"They might be in a motel in Casper, for all we know." I sounded angrier than I was, taking the frustration of the unknown out on my deputies. I made a conscious effort to be nicer. "We'll go ahead and dig it out."

Jim Keller hunting, why was that bothering me? Because, as near as I could remember, he didn't hunt. I started thinking back to that day he had brought in Bryan, how he seemed so hard on the boy. I remembered thinking what a mess this was for the young man and how it was strange that they hadn't just moved away. As far as I knew, they had no family here in the county, with no reason to stay other than to torture that boy. It was a pretty horrible thing to do to your child, and a pretty horrible thing to do to Cody and Jacob. Somebody ruins your life, your child's life, and his future . . . These were pretty powerful motives.

"I think we've got something here." Her voice was flat and emotionless.

I looked at Jacob for another moment, then got up and walked around the truck. Ferg stood to the far side, leaning against the truck bed and balancing the metal detector on his foot. I took up a position just in front of the passenger window and watched Vic work. I looked over at Ferg. "We get about four or five of those DCI guys to stand around here with us, and we'll have a real state job underway." He smiled, and my eyes fell back across the seat of Jacob's truck. I looked at the jumbled mess; was I the only one that actually put things away in my vehicle? I looked past Ferg at his little Toyota and the number of PVC containers he had strapped to the underside of his topper. "Ferg, how many rods do you take with you when you're fishing?"

He thought for a moment. "Seven, maybe eight."

"How many vests?"

"Just one."

I looked into Jacob's truck at the two vests that lay there, and that niggling feeling stopped.

10

"You blow one homicide, it looks like a mistake. You blow two, it starts looking like negligence. Or worse yet, stupidity." T.J. hadn't brought any investigators with her from Cheyenne, she knew me that well, but she had brought everything else in their mobile crime unit, including the kitchen sink, which was to my right.

"I thought I'd use that on the bumper stickers in the next election, VOTE LONGMIRE, HE'S STUPID."

"Well, don't worry about it. You blow this case, and you won't have to bother about the next election; they'll just run you out of town on a rail."

I took a sip of her coffee and tried not to make a face. "No hard feelings?"

"Hey." She smiled with the little wrinkle at the corner of her mouth. "It's your county."

Vic's rolls of film and DCI's digital camera sat on a table in the trailer next to the ballistic sample that Ferg had dug out of the hillside. It had flattened on impact to a mushroom-shaped disc about the size of the palm of my hand. I have a big hand. The feather was also there. I reached over and took the plastic-wrapped package from the table. "You mind?" She shook her head no, and I stuffed the piece of evidence in my jacket.

"You might get a phone call, later in the week."

"I get lots of phone calls. I'm popular."

The sun had overtaken a large breech in the storm, with blue skies and the odd snowflake that filtered down from high altitude. Digi-Sven, the computerized voice of NOAA, was warning that a real storm was on the way and would probably be here this evening. High wind and heavy snow. I was glad T. J. Sherwin had brought DCI's mobile unit. I was going to go back down, but at least Vic would be comfortable here.

"So, what's the story on George Esper?" she asked.

"There were two sets of fishing gear in Jacob's truck."

"Any possibility that he just hauls all that stuff around with him?"

"It's possible, but fly fishermen are pretty careful about their vests, with the flies and all. I just don't know if George would leave his vest in his brother's truck."

"Possibility they were together?"

"Contents of the cooler: two cleaned fish, one partially eaten cheese sandwich, and two empty cans of Busch Lite."

"Not enough for two."

"Not enough beer and probably not enough food. Besides, the passenger door was locked. It's my experience that people in this county only lock their doors when they visit Cheyenne." This got a sidelong glance. "Nobody was riding on the passenger side."

"What's your theory then?"

"I think that Jacob and George Esper were supposed to meet somewhere. That Jacob came up and spent the night, started his truck yesterday morning to go and meet his brother, and instead incurred a consummation devoutly to be wished."

"*Romeo and Juliet?*"

"*Hamlet.* All the death ones are *Hamlet*, at least the contemplative death ones." I unbuttoned my jacket a little; the propane heater in the camper continued to raise the temperature. "I suppose George could be with his parents, but we won't know anything about that till we hear something from them. We've got an APB out on their vehicle in both Colorado and Wyoming. I'd call Trinidad and Tobago if I thought it would do any good." We sat there, surrounded by all our technological wonders, hoping that some patrolman in Longmont would happen to drive by the right driveway. No matter how far you went into the modern age, it always seemed to come down to the guy on the beat. "I've also got the Forest Rangers, Smokey the Bear, and all God's little animals out looking for a black Mazda Navajo with the plates, Tuff 1."

She was watching me like a science experiment. "You look tired."

I sighed. "Yep, well . . . it's truly all my worst nightmares come to life." We sat there for a moment; "I'm 0 for 2." I looked at her for a while and then got up, trying not to tread on her feet, and sidestepped to the door. "You don't need me; Vic can be the primary again. You got ballistics stuff here in the Mystery Machine?"

"Yes."

"I've got a rifle out in my truck that needs to be tested; I'll leave it with Vic."

"Where did this one come from?"

I paused, with my hand on the door handle. "You wouldn't believe me if I told you."

"Walt?"

I waited. "Yep?"

"You're not being punished for your sins."

The air outside felt good, and I started getting just a breath of my second wind. I could smell the lodgepole pines above everything else, a sharp smell that really doesn't translate to air fresheners and cleaning products. It was also the altitude; the air just seemed to pull in a little more freely above ten thousand feet. I took a quick scope around, using the steps as a lookout, and called Vic over. "I've got another rifle in my truck that needs to be tested, and they've got facilities in the trailer."

She caught up, and we walked along. "Where are you going?"

"I'm headed down. I'll get things set up at the office, then I'll be back." I opened the door and took the Cheyenne Death Rifle from the seat of my truck and handed it to her.

She held it, carefully studying the sheath, then tightened her lips and looked up at me. "Henry?"

"Lonnie, by way of Henry."

She slowly exhaled and then pulled the rifle out, holding it up in the morning light. "Fuck me running through the forest."

"We already discussed that."

She ignored me and continued. "I've got a really bad feeling about this."

"That seems to be the general response to this particular weapon."

"It's beautiful."

"It's haunted. There are supposed to be Old Cheyenne hanging around the thing looking for people to abduct and take back to the Camp of the Dead."

She studied it some more. "Cool."

She went off to my truck, and I walked over to the back of one of the DCI Suburbans, where Ferg and Al Monroe were having an animated conversation concerning the relative advantages of the Bitch Creek Nymph over the Number Sixteen Elk Hair Cadis. I always wondered about men who spent their time trying to anticipate and know a fish in a world where man's knowledge of each other could only be called scarce. It just seemed to be gratuitously ignorant for any man to think that he could think like a fish. Then there was the high deceit of the artificial fly; subtlety, guile, and sly deception created and instilled only to lure a cautious and tentative fish to its death. They were as bad as drug fiends, living in their shadowy world of aquatic intrigue.

I sometimes fly-fished, but it was catch and release, and I always brought a book. "Ferg, have you looked at the equipment he was carrying?"

"Yep." He looked at Al for confirmation, and they nodded somberly to each other. "Yellow and Royal Humpies, Parachute Adams, Light Cahills, and a couple of wet flies, mostly Montana Stones."

"Nothing like a Royal Humpie. Any ideas on where George might have gone?"

"Some." I waited. "Meadowlark, West Tensleep Creek, Medicine Lodge, Crazy Woman, head of the Clear, maybe even north fork of the Powder."

210

"Well, that should narrow it down to about 189,000 acres. How long do you think it'll take you?"

Dejectedly, he looked at the skies west of us. "A little while . . ."

I followed his gaze to the dark lines of clouds converging across the Big Horn basin and the Wind River Range. This was the one that was going to signify that autumn was over. If you lived here long enough, you could sense them coming. The few leaves left on the aspens quaked, and you could almost feel the barometric undertow as the storm gathered momentum. The clouds looked flat and mean, and they stretched into the distance; it made my eyes hurt. I was having enough trouble operating a homicide investigation without a raging blizzard at ten thousand feet. As he started to go, I leaned over to him. "You got a rifle in your truck?"

He stopped dead and looked at me. "What?"

I glanced over at Al as he suddenly found DCI's proceedings of great interest. "Do you have a rifle in your truck?"

"Um, no."

"Get Vic's .243. Just because we don't know where George Esper is, doesn't mean somebody else doesn't."

The drive down the mountain wasn't too bad; the only place where there was ice was on the flats, where the wind had continually applied a fresh coat of melting snow. Any other time, swooping over the gentle hills of the high meadow was a mind-freeing experience, but my mind snagged on the teepee signs for the campgrounds in the Bighorn National Forest. Henry was right, there had been no Indians on the jury.

On Wednesday, the jury had come in dressed up and, in the back hallways, we all thought that after eight days of deliberation we were close to a verdict. I still remember the look on all of our faces when the red light went on. The family members took their seats in the first three rows, quietly, like it was church, as if how little noise they made would have an affect on their loved ones' fate: the Espers, the Pritchards, and Mrs. Keller in the front row, Jim Keller never attending; Lonnie Little Bird in the aisle with his trusting smile, the chrome on his wheelchair seeming shiny and out of place. Then there were the defendants, three of them smirking and Bryan Keller looking sad.

"Please rise." Vern's voice was steady and carried the patrician quality that resonated that fervent prayer, that desperate plea for justice. Whose justice we were about to find out. Bryan closed his eyes, Jacob and George remained emotionless, and Cody glared. Cody Pritchard was found guilty of two counts of first-degree aggravated sexual assault; one count was for assaulting a mentally defective woman, and the other was for using force or coercion in that assault. He was also found guilty of conspiracy in the second degree. Jacob Esper, same verdict. George Esper was found guilty of one count of aggravated sexual assault in the second degree and was guilty of second-degree conspiracy. Bryan Keller was acquitted of the more serious charges but was found guilty of second-degree conspiracy.

After Vern was through reading the verdict, Cody leaned over to Jacob and whispered something; they both laughed. I felt like going over there. I made a mental note to keep a closer eye on them from then on and, if possible, to take a personal interest in their miseries. Sentencing was set for three weeks. All four were released with nominal bail and, after two years of freedom following their crime, they were set free again.

When I made the final sweep of the now closed courtroom, there was only one person left. "Quite a show. Mm, hmm, yes. It is so."

I stood there in my cotton-poly-blend uniform, looked past him at the cheap paneling on the walls, and felt the fraud of human institutions. His eyes wouldn't let me go, wouldn't let me usher him out and get it all over with, so I went and sat on the armrest of the chair in front of him. He smiled, looking through the thick lenses in his glasses, and patted my leg. "Long day?"

I smiled back. "Yep."

He looked around, his hand remaining on my leg. "Doesn't take long for everybody to get out of here, huh?"

"No."

"Mm. Not like on the television."

"Is there somebody here to help you, Lonnie?"

"Oh, yes. Arbutus has gone to get the car."

"Do you need help getting down?"

"Oh, no. I use the elevator." We sat there in silence, as the radiators ticked and groaned. His eyes drifted down to the gun that also rested on my leg. "Those boys?" I waited. "They went home?"

I cleared my throat. "Yep, Lonnie. They did."

His eyes remained on my gun. "You will go and get them?"

I paused. "They'll be right back here in three weeks to be sentenced. That's when Vern decides what will happen to them now that they are guilty."

His eyes came up, and he looked profound. "That judge, yes, he looks like Ronald Colman. Mm, hmm. It is so."

By the time I reached the office, I had worked myself into a righteous rage, and I wheeled into the parking lot, the Bullet sliding to a stop. My emotional state was not improved when I saw Turk's car sitting next to the door. He came out of the office as I got out of the truck, his thumbs hitched in his gun belt as he came down the steps. I noticed how big he was, how young. "Damn, you keep drivin' like that, and I'm gonna have to . . ."

He didn't see it coming, nobody would have. He was used to my irascible moods and just thought he had caught the sheriff at a bad time. He had. I brought my hand up in a full-reach swipe that caught the side of his head and propelled it face first into the quarter panel of the Thunder Chicken, as my right boot scooped his feet out from under him. The impact was thunderous on the hollow flank of the car, and the dent it left was substantial. He didn't get up but lay there beside the rear wheel, a small pool of blood spreading from the side of his downturned face.

I stepped over his legs and rolled him to one side, brushing away his hat and grabbing his shirtfront, pulling his face up close to mine. "If you ever harm a prisoner in my jail again . . ." But he wasn't listening, he was out. I held his head there for a moment and then gently laid it down on the concrete. I felt sick. It was from the adrenaline, or at least I blamed it on that. It always hit me afterwards. I would have to walk it off. I became aware of some movement behind me as I stood and stepped away and continued up the steps and into my office. Whoever it was that had walked up had evidently decided that whatever they had to do with me wasn't that important.

The door to the office was open when I got there. Ruby held the knob with her other hand over her heart, her eyes wider than I had ever seen them. "Oh, my Lord . . ."

I breezed past her into the reception area and almost collided with Lucian. He teetered back and nearly fell as I caught him and stood him upright. I figured a good offense was the best defense. "You got something to say?"

His face broke into a broad grin. "Damn, what a lick!"

I left him there and continued down the hallway, through the door, and into the jail's holding cells. I slammed the door back, stormed through the open cubicle, and sat myself on one of the bunks, my back thumping against the wall as I clutched my shaking hands together and set my jaw. I concentrated on my hands, willing them to stop; it took a while. My breathing was returning to normal, and the flushed feeling was starting to fade. I licked my lips and exhaled, trying to push the rest of the adrenaline through my flooded blood stream. I hated it, I hated seeing it, I hated hearing about it, and I hated doing it. I brought my head up to find a terrified Bryan Keller looking at me from the other bunk. I wasn't quite sure what to say. He was crouched in the corner with his legs pulled up and his arms wrapped around them; only his eyes were visible over the kneecaps.

We listened as the commotion from the reception area carried down the hallway and bounced off the masonry walls. I had no idea you could hear everything so well from the cells. The front door was closed, but there was a scooting of chairs and a murmuring of voices. You could hear Lucian's voice above the others, "Bring 'im on in here, Ladies Wear . . ." More murmuring and voices, "How you like them apples, you little son of a bitch? You try and get up, and I'll kick your ass so far . . ." It trailed off with the roaring in my ears. It was like being underwater and, for a few moments, I floated there, letting the sinking feeling in the middle of my shoulders wash over me. I was tired.

A while later, Henry peered around the divider. His hair hung down, and his face looked at me sideways.

I took off my hat and placed it on the bunk beside me, running my hands over my face. "What?" It would appear that not all the adrenaline was gone.

"Nothing."

I sat there for a moment. "He all right?"

He stepped around the divider and ducked his head to look through the bars. "He will never play the violin with his nose again, if that is what you mean."

"Better call the EMTs."

"He is already gone; Ruby has taken him to the hospital. It seemed to be the best thing, since his uncle would not stop kicking him."

I waited. "You think I overreacted?"

He shook his head in mock earnest. "Oh, no. It seemed like a perfectly reasonable response to someone parking in your spot." He wandered over to the doorway of the cell. "How about we have breakfast?" He glanced down at Bryan. "How about you?" To my relief, Bryan declined, and we slipped out the back way. "Interesting office management skills, kind of a 'violence is not the answer so I'm going to beat the shit out of you' philosophy."

I was looking at the sky; still nothing, but I could feel the coming storm. My eyes continued up the South Pass to the snow above the tree line; I was looking for George Esper.

"Kind of like Indian foreplay."

He had to be up there, somewhere.

"What do ten Indian women with black eyes have in common?"

The fishing flies were the key and, if Ferg could connect the very specific lures to very specific areas, we might have a chance.

"They just won't listen."

If George knew about the weather, would he come down? Would he go looking for his brother?

"How was your date last night?"

The more time went by without finding him, the more likely it was that he was dead. I would have to deputize one of Ferg's buddies and send him out to sit at the Esper place to see if anybody was going to show up.

"You did not let her touch the wine, did you?"

And what the hell was going on in Longmont? I could have driven down there and looked for them myself by now. At least Bryan was safe, but I needed to talk with his father. There was something there, maybe.

"By the way, I got word on Artie Small Song."

I stopped. "What?"

"I thought that might get your attention." He was smiling and shaking his head. "I got a call from his mother, and she thought that we might want to know that Artie has been in Yellowstone County Jail, up in Billings, since Saturday."

That narrowed the field. "Charge?"

"Carrying an unregistered concealed weapon without a permit."

I nodded to Dorothy when we threaded our way through the three or four locals sitting at the counter, and we took seats on the end stools toward the back. They had looked up, and I didn't smile. "So, what're you doing following me around?"

"I thought you would be interested in Artie, and I have information about the feather." He propped his elbows on the counter and leaned in. "Something has happened?"

"What makes you think that?"

"Your manner is curt and slightly agitated."

"Jacob Esper is dead." I watched him very carefully, but there was no visible response.

"That answers some of your questions."

"You don't seem very upset."

"I am not. Should I be?"

216

I looked at him for a moment. "No, I suppose not." Dorothy brought over some coffee and a couple of menus.

She was looking at my winter gear, and she smiled. "The game's afoot?"

I tossed the menu back to her. "The usual." She raised an eyebrow and looked at Henry.

"I will have what he is having."

The other eyebrow rose. "He doesn't know what he's having."

"I will have it anyway."

She looked at the both of us, shrugged, and headed back to the grill.

"Tell me about the feather."

He sat back up straight, took a sip of his coffee, and made me wait, finally turning back and looking me in the eye. "Wanda Real Wolf. She used to head up the Cheyenne Artist's Co-Op."

"The one that went out of business?"

"Yes. It is much easier to get Indians to work together than artists."

"They're her feathers?"

"Feathers, plural?" I set my jaw and nodded, and he looked at me for a while. "Interesting. You have it with you?" I took the feather from my jacket and handed it to him. He turned the plastic bag over in the light from the windows and studied the contents. "It too could be Wanda's."

"I don't suppose Wanda keeps detailed records of her feather sales?"

He sat it down between us and took another sip of his coffee. "Worse than that, she does not sell them separately, only on objects she and her immediate family make."

"Like?"

"Dream catchers, flutes, pipes, dance headdresses, items like that."

"I don't suppose she has a limited clientele?"

"High-end tourist shops, all over the country."

"Great. So these things could be pulled off anything?"

"Yes. I asked her if there was any way of finding the location or age of the pieces, but she said no."

I started to take another sip of my coffee, but the smell informed me that I had had enough. "Any way to tell what pieces the feathers could have come off of?"

"She said that small pinholes at the base of the quill probably meant that they came off dream catchers or pipes, nontraditional usage." He caught me looking at the feather between us. "Both have such holes. I am afraid that does not narrow the field much."

"No." I took the feather and stuffed it back in my jacket.

He waited quietly. "There is more?"

I weighed my options and decided to clear the air. "How come you were late going running yesterday?"

He sat his coffee cup down, and a mischievous glint shaded his eyes. "I was out shooting white boys."

"I'm serious."

He turned and looked at me, square. "I know, and it is starting to piss me off."

Moment of truth. "Where were you?"

He turned on his stool, straightening his body and trailing a hand down to rest lightly on his leg. The smile was gone, and his eyes had flattened. "Are you going to hit me?"

My voice sounded mechanical. "I'm through hitting people today. Where were you?" It was a long pause.

"Sleeping with Dena Many Camps."

Two steaming plates of Canadian bacon and eggs, sunny side up, with grits, were slid under our noses. I glanced over and then looked again. "That's the usual?"

She looked at Henry. "Told you." With this, she freshened our coffee and moved down the counter to take care of the other customers. You had to hand it to her, she could tell when her clients wanted peace, if not quiet.

I started to work on my usual, but he was still watching me, and I was starting to feel ashamed of myself. "She's half your age."

He laughed. "Are you going to jail me for that now?" He turned and began eating.

"You should be ashamed of yourself."

"It is only premarital sex if you are planning on getting married."

I spoke out of the corner of my full mouth. "You should be even more ashamed."

He kept eating, finally replying between bites, "You are such a prude."

"Pervert."

"Jealous."

I told him about Al's description of the shooter, and we were through it, but he remained quiet for a while. I continued with the story of the two fishing vests, the flies, and Al Monroe. He agreed with the theory that George was probably up there somewhere. He asked if I'd checked the Forest Service sign-in sheets. I told him we had. He was thinking, "Largish with long maybe dark hair?"

"Um-hmm."

"Interesting." He ate some more of his breakfast. "Were they hand-tied or store bought?"

"What?"

"The flies. If they were new and store bought, then maybe they mentioned to someone where they were going?"

"I'll radio up and ask Ferg."

We finished breakfast, and I asked Dorothy to fix up a usual for an occupant. She put it in one of the Styrofoam containers and handed it to me with a worn smile but with no questions. I tried to mend some fences. "I'll probably be back for dinner."

"I'll set the name cards."

We climbed the stairs behind the courthouse; the weather hadn't changed, and I was beginning to think we'd gotten a reprieve. When we got back to the office, Lucian was gone, but Ruby was waiting for me. I handed her Bryan's breakfast.

"His nose is shattered."

"I'm feeling bad enough, you don't have to add to it."

"You're not feeling anywhere near as bad as he is. They patched him up, but they say he's going to have to go up to Billings to get it properly set."

"Yes, ma'am." I waited for more, but there wasn't any. "Could you see if you can raise Ferg on the radio?"

She flipped the toggle switches on the console and reached for her headphones, holding one side up to her ear. "Why, you want to beat on him, too?"

I continued into my office with Henry close behind. He occupied the seat in front of my desk and was smiling. I sat in my chair. "So, you wanna be a deputy?"

He looked at the accumulated clutter on my desk and the general disorder of the place. I had to admit, it didn't look all that inviting. "I think I might work better outside the framework."

"Well, we do have a moral turpitude clause."

The little red light on my phone began blinking, and I was starting to get an idea of how angry Ruby was with me; she never used the intercom, she always came to the door. I picked up the receiver and spoke cautiously, "Yep?"

"Ferg, line one." And she was gone.

I hit it. "Ferg?" The connection wasn't great, but I could hear him. "Where have you covered?"

Static for a while. "I started with Crazy Woman, middle fork of Clear Creek, and I'm headed up to Seven Brothers."

"I've got a question for you. Were those flies hand-tied or store bought?"

"Store bought, definitely." He paused. "I think they're from the Sportshop."

"That is good news. Thanks." I hung up the phone and looked at Henry.

"Do you want me to go out to the Espers and see who shows?"

"They also serve who stand and wait."

"Yes, but the pay is shit." He looked around the office. "Have you got any books around here?"

"I think I've got a paperback copy of *Crime and Punishment*"—I scouted out the bookshelves—"and I've got *Lolita* around here somewhere."

"I will pick something up."

As he left, Ruby appeared at the door, and I noticed he gave her a wide berth. "I need to talk to you."

I did my best to look repentant, but I had the feeling contrition wasn't suiting me. "Yes?"

"You need to talk to Bryan. I don't think he fully understands why it is he's here."

I thought of all the things I had to do. "Okay." She stayed there, leaning against the doorway and looking at me. "What?"

"You're a sheriff. You're supposed to stand against such things, not for them." I made the mistake of smiling. "It's not funny." She was really angry now, the blue in her eyes was neon. "You could have called him in and talked to him, you could have fired him . . . There's no end to the options that were open to you, but no, you waited, you planned, and you executed. Your actions were deliberate and with forethought."

I waited, then sighed, and continued on toward my doom. "Are you through?"

"No, I'm not." She was off the doorway in an instant and stood directly in front of my desk. She looked like she was about ten feet tall. "I'm thinking I should hand in my resignation."

"Ruby, I'm sorry." She glared at me, still not giving an inch. "I was sorry when I did it." I leaned back in my chair, just trying to get a little distance between us. "I'm mortified. It makes me sick." I sighed again, looking out my window to avoid those eyes. "How is he?"

"He looks horrible, both his eyes are black and his nose is . . . He has tubes in his nose."

"Ruby, please . . ." I got up and went around the desk, but she backed away, and the response was ferocious.

"Don't touch me."

I went ahead and stepped forward, opening my arms and pulling her in. She didn't struggle, and I wrapped her up. "I'm sorry. I really am sorry." I could feel how thin and fragile she was; her shoulder blades stuck out like sparrow wings.

"I am so ashamed of you."

"I know, I know." I held her there for a while, just listening to her breathe.

"You know this could be misconstrued as sexual harassment?"

"I hope so . . . How's Lucian doing?"

I felt her stiffen a little. "Don't make your problems worse by asking."

I let her go and held her out to look at her. "Yes, ma'am." The bell on the front door sounded as somebody pushed it open; we both looked toward the doorway. "You see to that, I'll go talk to Bryan." I gave her a quick kiss on the forehead and headed for the holding cells. When I got there, he was lying on his bunk, the remains of breakfast sat on the floor beside him, and the door still hung open. I went in and sat on the opposite bunk again. "Didn't like your breakfast?"

His arms were folded behind his head, but his face turned to me as I propped my Sorels up on the edge of his bed. "I'm just not hungry."

"I'd take advantage of the good stuff, we switch over to potpies on the weekend."

His attention returned to the ceiling. "I'm still going to be here over the weekend?"

"Unless I can find who's killing your friends." I waited for a moment, watching him. "Jacob Esper's dead." He didn't move at first, but then his arms came up and covered his face. I officially took him off the list. "I guess Mr. Ferguson didn't tell you." I looked at him. "You and George ever go fishing?"

He thought. "Yeah, I mean we have."

"Where?" He was aware of how important the answer might be, so he removed his arm and looked at me. "Anyplace special? A lake on the mountain he likes best?"

His eyes escaped mine and went to the floor. "Lost Twin, that's his favorite."

I was up and out of the cell before I remembered. "Bryan?"

He was already sitting up and looking at me. "Yes, sir?"

"You're not in here because you did something wrong, you're here because somebody is out there trying to do something to you, and I'm not going to let that happen."

I blew through the cell door and rushed down the hall but pulled up short when I got to the front. He did look like hell, with the rolled-up cotton and tubes sticking out of his nostrils and the gauze bandage plastered across the bridge of his nose and his cheekbones underneath both black eyes. He was sitting on the edge of Ruby's desk when I came in, and he started to get up, but I stopped him. "What're you doing here?"

"I'm here to work, unless you fired me."

His voice was thick and nasal; you could tell he was having trouble breathing. "Shouldn't you be at the hospital or on your way to Billings?"

He stood, even though I put out a hand to stop him. "I'm here to work."

"You think you can?"

He tried to stand up straighter. "I ain't hurt that bad."

I kept trying to see Lucian in him, that little glimmer of the old goat that would make him salvageable. Maybe he was what Lucian would have turned out to be if the old sheriff hadn't lived in such interesting times. A couple of years in a Japanese prison camp might be just what Turk needed, but I didn't have a bridge over the river Kwai for him to build, so we had to settle for Powder Junction. "Go out to the Esper place and relieve Henry Standing Bear. Tell him to come back to the office." He didn't say anything, just gingerly made his way out the door.

When I turned around, Ruby had her arms folded. "I suppose that's as close as we're going to get to an apology?"

"I didn't fire him." She rolled her eyes. "Can you get me the Ferg, please?" I gave her a dirty look of my own. "Then if you would be so kind as to try and get Jim Keller on the phone?" This got another questioning look. "Oh, and could you call the Yellowstone County Jail and see if they have frequent lodger Artie Small Song?"

While she attempted to raise Unit Three, I walked over to the window and looked back up the valley. The clouds were just beginning to creep over the lower peaks, and it didn't look good. We had an opening in the weather but, by my calculations, it was only good for about the next five hours. I needed help—as near as I could figure, about seven million dollars' worth.

"I've got him."

I turned back and took the mic. "Ferg, where are you?"

Static. "Up from the Hunter Corrals."

"Turn around."

There was a long pause. "What?"

"I think he's at Lost Twin." I shrugged for my own amusement and Ruby's. "Appropriately enough."

A much longer pause. "We'll never make it in there before dark, and with this weather coming in . . .'"

I keyed the mic and held it. "Yep, I know." I looked over at Ruby. "I'm gonna get us some help. I'll call you back. All I need you to do is get to the parking lot at West Tensleep."

Static. "Just the parking lot?"

Static again. "Hey, Ferg?"

"Yeah?"

"Anybody who's there . . . hold 'em." I handed the mic back to Ruby, loving it when she didn't know what I was up to. "Would you add Omar to the phone list?"

"What in heaven's name for?"

I waited a moment, then batted my eyelashes and stated the obvious, "I need to talk to him." I crossed the room and took out my keys and hung them on the rack, just in case anybody needed to move the truck. She shook her head and dialed as I made my way back to my office. I sat at my desk and made mental preparations for the coming conversations and for the plan that was just starting to fully develop in my mind. I glanced over at the doorway and around the corner to the safe where we kept the guns. I knew what was in there and made a few calculations on what we would need—all long-range weapons. There were a couple of battered old Remington 700s and a Winchester Model 70 and, as near as I could remember, the Remingtons were .30-06s and the Winchester was a .270. All good rifles, but I was thinking of the Weatherby Mark V .308 that was lurking in the back. Omar donated it to the library raffle about five years ago, and I had embarrassingly won it, and it had rested in the back of the safe ever since. I wasn't even sure if I had ammunition for the thing. I remembered the sign at the Marine Corps Scout Sniper School at Quantico that read THE AVERAGE ROUNDS EXPENDED PER KILL WITH THE M16 IS FIFTY THOUSAND. THE MARINE SNIPER AVERAGES 1.3 ROUNDS PER KILL. THE COST DIFFERENCE IS $2,300 VS. 27 CENTS. Shave and a haircut, two bits.

On a whim, I punched up Vonnie's number and listened to her machine tell me she was unavailable at this time but to leave a message and she'd get back to me as soon as possible. When I hung up the phone, Ruby was at the door; it appeared I was on the road to being forgiven. "Yes, ma'am?"

"Mrs. Keller says Jim's gone hunting with a friend in Nebraska. She also says that she's bringing Bryan his lunch and a few things and wants to know how long we are intending on keeping him."

"Oh, brother . . ." I placed my elbows on the desk and rested my chin on my combined fist.

"You're going to wish you hadn't stuck your hand in that hornet's nest."

I looked at the blinking red lights on my phone. "Do you think she was lying?"

She crossed her arms and covered her mouth, deep in thought. "It makes sense, doesn't it?"

"Yep, it does." She glanced down the hall toward the jail in an unconscious effort to conceal her thoughts. "When Henry gets here, tell him to go down to Dave's and get some real winter gear, altitude stuff, and some Winchester .308s." She nodded absentmindedly and disappeared back toward her desk. "Is this Omar on line one?"

She called back down the hallway, "Line one," then reappeared in the doorway. "By the way, Artie Small Song is in the Yellowstone

County Jail and has been there since Saturday. They want to know if you want him; they say he eats like a horse."

"Tell them it's a wonderful offer, but no thanks." She nodded and disappeared as I picked up the receiver and punched line one. "Omar?"

"Yes." It wasn't a happy yes.

I thought for a moment. "Are you aware of the term *posse comitatus*?"

"Yes."

I listened to the silence on the line and then settled into the plan. "Do you still have that Neiman Marcus helicopter?"

11

"I do not think the last one of these I was in was like this."

I looked around at the embossed, luxurious, Italian leather interior, but once again my attention was drawn to the swirling countryside as we ascended the east slope at over 160 miles an hour, a fact of which my stomach was acutely aware. "Don't talk to me, I'm concentrating on not throwing up."

"I did not know that they come with doors, and the little bud vases are a nice touch."

"I'm going to make a point of puking on you first and into them second."

Henry smiled and looked out the other window while balancing the Weatherby Mark V lightly between his powerful hands, completely oblivious to the speed and altitude. He had raided the small area of army surplus in Dave's sale department near the back door of the sporting goods store and was wearing fingerless wool gloves; one of the old, reflective-green, M1-style jackets with the genuine acrylic fur lining; a pair of Carhartt overalls; and a new pair of Sorels. He looked like a disco Eskimo. "Did Omar really buy this helicopter at Neiman Marcus?"

I sighed and attempted to put a good seat on my internal organs. "It was in the divorce settlement with Myra."

"So, she bought the helicopter at Neiman Marcus?"

I belched and placed a hand over my stomach. "He bought it for her when they were getting along. When they got divorced, he took it back." He was silent for a few moments, but I knew it was too good to last.

"Where exactly is the helicopter department in Neiman Marcus?"

I dipped my head and rested it against the barrel of the Remington pump I carried. "Please shut up."

He considered the rifle between his knees. "Did the Weatherby come from Nordstrom's?"

The metal felt cool against my forehead as I listened to the whine of the superchargers on the big Bell engine as it fought to carry us through the thermals the cragged peaks below were creating. I thought about my plan. I had to keep reminding myself that nobody else had thought up this harebrained stuff and that I was responsible for my own misery, but we couldn't have covered this amount of ground on foot. If we saw anything, if we saw George Esper, we would go down and snatch him up, dead or alive, and get out of there like a Neidless Markup bat out of hell. Just the thought of up and down made my stomach flip again.

He must have noticed me closing my eyes. "You want me to tell you about my first time?"

"Don't tell me it's Dena Many Camps."

He smiled, playing with the adjustments on the rifle's scope and then readjusting them back. "I remember the first time I rode in one of these things. We were doing a hot extraction out of Laos in '68 with this NVA colonel we were taking down to the magic fishing village on the coast. We had lost about half our patrol and were flying really low, under radar, maybe a hundred feet off the water. He was pretty sure we were going to throw him out, so sure that he decided to take things into his own hands. He must have tried to hurl himself out of that helicopter half a dozen times. On the sixth attempt, he kicked me in the chin. So, I just folded my arms and figured the next time he goes for the door, this fella better learn how to fly."

I opened my eyes and looked up at him. "And?"

He continued looking out the window. "He did not."

"What?"

"Fly."

I thought about it. "Is that story supposed to make me feel better?"

I looked up at the back of Omar's head. He wasn't happy about the current situation either. We were just cresting the meadows at the head of the valley, and the treetops swayed as the big rotors batted them away. I looked past the trees to the sky and made a few more calculations on the weather. I picked up the headset from the console beside me, held one of the cups to my ear, and adjusted the microphone. "Omar?"

He turned a little in his seat, and I could see him speaking. "Yes?"

"I figure about two hours before it hits?"

He studied the horizon ahead. "Maybe three, you never know."

"Let's make it two; I want to know."

He nodded his head, and my stomach did a half gainer with a full twist. I thought about all the light aircraft crashes I had investigated in my tenure as sheriff; it seemed like there was one every couple of years. Good pilots, good aircraft, but the mountain weather was always unpredictable. Between the thermals, downdrafts, and quirky winds, I wasn't sure how anybody kept the things aloft except with a liberal application of positive thought. "Doesn't this stuff bother you? Just a little bit?"

He looked at me, slightly swaying back and forth with the movements of the helicopter. "No, it does not." He watched me for a while longer.

"What does bother you?"

"You, thinking I might be capable of murder."

I looked at him, with the shotgun's barrel between my eyes, and tried to figure if this was really something he wanted to talk about or if it was just another distraction. In the end, I decided that it didn't matter. "You are capable of doing it."

He nodded. "Physically, technically, I suppose so." He leaned forward a little. "But do you think I would?"

"Do you think you'd be here if I did?"

He considered this. "There is the old saying 'Keep your friends close, and your enemies closer.'"

"You think you're an enemy?"

"I am trying to find out if you think I am." He leaned back in the cream-colored leather and looked up at the monitors on the ceiling. "Sourdough Creek."

We were more than halfway there. "Try to look at it from my point of view."

He closed his eyes. Henry could surrender himself to a hypothetical, even if it included making himself the suspect in an ongoing murder investigation. He never worked on a single level. "MMO?"

"Motive."

"One through three?"

We had played this game numerous times, but never with Henry as the perpetrator. "One?"

He was talking fast with his eyes still closed. "It cannot be conclusively shown that I have ever met Cody Pritchard or Jacob Esper or had reason to have feelings of ill will toward either of them."

Impossible. "Two."

"Not only have I met Cody Pritchard and Jacob Esper, but there are hard feelings between us since they took my niece into a basement and raped her repeatedly with their tiny, little, circumcised dicks, with bottles, and with baseball bats."

A chill was starting at the base of my spine. "Three."

"I was seen stalking through the courthouse after the trial with a Sharps .45-70 under my arm and muttering something about Cody Pritchard and Jacob Esper canceling their subscriptions to *Indian Country Today*." He opened his eyes. "I give motive a two."

"Two and a half."

He genuinely looked hurt. "Why?"

"Al Monroe's description of the perp, large with long, darkish hair."

He sighed and pulled the Weatherby back against his chest and folded his arms around it. "All right, two and a half, but I'm not going to be as easy on the next two."

"Means?"

He thought. "One: I have been stricken by a strange, tropical disease, which has paralyzed both of my trigger fingers."

"Uh, huh. Two."

"Both of these boys have been killed by a caliber of weapon of which I am in possession."

"Three."

"Ballistics matches this weapon with the slugs that killed both of these boys." He shrugged and looked out the window. "Two."

"Means, two." I studied the lines on his face, and it seemed as if some of the joy had receded from the game. "Opportunity?"

"One: I was in Vatican City with the pope at the time."

"Two."

"I was seen in the area of both murders, but no one can place me at the scene of either."

"Three."

"I am found standing over both bodies with aforementioned .45-70 in my hands as both Cody and Jacob respectively gasp out their dying breaths." He looked back at me. "Opportunity knocks twice?"

I shook my head. "One and a half. You had the argument with Cody at the bar, not too distant from the Hudson Bridge, but nobody saw you on the mountain."

"Al Monroe's description?"

"Not a positive identification; anyway, we already used it on motive."

"What about the feathers?"

"Circumstantial; fake feathers indicate a fake Indian to me."

He smiled. "I was late running yesterday." I stared at him for a moment. "No sense playing the game if you can't play it honestly. A two."

We sat there looking at each other. The theory was that three out of nine meant you should be looking for another suspect, and nine out of nine meant you started having the suspect's mail forwarded to Rawlins. Prosecutors usually liked higher than a six before going to trial, so Henry's six barely let him off the hook. "Looks like you're innocent, of the murders at least." I paused. "Honestly, who do you think is doing it?"

"Honestly?" He sniffed and dropped his chin on his chest. "I think

231

it is somebody we do not know. I think it is somebody we have not thought of."

"A sleeper?"

"Yes. Somebody that is doing this for very strong reasons, something we do not yet understand."

I nodded. "Do you know Jim Keller very well?"

He looked up, very slowly. "No."

"Which of the four boys do you consider the most innocent, and whose life's been messed up by this the most for the least cause?"

"Bryan." His eyes stayed steady. "The clever thing gets in the way in your line of work, does it not?"

"Sometimes."

"Is Jim Keller a shooter?"

"He's supposedly in Nebraska hunting with some friends."

I watched him turn the wheels. "Would you run off and leave your son here with all these things going on?"

"He never came to the trial."

The eyes didn't move. "Neither did I."

"She wasn't on trial."

"The hell she was not."

I didn't feel like pursuing that line of answering. "I guess we are back to you. Know your rights?"

"Yes, but it is the wrongs that keep getting me into trouble, Officer."

We watched the trees swing below as Omar and the department-store helicopter used a variation on the IFR, or I Follow Road, method of navigation to get us to Lost Twin. I thought for a moment and became aware that my stomach had settled. West Tensleep Lake lay at the base of the high valley that continued up the ridge until you got to Cloud Peak, the crowning jewel of the Bighorns. The Indians had named it Cloud Peak because, like most accentuated landmasses, it developed its own weather patterns. It hid from the plains below most of the time, peeking out at us from behind a haze of high-altitude cumulus.

Omar was rounding off the edges to get the most out of his three-

232

hundred-mile travel range. We had been up for the better part of an hour and, through the front glass of the passenger side of the cockpit, I could make out a few cabins that had been built before the government had acquisitioned the land. We were now technically in Big Horn County, but the less said about that the better. By the time we followed Middle Tensleep Creek below Mather Peak we would be back in Absaroka County and my proper jurisdiction. You could feel the lift and roll as the chopper followed the creek toward Mirror Lake and continued up the small valley to our final destination, the Lost Twin. They were both sizable. I noticed Omar's hand waving in the cockpit. I picked up the headset and adjusted the microphone. "Yep?"

"You've got a call on the single band; I'll patch it through."

A moment of static, and Ruby's voice was there in my ear. "Walt, the Game and Fish called. They said there wasn't anyone signed in at the trailhead to go to Lost Twin, but they said they've got a black Mazda Navajo with the plates Tuff-1 at the Tensleep parking lot."

"That part's good news. Anything else?"

"Affirmative."

"Affirmative? Hey, you really are getting the hang of this."

"Walt, I was going back over the duty roster so that I could write the Roundup for the week. There was a complaint phoned in yesterday morning that sounds suspicious."

"What's that?"

"Tracy Roberts, Kent's sister called; they've got that place down on Mesa road, on 115? Well, she and her dad were out feeding cows yesterday morning when the old man saw a porcupine that'd been doing some damage, so he makes her stop so he can shoot it."

"On the county road?"

"I know, she wasn't sure if she should call in, but she was angry. She says that somebody came roaring down the road and almost hit the old man." I waited. "She said it was a green pickup, an old one." I looked over at Henry, who continued to look out the window at the rushing scenery.

"What time?"

"A little after dawn." I continued to look at my friend who had just moved above a six. "Walt, do you copy that?"

"Yep, they get a look at the driver?"

"No."

Radio silence for a few moments. "Roger that. Over and out."

I pulled the headphone and rested it on my lap and studied him. After a moment he turned. "Something?"

I nodded slowly. "Yep." I explained about the black Mazda and the lack of sign-in sheet but neglected to mention the sighting of a green truck very much like his.

He smiled. "Lost Twin, how could it be anything else?"

We continued on as I tried to harness the thoughts that made the helicopter seem as if it were standing still. I looked out the side window and watched. I felt the blood in my body shift forward as Omar slowed the helicopter from 160 to nothing and poised over the small ridge that separated the two lakes. I could easily make out the pattern the rotors made on the surface of the water, spiraling dimples that rotated outward to feathering waves that agitated the surrounding shores. Without my asking, Omar began a slow, clockwise rotation to give us the maximum view. Henry went to the door on the other side as I hunched against the Plexiglas window and searched the area for any signs of human activity below.

The lakes are situated at the bottom of the Mather Peak Ridge that touches just over twelve thousand feet. Only through the valley in which we had made our approach could you make any kind of retreat and that was due northwest, the exact direction from which the storm was approaching. So far there were no real signs of the front, and I was beginning to think that the skin-of-our-teeth thing wasn't going to be an issue when my attention was drawn to the higher peaks to the west. It was still coming; it had just paused for a moment to gather its breath to make the run up the west slope of the Bighorns. The surrounding area was going to be swept into a frozen maelstrom a little before dark. I had every intention of being out of there by then but, just in case, there were two six-thousand-cubic-inch packs lying on the floor between Henry and me. They had extra clothes, food, a tent, two sleeping bags, and enough emergency supplies to keep us going for a little less than a week. Every time I looked at the oncoming clouds, I nudged my boot up against the packs and felt better.

"Hey." It figured Henry would spot something first. I turned and looked into the cockpit; Omar had seen something too and pointed to an area in a small gully hidden among the trees directly beside the farthest lake. His arm was decorated with three turquoise bracelets. Style. The nose of the helicopter dipped as we accelerated to the area and hovered just above the treetops. There was a small, green tent there, a little two-person job, with a rain fly staked to the ground. It was holding its own against the pounding of the Bell.

I reached up and tapped Omar on the shoulder. He nudged one of the ear cups forward and inclined his head toward me. "This thing got a PA?" He nodded and flipped the appropriate switches on the overhead console and motioned for me to pick up my headset and use the microphone. The helicopter had little bud vases, how could it not have an announcing system? I cleared my throat and listened to it echo from the surrounding mountainsides. I glanced up, as both Omar and Henry looked at me. "Shit." This too echoed across the peaks.

Henry shook his head. "You think he cannot hear the helicopter?"

I frowned at him and continued. "George Esper?" The volume gave me more of a sense of authority, so I continued. "This is Sheriff Walt Longmire of Absaroka County. If you are down there, would you please reveal yourself to us?" We watched closely as nothing happened, and the only thing I could think of was how difficult it was going to be to find his body in a snowstorm. We continued to scan the area, but nothing was moving down there except with the insistence of the helicopter's downdraft. I tapped Omar on the shoulder again, but he pointed to the headset and flipped the switches on the overhead. "You see any place you could set down?"

His head swiveled and the helicopter turned to the left. It was like being in Omar's head, and I wasn't so sure that was such a great place to be. His arm came up again, indicating a small meadow clearing to the north side of the lakes where the trail swerved and ran along the shore. "There."

The nose dipped again, and we sideslipped to a very small rock outcropping where the buffalo grass and the small alpine plants were plastered against the hard ground. There wasn't much room, and the tips of the rotors clipped the large pines that surrounded the area on the north side. I looked back at Omar, but he remained concentrated on the skids as they settled on the bald cap of rock perhaps two feet from a sharp ledge that sloped to the lakeshore below. It was good I didn't have to pay him, because I couldn't afford him or his helicopter. He took off his headset and turned in the seat to look at us; there was a large thumping noise as he unlocked the doors of the aircraft. "I want to be clear about this. We have consumed exactly one half of our fuel and, with current conditions, I can say that you have only about forty-five minutes to find George Esper and then have the ride of your life getting out of here." I scrambled out of the helicopter on the uphill side and waited as Henry tossed me the Weatherby and slid out after me. Omar was pointing at the bags. "Get rid of those; either you use them or we leave them here. When I get ready to head out, I want the least amount of weight possible."

Henry reached into the luxurious cargo section and pulled the packs across the contoured carpet out after us. As he dropped them on the moss-covered granite he took the .308 back and saluted Omar through the pilot door. "Sir, yes sir."

Omar ignored him and looked at me. "Forty-five minutes. You go check on the kid, and I'll do a run-through on this beast."

We threw the packs on our shoulders and headed off in a crouch toward the nearest lake. After a few steps, when we were assured we were beyond the slow deceleration of the rotors, Henry leaned toward me. "I do not think he likes me."

"You're an acquired taste."

The patchworks of snow led from all the high areas north, so we abandoned the covered trail for the banks of the lake and quick-stepped it toward the ridge. Once we got there, it was a short traverse to the other side where we had seen the tent. I looked back as we climbed. Somehow, I had gotten ahead of Henry. I stopped and waited as he made his way up in my footprints; if you were tracking him, it would have been as if he had disappeared. He held out his hand, and I pulled him up; to my surprise, he was breathing heavier than I thought he should, so I caught him as he shifted the Weatherby to his other hand. "You all right?"

He looked around at the collection of peaks that ringed the area; there was hardly any lower ground than where we now stood. "I do not wish to dampen your spirits, but this is a wonderful place to be shot."

"Kind of like being in a toilet bowl." We were in the open, with the deep cover of pines darkening into the surrounding area. I was having one of those creeping, grave-step feelings. "Let's go."

At the end of the ridge, the trail deflected into two paths that circled a large boulder and separated as one continued the high road around the far lake and the other dropped into the depression where the tent was pitched. It was a good spot, dry, but close to water. It didn't have too much of a view, but it was well protected from the wind. I looked back up the valley to the northwest and could more clearly see the dark line of clouds that continued to eat up the western sky. It was calm at the moment, but the intersecting triangles of black granite and fresh snow seemed to be holding their breath in preparation for what was coming. They looked like long teeth.

Henry put out a hand to stop me and looked down at the path. "Tracks." He lowered to one knee, shifting his shoulders back so that the weight of the pack wouldn't propel him down the hill. "How big is George Esper?"

I blew out a breath and thought. "Under six feet, maybe a hundred and seventy pounds."

"Size nine, Vasque hiking boots?"

I froze. "What?"

He looked up, his eyes very sharp. "Vasque hiking boots, looks like a size nine. Mean something?"

"Is there a little pattern on the arch, like a little mountain range?"

He didn't look. "Yes." His neck strained as he scoped the surrounding area. I leaned over his shoulder and looked at the print. "Is there something you would like to tell me?"

I was looking around now, too. "We had prints like these at the scene where Jacob was killed."

He stood. "So, George was there?"

"We checked them, and one of the guys that reported the incident wore size nine Vasques."

"What was Jacob wearing?"

I thought back. "The same."

"Size nine?"

"They are twins."

"Well, one set of prints is better than two, not that I'd be able to tell the difference." We continued down the trail to the tent. The rain fly was zipped, and there was a backpack leaned against a tree with the rain cover placed over it. The small ring of a campfire lay cold in the circle of rocks about ten feet from the tent; there was an aluminum frying pan and a plastic bag of corn flour resting on one of the flatter rocks. The heads of a few trout lay in the ashes, along with the strips of bone with connected tails. Henry kneeled by the fire and placed the palm of his hand in the ashes, gently pressing down. After a moment, his eyes came up. "It is old, but there is a little warmth here. Maybe this morning."

"Any more tracks?"

He nodded. "Vasques, size nine."

We looked at each other for a moment. "I don't like this, do you?"

"No."

He pulled his hand up and dusted it off as I continued over to the tent and slipped the pack to the ground, then crouched and unzipped the rain fly and the screen on the tent. I pulled back and turned to look at Henry. "Well, he spent the night here."

"But no fishing equipment?"

"No."

He looked around. "I will take one lake, and you take the other. Here." He tossed the Weatherby to me and extended his hand for the shotgun. He smiled as he took the Remington. "You are a better shot than I am." He scanned the surrounding hills. "Just in case there is somebody up there."

I nodded. "You got the rest of the ammunition?"

He patted his pockets and shrugged. "You only need one, right?" Henry turned and disappeared into the pines toward the eastern lake.

I looked at the rifle and considered whether it was loaded or not. For all I knew the Bear was standing just out of sight, listening to see if I would open the bolt action. I shook my head at the ridiculousness of the situation and pulled the .308 up onto my shoulder. If he was standing out there, I wasn't going to give him the satisfaction of hearing me check. Instead, I readjusted the forgotten .45 on my hip and made a face at a man I was sure had already begun the search around his own lake. I started off around mine thinking about what Ruby had said. Just because someone had sighted an old, green pickup didn't mean Henry was a killer. In my experience, smoke usually indicated smoke and nothing more.

There were coal-bed methane operations in the vicinity of the Robertses' place. To these men, time meant money and time in our part of the high plains meant driving, which to them meant speeding. From economic necessity, a lot of them drive older outfits, and any one of them could have been speeding to or from one of the many rigs in the area at that hour of the morning. I knew I was working up a grand rationalization but just because a truck was green and old didn't mean that it was Henry's. Even so, I once again had the urge to pull the bolt and see if the rifle was loaded. I looked back at the other Twin but kept the rifle on my shoulder, considering it a triumph of righteous logic, and wondered how many poor dumb bastards had died in the name of that particular line of thought. I stayed on the path that circled the lake, careful to avoid the wetter sections where the snowmelt had gathered and saturated the ground, but I didn't see any more footprints. I bolstered my spirits by reminding myself that I'd also not found any bodies.

Vasques, size nine. Had George been with Jacob? If he had, then why? And why would he be at the scene of his brother's death and then go fishing? Maybe Cody Pritchard did know his killer. My head was starting to swim with all the options, but one thing was starting to come clear: Just because you were a victim didn't mean you couldn't be a perpetrator.

I thought about Jim Keller. Mrs. Keller had come into the jail to check on her baby boy and had been somewhat disarmed at finding him in my office with his feet propped up on my desk. He was drinking a ginger ale and leafing through a stack of police supply catalogs. I guess she figured we'd have him chained up in the basement. I asked her about Jim, and she said that he was hunting down in Nebraska with some friends; geese, she said. There was a hesitancy in the way she said it that led me to believe there was something more there. So I used one of my age-old cop tricks and asked her if there was anything else she wanted to tell me. She used one of the age-old mother tricks and just said no. Cop tricks pale in comparison with mother tricks.

I looked back around the crescent ring of mountains and thought about what I would do if I wanted to kill someone here. I thought about how I might lure him into a remote area and then splatter him like a ripe pumpkin. It was about then that I decided to concentrate on taking in more of the scenery. Lost Twin is a lot like the other hundreds of pristine, alpine lakes in the Bighorns that seem to be sitting and waiting for calendar photographers. It lies in one of the mountain's few hanging valleys, and you could easily envision the tributary glacier that had gently cut this hidden one. With their beds of stone, the Lost Twins had given up little to the forces of erosion. It was as if their hearts had been broken by the retreating glacier, and they were not likely to allow such liberties again. These glaciers formed steps and benches, each successive one at a higher altitude. I had seen pictures of the Coliseum in Rome, and the similarity did nothing to ease my mind. I felt the wind and automatically looked back down the valley. The clouds were starting to move at a surreal pace; evidently, they had caught their breath. Maybe it was the altitude, but the weather always seemed to change more quickly on the mountains.

My attention was brought back to the trees, where I had seen movement. It wasn't a singular movement, but rather a collection of movements that I quickly dismissed as the wind.

Omar was still fiddling with the helicopter when I reached the hill leading up to the ridge. I stood there, and the air tasted good. I took a little bit of time to breathe in the smells of the pines, the rocks, and the water. There was a large patch of delicate, freeze-dried yellow flowers that lined the south side of the small ridge. Henry would know what they were. He was making his way around the scree-lined bank of the other lake, probably doing a much more thorough job than I had done with mine. I watched as he crouched down and studied a shallow area between the rocks. The acrylic fur wreathed his neck, and the scattergun was resting lightly on his shoulder as he held the pistol grip. He stayed that way, and I had the feeling I was getting a select view of the Athapascan race that had braved the Bering Strait in search of two bigger and better mastodons in each garage. Sometimes I didn't think his DNA thought things had worked out so well. I wasn't quite sure why I had decided on the shotgun, other than it balanced out the .308's long-range capacities; and, like a good scout, I was always attempting to be prepared, or reverent, or something like that. I continued to watch him as he studied a shallow area between the rocks and peered across the lake toward the area of the tent. As Henry made it to the top of the ridge, I asked, "Anything?"

He shook his head and looked back in the direction from which he had come, as if whatever he might have missed would be more visible from half a mile away. The wind was picking up, and the gusts were becoming more consistent. "Boot prints, same as before, but nothing fresh."

"What do you think?"

He stretched his legs and tucked the shotgun under one arm; I noticed the safety was on. "Difficult to say with all the scree; he could have gone off anywhere."

"Alien abduction?"

"Possible, but unlikely. They are usually looking for intelligent life."

I exhaled a lung full of the good smells, and we both looked down the valley to the trail out. "He's fishing."

"Yes, that, or a lyin' and a molderin' in the grave."

I looked back at him. "Let's concentrate on the fishing, okay?"

"Yes." He continued looking down the trail. "You need water for that." He finally looked back at me. "You thinking what I am thinking?"

"Three hours in good weather?"

His eyes watched the clouds; they were even closer than before. "I do not think that is going to be the case. Anyway, four, with the packs."

I tried not to put too much bass in my voice, "I wasn't planning on taking them."

He raised an eyebrow. "Do you mind jumping up and down so I can hear your big brass balls clank?"

"It's only three hours . . ."

"In good weather, which we are not going to have." He looked at his wristwatch as a particularly strong gust caused both of us to shift our shoulders. "Even then, it will be after dark." I continued to look at him. "We get caught in here without any supplies, we are the honored dead."

"Yep, but what a blaze of glory." I was enjoying being the tough guy for a change.

"I am more concerned with the freeze of agony."

"I have to find that kid, dead or alive."

I watched as he stretched his back and looked toward Omar, who stood at the nose of the helicopter with his arms folded. My forty-five minute window of opportunity already had the storm shutters closed and was prepared to depart at roughly twice the national speed limit. I briefly thought about telling Henry to go on back without me, but it would have been an insult. So I just stood there, waiting. "We find him dead, we leave him."

I lied. "Agreed."

"I will get some supplies from the packs. I refuse to leave here without water and some food."

"We could always eat George, if we find him." I watched after Henry as he crossed the ridge toward the tent where we had left the packs. His step seemed to have lost some of its natural spring. I called after him, "How long till snow?"

He called back without turning, "How the hell should I know?"

Maybe we were going to die. I trudged up the hill toward the helicopter and Omar. "You need to get out of here."

He pushed the Ray-Bans further up on his nose. "What're you gonna do?"

"We're going to trail out back to West Tensleep. That kid's here, somewhere, and I figure the only thing to do is follow the water out."

"You and the Indian?"

I looked at my reflection in his polarized sunglasses. "Yep." I didn't mean for it to have as much warning as it did, but that's the way it shook out. He didn't say anything, just opened the cockpit door and reached in to retrieve a handheld that he gave to me. The rotors pitched slightly as another gust rushed up the valley.

"It's already set at your frequency, so if you need to talk to anybody you should get through, as long as you've got reception."

"Thanks."

He looked at me for a moment as if memorizing me, and I can't say it was comfortable. "I notice you're carrying the .308."

"We traded."

He considered it for a moment. "Make sure he stays ahead of you." His face was stiff. "I'm not joking."

I looked at him and thought about saying a number of things. "We'll be all right." I waited a moment. "Get in touch with Ferg and Vic and tell them to meet us at West Tensleep parking lot, if you would?" We both looked back at the weather. "Tell them to bring hot coffee."

Omar sighed a deep sigh, climbed into the helicopter, and held the door open with a foot. He began flipping switches and from the center of the machine a high whine began slowly setting the rotors in motion. He started to place the headphones over his ears but stopped, leaned sideways through the still open door, and shouted to be heard over the increasing roar of the big engine, "You tell that Indian, if he comes out of here alone?"

I waited.

"I will see him dead."

I lowered my head, held the Weatherby in both hands, and quickly dropped over the ridge. The deep hues of the helicopter's exterior reflected the lakes; it quickly rose from the rocks and veered toward the center of the valley as a few pieces of the trimmed lodgepole pines scattered and dropped to the ground. A strong blast of the oncoming storm caught the chopper broadside, sending it in a cascading pitch that threatened to drop it in the lake below. Omar deflected the wind pattern and converted the stall into a rolling turn that carried it across the valley. I continued to watch for the next minute as he made the grade and slipped through the pass and down the mountainside toward the safety of Durant International far below. I walked the rest of the way down the hill and met Henry at the ridge. "Neiman Marcus decided not to honor our frequent flier miles."

"That is what we get for flying coach." He handed me an abbreviated version of my pack. "The tops disconnect from the rest to make a fanny pack. We both have two bottles of water and a little food, but that is all."

"A jug of wine and thou . . ." He didn't say anything but turned and started off down the banks of the western lake toward the trail that would eventually lead us out. A haze had begun enveloping the hills where the trail disappeared. The fog of low-flying clouds had begun eating the mountains, and we were headed down its throat. I wasn't quite sure why I was feeling as good as I was. Maybe it was because I had perceived a challenge and had accepted it, or maybe it was because I didn't see any other options. But I felt good and decided not to ruin it with too much recrimination. I caught up and pulled alongside of him. "He can't be too far, since he left all his stuff at the lake."

"Or he is dead."

"I wish you'd stop saying that."

He turned his head slightly toward me as he walked. "Would you go out this way fishing and leave all your supplies at the lake?"

"He's not the brightest bulb on the Christmas tree."

"Maybe."

"What's that supposed to mean?"

I notice that he had tied some tubular webbing from the packs to the shotgun, making a sling, which he now pulled up higher on his shoulder. "Do you remember what George Esper looks like?"

I thought for a moment. "Yep."

"I remember what Cody Pritchard looked like, I remember what Bryan Keller looks like, and I have a pretty good image of what Jacob Esper looked like, but whenever I think of George, I cannot seem to bring the image into focus."

I thought about the pictures, the ones I kept in the Little Bird file, the ones I had cut from the Durant High School yearbook. I had studied them enough over the past few years that I should have been able to tell you every significant feature of George Esper's face, but I couldn't. I shook my head. "Look, maybe we're getting worked up about nothing. Maybe he's just waiting for his brother."

He started down the trail and called over his shoulder, "He will be waiting for a long time."

We climbed the hillside in the Forest Service's zigzag pattern that led to a granite outcropping where the run-off from the lakes escaped to the rocks below. The wind picked up again, and the cold air found every inch of uncovered skin on my hands, ears, and neck. I looked down the valley and at the trail we would be using as the snow began overtaking everything within a quarter mile. In two minutes, it would be to us. Henry had stopped too, to pull up the government-issue parka hood and to look back at the lakes. I pushed his shoulder. "Considering the situation, why don't you talk about something happy?"

I watched as he tied the drawstring at his neck. "I thought I was." He shifted the shotgun from his shoulder and cradled it in his arms, first looking down the trail at the approaching wall of snow, then off to the distant lakes. His eyes softened at the view, and he seemed sad. "These . . . young men, when they did what they did to my niece? For me, they no longer existed. For good or bad, they were gone." His eyes returned to mine. "Do you understand?" His eyes stayed with mine. "It is the best I can afford them."

I waited a moment, but it seemed as if he wanted me to say something. "All right."

He smiled and once again threw the makeshift strap of the shotgun over his shoulder. "It is far from that, but it will have to do." He continued to smile, then flipped the flaps down on his fingerless gloves and twisted his fingers into the mitts. The smile warmed me even as the flakes began stinging my face. He threw a paw up and thumped my shoulder twice. "Anyway . . . Revenge is a dish best served cold." With this, he turned and walked into the low-flying clouds and the maelstrom of snow that had reached us.

I listened as the drums began a low rhythm and watched as the broad shoulders picked their way carefully down the trail. The world began to turn white, and the Bear disappeared.

12

Even in the snow-muffled air and the distance between us, I heard the gunshot.

We had been battling our way through the wind and the snow; it was an early storm, so the flakes were as big as silver dollars and, with the force of the wind, hit with the same impact. Henry and I had worked our way over the slight rise and outcropping, staying to the right as the trail followed the general path of the stream, and had moved past Mirror Lake with no results. The water continued to run fast from the hanging valley and you could hear it when the wind died down, which it did but with lessening regularity. The blizzard had arrived, visibility had dropped to about twenty feet, and you couldn't see much of anything except the creek.

The Forest Service path remained visible as it wound its way along the stream basin but, in another hour, the depression that made up the trail would be filled with the fast accumulating snow. I took a small measure of solace in the fact that the part that led to the West Tensleep parking lot was not only tree covered but downhill, and we didn't have that far to go before we would get to that section. But the farther we got, the farther my heart sank with the thought that George Esper was not going to be found. I had already summoned up the image of George's bones, scattered by all the little animals by springtime, their bleached white contrasting sharply with the green of the fresh, high-meadow grass. I watched as Henry's image faded in and out of the white swarm of the blowing snow. Every time he disappeared, I quickened my step a bit, wanting comfort from the dark shape that stayed just ahead of me.

Was the killer here? The last two murders had been within easy reach of roads, of quick access and egress, so I didn't think so. But what about the boot prints? It was a popular boot in a very popular size, and the possibility that George, Jacob, and some guy from Casper wore the same shoe wasn't out of the question. I had just about convinced myself that it was coincidence when I heard the shot. It was not the report of the Remington I knew Henry was carrying.

It was close, close enough that I thought I might have seen the muzzle flash. Hearing the sound of a gunshot when you're not expecting it is like sticking your finger in a light socket, but hearing this gunshot was more like sticking that finger into a fuse box. I know I jumped, because I had to catch myself from slipping on the freezing ground and falling into the icy water.

I wasn't aware that I had started running or how fast I covered the distance between us, but the next thing I saw were two distinct figures in the swirling haze of snow. One was seated in the path with his feet before him and was slouched forward, and the other was standing over the first and held something in his hands. With the keening of the wind, they didn't hear me coming even though I'm sure that the pounding of my feet and my ragged breathing alone was enough to get the dead to roll over. For some reason, I hadn't unslung the rifle during my run but was just now slipping it from my shoulder and gripping it with both hands.

It was like falling into an impressionist painting with the snowflake pointillism giving the image a surreal quality. As I surged forward I knew it was Henry on the ground. It wasn't a big person that I hit, and I didn't recognize a single aspect of his appearance as we collided. I know he didn't expect me, because there wasn't any resistance when I got there. I was carrying the rifle forward, but I didn't swing it, instead I used it as a battering ram. In hindsight, I suppose I could have used the thing with a little more strategy, but calculation didn't play much of a part in my reaction.

When he went, I went over with him into the cloud of snow and down the bank leading to the creek. When we hit the ground the first time, the rifle came up and caught me at the bridge of my nose, but the majority of the impact went directly into his head, which snapped back as the stock of the big Weatherby slammed into the side of his jaw. I'm pretty sure I heard the crack of bone as he went down with me smothering him as we went. The second time we hit the ground was the last, and the roll converted into a slow slide on the bank of the stream in axle-grease mud. I felt a sharp pain in my lower left-hand side; something dug into my short ribs and felt as though it had suddenly yanked on my insulated coat as I heard a muffled report. Even in the windstorm, the smell of spent gunpowder and quartzite stung the air. I slapped a hand down to the area where the gun must have been, and I could feel the small revolver that was wedged between our mutual diaphragms. The grip that held it was limp. There was accumulated moisture between us, and I couldn't tell if it was from the fall or if either of us had been shot. I stripped the revolver from the open hand of whomever it was that had held it and lay there for a moment to make sure he really was out and to catch my breath. After a moment, the bass of Henry's voice strained into the wind. "Are you hit?"

His voice was thick, and I could tell he was hurt. I grunted, rolled off the inert figure, and felt my side. I looked back up the hill. "No, I don't think so. I'm just trying to get my heart out of my throat. You?"

"Who is it?"

I pulled myself up on one elbow and looked down at my victim; his face was turned and buried in the hood of a Gore-tex jacket. I used the stock of the rifle to leverage myself up into a position more suited to looking and reached out to turn the face toward me. His chin grinded a little as I pulled the face around, indicating that some damage had been done but, aside from the askew jawline, it was the mostly intact face of a watered-down Jacob Esper. "George Esper."

Henry's voice was still thick, but there was a little more animation. "Is he hit?"

"I don't know."

"Check him. I can wait."

I sat up completely and looked in the general vicinity of where I thought George might have been shot and found nothing. The words were just coming out of my mouth when I noticed a small tear in his full-zip pants. "Shit . . ." I pulled off my glove and ran it over the black fabric; it was coated with his blood. "Shit."

"He is hit?"

"Yep." I tore the pants open to reveal an entry and exit wound at the front of his thigh. "Subcutaneous damage, possibly the thigh muscles. Missed the bone and major arteries though."

"Can you stop the bleeding?"

I sighed. "Maybe, but he's not gonna to be able to walk." I took one of my gloves, turned it inside out, placed the fleece-covered leather over both holes, and looked around for something with which to tie the glove in place. The small pack was still attached to my middle, so I stripped the water bottles off and emptied it out, wrapping it around his leg. I raised his head up and peeled back an eyelid. What showed was mostly white; he gave no sign of coming to. I had seen his chest rise and fall, but I felt his wrist just to make sure I hadn't killed him. The pulse was strong, but he remained still. I checked George's leg again and then scooped up a small .38 caliber Smith and Wesson Detectives' Special. I thumbed open the cylinders and looked at the two spent cartridges and at the two that remained. I removed the two empties, readjusted the wheel forward of an empty chamber, and snapped the cylinder back with the firing pin resting on the hollow chamber. I pushed it into my pocket, picked up the water, and climbed the hill to my friend who still sat on the trail.

As I got to the path, I had a clearer picture of him and saw that drifts of snow had begun building up against his outstretched legs. The Bear's arms were wrapped around his middle, and the hood on his jacket dipped low as if he were trying to sleep. The Remington 870 lay across his lap. I knelt down and looked up into his eyes; they were pinched. "Let me see." He slowly dropped his hands to the edges of his jacket, and it was only then that I noticed the dark red stains that had soaked through his woolen gloves. The jacket slowly opened to reveal a bloody mess at his abdomen, just above the navel and slightly to the right. The blood had saturated the lower part of his shirt and thermal underwear and was now leaking into his lap. I swallowed, and the word was out before I could stop it. "Shit."

He laughed but quickly stopped as the movement in the trunk of his body caused him who knew how much pain. "Please, you are overwhelming me with your optimism."

We had no idea where the bullet was or what damage it might have done on its merry little way. With abdominal injuries, there's always the possibility of traumatic tear in one of the vascular organs, which could easily lead to massive hemorrhaging into the abdomen. Percentages for gunshot mortality rates flashed through my head: liver, 30 percent; kidney, 22 percent; stomach, 18 percent; and bowels, 12 percent. These numbers geometrically progressed the more I concentrated on how far we were from a formal paracentesis, or peritoneal lavage, and computerized tomography, or CT scan. I also thought about how much time I had spent standing in emergency rooms developing an unwanted education, and how badly I wished my friend and I were in one of those very rooms right now. "We have to stop the bleeding."

He continued to smile. "Yes, we do."

I turned my other glove inside out and placed it over the wound. "Is the pain high or low?"

He grunted as I held the glove in place. "In the sense of tolerance or location?"

My eyes met his. "Where does it hurt?"

He chuckled very lightly. "No higher than the wound."

"Right, left?"

He thought, concentrating on the pain. "It appears to have stayed to the right."

I sighed and looked at his torn pack. I started unbuckling my belt, trying to remember if Henry still had his appendix. "You know, if one thing would go right in this case . . ."

I pulled my belt around him and cinched the notches through;

there were, of course, no holes where I needed them. "You got a pocket knife?" He began fumbling at one of his pant pockets, but I carefully took his hands away and placed them over the now saturated glove. "Hold this." I fished the knife from his pocket and pulled out a bone-handled stiletto with a five-inch switchblade. I shook my head as I flipped it open and gauged a hole in the spot I had indented with the belt's tang. He grunted when I finally buckled it over the glove. "Too tight?"

"No."

I pulled the radio from the clip at the small of my back, amazed that it was still there after all the acrobatics. I rolled the small dial on the side, listened to the static, and keyed the handheld. "Absaroka County Sheriff's Department, this is Unit One, come in Base? Unit Two?" I released the button and listened to the static some more. "Come in. Anybody out there?" Nothing. I looked around at the mountains that surrounded us and were covered in the visual static that was also taking its toll on our reception. I thought I heard a ghosting of some voice in the cover of radio frequency. "Come in anybody? I've got an emergency here. Anybody?" I listened, but the ghosting didn't repeat itself. "I've got two men down in the draw of Lost Twin, just past Mirror Lake?" Still nothing. I turned and looked at Henry. "What happened? The abridged version."

He cleared his throat. "He was standing on the trail when I looked up, so I stopped, and he fired."

"He say anything?"

"No."

"You?"

"I believe I may have gasped before clutching my stomach and falling to the ground, but that is all."

I punched the button on the radio. "Come in, this is Unit One of the Absaroka County Sheriff's Department, anybody out there?" I waited again. "If anybody can hear me, I've got two men down and need assistance on the trail of Lost Twin. I need backup and medical. If anybody can hear me, your assistance would be greatly appreciated."

"That would be an understatement."

I sighed. "Think you surprised him?"

"Yes, but all things considered I think he surprised me more." He glanced past me to George who was starting to gather his commensurate amount of snow. "He is out?"

I looked back over my shoulder. "Yep."

He raised a bloodstained hand to my arm. "You better get going."

I turned and knelt down to check George's pupils for any dilation or constriction; they appeared normal for now. I was concentrating, so it took a moment for me to process what he had said. "What?"

He gestured toward the prone George Esper. "You have to get him out of here."

It hit me all at once what it was he was saying. "I'm not leaving you."

He continued to slowly shake his head. "You do not have any choice. He is smaller, and you can make it out with him."

"I'm not leaving you."

He smiled. "Do not be mistaken, I have no intentions of dying. I will wait for you, here."

"It'll be after dark, in a blizzard. We won't find you."

"Then I will have to find you."

My shoulders sagged a little, but I kept my eyes on him. "All right, knock it off with the mystical horseshit. You are gut shot, and the chances of your surviving are narrow enough without you crawling around out here." His smile saddened a little. "What?"

"It is the mystical horseshit that is going to save my life."

I looked away and sighed. "Sorry."

"Do me a favor?"

I raised an eyebrow. "I'm not putting you out of your misery."

"I have a small bag in my front pocket. If you would please get it out for me?" I reached for the front pocket of his coat, unbuttoned the flap, and pulled out a small, green velvet satchel with a ledger horse and warrior stitched across the front. There were beads and feathers attached to the opening at the top, and there were a number of items under the soft fabric, some discernible, some a mystery. I handed the medicine bag to him, and we didn't mention it again. "You have to take him." His smile brightened again. "Who knows, perhaps the weather will cooperate." He grimaced and shifted his weight.

"Pain?"

"No, I have plenty, thank you."

I wanted to punch him.

In spite of our hopes, the wind had increased and, with an introduction of ground fog, visibility had dropped to within ten feet. I once again glanced back at George and considered the 170-odd pounds I was going to be carrying for roughly the next three-quarters of an hour. At least it was downhill. My attention was drawn to the foot that stuck up just above the drop off, and I wondered if it might be a Vasque, size nine. When I turned back around, Henry had pulled the hood back a little, and his eyes had sharpened. "You must go, now."

The longer I waited, the less chance he had. "You want me to move you up against one of the trees for a little shelter?"

"No, I am not moving until you get back." His jaw clamped shut, the muscles bunched like fists on both sides of his face, and I wished like hell that I were the one who had been shot. I slipped off my jacket, careful to take out the bottle of water, and placed another layer over his front. "What are you doing?"

"If I'm carrying him out, I'll be sweating like a pig once I get there. You'll need this more than me." I opened the water bottle and drained it in one continuous chug.

"Go."

I bent down to scoop up the water bottles that had fallen on the trail. He watched as I vented a lot of frustration by throwing each of them as far as they would travel. We listened as they glanced off the tree branches in the distance and landed with satisfying thumps. I turned and looked down at him and tossed the empty over the hill. "Promise you won't eat the snow."

"I promise."

I gave him a quick smile of my own. "I just thought I'd tell you, I'm taking you off the official suspect list."

"I am comforted." He didn't look it, but I placed my hand lightly on his shoulder, and we understood what it was that we didn't have to say.

I stood and trudged the small distance down the hill and paused at George's boots: Vasques, size nine. I brushed the snow away and tried to gently shake the still unconscious George Esper into some semblance of awake. If he came to, it was possible that I could assist Henry and we could all get out; but there was no response, so I reached into his pockets, found his keys, and stuffed them into my Carhartts. If nobody was there to meet us, at least I would have a place to put George. But if nobody was there, how was I going to get a gut-shot, 220-pound man out of the woods? I decided to tackle one problem at a time. Grasping George by one arm and drawing him over my shoulder, I leveraged him up. He didn't weigh 170, probably closer to a buck and a half, which reassured me a small amount. I stood with him over my shoulders and straightened my back, even though the majority of his weight seemed to remain on my right side. It wasn't going to be easy but leaving him in an unconscious state and making a mad dash for the trailhead didn't seem to be an option. He might die of hypothermia, even though I wasn't so sure that Henry wouldn't. But if I was betting on who could withstand the rigors of staying alive, my money was on the Bear. I was careful as I made my way up the small grade to the general flat of the trail and stopped to look down at my friend. "Couldn't you have shot him first?"

He didn't raise his head, but his voice rumbled, "What do you think?"

I thought about kicking his foot in response but was afraid that any unnecessary movement should be avoided, even a sign of affection. So I turned into the wind, shrugged George a little higher onto my shoulders, and kicked off the first steps of many to come.

Just a little away from all the action, I came across a nice fly rod and a creel resting beside the trail. I kicked the creel over, but it was empty. George's luck was holding. I was frustrated and getting angry, so I used that as fuel to get me going. The problem with anger is that once it burns out, you're left with empty tanks. I stopped and caught my breath. I thought about shrugging George off and taking a rest, but I didn't do it for fear that putting him back on might be more than I could manage. There was that, and then there was Henry.

As I had been making my way, I had heard him begin singing. It was a low voice that found a way to cut through the noise of the wind and join with it to carry its ghostly sound across the valley. I had heard Henry sing a number of times at religious ceremonies on the reservation and at powwows that he had dragged me to. I was always surprised by the tonal quality of his voice. The power and strength were a given, but the intricate patterns that it expressed, the infinite ability instantly to change tone, always made me smile. Good friends are the ones who can remain close without losing their ability to surprise. I listened as the driving rhythm of his song carried me farther, and his voice remained with me down the long descent into West Tensleep Valley.

I didn't know what kind of song it was, I didn't know what the words were, and I didn't want to know. I only listened to the complex melodies and carried them in my heart and mind, as other footprints seemed to join in with mine and share the load of George Esper. Old footfalls, old as the mountains and just as enduring. I listened as other voices joined in Henry's song, strong voices, voices that carried not only over the valley but through it. The Old Cheyenne were with me, and I could feel their strength as I continued along the trail, my heavy boots forming the snow as I went. The drums were there too, matching my progress in perfect fashion, providing an easy rhythm and keeping my legs moving. I felt strong, like I hadn't in many years, perhaps like I never had. I watched as my breath began blowing out ahead of me, and it was as if the wind did not affect it. The searing air felt good in my lungs, and I almost felt as if I could run; but the steady beat of the drums held, and so did I.

I felt as though the Old Cheyenne were challenging me for my friend, were attempting to take him with them back to the Camp of the Dead. It was a good, spirited challenge, one that pulled at my heartstrings, but one that I would not allow. I looked at their shadows as they walked along with me. Darting between the trees with closed-mouth smiles on their faces, nodding to me when I caught their eyes, they carried their coup sticks but kept them far out of my reach. Their steps were steady, like my own, and it was only after a while that I became aware that they were matching them precisely. I smiled back in the friendly assurance that their company was appreciated but their mission was not. They could see it as a smile, or they could see it as a showing of teeth. It didn't matter; I would pass this way again very soon, and they were welcome to join me, but they should not get in my way. They were dressed in their summer loincloths with only low moccasins on their feet, but the cold didn't seem to affect them any more than it was affecting me. One of them nodded in a knowing fashion and dipped his shoulders sideways to slip between the close-knit lodgepole pines only to disappear on the other side.

There was a small rise ahead, and it was only when I realized that my gums were freezing that I knew I was smiling in full anticipation of it. My stride lengthened, and the songs kept step. I had slept little in the last twenty-four hours, I was over five decades old, and yet none of it mattered. The young man on my shoulders felt like an oversized bag of baking potatoes as I kept the pace and continued on.

Even with the cloud cover, I could tell the sun was setting; there was the slightest darkening of the valley. I concentrated on my feet, leaving the Old Cheyenne to their devices, and tried not to slip into the icier areas of the trail. I had been right about the heat I would manufacture, and my clothes began attaching themselves to every outline of my body, causing an impediment to my speed as they started to harden. My muscles felt just the slightest twinge of ache and fatigue as I stayed on the high side of a sweeping turn that opened into a small meadow that I remembered from years ago. The wind hit me like a swinging door, knocking me back a half step before I caught myself and surged forward, still concentrating on my feet.

The weight of my burden was just beginning to take a toll when I noticed something else besides my boots in my line of vision. It was a hide-wrapped knob with pony beads and what I now knew to be owl feathers. I raised my head as the little rivulets of sweat raced down the middle of my back and from my face. Someone was there, in the trail before me, walking backwards with every step I took. It was a large man with hair like Henry's and, when I squinted my eyes through the stinging snow, I could see even more of a resemblance. The face was harder and leaner, and there were scars where Henry had none, but I had no doubt it was family. His eyes were sharpened to slits of chipped obsidian that shifted to the left and then to the right. He had the same look as dogs have when they stand over a bone.

I shrugged George farther up on my shoulders and kept my pace as the warrior continued to back away, keeping the end of a stick only inches from my stomach. Every time I surged ahead in an attempt to run into the staff, he would back away at exactly the same speed. The clouds of his breath seemed to pour forth only to be caught in the suction of my own breathing, and it was as if we were sampling the same air. It agreed with both of us as we picked up the pace again, and I moved forward, stepping like some strange four-legged animal.

He smiled a tight-lipped smile, and the light that reflected from his eyes brightened the trail ahead. He caught me looking at something large and square that loomed in the distance over his right shoulder. He motioned with the staff, only missing my stomach by a hair's width, and I could smell sweetgrass and cedar. I looked back as he smiled, and his words were the whisper of many voices, "Sometimes dreams are wiser than waking."

I nodded my head and laughed so hard that the weight of George Esper pressed on the back of my neck and forced my head down. When I resettled the young man and raised my eyes, the brave who had been in the path was gone. I looked around; the only thing I saw was the back of the trailhead map that indicated the path leading to Lost Twin. I laughed some more as I trudged around the two poles that supported the eight-foot sign, leaned against it, and looked at the snow that had plastered the north-facing side. I lunged on as the pressure of two men ground the gravel of the parking lot under the surface of snow.

There are two levels to the gravel lot, and I was hoping that the lower one, which also happened to be the closest, was where he had parked. There was a rise where the Forest Service had used railroad ties as bumpers, and I walked alongside of them until I literally ran into the fender of a snow-covered vehicle, almost dropping George onto the rear deck in the process. I caught my balance and turned toward the back of the small SUV, fished for George's keys in my pocket, and prayed the car was his. When I got to the back of the vehicle, I wiped a hand across the deck and looked in satisfaction at the partially exposed chrome letters, MAZDA. Just for the heck of it, I tried the handle, and sure enough the tailgate let go with a small click. I raised the lid and gently slumped George in like so many groceries. There was a travel blanket that I wrapped around him and, after checking his leg, I closed the back, staggered around, and opened the driver's side door. I slid into the seat. The steering wheel pressed against my stomach so I released the catch, allowing the seat to slide back with a thump. I took the keys in my hand and, as quickly as my frozen fingers would allow, separated the Mazda key from the rest and slid it in the ignition with a determined warning. "You better start."

I turned the switch, and the engine roared to life along with some indiscernible heavy metal band that had been lurking in the CD player at full volume. I slammed my hand against the dash, splitting all the knobs from the deck, and they fell to the floorboards. I sat there for a moment in the relative quiet, then reached down and turned the heat on full, adjusting all of the louvers toward the back.

His gas gauge was at three-quarters; I figured I could leave the truck running, get back with Henry, and still have plenty of gas to get us all out of here. Where was my backup is what I wanted to know. I would have thought that once everybody had gotten the details of the plan somebody would have been here. I rolled down both front windows about an inch just in case George's luck stretched to carbon monoxide poisoning. I heard a low moan come from the back. I threw my arm over the passenger seat and stared at the lump under the blanket.

He began rubbing a hand over his jaw while simultaneously holding his leg with his other hand. "Ohl, gawhd . . ." It was garbled, but you could still make it out.

"George?"

One of the eyes opened a little, then rapidly closed. "Pwhlat?"

"Do you know who I am?" The eye partially opened again, and he strained to remember my face. "I'm Sheriff Longmire, remember me?" He nodded, slightly. "George, we're in a really bad situation here, so I need you to understand what I'm saying."

He grimaced and raised his head a little. "Whmy laghwurts . . ."

"Yep, I know your leg hurts, and I'd imagine your jaw doesn't feel too good right now, either. But I need you to listen to me. You're hurt, but I've got you stabilized. There's not a lot more I can do until we get you out of here. The problem is, I've got another man injured, back on the trail, and I need to go get him."

"Thehindiyan?"

"You remember him, huh? Do you remember shooting him?" He remained silent and didn't move. "Well, you did, and now I've got to go back and get him."

His eyes widened a little, and he blinked. "Whtryed tookill me . . ."

"No, he didn't. It's Henry Standing Bear, and he came up here with me to try and get you out safely." I sighed and tried to wrap it up. "George, we're stuck in a snowstorm, and I've got to go back and get Henry before it gets so I can't find him . . ."

"Whtryed tookill me . . ."

"No, George, he didn't try and kill you because, if he had tried, you and I wouldn't be having this conversation."

"Swhotme?"

"No, you shot yourself while you were trying to shoot me."

"Whtryed to . . ."

I leaned forward and glared at him for emphasis. "George? I need you to shut up." It must have worked because his eyes widened, but that was the only part of him that moved. "Here's what I need you to do; I need you to stay here and try and stay awake. Do you understand?"

He nodded his head.

"Good. I've got your truck going and the heater is on so it's going to warm up in here pretty quick. Now, here's the important part." I leaned in even farther. "No matter how long it takes me, you wait here. Got it?" I kept my eyes steady on him for a moment. "Good. Now just stay here and get warm. I'll be back, okay?"

I pulled the seat cover off from the passenger side and dragged it after me as I slid out into the snow and wind. I shut the door and wrapped myself up in the cover, pulling it high and making a hood. I pulled the radio from the small of my back and shook the condensation from it before it could freeze. "This is Walt Longmire, sheriff of Absaroka County, I've got an emergency with men down. Is there anybody out there? Over." I waited, but the static seemed fainter than it had before.

I looked back across the lot in the general direction of the trailhead, but the only thing visible over the top of the truck was my rapidly filling footprints that led into oblivion. I drove the radio back in the clip at the small of my back and started off. I clutched the seat cover tighter around me and discovered a series of vinyl pockets that ran along the front. I tucked my stiffening hands into two of the pockets and silently thanked George for spending the extra twenty on the luxury model. I felt around and found what felt like a church key and a large shop rag, which I pulled out and wrapped around my face. I'm sure I looked like a Bedouin: Ben el Napa. I chuckled to myself at the thought of Henry seeing me like this; he could just laugh himself to death.

There was a sudden grade as the parking lot ended and I thought the trailhead began. I peered through the snow as it dove around my makeshift hood, but I couldn't see the sign. The fact that it was eight feet high and at least six feet wide was less than encouraging. I tucked my head back into the nylon tweed cover and continued to trudge ahead. I was thinking that this was a poor excuse for a search if I couldn't even find the sign, when I ran my head into one of the telephone poles that supported the damn thing. My head really hurt, but at least I'd found the first indication that I was going in the right direction. The gusts pressed against my back and slapped the ends of my autoponcho around me.

What was I doing, what had I done? It was hard to think. It was darker now, and the snow had gotten worse. The flakes were smaller than the silver dollar ones of before, and they became tiny flat discs that hovered in the air, moving with its currents. They swirled, paused, and then dove into the distance, making me feel that I was falling backward no matter how hard I lumbered forward. I closed my eyes to clear my head, but the disorientation continued. It was definitely darker now; the depression of the path continued up the hill, and the shadows of the trees remained consistent on both sides. As long as I stayed between them and continued uphill, I would eventually get to him.

Henry hadn't been at the sentencing, but this hadn't been a surprise since he hadn't been at the trial at all. We hadn't been in touch during the case and, even though I was continually busy, I had gotten the distinct feeling that he was distancing himself from me. I don't know if I would have done anything different if I had spoken with Henry, and it was like he had said on the trail, in what seemed like another epoch, ignoring them was the best he could do. I wasn't sure if I could have shown that much restraint, given the circumstances.

Vern said that he had received about seventy-five letters about the sentencing, that they were split fifty-fifty on whether the boys should be granted some semblance of leniency or whether they should be horsewhipped all the way to Kemmerer. After he had taken his place on the bench, the defense pled for a sentence that would "reflect the homegrown values and sense of forgiveness that were a hallmark of frontier civilization." Even Ferg had to glance up at Steve Miller as he delivered that one, but his righteous tone and openly displayed conviction kept anyone from laughing out loud.

Each of the boys was allowed to stand and make a statement; it was the first time Bryan Keller had spoken in public about the rape. He stood and fanned his fingertips across the table before him. The whitening at his knuckles betrayed the fact that he needed assistance to stand, and we all waited. After a few moments, Vern spoke to him. "You wish to make a statement, Mr. Keller?"

"Yes . . ."—he cleared his throat—"I do, your honor." His head dropped as he studied the dull oak finish of the table. He took a deep breath and raised his head. "Your honor, my lawyer has advised me to remain silent, but to be honest with you I feel that I may have said nothing for too long." It had taken all the air out of him to get that far, and I wondered how much more he could get out before he hyperventilated. "I've thought a lot about all the things I've wanted to say, and I've had a long time to think about all of them. I've thought about the poor judgment I used that day, and how I'm older and that I hope you'll let me learn from this horrible mistake that I've made . . . But none of that seems important now. There's only one thing that's important for me to say now, and that is that I am sorry." He tilted his head back, and you could just see the beginnings of a shine to his eyes. "I want to tell Melissa that I am sorry; I want to tell her family that I am sorry for what I've put them through, to the people on the reservation for the things that have been said, to my family . . ." He stopped for a moment, then stood up straighter and allowed his hands to fall to his sides. "But the most important one is Melissa. I just want to tell her how sorry I am for what I've done to her and her life." He stood for a moment longer, then sat, with a hand shielding his eyes.

"George Esper?"

George stood and placed his hands in his pockets but quickly extracted them and allowed them to drop. His voice was soft and faded out at the ends of his sentences like someone unaccustomed to public speaking. "Your honor, you can't go back and change things that happened . . ." The majority of his apology was to the parents that sat behind him and tapered off from there.

"Jacob Esper?"

Jacob stood with fists at his sides. "Your honor, I'd like to say that I can't express the sorrow I feel." So he didn't. Instead, he made a general appeal at how sorry he was for everything and left it at that. I wondered mildly what everything entailed.

"Cody Pritchard, do you have anything you would like to say?"

He didn't move and remained seated with his hands in his pockets. After a moment, he smirked and said, "No." And I thought about how far I could get him through one of the second-story windows on one try.

Then Kyle Straub, the prosecuting attorney, stood and began the statement he hoped would assure that the defendants would serve significant jail time. He argued like a man on fire that these young men must not go free and that anything less than strong sentencing for all four would be the final punch line in the unending joke that this trial had become. Vern looked up at that one, too.

Because of their ages when they had raped Melissa Little Bird, Kyle anticipated that Vern might sentence the three young men convicted of rape to a youth facility rather than to a prison. Offenders sent to youth facilities were usually not given a minimum sentence, which placed the duration of imprisonment squarely on the shoulders of prison officials. All of which meant that the prosecution needed a five-year minimum sentence or the convicted would be available for parole in a much shorter period of time. The judge must set a minimum; even I got that.

I tripped but caught my balance before I buried myself in the snow. It was getting deeper, about at midcalf, and my plodding was becoming more forced. Other than my feet, the only part of me that consistently felt warm was my chin and nose. The smell of gasoline and used motor oil from the shop rag was beginning to get to me. My legs were tired, my back ached, and the seat cover was doing little as protection. With my hands embedded into the nylon pockets, I had been unable to keep the wind from periodically lifting up the rear of the poncho and sending a brisk nor'wester up my back, so my fingers became victims to my attempts at keeping the seat cover wrapped around me. They caused me the most pain, until they lost all feeling. The problem with stepping in the rut of the path was that my boots kept slipping on the angle, sometimes causing me to slide on the frozen, uneven ground. When this happened, I was forced to throw out my arms in an attempt to maintain my balance. It was in one of these equilibrium episodes that I lost it.

I hit the ground face first because my hands were tangled in the seat cover. It didn't hurt as badly as I thought it would, so I lay there for a moment as the snow next to my face began to melt. The stinging in my eyes bothered me, but it felt like a good place to rest. Somehow, it didn't feel as cold there on the ground, and a comfortable, dreamy quality began seeping in with the melting snow. I exhaled a breath to clear the snow away from my shop-rag veil, but it didn't clear very well. It should have bothered me, but it didn't. It felt like I was getting enough air, and enough was all I needed. I became aware of a weight that pressed down on every part of my body, like a warm blanket. I struggled a little to clear my hip from a rock that was pressing up from underneath the snow pack and felt a burning sensation in my right ear. Somehow it had gotten uncovered, so I jostled my right arm loose from the nylon and started working my hand up to the exposed flesh.

I listened to the wind and was thinking about just taking a short nap when I heard them. Their voices were high, shifting in and out of the wind along with the sound of chimes or maybe very small bells. It was bells, the sound of thousands of miniature bells, not finely tuned ones, but lesser bells, handmade bells. I listened as they swirled and rounded with the wind and snow. It was as if the bells were not ringing unto themselves but were brushing against something as they continued on their way, turning and stepping with the wind, starting a rhythm that overtook their circular motion. They had started in the distance, but it now seemed as if they were all around me, and they were insistent.

There were shadows too, but these were different from the ones I had seen before. These shadows moved in and out of the snow-covered trees with a different purpose, one that seemed more complicated than that of the ones before. Where the others had moved in a single line along with me, these seemed to enjoy the infinite patterns of the wind, the snow, the trees, and maybe other things that I could not see.

I lay there with my loose hand ready to close the small aperture of the seat-cover hood like a small child afraid to look yet afraid to look away. It was hard to see because my eyelids were trying to freeze shut; my fingers no longer moved individually so I rubbed the butt of my hand across my eyes and blinked to clear my sight. The swirling was right in front of my face now, and it carried the rhythm of many. The patterns swooped in close to the ground and then snapped back quickly as if teasing the ground to follow. I reached my hand out to touch one of the strands, but it slipped through my fingers with the snowflakes. I reached out farther but, every time I got close, the white tendrils whirled away. I placed my arm under me, pushed myself up on one elbow, and looked through my tunnel of snow-coated cloth. They were small, cone-shaped bells that chimed lightly as they moved in tiny rows across well-rounded cloth, which draped from opulent forms. The bells continued to ring even when the wind-fringe swept them away.

I pulled myself over to one side of the walking trench and sat there for a moment, listening to the voices, to the bells as they ascended into the treetops. These voices were in a higher register than the ones that had accompanied me on my way down, and they comforted and stimulated at the same time. I pulled the makeshift hood back and felt my head loll sideways onto my left shoulder. The long fringed fingers traced fire trails across the length of my shoulders, but when I turned they snapped into the retreating snow. I felt another set cross the small of my back, but when I straightened, they too continued up the trail. I pulled a leg under me, toppled into a crouch, and then stood. It was difficult to walk at first, but the rhythm of the tiny bells and the way the tassels and cloth stretched across languid muscles drew me forward.

Voices were speaking into my exposed ear, whispering in tongues that I didn't understand. I could never hear the beginnings or the ends of the sentences, only the smoldering playfulness that fueled them. The words simultaneously tickled and burned. Some were lugubrious and extended; others were short and sharp like surprised snatches of breath. I listened to the words and the melody and staggered upward, the hillside rising to meet my feet as they sank into the receptive snow. It was much deeper now, and the wind flattened the hanging cloth of the seat cover to the back of my legs and froze it there, pulling at the top of my head whenever a hind step lingered an instant too long.

I didn't pay any attention to the path any longer. I just followed the tinkling silver bells and the swirling deerskin as they continued in their circular pattern up the hill. Their mouths didn't smile, but their eyes did. The same glittering obsidian as before, but with a great deal more promise, with promises of everything under arched eyebrows and thick lashes.

The ground grew flatter for a while and then steepened in the opposite direction as my heels began striking the muffling snow before my toes. The momentum carried me forward, and I only slowed as the other voices joined in, the voices from before. They provided a strong bass counterpoint to the ascension of the bells and harmonized with the wavering beauty of the voices that had gone before me up the hill. Then, on the path ahead, I could see them standing in a group, looking down at something on the ground. They all smiled the close-mouthed smile and looked back to me. I trudged on and stood there among them, looking around and smiling, too. But there was something at the middle of the group, something that didn't move, and I rested my chin on my chest to look at it. It was large and it looked heavy, but they seemed to prize it in some way, so I leaned down and brushed some of the snow away. When I finished brushing the majority of the snow off it, I stood back with the others and listened to a new song, one that sounded much closer, with words that I remembered. I could hear all of this song, the beginning, middle, and end. It was a very forceful melody, and it was coming from the thing in the path.

We listened to it for a while, all of us smiling, and then they began breaking away. But before each one of them began their swirling and swooping and snapping, they motioned for me to take the thing in the trail as a gift. I stepped back as they offered it to me. Two of them each took one of my hands and placed them on the object before us. It sang louder as I touched it, and I reached around and pulled it from the ground, as the remaining snow sloughed off. It was heavy and cumbersome to carry, but it seemed ungracious not to take it. Its song became strained as I loaded it onto my back.

The snow seemed to part as I moved forward in time with the bodies in the shadows to my left and right. There were small flashes in the darkness ahead, as if they were clearing a path for me, muted flashes of crimson and cobalt within the smothering white. My legs began to shake with the weight of the gift, but dropping it in the face of such hospitality would be unendurable, so I kept walking. Soon the flat gave way to a gentle downward slope, and the images tilted the world in my favor, allowing me longer strides and easier breathing through the cotton cloth that was now frozen to my face. I didn't feel the cold anymore and noticed a jaunty quality accompanied my step as I matched it with the music of the small jingle bells and with the pace of the darting figures all around me.

The best part of the song emanated from the gift I carried. It caught all the complex rhythms and melodies of the group and conveyed it in a singular fashion so that it was easier to understand. Its voice was right behind my head, and its strength reverberated through me and into the ground with each step. But, after a while, the song changed and became more maudlin and extended. I shook the weight on my back to get it to switch back to the melody from before, but that didn't work. It was harder to get my stride back with the new song since the patterns were not even and my steps wouldn't match. I was beginning to wonder what was so great about the gift they had given me when I passed the spot where I had taken the little nap on the way up.

I was thinking about taking another one, but others had joined in with the song on my back, and the whole thing took on the feeling of a processional. I didn't want to be the first to break step, so I just kept going. After a while, I became aware of a large shape up and off to my right. I remembered it as being something important, but I couldn't remember why or what it was. There was a sharper drop off as I made my way around that shape, and I almost lost my footing as I skirted it. I had a vague recollection of it having hurt me in the past, but it seemed benign enough now. I stood at a flat spot and struggled to stay upright. I remembered that there was something waiting for me just a little ways ahead, so I started off once more, but the voices lingered in the shadows behind me. They had elected to stay in the forest, and I would have turned to look back at them, but it would have taken more energy than I had. I felt bad about not saying good-bye. The song on my back continued, although the quality of its tone had weakened. I had to get where I was going before the song on my back stopped. I wasn't sure how I knew this, but I did.

I started forward again and, as I came across an area where the snow was shallower, I remembered a promise that had been made to me. It was something important, too. It was a promise about leaving. All the important promises are about leaving or not leaving. I thought about turning around to see what it was that I was leaving, but if you did that enough, you didn't leave, and then what were all the promises about? I kept walking. I could barely hear the song on my back now, so I shook it to try and get it going. It stopped. I shook it some more, trying to get it going again, but it still wouldn't start. I thought about dropping it since it didn't work anymore, but they might be watching from the trees.

I guess they figured I needed some help, because the flashes were back, crimson and cobalt flares that lit up the snow in a rhythm of their own, but the spirits must have been getting tired too, because the lights seemed to have lost their individuality and were blinking in a monotonous and irritating fashion. The music was gone, the bells and the drums and the voices had drifted off with the wind. I listened, but there was only an ugly squawking. I shook the song on my back, but it remained obstinate. I figured it was probably the cold, that some part of it must have frozen. I would have to see if I could fix it once I got to where I was going. I tried to remember where it was I was going, but all I could think of was that it was warmer there. I was about ready to set the song down and take a rest, but the shadows were there again. Some of them stepped out from the snow clouds to my right, and I was just starting to see the ones to my left when I noticed that, unlike the others, they were coming straight at me. The only thing I could figure was that they wanted the song back.

Indian givers.

I stopped and stood up straight. I was a lot bigger than they were, now that we were on level ground. They stopped as well, but their arms reached out to the song; I whirled around a half step to let them know that they couldn't have it. I tried to speak, but it was as if my vocal chords were frozen, so I just roared and took a few quick breaths to get ready for the fight.

The smallest one was directly ahead of me; it was the one that had backed off the least. I focused on that shadow and leaned in to smash it. It still didn't move, but just stood there, hipshot and kind of crooked, like most of its weight was resting on one side with a hand on its hip. You had to be careful, because the little ones might be just as powerful as the big ones. It didn't really matter how big they were, or how many of them there were though, I wasn't giving up the song. The little one still didn't move, and I was just getting ready to crush it when it spoke in a sharp and unpleasant yet strangely familiar voice. "Nice fuckin' outfit."

Later, when I rolled my head over and found Henry looking at me through barely open eyes, as the EMT van slowly made its way through the drifts that had accumulated throughout the evening and on into the night, I asked him if he thought it had been wise to be singing all that time with the internal injuries he'd sustained.

Groggily, all he said was, "What singing?"

13

"What do you mean, you released yourself on your own recognizance?"

"I rang the bell a bunch of times, but nobody came around." I was trying to look reputable, but it was difficult with the clothes I was wearing.

"So you just left?" We stood there for a moment, looking at each other. "They're on the phone, and they want to know where you are!"

Ruby had a point, and in hindsight it did seem a little irresponsible. I straightened some of my papers and tried to look busy. "Well, tell them I'm here."

"You tell them. Explain to the doctor why it is he can't find you anywhere in his hospital."

I stared down at the blinking red light; I had to get a different color. It was still early, and the sky was getting a little bruised yellow to the east. The tail end of the storm was tapering off to the Powder River country, but the skies still stayed mostly gray. They said it was over, but I felt like it might be stalking me. I remained there for a while, not allowing the pain in my fingers and ear to get the best of me. I could hear Lucian chuckling to himself in the hallway. Changing of the guard. I had timed it poorly; if I had arrived earlier, I could have gotten things going and hit the road before Ruby had shown up for duty.

I woke up very early and couldn't get back to sleep, so I lay there and thought about Henry. I rang the little bell for the night nurse and waited about five minutes. Then I rang it again and again. A half an hour went by, and I decided to go look for the Bear myself. The IVs were the biggest pain in the ass, but they came out pretty easily, and the tape covered the holes so that the bleeding stopped. I had dismissed the idea of dragging them along with me, as they would cut down on this particular mission's stealthy quality. The nurse had hidden my personal belongings, but I found them in a locker near her station, which was, I had learned, the safest place to avoid her. There was a little cardboard sign on the desk that said, IN CASE OF EMERGENCY, CONTINUE TO THE CLINIC OR RING BELL. I'm cagey that way, so I didn't ring the bell or go to the clinic.

There was a guy who might have been part Crow mopping the hallway when I came back to my room to change into my clothes. He had the sickly look that everybody adopts after working nights for a while; I had had that look before. "How you doin'?" He stared at my gown and the clothes I clutched to my chest but didn't say anything. He leaned on his mop and stared at me some more. "You know where they stuck Henry Standing Bear?" He motioned the mop handle toward the room across from mine: 62. We stood there for a moment longer. "Thanks."

He continued mopping, and I ducked into my room to get dressed. My hands were swollen and starting to blister, and it was only with a great deal of difficulty that I snapped my shirt. The rubber boots were the hardest part so I finally left them unlaced. My hat hadn't been with the rest, and I paused for a moment to think about when I had seen it last. I thought it was on the mountain, but I couldn't be sure. I fingered the glob of tape attached to the side of my head and felt the tenderness that must have been my ear. It hurt worse than anything else, but at least they hadn't cut it off.

By the time I opened the door and looked around, the guy with the mop had moved on to another hallway or had gone to fetch the elusive nurse. I quickly moved across the hall and into the room opposite, hoping it was the right one. I stood there in the dark, letting my eyes adjust. It was a mirror image of mine, with the exception that it did not look out on the parking lot. The breathing was heavy, regular, and familiar. I moved carefully to the bed and looked down. He seemed to be all there and, short of pulling down the sheet and examining the wound myself, I would have to go on the assumption that he was doing all right. He had a couple of IVs stuck in him too, but there weren't any monitors attached and that gave me hope. I looked around for a clipboard at the foot of his bed that would tell me how he was, but there wasn't one. Durant Memorial Hospital was doing little to live up to the expectations I had developed as a teenager watching *Ben Casey.*

I wasn't sure what else to do, and I wasn't certain why I was here, other than to just make sure he was alive and well. They lie a lot in hospitals; it's their job, to supercede the power of the Almighty with half-truths. Better to check things out for yourself. I was about halfway to the door when he spoke. "Thank you for the visit."

I stopped and crept back. "I left the Whitman Sampler on the nightstand."

"Very thoughtful."

I took a breath. "How do you feel?"

"Doped."

"Must be nice; all I got was some Tylenol."

He rolled his head toward me a little, looking at my clothes. "Where are you going?"

"To look for George Esper."

"You want to kill him before somebody else does?"

I continued to look at him. "You aren't that doped up."

"I was just thinking of calling and asking for some more."

"Good luck." I patted his arm and started to back toward the door. "Get some rest."

"Walt?" I stopped. "Thanks."

When I got into the hallway there was still nobody there, so I quickly made my way around the corner. To my utter surprise, a nurse sat at the nurse's station. She was looking at me so I marched straight over to her, crossed my arms, leaned on the chest-high partition, and draped my hands by my side where she couldn't see them. There was nothing I could do about the ear. "Hi. I was just checking

on a patient here, Henry Standing Bear. You've got him in room 62."
She had sandy hair, china-blue eyes, and looked like she was about
fourteen.

"Yes?"

"He was complaining about some pain, and I was wondering if
somebody could get him more medication?"

She seemed a little distracted as she picked up a phone. "Certainly."
She looked at me a little more closely. "Aren't you in room 61, Uncle
Walter?"

I glanced around as if it were obvious. "No, I'm not." I looked at
her more carefully. "Do I know you?"

"I'm Janine Reynolds. I'm Ruby's granddaughter."

The eyes started to look more familiar, so I smiled. "How you
doin', Janine?"

She didn't smile back. "What are you doing out of room 61?"

I thought for a moment. "Official business."

The brat, she had called her grandmother and told her everything,
especially the part where I didn't know her from Adam. Maybe they
had given me more than Tylenol; at least that's what I told Ruby. I sat
at my desk and watched as Lucian ambled in on his man-made leg and
occupied the chair opposite mine. He was studying me with more
scrutiny than I was comfortable with. "What?"

"I bet'cha they take that ear."

I sighed. "Just because they're always taking parts off of you . . ."

"'At's what they do best, take parts off."

"I'm pretty fond of this ear."

He scratched his stump. "Yeah, well I was pretty damn fond of
my leg."

I waited. "Anybody got any idea where George might've gone?"

He leaned back in the chair, hands spread onto his thighs with the
fingers stretched. "Got an APB out, but them HPs are about as useless
as tits on a boar hog."

"How did he get out before Vic and Ferg got in?"

He shrugged. "Must 'a left right after you left him, in that little Jap piece of crap." His head leaned to one side, and he was the perfect picture of disgruntled as he gazed at the floor. "Little shit bird." He looked back up. "Stop playing with your ear." I had been. "Yer gonna do more damage playin' with it than you did freezin' it."

I decided to change the subject. "Where is everybody?"

"Turk's still out at the Esper place. Guess he's tryin' to work his way back into your good graces. Ferg was running some food out to 'im, but that was an hour ago." He grunted. "Ferg's got your hat."

"I was wondering where it had gone off to."

"You're gonna need it to hide that half ear you're gonna have."

I sighed some more. "Vic?"

"Up at the DCI compound." He said it with the same derisive conviction he had for the highway patrol. He looked out the window at the frozen sky. "What'd the little pissant get shot with?" I felt around in the jacket I still had on and tossed the gun onto the desk with a satisfying clatter. I was showing Lucian that I could be tough, too. Next thing you knew, we'd be breaking out the bourbon and calling Ruby a twist; then the real fun would start. He looked at the little revolver. "That ought'a do it." His eyes came up to mine. "How bad?"

"Not bad enough to keep him from jumping in the driver's seat and leaving us in the lurch."

I leaned forward on the desk and told Lucian about the Vasques, size nines, and about the conversation I had had with George before I had gone back for Henry. He neither responded nor remarked until I was through; just sat there looking at me. I was remembering what a good lawman he was when he finally spoke. "Well, he's gotta get doctored somewhere." He cleared his throat. "Seems to me you just left the place where you should 'a started looking for him."

"You don't think he's stupid enough to go to the hospital?"

"He was stupid enough to be up there fishing in a blizzard, stupid enough to try and shoot you and Ladies Wear, stupid enough to try and make a run for it." He stopped, shook his head, and folded his arms over his chest to signify the particular gaps in my line of thinking. "I'd say the depths of his stupidity have yet to be plumbed, and yours is comin' up fast on the inside turn."

I had gotten a lot of tirades like this when I was a deputy under Lucian, but I didn't take them personally, much. "So, we've got the hospitals and doctors' offices, but they have to report any kind of gunshot wounds."

"You couldn't get 'em to answer a bell, how long you think it'll take 'em to file a report?"

He had a point. "You want to take a ride?"

"I'm saddled and, if you're waitin' for me, yer backin' up."

It was like working with Louis L'Amour.

Ruby stopped me as we tried to make our way out of the office. "Do you think you should make an attempt at cleaning up?"

I looked down at the stains and rumples that made up today's and yesterday's ensemble. "Lets the citizens know they're getting their money's worth."

"You have dried blood all down your back."

I dodged out the door before she could say anything else, with Lucian cadging along after me. I gave the old sheriff a hand as he pulled himself up into the truck. He took out his pipe and a small, beaded leather pouch of tobacco and began filling the cherry-wood bowl. I noticed the pattern on the small bag and recognized it as the same as the Dead Man's Body on the Cheyenne Rifle. I informed Lucian of this. He looked at the pouch anew as the smoke drifted around his head and his dark eyes and out the window he had just cracked. "Well, I'll be damned."

Going back to the hospital was risky business, but it was a chance I was going to have to take. Lucian waited patiently as Isaac Bloomfield looked over my hands and examined my ear while I questioned him about any other gunshot wounds that might have popped up last evening. He said there had been nothing suspicious to report, but that if anything came up he'd be sure to get a hold of me as quickly as possible. I asked about Henry, but all he did was kind of chuckle and said the nurses were taking very good care of him. I feared for Janine Reynolds's virginity. Much to Lucian's dismay, he, my entire ear, and myself left shortly thereafter. We continued our search to the drugstore downtown where they reported that they had not sold a single Band-Aid since yesterday afternoon. It was a tough economy on the high plains. I turned and looked at him as I started the truck. "Veterinarians?"

"Taxidermists."

I'm not sure why, but it made sense. "Which one?"

He pulled on his pipe and studied the problem; one thing we had no shortage of in Wyoming is taxidermists. "How 'bout that outfit of Pat Hampton's down on Swayback Road?"

I wheeled the Bullet into a U-turn and headed south; a few vehicles slowed and the drivers gave me irritated looks. Lucian shot them the bird, and I slapped his hand down as he snickered and told me to turn on the lights and siren to show them we meant business. I figured he just wanted to run them again, so I did. I navigated the entrance ramp of the highway at the south side and, since there wasn't any snow on the road, took the truck up to about eighty-five. He didn't say anything, just looked ahead, and I figured I was going to hear about it. I was right, but it wasn't what I thought it would be. "What you did up there?"

"Yep?"

"That was a hell of a thing." I nodded and looked ahead too. I didn't tell him about the Old Cheyenne.

Pat Hampton's was an odd mixture of taxidermy and game processing. It was said that no matter what you wanted to do with an animal, Pat could assist you. When we pulled up to the ramshackle complex of dilapidated buildings, you could have knocked me over with a feather. Pulled around to the far side of one of the buildings, covered with mud and with the side caved in, was a black Mazda Navajo with the plates, Tuff-1.

"Bonzai." The old sheriff smiled and pulled the pipe from his mouth as I eased the Bullet up to the other side of the building. "You got a gun I can borrow?"

I unlocked the 870 Wingmaster from the dash. "This kid is a victim."

He looked at the shotgun. "Fugitive from justice."

"Lucian, do me a favor and don't shoot anybody."

He jacked the pump action and fed a shell of double-ought buck into the breech. "Ain't nothin' wrong with shootin' folks, long as the right ones get shot." The next five minutes promised an inordinate variety of excitements. I pulled out my .45 and checked it, like I always did, then reholstered it, snapping the leather strap over the hammer. The old outlaw smiled. "Front or back?"

I looked at the accumulation of buildings, trying to figure out which was which. "I'll take the front." The Remington waved in my direction as he navigated the door, and I was acutely aware that he had not put on the safety. I walked across the muddy slush of the lot to what looked like it might be the front as Lucian swung-stepped his way around the corner of the ratty, brown-painted building. There were boot prints leading up to the aluminum screen door that had only some battered strips of screening still attached. There was a plastic sign in the window, flyspecked and bleached by the sun. In swirling letters it read, SORRY, WE'RE CLOSED.

There were ancient blinds in the windows, but there was a small, diamond-shaped pane in the door that was unshaded. I poked my head through the empty frame of the screen and looked through the dirty glass. I could see an odd combination of living room and reception area with sofas, a console television, and some sort of strange reception desk. I noted the hallway leading to the right, after you got past the desk, and figured that was where I should go once I'd gotten through the door.

"Sheriff's Department!" I pounded on the door with the flat of my hand. "George, if you're in there? Let's not make things worse!" I listened as a shuffling noise came from the center of the building. I took a deep breath and checked the knob. It was locked. I banged on the door again. "Sheriff's Department, I'm coming in!" I took another couple of breaths and unsnapped the strap from the top of my holster. I only had a certain amount of time before Lucian came in the rear, but I figured having only one leg would slow him up in kicking his own door down. I carefully swung back the screen-door frame so as to not get caught in it and pulled the Colt from my holster, clicking the safety off and holding it in the air. I leaned back and put everything into a fourteen E width.

I guess I was expecting a little more resistance from the rotting, hollow-core door, because I followed it rather rapidly as it folded up into two main pieces and blew us into the room and onto the sofa at the opposite wall. I heard a loud thumping at my right and pushed off the couch, cleared the doorway at the hall, and ran toward the noise. When I got to the entryway at the opposite end, somebody was coming the other way but didn't see me until it was too late. I just kept running and carried him back into the room as I led with the point of my unarmed shoulder. I heard the air leave his body as we went back through the doorway, and he felt familiar. Hello, George.

We bounced off a large table at the center and slid to the cool, tile surface of the floor. I steadied myself against the countertop with one hand and stood. It was George all right, and he was out again. He was only partially dressed and still held his pants in his hands. There was a large wrapping of bandages at the middle of his right thigh and another set around his head that was holding his jaw secure.

I stood the rest of the way up, pulled out my handcuffs, and secured George to the table. As I finished this, there was noise down the hallway, and an explosion that was unmistakable as the sound of a 12 gauge shotgun being discharged filled the air. I started to head down the corridor when another young man with a pale face came bursting through the doorway with what looked like a rifle in his hands. When he saw the barrel of the .45 about a foot from his nose, he pulled up short and froze. "Sheriff's Department, you don't move."

His hands went straight up, along with the rifle. "I won't."

"You just did." He looked confused for a moment. "Drop the rifle." He hesitated for a second. "You got a problem?"

He was still frozen. "It might go off."

"All right, you keep it pointed away from me and set it down on the table." He did as requested, and I told him to stretch forward and place his hands on the counter, palms down. He did this, and it seemed like he was going to cry. I had a moment to look at him; he was just about George's age. It all figured.

"Lucian! You all right?" There was a little more clatter, and he answered from the distance, "Yes, goddamn it!"

I went around the corner of the table and looked at the kid's rifle and propped the butt against my hip. "A pellet gun?"

His face turned toward mine. "It's all I had, and I didn't want to hurt anybody . . ."

Lucian appeared in the doorway, shotgun at the ready. "Damn door was locked."

I sat on the edge of the table and stuck the pellet rifle under an arm as I put my sidearm back in the holster and looked at the kid, trying to place him. "Well, where's Pat? He away?"

Lucian planted one of his formidable claws at he back of the kid's neck. "Yeah." I watched as Lucian's grip tightened. "Hey!" His voice strained.

"You say 'sir' . . ." Lucian leaned in over the boy's head. "Yes, sir."

The voice was even more strained. "Yes, sir."

"Lucian?"

He let up a little bit and looked at me questioningly. "What? I ain't hurtin' the little pissant." He rolled his eyes, stepped back to the doorway, and poked the kid with the barrel of the Remington before resting a shoulder against the facing. "Don't you forget that I'm here, son." Even from my perspective, I could see that the safety was still not on.

"He's down in Casper, buying a truck."

"Are you Petie Hampton, Bruce's boy?"

He smiled at being recognized. "Yes, sir."

"I thought you were in school down in Colorado?"

280

The smile hung there. "I'm home to hunt for the weekend."

"How did George know you were coming up?"

"I called him last week; he was going to go with me."

I pulled the pellet gun from my underarm and broke the barrel down, used a fingernail to pull the pellet in the tiny gun out, and let the small, mushroom-shaped projectile fall to the floor. I tossed the rifle onto a desk filled with taxidermy supplies, which made a tremendous noise. "Okay, Petie. We've got two options here. Number one is me reading you your rights and taking you up to town and booking you on at least resisting arrest and with a criminal conspiracy charge that's gonna look really good on your transcript, or you and I just have a little chat and we don't tell your school or your daddy and uncle what you've been up to."

It didn't take him long to answer; maybe the college thing was working out. "What do you want to know?"

It was about that time that there was a clamoring at the other end of the table; George Esper must have awakened, heard a little bit of what was being said, and decided once again to make a break for it. The table moved about six inches, even with my weight on it, when George reached the end of his stainless-steel tether. A low moan emanated from below the other end of the table as Lucian walked around and looked down at him. "Son, I have met some sorry little bastards in my life . . ."

"Lucian, don't abuse the prisoner."

He looked up with his mouth pulled to one side. "Hell, I ain't the one that shot 'im and broke his jaw."

"He shot himself."

"Yeah, that's your story . . ."

I turned back to Petie, who had not moved, but whose eyes seemed a little wider. "What's the story on Houdini down here?" He looked confused, so I nodded toward the moaning. "George."

He cleared his throat. "He called me this morning, real early. He said he had a hunting accident and that he didn't want to go to the hospital because it was going to cost a lot." I nodded. "He showed up, with his jaw and all? I started thinking that there might be something else going on."

"You doctored him up?"

"Yes, sir."

"He got here when?"

"About an hour ago."

"What all did he have to say?" Petie looked at the ceiling, and I sighed. "Petie, I think you are considering lying to me, and I would advise you against it."

"He said he ran his car off the road."

"Anything about his parents?"

"He said they were in Deadwood." Well, that answered a few questions.

Outside, I placed George in the passenger seat of the Bullet and found his keys in the bunched pants he still had on his lap. I tossed the keys to Lucian. "What am I supposed to do with these?"

"He drove the thing with one leg, I figure you can too. Go get Turk out at the Espers. I'm headed to the hospital to get George here looked at."

"You ought to kick his skinny little ass, but you do as you see fit."

When I got in, George was looking at the steering column for the keys to my truck. When he caught my eye, he leaned against the door and began moaning, with his eyes partially closed. "George, so far your situation is not irretrievable. Henry Standing Bear is unlikely to press charges, and I'll do what I can about the mandatories if you tell me everything I want to know." One eye opened a little more. "Where are your parents?"

He started to speak, then put a hand to his mouth in an attempt to still the pain. "Dehdwoo."

I keyed the mic on my radio. "Come in Base, this is Unit One." I waited as Lucian backed the Mazda out and pulled up beside me with a questioning look. I held up the mic to show him what was up; he nodded and headed off for the Espers. The entire side of the little truck was dented from one end to the other. "Come in, Base."

Static. "What do you want now?"

"Ruby, the Espers are in Deadwood, South Dakota. Can you make the appropriate inquiries?"

Static. "How did you find that out?"

"I am sitting here with the elusive George Esper."

Static. "Does he know where they're staying?"

I looked over at George, who was now watching me with both eyes. "Lowsla."

"Loadstar?" He nodded. I keyed the mic. "The Loadstar. Any word from up on the mountain?"

Static. "They're on their way down."

"Roger that. I'll be over at the hospital."

Static. "Ten-four."

I stared at the radio. "What'd you just say?"

Static for a moment, then a sharp response. "I wouldn't press my luck, if I were you."

I started the truck, wheeled around, and headed back for the highway. The gravel road wasn't too bad, but George moaned with a little more persistence every time the truck bounced. He was back in full victim mode. "Your parents gambling in Deadwood?" I glanced over at him. "Just nod your head yes or no." He nodded yes and looked out the windshield. "Your brother with 'em?" He shook his head. "Was he supposed to meet you fishing up on the mountain?" He nodded, then, after a second, turned to look at me. I looked back at the road and nodded a little myself. "We'll talk some more about that at the hospital."

His eyes stayed on me, and I was convinced he wasn't the Vasques, size nines we were looking for. "Eesurt?"

"No, he's not hurt." It wasn't a complete lie. "We just need to get you repaired." I changed the subject. "Sorry about the jaw."

He nodded and slouched farther against the door. He really was a mess. I don't think the second altercation had done him much good, and the symptoms of the first were plainly evident. The discoloration from his jaw had spread to his eyes, and the swelling had puffed his face so that he was almost unrecognizable. There was that, and the fact that being confused with his brother wouldn't be an issue anymore. The radio interrupted my thoughts. "Come in Unit One?" Static. "I've got the Espers on line one. You want me to patch them through?"

I glanced over at George, who was studying me very closely. "No, just get the number, and I'll call them back in about five minutes."

Static. "Roger that." I looked at the radio and smiled.

By the time we got to the hospital, it was looking like a cop convention; both Vic's and Ferg's vehicles were parked in the official spots at the emergency room entrance. I pulled up to the door and walked around to get George. There was a small crowd at the desk when I made my way in. "You know, just because you're as big as a bus, doesn't mean you have to provide service like one." I casually bumped past her and sat George in the wheelchair that Janine had pulled from the wall.

"He's got a gunshot wound in his left thigh, and I think his jaw's busted. You better check his ribs. Thanks, Janine." She rolled George away, and I nodded for Ferg to follow them. As he passed, he patted my shoulder and smiled. I called after him, "Hey, you got my hat?"

He smiled some more. "It's on the desk."

I watched them go down the hallway, then walked over and picked up the now disreputable piece of 10X beaver felt. It needed a little work. I was dusting it off as a sharp index finger punched my stomach. It didn't go in as far as it used to. I turned to look at her. "Yes, ma'am?"

"What are you doing out of here?"

"I released myself."

She shook her head, but the poking stopped. "You looked like you were going to die last night."

"They gave me Tylenol. I'm feeling much better." I gave her a thumb's up. "What's the story on DCI?"

She looked at me for a moment longer. "Headed for Cheyenne with Jacob." She looked down the hallway after George and his entourage. "What's the word on him?"

I walked past the glass partition at the reception area, over to the waiting room, and sat back in one of the chairs; she followed along and did likewise. I looked at the soothing gray that must have been chosen, along with the muted mauve of the walls, to calm upset relatives and loved ones. It made me want to take a nap. "I honestly don't think he knows anything."

"What about the size nine Vasques?"

I studied my coveralls and thought about a shower and a change of clothes. "I don't think it was him. It could be the guy from Casper, or Jacob, or it could be somebody else . . ."

Vic studied the side of my face in the humming fluorescence. "You make it sound like somebody else."

I turned to look at her. "I want to talk to Jim Keller."

She raised an eyebrow. "About?"

"Things in general, nothing specific." She looked tired too, but I decided to keep that to myself. "You get a ballistics check on the Cheyenne Rifle of the Dead?"

"Yes, I did."

I had started to turn and study my dirty pants, but the tone of her voice pulled me right back around. "Oh, now, why do I not like the sound of that?"

"No match, but it's been fired."

I was glad I was sitting down. "How long ago?"

She inclined her head. "Difficult to say, anywhere from three days to three weeks."

"Did DCI take the rifle?"

"No." She smiled. "Everybody's real nervous about handling that thing."

"Because it's haunted?"

"Because it's probably worth millions"—I hadn't told her about the Old Cheyenne and their assistance on the mountain—"And it's fucking haunted." She was looking at my hands. "I put it in your truck and locked the doors."

"Thanks a lot." I smiled at her because I liked her. Vic was like some exotic eastern bird that had accidentally landed in our high desert and had taken it upon herself to stay, and I don't know what I would have done if she hadn't. It was a profane little song she sang, but I had grown fond of it, like the first cries of the meadowlarks in the early spring. She had a quirky perspective on things and a foul mouth, but she would make a fine sheriff, no matter what anybody said or what words they used to say it. "How's your love life?" That caught her off guard.

"Shitty, how's yours?"

I shrugged and looked at the carpet. "How should I know?"

"She was here." I turned and looked at her with a questioning expression. "Vonnie."

"Oh, shit."

"Yeah." She crossed her arms and looked at her legs stretched out before her. "She brought flowers, but I told her you weren't dead. I don't think she thought I was funny."

"Most people don't."

"Most people around here got no fucking sense of humor." She didn't move for a while. "Can I ask you a question, without you getting all pissed off?"

"I'll try."

She pursed her lips. "What is it you see in her? I mean, other than she's beautiful, intelligent, and rich? I just don't get it." I pounded the crown back into my hat and made an attempt at straightening the brim. Relatively satisfied with the results, I placed it on my head and pulled it down. She finally spoke again. "I always wanted to be a woman like her. I think it's because she's tall." She turned and looked at me. "It doesn't seem fair that somebody should be beautiful, intelligent, rich, and tall. That's bullshit."

I waited. "How's my hat look?"

She considered. "Like Gabby Hayes."

I tried for another subject, the third being a charm. "You been in to see Henry?"

"I was, but then Dena Many Camps showed up, and I started feeling like a third wheel."

I moved my head back and forth like a disco dancer. "He gettin' some sweet medicine?" I put my arm around her shoulders and pulled her in. It was a risky move, but she didn't resist, and I rested my chin on the top of her head. "Thanks for coming up after me."

Her voice was muffled and sounded strained. "You're the only friend I've got."

"I bet you say that to all the sheriffs." I held her there for a while. Her husband was an idiot. We stayed that way until I became aware of somebody looking at us through the glass partition. It was Vonnie. She didn't say anything, just nodded and disappeared around the desk and down the hall where everybody else had disappeared. She was carrying a shopping bag and the aforementioned bouquet of flowers. I pulled Vic back up and looked at her. "You okay?"

She smiled, but it seemed as if there was a little more ocean at the corners of her eyes. "Yeah, I'm good."

I leaned her back and kissed her forehead. "Yep, you are." I staggered up and steadied myself on my increasingly sore legs. "Vonnie just walked by."

She nodded. "I get you into trouble?"

"I don't think we're to a place where I can get into trouble."

She stood. "That's what most guys think when they're in trouble." She turned the corner and walked toward the automatic doors. As they opened, she paused, making them wait. "I'll be at the office. It's getting crowded in here."

I followed Vonnie's trail and found her leaning against the wall outside room 62; she was holding the flowers with the shopping bag at her feet. Her long hair was pulled back in the single ponytail that she had worn to watch football with Henry and me, only a few days ago. The lines in her face were more evident today, in the harsh lighting, but they gave her a delicate appearance like some fragile and beautiful tapestry. Seeing her again was like unearthing an emotional library card with a lot of overdues. I slowed as I got nearer, a little worried about what might be coming. She looked up as I approached. "Thank God you're all right."

It was good that I stopped, because those eyes were just a little bit hard. "How did you find out?"

Her jaw set, and an awful lot of the wrinkles disappeared. "I bought a police scanner at Radio Shack, thinking it would be nice to hear your voice once in a while."

We stood there for a moment and listened as a female giggled through the walls of the Bear's room. "I didn't call."

"No, you didn't."

I nodded and looked at my boots. "I've been kind of busy."

She stood away from the wall, the flowers clutched in her hand like a Louisville Slugger. "Did you know that they could hear you? That I could hear you? We heard every word you said, and you couldn't hear anything when they answered?"

"No."

"I could hear it all." Her head nodded in a tense fashion. "I could hear everything. Do you know what that's like, hearing those words and not being able to do anything?" She threw the flowers, and they hit me in the chest. "I have spent my whole life getting to a place where I don't have to put up with things like this."

"I'm sorry."

"I will not let you do this to me; I will not." She stormed past, and I raised a feeble hand to stop her. She yanked her arm away and pointed to the shopping bag on the floor. "I thought you could use a change of clothes." She stood there for a moment, and I thought there might be some kind of opening, but there wasn't, and she continued down the hallway as I turned and watched her go.

I sighed and stooped down to pick up the flowers. As tired as I had been before, I was twice that now. I figured there were better places to take a nap, but fatigue set in and I sat down with my legs stretched out in front of me. It felt good to stretch them, and my back was starting to hurt, so I just laid back and sprawled out on the tile floor of the hallway. I placed the flowers on my chest in a fit of symbolism and closed my eyes.

More giggling slipped from under the door of the Bear's room.

I lay there for a while, thinking that what I ought to do was get up, find a shower, and change into the clothes Vonnie had so thoughtfully provided. I wondered how she knew my size and thought about what she had said. I was feeling sorry for myself, and it felt pretty good; so, I just lay there musing in self-pity, thinking about life, death, and a shower, in that order.

More giggling.

I had to eat something. I had to talk to the Espers and tell them about Jacob and try to confirm all of the suppositions as to what Jacob and George's plans had been, where they had been, and what had happened. My five minutes had run out a half an hour ago. I had to speak with Jim Keller, and it wouldn't hurt to have a word with Lonnie Little Bird about the last time the Cheyenne Rifle of the Dead had been fired.

Even more giggling.

I could also talk to the Little Wolf woman to see if there were any more clues as to where the feathers might have gone to and come from. I needed to follow up on the Vasques, size nines, and get a better idea on who might have been leaving tracks all over God's little acre in them. I didn't think it was George, but there was the disturbing habit he had of running off every time he got the chance. He had been so sure that Henry had tried to kill him on the trail that I began wondering if that might have been one of the motivations behind his constant state of flight. I also wanted to check on Henry and get a more thorough diagnosis on how he was doing. The first part was in getting my eyes to open and, when I did, an upside down Janine Reynolds's blues were there to meet me. "Hi, Janine."

She looked a little worried. "I thought you might want something to eat?"

"Bless you."

She looked around and then back down to me. "Are you okay?"

"Just thinking." I reached over and picked up my hat where it had fallen during my dramatic interpretation. I looked at the flowers, still clutched in my other hand. "You want some flowers?"

"No, thanks."

I pushed up and slid over to the wall as she handed a tray down to me. It was some sort of supposed egg matter that I'm sure had never seen the rear end of a chicken and two grayish meat patties that had never oinked. I placed my hat beside me with the brim up and placed the flowers in it. I rested the tray on my lap and picked up a piece of dry toast and began chewing. No wonder so many people died here, they starved to death. Whatever this was, it was not the usual. "Janine, is there a shower around here?"

She blinked. I guess it was a strange request. "There's the one in the staff locker room."

"Would anybody mind if I used it?"

"I don't think so; you're kind of a local hero."

I continued chewing my toast and began wondering if it was real bread. "Why's that?"

"Because of what you did up there."

Everybody talked about the mountains as if they were on the second floor. I was uncomfortable with flattery, so I asked her how the Cheyenne Nation was doing. She said that he had turned out to be remarkably resilient and was lucky in that the bullet hadn't done any serious damage to any of his solid organs. While the doctors were in there, they had taken his appendix. I asked about his index but didn't get a laugh, at least not from Janine, as a sultry giggling erupted again from room 62. We looked at each other as I continued chewing my toast, and her face reddened. "Well, it's good to know all his solid organs are functioning properly."

Janine made a hasty retreat down the hallway. A few moments later, Dena Many Camps came through Henry's door. She straightened the same fringed dress I had seen her in a few days earlier and fine-tuned the lipstick at the corner of her open mouth with the tip of a middle finger. She froze for an instant when she saw me. I pulled a beaten tiger lily from my hat and held it up to her. She smiled and took it, bestowing a ravishing wink back over her shoulder as she sashayed down the hall and turned the corner.

I figured that about a dime's worth of Dena Many Camps and a Fresca would kill my ass.

14

"What do you mean he's gone?" George Esper was, once again, at large. I dried off my damp hair, made sure the towel around my middle was secure, and sat beside my set of new clothes that were still in the green paper shopping bag from the Sportshop.

Ferg looked like he was going to die. "He said he wanted something to eat, so I went to get a nurse . . ."

I draped the towel from my head to over my shoulders and examined my fingers. The first layer of skin was pretty well shot, and the next was pink and sensitive. My ear hurt, and I hadn't taken the bandage off for fear of disturbing it, but mostly I felt good, being clean for the first time in a couple of days. "Why didn't you just ring for a nurse?"

"I tried."

I thought about going back in the shower and drowning myself. "Where did you see him last?"

"In his room, about five minutes ago."

I handed him the portable radio, still amazingly clipped to the back of my mud-encrusted Carhartts. "This building is not that big. Have somebody go stand at the northeast corner of the hospital, and you stand at the southwest; either of you spots him leaving, call in. You use your truck radio." I looked up at Ferg and thought about how he had worked through the better part of the night, probably hadn't had anything decent to eat in days, and more than likely needed to phone his wife and let her know he was still alive. Donna worked at an insurance firm in town and, after thirty years of marriage, they were still madly in love. On Sunday afternoons, you could see them walking, holding hands, along Clear Creek in the park. "He got away from me, too, don't feel bad." I picked up my hat to keep him from feeling self-conscious. "I think I need a new hat. What do you think?"

He looked at me with hazel eyes not too disturbed by self-analysis and struck out for the southwest corner of the building. "Definitely."

I sat the hat back down on the polished surface of the wooden bench, which was anchored to the floor with three-inch pipe. I guess the administrators figured the doctors and nurses weren't making enough money and might try to run off with the furnishings. I looked in the bag at my new clothes with a sense of trepidation. If she was angry when she bought them for me, I wasn't sure if I wanted to see what size they were, but the jeans were an exact fit, as were the jacket, shirt, socks, underwear, and undershirt.

After I finished dressing, I put my gun belt on, carefully adjusting the jacket so that it covered the majority of it. Then I stuffed my dirty clothes into the bag for later washing or burning, placed my hat on top, and carried it with me into the hallway. Friday, midmorning, and there still wasn't much traffic at the hospital, which meant that George would have less cover. But, even though the building was small and the staff sparse, there were probably hundreds of places where he could be. I decided to drop my clothes off in Henry's room, if he was between female visitations, and use it as a base of operations for the hunt for George Esper, take two.

When I got to Henry's door, I paused to listen and hear if anybody else was in there. I heard voices but, whatever they were saying, it wasn't postcoital, so I pushed open the door and found George Esper seated in a chair beside Henry. I walked up to the bed opposite George and noticed that he had been crying. "Did it occur to you to say something to my deputy before you went wandering off, George?" He looked sufficiently sheepish and wiped the tears on his bare arm. "I mean, before I put out an all-points bulletin and file a missing persons with the FBI?"

"Thsorry . . ."

"George, here's the way it works from now on. When I put you someplace, anyplace? I want you to stay there until I come and get you. Do you understand that?" He nodded. "Good, now go back to your room." He got up and limped toward the door, but before he could get it open I called out, "And stay there." I listened as the door closed behind him.

"I think George might be a little confused."

I looked down at him. "Really. I think George is a lot confused."

"I am serious. I think something might be wrong with him."

"Other than continual flight syndrome?"

Henry paused for a moment, then folded the sheet down and smoothed the edge. His hands looked strange in this setting, like wild birds accidentally indoors. "Does the family have any history of mental illness?"

"Not that I know of."

He shook his head. "He seems scattered, and he has no attention span."

"Concussed?"

"Possibly." He looked at the empty chair where George had sat. "He wanted to know what he had to do if he wanted to live on the reservation. He thought he might be safer there."

"That's confused. He wasn't that bad on the mountain." We thought that one over for a moment.

His eyes stayed steady on mine. "He knows about his brother."

I felt like sitting down. "What did he say? How does he know?"

He shrugged. "It was not anything he said, it was just a feeling. But he knows."

I studied the polished railing at the side of the bed. "Do you think he was with Jacob when he was killed?"

"I do not know that." Henry smiled. "I am sorry to be so little help to you, but it is just a feeling. They are twins."

I leaned against the foot rail and peeled a small piece of the skin from the side of my hand. "How are you feeling?"

"Very well, and yourself?"

"My hands are falling off and my ear hurts."

He nodded. "Things could be worse, your ear could fall off."

"There's an intraoffice pool; odds are the doctor is going to cut it off."

"That would be a shame. Your ears are one of your finest features."

I looked out the window with him. "My thought exactly. They're gonna get a fight when they come for it."

He smiled and nodded. "Put me down a fifty on keeping the ear."

"You're up against Lucian."

He continued to look out the window. "He is still calling me Ladies Wear?"

"Yep."

"Make it a hundred."

I laughed. "Well, I better call off the manhunt and go talk to George." I looked down at him again. He really was recuperating quite well and looked as though he could get up and follow me out. "How's Dena Many Camps doing these days?"

"She is a wonderful and caring young woman."

I paused at the door. "I don't suppose George mentioned what room he was in?"

"No." He still looked out the window, and I wondered how long they would be able to keep him. "He was probably afraid I would come looking for him."

I watched him for a moment longer and then went out into the hall. Doctors and nurses are human, and humans are creatures of habit, so I walked across the hallway and pushed open the door of my old room. George was sitting at the side of his bed, looking out the window at the parking lot. "Hey, George. Mind if I come in?" He didn't say anything but kept staring out the window. The snow swept across the asphalt surface, piling up wherever the concrete partitions divided the lot. Nobody wanted to be here, and everybody was looking out the windows. I pulled a chair from the wall and sat down in his line of sight. I turned my head and also looked out the window. "Well, I'm glad to be inside, how about you?" He nodded but continued to look at the lot. I could see the Bullet from here; he was probably trying to figure out how to hot-wire it. "I'd say winter is here . . . George?" He finally turned his face toward me. I studied him carefully and noticed he was shaking. "George, are you all right?"

"Chjakeb's ded."

I could feel my eyes sharpen as I looked at the young man. "What makes you think that, George?"

"Thsaw himb." His lips moved, but no more words came out.

"You saw him?" He nodded his head. "Saw him where, George?"

"Othwe montan . . ."

"You saw him up at Dull Knife Lake?" He shook his head as violently as his bandaged jaw would allow. "Where then?" The tremors continued to wrack his body as his naked legs hung from the bed and shook, the nearest thigh wrapped up in a winding layer of gauze. I wasn't sure if they had him on anything, but with the head injury it was unlikely. "George, if you know anything? I need you to tell me about it. I'm trying to stop who's doing this, but I have to figure out who it is before I can do anything."

"Yhew kan'tsopthm."

I nodded. "Stop who, George?"

I watched as a finger crept from his hand and pointed toward the window. "Tthemb."

I felt a continuous charge run up my spine as I turned my head and looked out the window again, my reflected image only inches from my eyes. There was a minivan parked a little farther out, but I could almost swear that George Esper was pointing at my truck. "George, there's nothing out there but my truck." He continued to look, but the finger disappeared into his fist. I checked again and looked out to the municipal golf course. Maybe Arnie's Army was after George. "George, who did you see up there?"

The only thing he said was, "Yhew kan'tsopthm."

I stood up slowly and gently lowered the Venetian blinds with the cord that had been at my back. George still didn't move, so I pushed him back in the bed with a hand on his shoulder and pulled the blanket and sheet up to his chin. He still shook as if he were freezing. "Why don't you try and get some sleep?"

"Yhew kan'tsopthm."

I looked down at another human wreck and patted his chest. "Well . . . I might just surprise you."

I made my way through the automatic doors of the emergency room and waved at Ferg, who joined me. We used one of the blond brick walls as a wind block and stood against the building's entrance. "He's back in his room. I found him in Henry's, but he's back in his." The air was more than a little brisk, so I flipped the collar up on my new jacket and pushed my hands farther into the pockets. "He's acting a little strange, so you might want to keep an even closer eye on him. I don't think he's dangerous, but he might wander off again."

"You bet."

"I notified them at the desk. I'm going to head back over to the office and get things sorted out."

"You bet."

I was also willing to bet that Ferg would be sitting on George within the moment. I pulled my keys out, headed over to the Bullet, and looked through the window. I'm not sure what it was I expected to see, an entire Old Cheyenne war party riding shotgun or what. I stood there in the wind, the blowing snow peppering the side of my face with its sting, as I looked into my truck. The rifle was there, a palpable reminder of things I could not see and, beside it, sat a black-and-white box of ammunition for things I could. Vic must have left the box after the tests, a little joke, or maybe she thought I might need it. I wondered mildly what had happened to the Weatherby I had on the mountain or to the Remington that Henry had been carrying.

Was anybody in there? Ever since the mountain, I was careful to look for them out of the corners of my eyes. It seemed as though, if I stood there long enough, they would begin to appear, sitting easily on the leather seats and looking back at me with their hair-bone chokers, their trade cloth tied in their hair, and their closed-mouth smiles. They held the rifle in their laps, waiting for me to get in so they could hand it to me. I leaned against the door and closed my eyes; the glass was cold, but I could think again. I opened my eyes, and they were gone. I stood there for another moment, and I'm not sure if I was making sure they were gone or hoping they would reappear. I turned the key, opened the door, and slid in next to the Cheyenne Rifle of the Dead. My hand shook a little as I slid the rifle over and placed the box of ammunition on the seat next to me. The box looked old, as if the edges had been roughed off and the printing had been done by an antiquainted press. The date on the box even read 1876. It felt heavy, and I thought about pumpkins.

By the time I got over to my desk, the Espers were waiting on line two. I had told Ruby I would get it in my office and passed by Vic's open door. She was on the phone, and it looked like she was enjoying her call far more than I would mine. It was probably her friends at the Department of Justice, and I had a brief twinge of panicked jealousy. If Vic weren't married to Wyoming anymore, she'd be a fool not to go back east and get a job with a large, urban department or with the Feds. As I sat there in my office, my plans for the first female Wyoming sheriff evaporated into thin, high plains air.

I picked up the receiver and punched line two. "Longmire." I sounded busy and possibly a little angry.

"Sheriff?"

It was Reggie Esper. "Yep, Reggie. Are you still in Deadwood?"

There was a pause. "We are. I told the mine I'd be back yesterday, but we had a lucky streak and decided to stay on 'til Monday. Then this South Dakota Highway Patrolman came to the casino and got us." Another pause. "Walt, if this is about that damned Pritchard kid, I haven't let the boys have anything to do with him . . ."

"It's not about Cody Pritchard."

Yet another pause. "Well, is it important? I mean I don't want to cut a weekend short if I . . ."

"It's important." I stared at the blotter on my desk and picked up a pen. I looked up at the old Seth Thomas clock on my wall, a plugged-in leftover from Lucian and Red Angus before him. I adjusted it twice a year, and it never lost or gained a second. "It's a little after eleven, and you could be here by three or so?"

There was a discussion going on in the background. "We'll leave right after lunch."

He started to hang up. "Reggie? Make sure you come straight to the sheriff's office." He said he would.

I put the phone back, leaned an elbow on my desk, and accidentally hit my ear. I swore and readjusted my hand to my cheek. It hurt to hold the pen, and I clutched my tender fingers in a half claw. I put the Espers down for four o'clock and wrote a note to ask Vic about ballistics. I had to talk to the Curator of Firearms at the Buffalo Bill Museum in Cody, talk to Jim Keller, and call Dave at the Sportshop about Vasques, size nines. I was also beginning to wonder about Lucian and Turk. I started to punch the intercom on my phone, but all the lines were busy. Probably Vic, faxing her resume. I got up and walked out to Ruby's desk.

She was on the phone too, but she hung up. "Lonnie Little Bird was here looking for you." She laced her fingers together and rested her chin on them. "He's sweet."

"Yes, he is." I paused for a second. "I've got the Espers coming in this afternoon. If they're running late, can you stick around?"

"Yes."

"Anything on Jim Keller?"

"Not back from Nebraska yet. But Mrs. Keller has been here twice already today."

"How's the kid doing?"

"He's in the back, asleep. I gave him the old sheriff report books to look at, which would put anybody to sleep. By the way, you have the worst penmanship of any sheriff we've ever had since 1881. I thought you'd be glad to know."

"Who was before 1881?"

She raised an eyebrow. "Nobody; that's when we first became a county in the territory, about nine years before we became a state. You did hear about that?"

I scratched at my ear and immediately regretted it. "Yep, I remember reading about it in the papers."

"Stop picking at your ear."

"Yes, ma'am." I slouched a little bit. "Do you know what's happened to Lucian and Turk?"

"They are having lunch down the hill at the Busy Bee. Lucian mentioned something about having a Come-to-Jesus meeting with his nephew."

"Oh, boy. Anything from Vic on the ballistics at DCI?"

"Why don't you ask her?"

"She's on the phone." I looked down at all the blinking lights on Ruby's console. "She's on all of them."

"Then she hasn't, or she is now." She stayed looking at me.

"We're not going to be able to keep her, are we?" It was out before I knew I had said it and, when I looked up, Ruby's electric blues steadfastly joined with mine.

"Why don't you go have lunch; she'll be off the phones by the time you get back. Besides, you could use a little religion."

In its usual perverse manner, the sun had decided to come out and cast a glare without providing any heat. It might get warmer by the end of the afternoon but, for now, it was just plain cold. As I navigated the courthouse steps, I looked up at Vern's window. He was probably up there still waiting for our lunch, but I could bet that he wouldn't want anything to do with Lucian's type of revival meeting, even though I was sure it would carry its own unique version of fire and brimstone.

Cody and Jacob, convicted of two counts of first degree sexual assault, could have been sentenced to as much as forty years. The sentencing date hung over all of us for two solid weeks, but over nobody as much as Vern Selby. The jury had lived with deciding, and now they had passed it on to Vern like some communicable disease, and the fever of justice ate away at him.

He had taken it upon himself to merge the two counts into one, which was his judicial latitude, and sentenced Cody and Jacob to a maximum of fifteen years in prison, far to the low side of the five- to fifty-year sentencing guideline. George had gotten the minimum of ten, but it all became academic when the judge had pronounced that the offenders would be incarcerated in a young adult institution in Casper and would therefore receive indeterminate terms. I guess Vern had decided that since they were all first offenders, the rape shouldn't cost them the rest of their lives; never mind what it had cost Melissa.

Cody Pritchard had turned to his friends in the back of the court-room and playfully tossed his hat in the air and smiled. With time off for good behavior, Cody, Jacob, and George could see less than two years of soft prison time. Bryan Keller would receive two years of pro-bation and one hundred hours of community service. The young men were once again released without bail, and Vern had nodded quietly in his chambers when I personally volunteered to drive the three of them down to Casper.

When I got to the Busy Bee, I glanced through the window. Turk was slouched on his stool and was against the wall about as far as he could be. Lucian, with his lips barely moving, was leaning in and glared at the side of Turk's face. Any thoughts of hunger passed, and I continued along the sidewalk to the Sportshop. When I went in, David was punching something into his computer behind the counter, and his wife, Sue, was waiting on an overweight middle-aged woman in the shoe department. I strolled up to the counter and leaned a hip against it.

He looked up through the top of his bifocals. "Hi, Walt."

"What's the number one selling hiking boot?"

"Here?" He thought. "Vasque, maybe Asolo."

"Most popular size?"

"Nine, maybe ten."

"Any way to track how many Vasques, size nines you've sold in the last year or so?"

He looked at me and sighed. "You're lucky Sue's here today. I don't have time for . . ."

"Make time." I looked at him for a moment to reinforce it.

"I can ask Sue to go back through the special orders and check the stock, but I wouldn't hold my breath on names if I were you. If they paid cash . . ."

"I need you to do it now."

He pulled a pen from behind his ear and tossed it on the counter in defeat. "All right."

"One other question. Do you remember Jacob or George coming in to buy flies?"

He crossed his arms and exhaled a long, slow hiss. "Maybe a week and a half, two weeks ago?"

"Anybody else here when they were talking about where they were going?" It was a long shot, but I had to play it out.

He shook his head. "I have no idea."

"Will you think about it?"

"Sure."

"I mean really think about it."

"Sure." Before I could get too far from the counter he said, "Nice clothes."

I stopped and looked down at my fancy duds. "You help her with the sizes?"

"Did it all on her own." He smiled. "Somethin', huh?"

"Yep." I continued to the door and rested my hand on the brass handle.

"You should be proud of yourself, she's quite a catch."

"Yep." I pulled open the door and started out. "Call me."

By the time I got back to the Bee, Lucian and Turk had vacated the place and nobody was visible, not even Dorothy. I went in and sat at the corner stool, next to the cash register. After a moment, a shadow cast across my plastic-covered, vinyl menu. "What are you having?"

"Anything but the usual." I closed the menu in one hand and reached it over to her. "I want to apologize for being sharp with you yesterday."

She took the menu and looked at my fingers. She had been talking to somebody because her next glance was up to my ear. "Feeling experimental, are we?" She reached down and threw two meat patties from a small Tupperware container onto the grill, then dropped a basket of hand-cut potatoes into the fryer. It appeared that hamburgers and french fries were not today's usual. I asked her about Lucian and Turk. She raised an eyebrow. "I think you're due a formal, verbal apology. Then I think the former, yet attending, sheriff intends to take a nap in the jail." Her voice softened. "How's the Bear?"

I looked up. "I bet he's out of there by this afternoon."

"Hard to keep a good man down."

I reached up to feel my ear. "You have no idea . . ."

She slapped my hand away. "Stop that." She turned back around and flipped the sizzling patties. "So, where are we on the case?"

"Well, I'll tell you, Inspector Lastrade . . ." And I did. I left out any suspicions I had about Jim Keller, but that was about all. I was looking defeat squarely in the face, and pretty soon the county would be crawling with DCI investigators and Feds. I honestly didn't think they were going to get any further than I had. Nonetheless, I told her I was considering a career in telemarketing.

She filled a glass with ice and then with tea from a pitcher that sat on the cutting board. "You can make a lot of money." She flipped a couple of slices of cheese onto the burgers, prepared the buns for reception on an oval-shaped plate, and pulled the fresh basket of fries from the deep fryer, hooking them on the rack to drip dry. My stomach gurgled in response to all the activity, and I was glad she had put on two cheeseburgers. "Okay, unlucky at cards . . ."

I took a long sip of the tea. "Don't even ask."

She scooped up the patties, scooting them expertly onto the bun beds, and covered the rest of the plate with french fries. "That bad?" She slid the dish in front of me. "Careful, hot."

"You know, I used to think I was pretty good at this relationship stuff . . ."

She wiped her hands on her apron. "Oh, Walter." She shook her head. "You know she's had a rough life."

"Yep, I know. She's having a rough time buying the White Mountains in Arizona right now." The food, as always, tasted marvelous. Maybe when I was unemployed, I could work part time for Dorothy. She was still looking at me, and I had the feeling I was going to have to go seek employment elsewhere. "What?"

"When her father killed himself"—she had placed the pitcher on the counter, anticipating another fill—"there were some things going on out there." The hazel eyes stayed steady under a salt-and-pepper lock.

"What's that supposed to mean?"

She shrugged. "Just talk. I don't think her marriage was very happy, either." She looked down at my rapidly vanishing meal. "How's the food?"

I stopped chewing long enough to reply, "Marry me?"

"That good, huh?"

I looked up to check, but there wasn't a cloud in the sky. The wind was still kicking up, so I figured the snowflakes that kept waltzing around my head must have just hitched a ride; their changing patterns reminded me of the mountain in an unsettling fashion. I thought about the visions I had been having and chalked them up to strain and just plain fatigue.

Turk was sitting in one of the reception chairs and stood when I came in. Ruby was seated at her desk with her lunch of a watercress sandwich on low-fat seven-grain bread, carrots, and a sliced apple unfolded before her, which looked fresh, healthy, and completely unappetizing. "What's up?"

He glanced over at Ruby, who was watching him. "Could I speak with you, Sheriff?" His voice was still nasal with the muffling of the packing and bandages.

"Yeah, sure. You wanna talk in my office?" He nodded and followed me in. I sat at my desk and gestured for him to have a seat. He shook his head and continued standing. He looked like nine kinds of hell; the bruising around his eyes had spread as far back as his side-burns, and it hurt to look at him. "What can I do for you?"

"Uncle Lucian says this is a bad time to have this conversation with you, but I thought you ought to know about my intentions? I put my application in with the Highway Patrol."

I had to laugh; I couldn't even keep a hold of Turk. "Really?"

"Yes, sir." He twitched his face to stop an itch I was sure he was going to have for a while. "Uncle Lucian said it might be for the best."

I nodded and crossed my arms. "He's a smart fella, that one-legged bandit uncle of yours."

"Yes, sir." He looked back up at me. "He also said that if I ever ran for sheriff, you'd just run against me, win and serve a half a term, and then step down, giving her two years to prove herself."

"He's right, I would." Pretty soon I'd be running the place by myself. "He say anything else?"

I thought I saw just a glimmer of a smile at the corner of his mouth from underneath the droop of his mustache but, with the ban-dages, it was hard to tell. "He said that masturbation is a wonderful form of stress relief in the workplace and that the wildflowers are beautiful along I-80 in the spring."

I stuck a peeling hand out to him. He looked at it, then to me. I'm sure we were a handsome pair, him with his nose and me with my hands and ear. "I won't give you a bad letter of recommendation."

He took my hand, hesitantly. "Thanks."

I knew the colonel down in Cheyenne, and he owed me a few favors. "I'll make some phone calls."

He shook my hand a little more and then released it. "You really do want to get rid of me."

"Let's just say I think it might be a better fit." I really did. The nar-rower limitations of vehicular law enforcement along with a more regimented style of department could be just what Turk needed. That or the colonel would never owe me another favor for as long as the state had paved roads.

I looked past him and saw Vic appear in the doorway. She glanced at Turk when he turned to see what I was looking at. "Jesus, you look like shit."

He turned back to me before he left. "Good luck." I had no idea he had a sense of humor. I could have asked him about his .45-70, but it didn't seem pertinent. It wasn't him, and it wasn't going to be.

Vic sat in the chair opposite me, propping her feet onto my desk as usual, and arranging a sheath of papers in her lap. I sat back down. "Don't play with your ear."

"Sorry." I returned my hand to my lap. "Henry and Lucian are going even money on whether I'll lose it. Ballistics?"

She shuffled the papers. "Both leads match, which does not come as a great surprise, both contain the same chemical compound, and both are from the same slug batch, 30 to 1 ratio . . . Same shooter."

"How are your friends back in Washington?"

She looked at me for a moment. "Quantico."

"Whatever." I pulled out a pen, uncapped it, and underlined Jim Keller's name. "I've always wondered why they haven't tried to lure you back."

"There's an opening with the National Center for the Analysis of Violent Crimes Services in the Criminal Investigative Analysis Unit."

I nodded. "Do you have to say all that every time you answer the phone?"

"There's also an opening in West Virginia at the FBI Fingerprint Analysis Lab, and there's always Philadelphia."

I exhaled slowly. "Well, I didn't think we were going to be able to keep you forever."

She looked up from the papers then returned to them, and it was very quiet for a while. "We ran a check on Roger Russell's gun . . ."

"I didn't even know you had it."

She looked back up, allowing her head to drop to one side in dismissal. "Somebody's gotta run the place while you're out traipsing around in the woods."

"And . . . ?"

"Doesn't match. And we got a call back from the Buffalo Bill

Museum. They did acquire a Sharps .45-70 from Artie Small Song more than a year ago."

I shrugged. "Artie has also been locked up in the Yellowstone County jail since Saturday."

She made a big show of pulling a pencil from behind her ear and scratching through his name on her papers. "Jim Keller?"

"Nothing." I put the cap back on the pen and tossed it onto the blotter. "Which brings us to the Cheyenne Rifle of the Dead."

She looked at her notes. "No match, but it's been fired numerous times. Like a box of shells."

"Twenty rounds?" She nodded her head. "When?"

"Just over a week ago."

"Right before the murders?"

"Have you ever looked down the barrel of one of those things after they've been shot?"

I thought back to Omar's. "Yep, once."

"They lead up real bad. You throw twenty rounds through one of those things without cleaning it, you're looking to get it blown up in your face." Her hands rested on her lap. "I looked down the barrel, and you could hardly see daylight."

My ear itched, but I figured it was a good sign. "So why would somebody do that?"

"Practice?" We looked at each other.

"That lets your friend Henry off. He doesn't need practice."

I leaned back in my chair. "When we were up on the mountain, he took the shotgun and gave me the rifle. He said something about not being as good a shot as me." I stood up. "I better go get that damn thing out of my truck and bring it in here. It turns up missing, I'm gonna be even more cursed than I am now."

"It's still in your truck?"

I started around the desk and looked down at the top of her head as she studied her notes. "I forgot about it." She shook her head, and I reached over and touched her shoulder. "By the way, thanks for the shells."

"What the fuck are you talking about?"

"That old box of shells in my truck, the ones that look about a hundred and fifty years old?" She didn't move, but the tarnished gold came up slow. "Please tell me you left an aged box of .45-70 ammunition on the seat of my truck?" I waited. "Next to the rifle?"

She didn't say anything, just sat there looking at me. I think she was checking to see if I was really there. I wasn't sure myself.

15

When we got to the truck, I was relieved to look through the passenger side window and see the cartridge box there. I was beginning to think that I was having some sort of mental breakdown and that the box lying beside the rifle on my seat was another phantom apparition. "Do you see that box on the seat?"

She peeked past my shoulder and turned her face to look at me. "What box?"

I nodded my head, ever so slightly. "Very funny." I unlocked the door and opened it; the barrel of the Cheyenne Rifle of the Dead was pointed directly at us. The box was on the seat in the exact spot where I had placed it after my brief examination. Using the inside liner of the pocket of my jacket, I reached in and showed it to Vic. "Was this in here when you put the rifle on the seat and locked the truck?"

"No."

I looked at the box. "Anybody drive my truck while I was gone?"

"Nobody. Did you leave your keys?"

"On the rack, in case somebody had to move it."

"This is getting exciting."

I placed the small cardboard container on my desk along with the rifle and sat in my chair as Vic leaned against the desk with her thighs flattened on the edge and her arms crossed. We were both looking at the damn thing like it might jump up, do back flips, and run away. It was a battered little box with the corners dented in and the edges fuzzy. The black printing was faded and scuffed, but you could still make it out. The print was in assorted fonts and at least as ornate as the handwritten addition. There was a floral pattern and a series of lines on each side that encapsulated the words "This Box Contains 20 Metallic Cartridges, Manufactured by Sharps' Rifle Mf'g Co., Hartford, Conn." There was a large hole, exactly the size of a .45 caliber slightly low and left of center with "400 yards" scribbled in pencil beside it. The writing was old, with a flourishing hand and detailed penmanship. It looked like the writing in the old sheriff's logbook. There was something familiar about it and, if the distance was true, it was scary shooting.

When I looked up again, Vic was staring at me. "Well, are we waiting till Christmas?"

I took two pens from my broken Denver Broncos mug and carefully held the box down with one and worked the flap open with the other. No sense in getting even more fingerprints on the thing. I slumped a little and rested my chin on my arm as I continued to look in the box. "If you were cartridges over a hundred years old, wouldn't you be tarnished?"

"Yes."

"They're not."

She leaned around the corner and peered into the box like something might come out. "Look like they were loaded yesterday."

I flattened one of the pens on the cardboard divider and slowly coaxed the box back, allowing two of the cartridges to roll out onto the blotter; they were both empties that had been fired. I spun one of the cartridges around with the pen so I could see the indentation at the primer. I turned the other one, and it was identical. "Two down." I pinned the divider to the blotter again and nudged the box back, allowing two more shells to roll out. These were live, with lead and primers intact, as were those in the rest of the box. "Does it worry you that there are two of these shells spent?"

"You mean how it matches up with our current body count?"

"Something like that." I looked along the shiny lines of reflection on the surface of the casing nearest me and clearly made out discolored spots whirling in the pattern of fingerprints. Whoever had handled these cartridges had not done it with any great care and, as I glanced at the other shells, I began to see more prints. With my luck, the individual who made them had been dead for seventy years. "Do you still have that shell of Omar's that I gave you?"

"Yeah." She retreated into her office and returned with the cartridge. While she was gone, I flipped the box over. On the other side was another hole where the shot had passed through: impressive to the point of being mythic. I looked at the handwriting and was sure I had seen it before. When she returned and handed Omar's bullet to me, she leaned over to peruse the shells on the blotter. "These are different."

His shell had a rounded line at the butt end that ended with two small stars and writing on the other side of the primer that read .45-70 GOVT.; on the mystery shells, there was nothing. The edges at the butt plate weren't as sharp either, as if the machining had been done in a hurry with devices under pressure to produce in difficult times. I scooped up one of the spent shells at the open end with the tip of the pen and held it up to my nose and sniffed. There was no quartzite, but traces of black powder were evident.

"They are originals." I wasn't surprised when the baritone rumble of his voice interrupted our conversation. I had seen Henry walk up and lean against the doorway, but Vic hadn't, and it was just a tiny bit amusing when her back stiffened.

"What're you doing out of the hospital?"

He crossed over and eased himself into the chair opposite my desk. "I see you still have your ear."

I laid the cartridge down on the blotter and tossed the pen back in the mug. "Yep, I've removed all the scissors from the office, and I'm just not going to take any naps when Lucian's around." I nodded toward the scattered shells on my desk. "What do you know about these?"

Vic refolded her arms and looked at him, and her glance seemed to carry a little more professional interest than I would have found comforting. Henry simply smiled at her. "Hi."

She smiled back. "Hi."

I looked at the two of them for a moment. "Okay, before the two of you get into a pissing contest, how about you tell me what you know about these?"

His eyes continued smiling at Vic for longer than they should have, then he turned to me. "Where did you get them?"

"They were on the seat of my locked truck this morning, alongside the rifle."

"Interesting." He waited a moment. "They are originals."

"How do you know that?"

"I am the one who polished and reloaded them, but I did not reload them for myself." He took a deep breath and exhaled it slowly as he turned his head toward the window. "Lonnie." After looking up at Vic, I turned back to him and waited. "Lonnie said that he wanted to shoot the rifle, and I was concerned that he might run some of those hot, modern cowboy loads through it. I took forty of the original cartridges he had and hand loaded them so they wouldn't damage the rifle."

I sighed and raised my eyes up to Vic. "Get a preliminary on these shells, then ship samples down to DCI." She nodded, and I stood. "How far do you think you can get, within our obvious technical limitations?"

"Pretty damn far." She looked at me as I scooped up the rifle. "Where are you going?"

I glanced over at Henry who was studying me. "I'm going out to talk with Lonnie Little Bird and get some fingerprints."

"You sure you don't want somebody to go with you?"

I looked back at him. "I got somebody."

The heat of the day had begun to melt away what remained of the snow, and the clouds were just beginning to break up in the face of a mild, Wyoming autumn afternoon. As we drove out of town, I looked in the rearview mirror at the Bighorns. The fresh coat of snow had done them some good, even if it hadn't done either of us any. We rode along in silence. My sheepskin jacket was draped over Henry's shoulders; Dena Many Camps had forgotten to bring him a coat along with his fresh clothes. He didn't particularly look irritated, just preoccupied, so I left him alone with his thoughts. I had picked up a fingerprint kit from our minilab and informed Ruby where we were going, asking her to relay any information gotten from Dave at the Sportshop, from the Espers, or Jim Keller. Lucian was still in the back asleep, and I told her to wake him up if anything happened. She had looked at me and withheld comment.

There was one question on my mind, and it concerned a box of aged .45-70 shells that had been left on my truck seat. I broke the silence by asking, "Why did he leave them?"

"I do not know." He didn't turn but slouched a little against the door, the Cheyenne Rifle of the Dead leaning gently against the inside of one of his knees. "Unless it was good fortune."

"For whom?"

"You." He still looked out the windshield at the sunny afternoon. "Lonnie has grown very fond of you over the last few years. The last time we were there? He asked me if it would be all right if he gave this rifle to you."

"The Cheyenne Rifle of the Dead? Thanks a lot, but no thanks." He rode along quietly, and I was pretty sure I had hurt his feelings. "If it's all the same with you and Lonnie, I think I'll just hang around here in the camp of the living for a while."

"That is not why he wanted to give it to you." He turned and looked at me for the first time. "He wanted to give it to you to shield you."

"From what?"

He shrugged and looked back out the windshield. "He said that you need protection from something very powerful and very bad." The rest he spoke in a monotone. "He said that you are a good man and that there are those who would assist you if they could. That they had spoken with him, and that if you would allow them, they would help you."

"Help me what?"

He sat there for a while, and I was getting worried that he might have left the hospital a little prematurely when he spoke. "Live."

As we passed the cutoff to the Powder River Road, I thought about what Vonnie had said, that she had assembled herself so that she didn't have to deal with all the things I had suddenly reintroduced into her life. I thought about caring about somebody more than life itself. As I looked back, I was pretty sure that Martha hadn't loved me that much. She had been fond of me but had settled for me and had made the best of her situation. She had stayed because of Cady, and I had stayed because I loved Cady that much. I simply couldn't conceive of doing anything else. I figured what I'd do was go over to Vonnie's tonight and have a long talk with her. Maybe we could put things off until this case was over. The time when I had held her long toes, fitting the high arches of her feet in the palms of my hands, and had driven her home in the dark of the night seemed very far away and receding.

Henry dozed as I drove away from the sun, and the ruffling of his breath became steadier as we took the cutoff to the reservation. I saw Brandon White Buffalo looking after us as we went through the intersection. He stood behind his counter. It was hard to miss him as he looked through the clinging soda, chips, and candy advertisements. I extended a hand across the cab toward him, and he watched as we passed without slowing. He raised his hand also and pressed it against the heavy double glass of the convenience store window. Brandon White Buffalo stood there in the maelstrom of modern consumerism like a sentinel, like a warning in a mystical undertow. I looked back through the rear window of the truck to catch a last glance; he still stood there palm out and fingers spread like an orchard basket against the glass. He looked after us until we were gone, and I thought of Melissa at the Little Big Horn.

I reset my shoulders, concentrated on the road, and considered my dwindling staff. Turk would be out by January, Vic could possibly be gone before that, and the chances of me getting Ferg to return to full duty were slim. He would probably just retire. I was thinking about it myself. I picked the mic off the dash. "Base, this is Unit One, come in?"

After a moment there was static, then Ruby's voice. "Leave me alone, I'm busy."

"Any word from Dave at the Sportshop?"

Static. "His wife called. She's about halfway through and will fax the stuff over when she gets done. Stop bothering me."

I hung the mic back up and watched the trees pass by along the irrigation ditch. I expected to see the Old Cheyenne again, standing among the cottonwoods. But there was nothing there and that worried me a little more; maybe even they had abandoned me. I thought about where we were going, about Lonnie. Yes, it is so . . . I didn't think that Lonnie had killed Cody and Jacob, but I wanted to talk to him directly and find out if there was anything more to his story than Henry had been able to tell me. I looked over at my friend. It seemed that his breathing had gotten a little rougher, but he still slept, his body attempting to repair itself while he wasn't looking.

There was a maroon minivan with a bumper sticker that read FRY BREAD POWER in Lonnie's driveway, and there was someone sitting on the passenger side. Even from the distance and angle, I knew it was Melissa. I brought the Bullet to a stop alongside the van. Henry woke and placed a hand on the dash to steady himself. "You all right?"

"Yes." He blinked. "Just sleepy." He looked out the passenger side of the Bullet, and I saw the muscles at the side of his face bunch as he smiled at her. His hand came up to the glass, and I knew hers was extended toward him. He handed me the rifle. I took a moment to collect myself, giving them enough time to be together before I opened my own door and came around the back of the truck. It was a moment I had avoided, this personal contact, but here she was, and here I was with her.

She was holding him, and I was amazed at how she had grown. Melissa was taller, still lean but muscled now and, even though she hadn't lost all of the stunting qualities of Fetal Alcohol Syndrome, the graceful quality that was indicative of the Cheyenne and their personal beauty was there. Her face turned to me. I hadn't seen that face, with the exception of that fleeting glance at the powwow, for more than three years. Her eyebrows still arched in a questioning fragility, and the folds at the insides of her eyes still attempted to betray her. In honor of the golden fall afternoon and despite the oncoming winter, she was dressed in a pair of gray flannel athletic shorts and a T-shirt that read SWEET MEDICINE TREATMENT CENTER, SOBRIETY RETREAT. I stood there for a moment with the rifle in my hand, unable to move, as she loosened herself from Henry only long enough to attach herself to me. I held the rifle out so that it could not touch her and looped my other arm around her shoulders. Henry quietly took the gun. After a moment, she pulled back to look up at me. "You are sad?"

I laughed as a tear threatened to escape the corner of my eye. "I guess I'm just happy to see you."

She smiled back, and it was like sunshine through a church window. "I am happy to see you, too."

Henry retreated and headed up to the house with the Sharps as Melissa and I talked. She kept a hand on my arm as we spoke, as if the connection might be fleeting and neither of us could take the chance. She had received a partial basketball scholarship to a community college in South Dakota and was only back from her special classes for a tournament. She wanted to know if I could come home with her in a week and a half and spend Thanksgiving with her and her aunts. She assured me that Lonnie would be there, too. I asked her where Lonnie was now. "He is inside, arguing with my aunt Arbutus. She said that I should come out and sit in the car. I'm glad you are here. I was bored."

As she spoke, I became aware of a commotion. The screen slapped open and the most formidable of the aunts made her way from the porch and headed toward us. Henry was wheeling Lonnie out the door after her with the buffalo rifle in Lonnie's lap along with a small, black plastic box. Melissa's aunt pulled up short when she saw me. I hadn't formally met Arbutus Little Bird and had previously withstood her cast-iron gaze from afar. She didn't like me, but I think it was less because I was a white man with a badge and more because I associated with Henry. "Hi, Arbutus."

She redirected her gaze at Melissa. "Get in the car."

I took a deep breath and took Melissa's hand in mine. She was trembling. "Arbutus, do you want to tell me what's going on?"

She didn't respond but stood there with her hands at her sides as Henry wheeled Lonnie up behind her. She turned slightly and spat out the words, "I hope you're happy, now that the sheriff's here."

Lonnie's eyes did light up when he saw me. "Hello, Sheriff."

"Hey, Lonnie. What's going on?"

"Oh, my sister isn't going to let me have my daughter for the holidays. Yes, it is so."

I glanced up at Henry, who shrugged. I looked back at the galvanized aunt. "What's the story?"

"I'm taking her home."

"Well, do you mind telling me why it is you're not going to let her have Thanksgiving with her father?"

A moment passed. "I don't have to talk to you."

"No, you don't, but I can get on the radio and get one of the IPs over here and you can talk to him." I was playing an angle, but most inhabitants of the reservation hated Indian Police even more than us. We were just whites. They were apples, red on the outside, white on the inside. She didn't say anything. "Whatever it is? I'm sure we can work it out."

"I found a beer in his refrigerator."

I turned and looked at Lonnie. "Is that true, Lonnie?" God, like I didn't know the response.

"Yes, it is true. Yes, it is so." He continued to smile. "I keep it there as a reminder and to keep temptation at hand. Temptation out of reach does you no good."

"How long's the beer been in there?"

"About a year and a half."

She crossed her arms, but she turned to look down at him. We were making progress. "How come I haven't seen it in there before?"

He blinked his eyes through the thick glasses. "It was behind the pickled pigs' feet. You don't ever move them. Um-hmm, yes it is so."

The look on her face told me he was telling the truth. "Arbutus, do

317

you think it would be all right if Lonnie came over for Thanksgiving dinner at your place?" I waited a moment myself, for the next one. "And do you think it would be all right if Melissa came over here and spent the night with Lonnie, maybe on the Friday after Thanksgiving?" She didn't say anything but turned to look at me. "Friday night, then?"

"Get in the car, Melissa."

She started to open the door, but Melissa's voice stopped her. "Would it be okay if the sheriff came over for Thanksgiving dinner, too?"

Arbutus stopped and turned to look at her, then at me. She was a hard old gunboat, but I saw the steely eyes soften a little. "Walter is always welcome at our table." She started to open the door, but her eyes steered clear of mine. "You know where I live. Melissa, will you get in the car?"

The hand loosened in mine, and she leaned in to give a slight peck on my lowered cheek. "I'll see you in a couple of weeks."

"I'll do my best." She stopped. "I'll be there." The smile returned, and I watched as she turned the corner and got into the van, or almost did, before she jumped out, ran around the front, and gave her father and uncle a good-bye hug.

I leaned against the bed of my truck, crossed my arms, and looked down. "How you doin', Lonnie?"

"I'm good, and how are you?"

"I'm all right. Did you leave me a little present?"

He looked up at Henry through the split lenses, and the mid-afternoon sun glinted off his metal-framed glasses. Then he turned back to me and smiled. "Um-hmm, yes, I did."

I nodded. "How did you get in my truck?"

"Oh, those new ones are easy to break into, that and the keys by the door of your office. Yes, it is so."

I had to relocate the key rack. "Why did you leave the ammo for me?"

"You're gonna think I'm crazy if I tell you." The smile was a little weak when he looked up.

"Lonnie, I've seen an awful lot of crazy stuff lately, so why don't you try me?"

"The Old Ones told me you would need them." He nodded. "Yes. When I lost my legs, they began talking to me. I think it is because my legs are with them, now. They tell me half things."

"Half things?"

"Yes, because I am only half with them. Someday, all of me will be with them, and they will tell me everything."

I smiled. "I hope you don't get the whole story too soon, Lonnie." I looked down at the rifle in his lap. "Lonnie, did you take the gun out and shoot it a bunch of times?"

He looked genuinely ashamed. "I was angry, so I shot one of the fence posts out back."

I thought of the things I might shoot if somebody had done to my daughter what had been done to his. The image of Lonnie out on his back porch late one night shooting at a singular fence post hung there just out of range. I'm pretty sure I jumped a little when the radio crackled in the truck. I could hear Ruby's voice through the glass and the transceived miles. "Come in, Unit One."

It was probably word from the Sportshop or on the Espers but, when I looked up at the clock on the dash, it was only two-thirty; maybe it was Jim Keller. I opened the door and keyed the mic. "Base, this is Unit One. Go ahead?"

Static. "Walt, George Esper is gone again."

I slumped against the doorjamb of the truck and rested my head on the mic in my hand. "You've got to be kidding."

Static. "He stole Ferg's truck. Vic's in pursuit."

"Where?"

Static. "Out 16, probably on the highway. He already ran into somebody near the co-op. Turk's out there now."

"Did anybody notify the HPs?"

Static. "Yes."

I waited a moment; chances are Vic was still in range. Static, then a fainter signal broke through. "I'm at Mile Marker 113, and if the little fucker was up here, I would have caught him by now."

"Vic, leave the highway to the HPs, I got a sneaking suspicion that he's headed out this way."

Static, and I listened as she slowed the five-year-old unit down to under a hundred, negotiating the divider with one hand. "I'm on my way back, but if that's the case he's got a hell of a lead on me."

"We'll get him from the other direction. Unit One, out." I hung the mic back up and leaned out to look at Henry. "You coming?"

He nodded and started pulling Lonnie back up to the house. Lonnie grabbed the wheel rails of his chair and slid himself to a stop. "You go ahead, I can get back in the house myself. Yes, it is so." Then he reached down and handed the rifle up to me. "Take this." I took the rifle as he handed the black plastic box to Henry.

Henry looked at him, nodded, and came around to the passenger door. As I crossed in front of the truck, I stopped. "Lonnie, you know that cartridge box?"

He continued to smile. "Yes?"

"It has writing on it, next to the bullet hole?" He nodded and smiled. "Whose handwriting is that?"

"You should know that handwriting."

"Lonnie, I don't have a lot of time . . ."

"Nedon Nes Stigo, He Who Sheds His Leg."

Lucian.

"He used to shoot with us out at the Buffalo Wallows, back in the day. One time, my father challenged him to try to hit a target as small as the cartridge box at four hundred yards, and he did it. Yes, it is so."

It took me a minute to get myself going. "Thanks, Lonnie."

I climbed in the truck and, reaching for my seat belt, motioned Henry to do the same. He placed the small, black plastic case at his feet and held the rifle as easily in his hands as he had held the one in Omar's helicopter. By the time we got to the end of the state route that joined with the main drag, we were doing about a hundred with the sirens and lights at full tilt. It was still going to take us more than twenty minutes to get back to the other side of the reservation, and my knuckles tightened around the wheel. I concentrated on the road as we passed the cutoff down to the Powder River. "I think he's headed toward us."

"Because of what he said at the hospital, about living on the Rez."

"It's as good a guess as any."

He braced a hand against the dash as the gravitational pull of a sweeping turn almost slid us into the barrow ditch. "What did Lonnie say about the writing on the box?"

"He said it was Lucian's . . . You never heard that?"

"I never asked."

"I guess it was done a long time ago, when Lucian was shooting with Lonnie's father." At the next straightaway he opened what looked like a cleaning kit and pulled out two long stems and began threading them together. "What're you doing?"

"I am cleaning this rifle."

"That's evidence."

"No, it is a weapon."

It took awhile, even at our speed, but we finally made it to the northern end of the Powder when another vehicle popped over the horizon that was traveling at a pretty good speed of its own. From the distance, it was hard to tell who it was but, after a moment, I could see the lights. I grabbed the mic. "Vic, is that you?"

Static. "Fuck yes, it's me. Where in the hell did that little shit go?" I slowed and stopped. By the time I had, she was pulling up alongside us and was rolling down her window; she had to crank. I cut the siren, and she leaned an elbow on the sill. "What now?"

I thought. "Well, if he didn't take 14 back toward Sheridan, the only other main road is Powder River back here."

"North or south?"

"We'll take south, you take north." She was gone in a billowing cloud of blue burned oil and tire smoke before I could finish my sentence. Maybe, if I bought her a new unit . . . I turned the Bullet around and laid a little strip of my own, accelerating back to the Powder. When we got to the cutoff, the only thing headed north was a drifting cloud of dirt that hazed the gravel road into the distance. We made the turn and headed south as the back end of the Bullet attempted to get ahead of us. I countersteered and hit the gas again as we slid around the first turn just about sideways and clipped a few mailboxes. I noticed Henry struggling to hold onto the Sharps and find his seat belt with one hand. "What's the matter?"

"Just buckling up. It is the law." This was the first time I had taken the big beast up to speed for any length of time; there hadn't been any reason before. It was heavy, but I was surprised by the agility it had. "All right, you can crash now." He had gotten his seat belt on and was studying the road farther ahead as I dealt with the ground at hand. "I see dust."

If it was George, he had just jumped off the highway. A thought snagged in my mind. "Do you think he's got the radio on in that thing?"

Henry turned to look at me as I negotiated another turn and another quickly afterward. "That would explain why he got off the state routes."

"There's something else."

"What?"

"The old Esper place is out here somewhere, the one that Reggie's great-great-grandfather settled. I remember Vonnie telling me about it. She bought a bunch of property on a speculation that they were going to put that power plant out there someday."

"How does romance bloom?"

"Don't ask." I could feel his disapproving glance as we crossed a cattle guard and momentarily became airborne. We made for the washboard curve that lay ahead, and he braced himself. "Hey, I thought you guys always thought it was a good day to die."

"Attributed to Crazy Horse who was often misquoted."

* * *

The road straightened after the washboard, and I was able to bring all ten cylinders on line. The speedometer was creeping back up on eighty, and we were starting to get that light, floating feeling on the ball bearings of loosely packed dirt. My testicles felt as if they were somewhere in my chest cavity, and it wasn't a pleasant feeling. If we missed one of the curves at this speed, we were most assuredly dead. All Henry said was "Ooh, shit."

We hit the next turn at just about a hundred, and the sickening feeling in my stomach magnified as the laws of geometry exerted themselves on the velocity of all that Dearborn steel. At any reasonable speed it wasn't much of a turn, certainly nothing worthy of a Jan and Dean ballad, but it was enough to slam the side of the truck into the red clay embankment. When we bounced off the wall, I overcorrected, and the Bullet shot for the river. I turned ever so slightly, trying to urge our velocity forward, and only the left rear wheel slipped off the road. The truck tipped slightly back to center where we gained purchase and shot into the next straightaway. He looked over at me, the passenger-side mirror beating against his door. "You want to wreck? Do your side, okay?"

George had obviously had a little trouble getting around that one, too; his side-view mirror bounced and clattered under the Bullet. We had gained a good amount on him. When we saw him next, he had topped a hill and was bouncing immediately through another cattle guard that was on his right. The road continued a steady climb until we got to where he had been, and I slowed just a little because there might be a slope on the other side. It was a good thing I had, because the road did make a sharp cut to the right and there was a reasonable drop-off. George had not made it.

You could see where the Toyota had gone through the fence sideways, taking the majority of the barbed wire and aged posts with it. The little truck had most certainly gone over, but it had landed on its wheels, and George was still bumping his way across the bottomland where the pasture ended in a gate only about a quarter of a mile ahead. If we kept our speed up, we would get there before him and arrive in a large wash that opened to the east with a rise of about eight feet in more than a mile. This was the part of the river that admitted honestly to the moniker "a mile wide and an inch deep." There wasn't much in that direction other than the access road to the Burlington Northern/Santa Fe tracks. There wasn't anywhere else for him to go. He couldn't turn back and try to climb the hill he had just slid down, and the river blocked him to the left where the water might only be an inch deep but the mud was bottomless. He had to go for the gate, and we were going to be there before him.

I slowed just a little, since time and topography were now on our side. The Toyota leapt in and out of the hillocks and sagebrush. You could see him in there, sawing at the wheel in an attempt to keep the pickup on a relatively straight line, his head beating against the head-liner as he topped each rise. I cringed a little at the thought of what he was doing to his leg, his jaw, and other assorted and sundry injuries.

We made the last turn before the gate, and I accelerated briefly before sliding to a stop and blocking his path. I figured the faster I got there, the sooner he might pull the battered little Toyota to a stop, but he kept coming and I was beginning to wonder if he could see us or if he had beaten himself senseless. I waited as he approached, and it was only when he was about seventy feet from the gate that I saw the wheels turn and the vehicle lurch down the hill. George had decided to test the waters.

"Jesus H. Christ . . ." I gunned the Bullet farther down the fence line till I found a likely spot and cut the wheel myself, this time pulling a couple of yards of barbed wire and stapled posts after me. We followed him to the cut bank of the river and watched as the underside of his truck suddenly became visible. The jump didn't get very far and, as anticipated, the wheels and most of the front of the Toyota sank into the soft mud of the Powder River, effectively ending the vehicular portion of George's getaway.

I pulled up sideways and watched in absolute exhaustion as George climbed out of the window of his truck, fell into the water, rose up, and began quick-slogging away from us as fast as his bandaged leg would carry him. I looked past Henry in disbelief as he turned to hand me the rifle. "If you do not shoot him, I will."

"We don't have any bullets, or I would seriously consider it." He laughed and pulled a gleaming .45-70 from his shirt pocket and held it up. "Where did you get that?"

"Off your desk, where do you think?"

I pulled the handle and opened my door. "We're trying to keep somebody from shooting him."

He started out on the other side. "I am beginning to question the logic in that."

George had gotten a good start, but his injury and the mud were slowing him quite a bit, and I could see the gray slime of the riverbed clinging to his pants well above his knees. I stopped at the cut and stood at the edge; he was about fifty yards out. I cupped my hands around my mouth and yelled, "George, where do you think you're going?!"

Henry joined me at the dark crust edge of the bank. He was still carrying the rifle. "If you shoot him now, we do not have to bury him."

I cupped my hands around my mouth again. "George, that's enough, get back over here!"

George continued on. I started down the bank and slipped, barely catching myself before I fell into the river. I looked down into water that I was sure was just above freezing and tried to figure out what the best approach might be. I was never an all at once guy, preferring to ease myself into things, but I was about ready to throw prudence to the wind when Henry spoke. The tone of his voice ran a chill colder than the Powder had ever run. "Walt, there is somebody over there."

I raised my head and searched the opposite bank, but all I could see was George slowly making his way across. "Where?"

"Long way out. See that pointed clump of sage to George's right? Just to the right of that, all the way out at the horizon."

I stopped breathing, strained my eyes, and there it was. A small vertical figure in a horizontal landscape. "You sure that's not a pronghorn or a mule deer?"

"No, it is a man, and he is armed."

As Henry spoke, a small burst of smoke erupted from the figure. Just over two seconds later, George was cartwheeled backward into the frigid water. I took an involuntary step forward and splashed into the river water as George hit the mud. He struggled to get up, rolling himself sideways as he attempted to sit. It was a slow, grinding motion before things slipped into the adrenalin-induced rate where the real world cannot keep pace. I yelled with everything I had, "Stay down!" He couldn't hear, or it didn't matter. I had seen it in Vietnam, and I had seen it here. When you are a standing animal and you suddenly discover that you are not, there is an overriding need to rise and prove to yourself that you are intact.

"Reloading."

When I turned, he had already thrown me the rifle. I caught it and quickly jacked the lever down and extended a hand up for the shell as he fished in his shirt pocket. At that point, all I could think of was the penny he had tossed to me at the bar that night. He threw me the round; it hit the side of my palm and started to ricochet off, but I caught it against my chest and quickly inserted it past the dropped block and brought the lever up. I squared myself for the shot, and my shoulder jarred as the stock came up and slammed against it. I had to calm down and bring it all together in a fluid motion; that's when it occurred to me to breathe. I filled my chest cavity and felt the burn of flooding oxygen as I flipped up the Vernier sight . . . "Six seventy-five . . ."

"Seven hundred if it's an inch."

"Damn it." I readjusted as quickly as I could. "Where's Omar when you need him?"

Henry laughed as I brought the rifle up again, and it was just what I needed. All the tension faded from me. I pulled the set trigger and paused for a moment to check my target. Even at this distance, there was something familiar, something I knew, someone I knew. I adjusted my figures to encompass the season, general elevation of the shooter, and mean temperature. An approximation of one twenty-one-hundredths of an inch was the starting point, but I would have to go higher with current conditions. I peered through the pinhole of the Vernier's tiny disc, which was capable of measurements as small as one one-thousandth of an inch, and through the knife-shaped, German-silver blade sight.

He was waiting for me there, whoever he was, a mirror image at seven hundred yards with the same off-hand positioning. It occurred to me that the first one of us to find something to rest against might be the one who would still be standing, but there was no time. I had an ace in the hole because I wasn't the one he was shooting at, at least as far as I knew. I considered how many unfortunate individuals had held that as a last thought. George was clearly in my peripheral vision as I closed my left eye and blocked out the sight of the suffering youth. He had struggled up into a sitting position and now cradled his right arm in his left. It was difficult to tell what was blood and what was darkened from the water. I could hear him sobbing and only hoped it would continue.

I allowed my breath to slowly drift out with the faint breeze and it blended with the rounded river stones, the rustling of the dying buffalo grass, and with the faint wisps of high-altitude clouds. I could hear the song I had heard before on the mountain, the one that had shaken the trees and resonated through rock. The Old Cheyenne were there now with me, and I could hear their voices ascending as I held their rifle. I pulled the trigger of the big Sharps, and they whistled across the Powder River and beyond with a deadly accuracy that begged forgiveness as they went. They imparted death as a release and an involuntary shudder in the ongoing action of things. I hardly felt the kick and lowered the rifle in acceptance of a forgone conclusion. The figure dropped, and I listened as his wayward shot passed just above our heads. It screamed like misplaced vengeance and slapped through both sides of the Bullet's double-sided bed.

George continued to sob, and I was glad that he was alive. After a few moments, I became vaguely aware of Henry as he took the rifle away from me and leaned it against the bank. He stood there for a moment, and I think he touched my arm. He continued on into the river. The voices of the Powder would continue to tell the stories they had told before I was born and would tell long after I was gone. Henry carefully picked his way on the large, flat rocks that George had had no time to look for. I watched him for a moment and then looked back in the direction of the shot. My jaw set, and sadness overwhelmed me.

I knew who it was.

16

The bullet had shattered the clavicle, passed through the muscle and tendons of the shoulder, and had exited through the blade, taking most of it as it went. The tissue damage was tremendous, and it was unlikely that George's arm would ever operate properly again. His pulse was weak and rapid, his breathing was shallow, and it seemed as if he was doing everything possible to lower my odds below fifty-fifty.

We had wrapped him in the wool blanket that I kept behind the seat of my truck and had carried him back to the tailgate. He lay there, trembling from the cold of the water and the loss of blood. Shock had dulled his eyes, and the pupils were dilated as he stared into the late afternoon sky. He had lost a lot of blood in the river and continued to ooze his life out onto the scratchy surface of the gray blanket. I folded my fleece jacket around his shoulder in an attempt to compress the wound and quell the blood flow. I leaned over him and smiled with my mouth, even though my eyes refused to join in. "You're going to be okay, George."

Along with the difficulty in thinking clearly that accompanies shock, his jaw was still wired shut, and his lips shuddered along with the rest of him, so that it was doubly difficult to understand what he was saying. "Shoshmeee . . ."

"Yep, somebody shot you, but I shot them. You just relax, everything's going to be okay." I pressed on the jacket at his shoulder and calculated the miles back to Durant. If you continued down the Powder River Road to Tipperary, you could cut back up 201 and get to town faster than doubling back to 16 and the paved roads. I couldn't help but think that time was more important than macadam. Henry returned from the front of the truck where he had gone to raise Vic on the radio. "Henry's here. He was with me in the truck when we were trying to find you."

"Ya te he, George." He put his hand down on the dying boy's chest and smiled with his whole face. "You really had us scared there for a moment." George was bleeding and would continue to bleed until he got to an emergency room. The important thing now was to keep his mind working in a positive direction, to speak calmly, and to reassure him, so that he could counter the effects of the shock. We had to get him thinking about other things, and I truly believe I could have searched the world over and never found someone better at diversion than the man who now stood beside me. George's life hung on Henry's every word, and I watched as the dark eyes peered into the dilated pupils and scooped up a subject that would carry the young man to safety. "George, I need to talk to you about being an Indian . . ." He glanced toward me and whispered, "She will be here any minute." He looked back down. "George, if you are going to live on the reservation with us I have to teach you some things . . ." We transferred hands, and he held the makeshift bandage against George's crushed shoulder. He continued to talk to him in a hypnotic rumble. "We need to talk about finding a harmony and a wholeness within yourself that you can share with all your relations, but I need you to listen carefully because the things I am going to say to you are very important. You need to hear every word, yes?" The trembling subsided, and George actually nodded his head. "Good." Henry continued to smile. "You are going to make a good Indian."

I tried not to think of the rest of that old statement and pulled away to look back up the road in time to see Vic's unit come over the hill. She barely made it through the curve where George had gone off the road, cut her truck through the opening, and pulled up alongside the Bullet. With her sunglasses, she looked like a fighter pilot; she drove like one, too. "You shoot him?"

"No."

"Who did?"

"I'll tell you later. We need to get him into Durant. Now." She followed me around her truck and opened the passenger-side door, and we laid George across the backseat and trussed him up carefully with the seat belts. I looked at Henry as she rounded the truck and got in. I noticed he was holding something out to me. It was another .45-70. I stared at it for a moment, then back up to his face. His eyes were grim. We both knew the ending, and it was a bad one. "This land used to belong to the Espers . . ."

He didn't move. "Yes."

"You know who it is."

He nodded and then looked off into the distance of the shot. "Yes."

I took the bullet and stuffed it in the pocket of my jeans. "Get him in there alive, would you?"

"Do not worry about him." He climbed in and sat on the floor beside George. He continued to apply pressure to the wound. I closed the door as he turned back to me and looked through the open window. His eyes were a warning. "Be careful."

Vic looked at me questioningly, but I only nodded to her and slapped the side of the door in dismissal. I turned and walked back to the river and the rifle as she backed around the corner of my truck and rushed away to Durant. She took a left and continued down Powder River Road without my even telling her. I watched as the dust receded into the distance, and then the only sound was the water and a wandering band of Canada geese staging a late season getaway south. I watched them for a moment as they made their way along the water, keeping a steady pace between the darker hills on both sides of the storied river. The hills were contusion purple, and there were lengthy wounds of burnt-red scoria. It seemed like the whole valley was bleeding.

I picked up the Sharps at the cut bank and noticed a slight discoloration around the breech as I held it. It was still warm. I looked into the distance of the shot but could see nothing but rough terrain. I pulled the lever down, plucked the spent shell from the receiver, and replaced it with the live round Henry had given me. I tossed the empty into the river so that it would never be reloaded again. I crouched over the three inches of rushing water, cradled the rifle on my legs, and took a moment to wash George's blood from my hands. The blood mixed quickly with the clear, cold water and disappeared north toward Montana.

I crossed the river and kept a straight path, even as the current attempted to drift me northward in its direction. When I got to the other side, I paused to steady myself and to breathe away the nausea that had overtaken me. I looked back at the Bullet to triangulate my shot's trajectory, took a reading on the horizon, and began walking. I could feel the warmth of the setting sun on my back as I negotiated the clumps of sage, buffalo grass, and cactus, and I scared up a few western cottontails as I went. Just at the foothills, there was a small band of pronghorn antelope.

It didn't take as long as I had hoped. I stood there with the rifle in both hands and looked at the elevated section of tracks marking the coal freight line's direct path farther on east toward Gillette. It was lonely country and was a good spot, no matter what your intent, with a clear line through the wash that made for a perfect view of the river.

I kneeled down by the dark stains in the dirt and pressed my hand against the coarse texture of the land. It was sticky where blood had already begun drying into the earth. The Powder River country would accept moisture from any source, no matter what the cost. There wasn't a lot, but there was enough. I stood up and took another look around before checking the road. There was a depression on the ground where the shooter had fallen, and I could tell from the pattern of the blood that the shot had hit left. Vasque, size nine tracks were all over the place, and as I knelt to examine one I saw the faintest glint of brass underneath a patch of sage. I went over and picked up the empty casing. There was no need for gloves or pens, so I held the spent shell up to the fading sun and looked at the dented primer and the base, which read .45-70 GOVT. I was feeling a little sick again, so I stood and deposited the shell in my shirt pocket.

I followed the blood trail back to the access road and knelt by the last splatter. In the dry dust it looked black, just like the ones at the center of the road. A vehicle had been parked here long enough to leave traces of motor oil and transmission fluid; a vehicle with a pretty wide axle spread and, from the spin, it wasn't positraction. The tires were a narrow ranch ply, and the depressions told me it was heavy, approaching a ton at least. There was a single exhaust blow where it had been started: carbon and condensate, with a little oil mixed in. I was willing to bet it was an older truck, and I was also willing to bet that it was green.

The shadows were lengthening, and I had someplace to go. I worked my way back across the Powder and to my truck, leaned against the bed, and thought about what was going to happen in the next few hours. My stupor was broken by the radio.

Static. "Come in, Unit One." Static and a worried, "Walter, are you there?"

I swallowed, reached in, and grabbed the mic. "Yep. What's the word on George?"

Static. "They made it in; he's at the hospital right now."

"Alive?"

Static. "Yes. Ferg took the Espers over there just a few minutes ago. Turk is getting ready to leave now, on his way out to you."

"Don't send anybody out. I'm on my way in, but I've got to take care of a few things." I waited for a moment. "Is Lucian there?"

Static. "I think he's still in the back with Bryan."

"Will you get him for me?"

As I waited, I thought about how personal and ugly things had gotten over the last forty minutes. A breeze picked up a little in an attempt to scour the countryside. I wished it all the luck in the world.

Static. "What the hell do you mean don't send anybody out?"

I smiled. "Good to hear your voice, old man. How're you doin'?"

Static. "You woke me up to ask me that?"

I took a deep breath and laid the Cheyenne Rifle of the Dead on the seat. "Lucian, do you remember back when Michael Hayes killed himself?" A long pause.

Static. "What the hell does that have to do with the price of tea in China?"

"What kind of gun did he use?" There was another long pause.

Static. "Son of a bitch."

There were clouds at the mountains, and the snow pack reflected the sour-lemon sun into one of the most beautiful and perverse sunsets I had ever seen. The clouds were dappled like the hindquarters of an Appaloosa colt, and the beauty kicked just as hard. The head wind rattled the bare limbs of the cottonwoods as the longer branches swayed, and the remnants of grass and sage shuddered close to the ground. The buffeting of the wind against the truck reminded me that I had lost both of my jackets.

I started at the beginning, working with the most innocent facts and making my way toward the most damning. I thought about the history first. No one knew exactly why Michael Hayes had killed himself. I was just a teenager when it happened, but I remember her saying that he had killed himself in the tack shed. Someone at the time had said he had done it with a large-caliber rifle, and anyone who knew Mr. Hayes would be happy to tell you he was not the type to take half measures. I remember someone making the statement that his brains had been scattered all over the walls.

I thought about the night I had gone to her house for dinner, and how she had made me leave the rifle by the door. Could she have been responding to the weapon itself? I remembered how the dog had continually looked at the door that evening. Could he have seen the Old Cheyenne?

I thought about the Vasques, size nines, and about holding those lengthy, supple feet in my hands. I thought about how she was only a head shorter than me, and how that sandy hair hung past her shoulders. It could have easily been she in the early morning light at Dull Knife Lake, and it would have been easy for her to carefully wind her way through the twisted branches at the second crime scene.

I looked longingly at the bar as I passed. The lights were on, and there were a few aged pickups parked in equal distance around the building; in Wyoming, even trucks have personal space. Dena was in there, fleecing the local cowboys out of their $163 a week. I guess with the current events, she had decided to bag the Las Vegas tournament and take care of some of the local talent. It was well past the end of the working season; for some of the cowboys it would be the last check they would see until things picked back up in the spring. It would be a hard winter for them too, but for now, they were having fun losing their money to Dena Many Camps. I envied them the privilege.

When I got to Portugee Gulch at the Lower Piney, the gate to the house was open. I picked up the rifle and listened for drums, bells, or voices of any kind, but the only sound was the wind as it swept down, undulating along the foothills of the mountains. I stepped out of the truck, and the halogen spotlights of the courtyard tripped on. It took me a second to remember how they had done the same thing when I had brought her home a couple of nights ago. The red shale crunched under my feet as I approached the house. When I got to the door, it was unlocked. I pushed it all the way open and looked in at the empty living room. Things were a great deal as they were when I had made my hasty departure the other night. The blanket was still crumpled on the sofa, but the fire was dead and cold. I thought about the dog and looked behind me. I listened very carefully as I glanced across the openings of the archways to the dining room and looked down the hallway that led to the kitchen. This was where I had seen him the first time, but the only sound was the wind in the courtyard and a soft whistling coming from the still open flue of the fireplace.

I closed the door softly behind me and looked down at the Cheyenne Rifle of the Dead; it had taken on a much more articulate quality with the amount of handling it had endured in the last week. The oils from many hands had given its ghostly finish a peculiar gleam, and the wood and Italian beads shone with a warning that it had come to life once again. The small, gray feathers looked soft and invited my touch. I jacked the lever down and checked the round just above the sliding block and then pulled the lever back up. I leaned the rifle against the wall and slid the action back on the Colt, releasing a live round into the chamber of the .45. The hammer kicked back like a hitchhiker's thumb. The sound of the thing was enough to wake the dead. I looked back at the Sharps; I didn't want to take it, but I couldn't leave it behind.

I moved across the room and went up the couple of stairs into the dining room, still listening and looking for any signs of blood. I paused at the opening to the kitchen and raised the sidearm up into a ready position, holding the rifle behind me. The kitchen was empty, but I thought I heard a slight noise and looked around the room again. The copper pots and stainless steel appliances remained mute until the refrigerator kicked on with a low hum. I heard the noise again. It was like the shifting of weight against something solid. I glanced toward the mudroom, where the dog had been kept before. Something very large moved, and a second later he crashed into the door. He barked and snapped over and over again at the other side as he leaped and the center panel pressed out toward me. I raised the pistol, holding the rifle in reserve, but the latch held.

I waited a moment for my heart to return to its regular pattern. It was going to be tougher from here on; I didn't know the layout of the rest of the house. I went back out the opening to the kitchen, and there were four different hallways and two separate sets of stairs where I could continue my search. I had to think about where it was she might be, where it was that I would go if I were in her condition. I knew she was hurt and losing blood. Where would she go to doctor herself? There was no blood trail on the slick surface of the clay tile. She had not come this way, nor had she gone the other way into the living room or to the bedrooms beyond. She didn't appear to have come into this part of the house at all.

I went down the back hallway that led farther into the compound. It was lined with bookcases and opened into an atrium with hanging baskets and large pots filled with plants I didn't recognize. There were Turkish rugs and wicker furniture, and the air felt moist. Here was the pool, about fifteen feet long and seven feet wide, with a motorized unit that must have created an artificial current to swim against. I looked around at the lead framework that was filled with the panels of glass that made up the majority of the back side of the house. I moved toward the end of the right side of the room to an exterior door, put the Sharps under my arm, opened the door carefully, and looked around. The yard was filled with the same red shale as the front, and there was an opening that lead into an indoor riding arena that was about forty feet across the courtyard. There were depressions at the center where a truck had been driven. It was getting late, and the skies above had dimmed to where the strong angles of the sun set everything on dramatic edge. It would be dark very soon, and I had to find her before then.

I walked down from the slate steps and started to cross, keeping an eye on the surrounding windows and doors. When I got to the side of the large open doorway, I stopped and placed my back against the tin surface of the wall and propped the butt of the buffalo rifle carefully on the ground. The owl feathers moved very slightly, and I had a feeling the messengers were calling. It was the stable section of the arena, with horse stalls on both sides. There were opaque skylights that allowed a certain amount of the failing sunlight to spill through so I could see red shale tracks where a truck had crossed the concrete floor to the right. It was a large building, one of those prefabs at least fifty yards long and about twenty yards wide. Two horses came over to the gates to see if I had treats. One was a grade bay with Chinese eyes, and the other was a big thoroughbred, at least seventeen hands. The big one stuck his head through the stall door and reached his soft nose out to me. I reached up and petted him but continued to keep an eye on the opening ahead. When I got past him, he whiffled at me, and I turned to give him a dirty look.

Inside the large sanded space of the arena itself, there was a green Willys pickup, circa 1950, with the driver's-side door hanging open. It wasn't a '63 Ford, but it was close enough. They were Arizona plates, antique. It was parked in front of another opening, and I could see lights on in the hallway beyond. I stayed along the plywood partitions that kept a rider from getting brushed off as he circled the arena on horseback and worked my way around to the truck. There was dried blood everywhere, and a small cotton bag of .45-70s had spilled onto the floor. Wedged in the crease of the bench seat was a bloodstained, fake eagle feather. The ignition had been left on, although the motor was not running, and the dash bulbs had grown dimly yellow like the bug lights on an old-time porch. I turned back toward the opening and noticed that the architecture had changed in the hallway beyond.

This stable way was different from the others; it was assembled with rough-cut lumber and river stone. The corners of the wood were hand-worn, and the surface of the planks was weather-stained as if they had originally been outdoors. There was a row of dirty windows to the right. The dying light made angular, sharp-edged patterns down the walkway and reflected small seas of floating dust motes. Everything here was old, even the tools on the walls, and it looked like a small rural museum that had gone to seed. There were cobwebs in the overhanging rafters, and ring shank nails punched through the stained plywood where someone had not bothered to check their length when nailing down the tarpaper above. A fine patina of dirt had settled over everything and, except for the tang of blood, it smelled moldy, old, and mousy.

There were dark stains in the sand and a few on the stones that made up the walkway leading down the forty-foot hall. A Dutch door was open at the far end, and there was a light on. I stopped and listened; there was a brief crackle of what sounded like a radio frequency, but then it was gone. You could see a row of old saddles in there, but that was about all. I moved carefully past the abandoned stalls. Nothing had been in any of them for a long time, and I could just make out the scurrying movement of field mice as they busied themselves. I paused a little away from the door and noticed the blood on the galvanized handle. I started to speak. If I was going to be shot, it wasn't going to be by mistake. There wasn't any sound, so I inclined my head a little bit to see more of the room. "Avon calling . . ."

She laughed, a wispy, hollow laugh like air escaping from a tire, and the sound went through me. I turned slightly to the right and leaned in a little more and, through the dim light of the dusty, forty-watt bulb, I could see her. She was sitting on a series of wooden steps, the kind that grooms use to assist foxhunters in mounting their horses. They were a dark, hunter green with gold trim and looked as if they hadn't been used in a while. I couldn't remember the last foxhunt in the county, but I remembered the white-painted fences, and I remembered the glasses of pulpy lemonade that Vonnie's mother had brought out to us when my father had shod their horses. She had put Maraschino cherries in the bottom of each glass, and I remembered how her hand had lingered on my father's arm as he had taken his.

Vonnie was wearing a pair of dark coveralls that had been unzipped and peeled down to her waist and tied with the sleeves there. She had on a pair of Vasque hiking boots, and the blood had dribbled on them too. I wondered how she was still conscious. Then I noticed the Sharps buffalo rifle that was propped up between her knees with the butt resting on the floor. It was angled slightly in my direction. I knew how heavy the things were, but those fingers still wrapped around foregrip and trigger with a terrible determination. I could see that the massive hammer was pulled back and the rifle was ready to fire.

I eased the rest of the way into the room. She was against the wall, and there was a counter to her left where her shoulder was. The surface was strewn with medical supplies, most of them for horses. There were blood-saturated gauze pads, plastic bottles of topical antibiotics, and even a couple of syringes. They looked as if they had been pushed aside with a sweeping gesture when she had lost interest in the procedure. There was also a police scanner sitting on the table and, from the illuminated dial, I could see that it was set to our frequency of 155.070.

More saddles rested on log racks to her right, and the layers of grime made it clear that they hadn't been disturbed in years. The ceiling was low, and I had to lean to one side to see around the naked light bulb that hung there. The glare from the proximity of the bulb was irritating. I was standing in the only door in the room, and there were no windows. There wasn't anywhere to go, for either of us. I looked down and studied her face and could feel the sympathy twinge in my own. The damage to the left side of her head was only slightly evident in the tangle of blood-matted hair that stuck to the side of her face and strung down past her shoulder where the blood continued to drip. I was pretty sure her ear was gone and could only guess as to the extent of the rest of the damage.

"Hello, Walter." She stared at the automatic in my hand that pointed down at the wooden plank floor and then to the Sharps that hung loosely in my other hand. "Are you going to shoot me again?"

I glanced down at the hammer of the Sharps she held but quickly looked back up at her eyes. With the dim light, I could barely make them out and wasn't sure if they were dilated or constricted. "No." I slowly lowered the hammer, placed the .45 back in my holster, and pulled the snap over and clicked it shut. I raised the Cheyenne rifle muzzle up and leaned it against the wall beside the door. "It's department policy to only shoot people once a day; it's a budgetary thing."

"I'm glad to hear that." She laughed. "At least what I can hear . . ."

"Got your ear?"

Her blood-covered hand started to come up but then rested back on the rifle beside the set trigger; if it had already been pulled, it wasn't going to take much to set the thing off. "Yes."

I watched her hands for a moment. She was hurt and the effect was gruesome, but her movements were still sharp and, so far, the loss of blood hadn't robbed her of any of her mechanical skills. "Pretty impressive. Getting hit like that would knock most people down and out."

"It did." Her eyes twitched in response to the wound, but she rolled her head back a little so that I could see more of her eyes. "I was out for a minute or two . . ."

"Pretty tough." I waited for a moment, but she didn't say anything. "We're a pair, aren't we? You with your ear and me with mine?"

She nodded slightly, smiled, and the effect of the bright white teeth against the blooded gore made my heart trip. "I don't think this relationship is going to work out." The smile broadened and then relaxed, as the muscles in her face must have disturbed the ear. "You play too rough."

"Vonnie . . ."

"I'm glad you're here, though. It wouldn't have been right if you hadn't been."

I nodded and stepped to the side just enough to get the light bulb out of my face. "You've lost a lot of blood."

She nodded slightly and glanced at the medical supplies scattered on the counter. "Not much of a Florence Nightingale, am I?" A moment passed. "I suppose my talents lie elsewhere."

As I started to move again, the muzzle of the Sharps leveled up between us and hung there. "No." I stopped, still too far away to grab the gun. She leaned a little, the slope of her back resting against the wall. "We could just . . . talk."

"Well, we've got an awful lot to talk about."

I waited, and after a while her face shifted a little, saving me the view. "Why couldn't I have met you a day earlier?" She readjusted her weight against the wall and turned a little farther. Almost none of the damage showed now, except that the blood continued to saturate her thermal top. "Maybe none of this would have happened."

"Vonnie . . ."

"One day earlier, that's all we would have needed."

"I don't . . ."

"Twenty-four hours, and maybe I wouldn't have made all this mess." She glanced over at the medical supplies. "Why you? Why did all this have to do with you?"

"It's my job."

She looked back at me. "Yes." Her attention dropped to the barrel of the buffalo rifle. "We all have our jobs, don't we?"

I tried changing the subject. "What's the story on the feathers?"

"Oh . . ." She blinked and refocused. "A bit of dramatic effect, symbolic really . . . life and death . . . I had hoped that the eagle feather would heal Melissa, the breath of life to make her better."

"You took a lot of chances placing them."

She didn't move. "That was the hard part, seeing them up close . . ."

I thought about not telling her, but we were telling the truth and maybe it would keep her going. "They aren't real. The eagle feathers, they're fake."

Her eyes glazed over, and the stillness of her was betrayed only by a sharp nod. "Well, doesn't that fit . . ."

I glanced down at her feet. "The boots?"

"I was in the store when George was buying his. We have the same shoe size and I thought it might be handy later."

"You knew where he was going?"

"I told him and his brother that they were welcome to fish at the old family place on the Powder if they wanted to." She glanced at the scanner. "I also knew it was where you thought he was going." Her eyes returned to the rifle. "Is he going to live?"

"Probably." I waited what seemed like a long, long while. "We need to get you into town . . ."

"Walter, don't."

I waited. "Okay." I looked around and gave it a resigned quality. "Why are we in here?"

"Why not here? This is where everything happens." I looked at her, hoping that if I kept my eyes on her, she wouldn't drift. She smiled just a little, started to laugh, and then stopped herself. She kept her eyes away from me. "He built it himself. He never built anything else in his life; he just wasn't good at it. But we had this older cowboy who was working for us at the time who helped him . . ."

I smiled. "Jules Belden?"

Her eyes returned to me, but her head didn't move. "Yes." She stayed like that. "He's still around?"

"Yep, he's still around." I started formulating a plan to keep her talking. If I could get her to go long enough, then maybe I had a chance.

She was looking into my eyes when I focused on her again. "He gave me quarters."

"Me too."

She laughed the wispy laugh. "He used to drink when he was here, and that's why Father finally fired him, but he was a good carpenter."

I looked around. "So he and your dad built this?"

"Yes." She glanced at the tack. "When I decided to have the arena built, I just didn't have the nerve to tear it all down, so I left this part." I waited. "I still see him, sometimes . . ."

I watched as her eyes dulled a little. "Your father?"

"Yes, I sometimes see him. I'll be out riding in the arena and I'll look over and there he stands by the door, waiting for me."

I couldn't help but laugh. "I've been having a little problem along those lines myself lately."

The eyes narrowed. "I'm not being funny."

"Neither am I."

She continued to look at me but then broke it off to glance around. "You see him too?"

I shrugged. "No, I've been seeing Indians." I placed my hands in my pants' pockets, so she could see that I wasn't going to try anything. Yet.

She gestured toward the buffalo rifle. "Is that their gun you've been carrying around?" She continued to study it. "The one you shot me with?" She didn't show any signs of weakening, and I was beginning to think this was going to take awhile. "It's beautiful. What was it you called it?"

"What?"

She continued to look at it. "The rifle?"

"Oh." The barrel of her Sharps had shifted a little. "The Cheyenne Rifle of the Dead." She nodded, and I smiled back. "It's haunted."

"By the Indians?"

343

"The Old Cheyenne."

"Why?"

I studied her and tried to think if this was a good line for our conversation to take. "The Old Cheyenne stay near the rifle, and every once in a while they get the urge to take somebody back to the Camp of the Dead with them."

"The Camp of the Dead." It gave me time to look into her eyes. The pupils were dilated, but it was difficult to tell if it was from trauma or from the darkness of the room, or both. I watched her very carefully as I spoke and noted the continuing tremors in her long fingers. "So, the Old Cheyenne have come to get me, huh?"

"I started to leave the Old Cheyenne inside your door, but you said you didn't allow guns in the house."

I wondered how long it would take for her to get to the fact that her father had killed himself, probably in here. I looked at the wood behind her head, but the planks had been replaced. It had to be here, but I didn't want to discuss her father's suicide with her as she sat there with the loaded and cocked buffalo rifle in her hands. I didn't say anything, and I didn't move. She gestured gently with the Sharps. "This is the one he did it with." I still remained silent. "They really are exquisite guns, aren't they?"

It seemed safe enough. "Well made."

"Yes, well made." She looked back up from the barrel. "I was thirteen." She puzzled for a moment, nodded, and then stared off into space as more blood dripped from the side of her face. "Did you ever wonder why it was he did it?"

I lied. "No."

She was looking at me again. "You're lying. You're afraid I'm going to shoot myself."

"The thought had crossed my mind."

"You ever wonder why he did it here?"

It seemed like an odd question, but as long as she was talking. "I think you said it was because he didn't want to make a mess in the house?"

She looked around. "He didn't, but this place had special meaning for him."

"Because he built it . . ."

She was perfectly still. "More than that."

I looked at her, and the pieces started to fall into place. "What happened, Vonnie?"

"You're a smart guy, Walter. I bet you can figure it out without all the horrid details." She took a deep breath. "Daddy's little girl . . . I was nine years old, I mean for the physical act. It started a long time before, though." She looked back to me. "Can you imagine?" Her eyes welled. "No, I don't suppose you can." I towered there like a stacked-up wreck and watched as tears fell from her dull eyes, diluting the blood on her face. I could feel their heat from where I stood. "I hated him. How could you not hate somebody that would do that to you? Somebody you trusted, somebody who was supposed to protect you? Someone who was supposed to love you." She paused, and some of the heat died. "I tried. I really tried to have a life with a husband, family, children, and dogs even . . . I tried, but no matter how long or how hard . . . No matter how much therapy . . . I couldn't get past it. No matter how strong I'd be, I'd remember him. I'd remember this place and what he did." She had run out of air with a hissing finality, and I listened as she breathed. I waited as she continued to look at the rifle that leaned against the wall. "He didn't kill himself because of me . . . I didn't even get that satisfaction." She sniffed and winced in pain. "He did it because my mother was going to tell . . . I moved back after a lot of years to take care of her and to try and get my life back from him, from here . . ." Something struck her as humorous. "I came back so I could hate him with her."

"Vonnie . . ."

"And then, when Melissa . . . When it happened to her? She's a child, Walt, just like I was . . . I thought surely now, now there'd be some kind of punishment, some kind of justice. Something for her, something for me. But they got off. Hardly any time served." Her eyes turned toward me. "I didn't let him off . . . I couldn't let them." I started to move but the barrel of the rifle was still there, and I had to wait and make it count. After a moment, she spoke again. "So, do you think the Old Cheyenne can get me in here?"

I cleared my throat. "I don't think they're out to get you."

She half-nodded. "That's too bad, I rather hoped they would be. But maybe I just don't make the cut, huh?"

I took a deep breath. I thought about how it is a woman's lot to be dismissed by men. "I think they could hardly do better."

Her voice was small and distant. "Thank you." The little corner of her mouth kicked up again, and the barrel of the Sharps shifted a little and came back closer to her chin. I took my hands from my pockets and gauged the distance to be about eight feet. We looked at each other for a while, and it's possible she was reading my intent. "I don't think anything will ever get me here again." She was learning to smile with the undamaged side of her face. "But I suppose they can get you anywhere." She paused for a moment, and I thought I might have a chance. "You understand, don't you? I mean, you said that a part of you wished you had done it?"

"I think that a lot of people feel that way."

"You know, I have a hard time telling which part of you I like most: your smile, your sense of humor, or the fact that you lie so poorly."

"What do you want me to say, Vonnie? I don't think the county's going to have a parade for you . . ." Her eyes stayed steady. "There's a difference between talking about it and doing it."

She looked sad. "I was hoping we were past the moral portion of the conversation." I wanted to hold her, to patch the ear up, and to make it all better. "Please, let's not talk about what people deserve."

"I guess it doesn't make much difference, does it?"

"Not now." Her finger twitched on the trigger. "Walter, I need you to not look at me . . ."

"Vonnie, don't do it." There was a long pause.

I froze the image of her then, with her head turned just slightly in the light of the dim, forty-watt bulb, the angle of her head accenting the fine bone structure of her jaw and the strong muscle tone of her throat. It might have been the night I saw her at the bar, the morning with the pancakes, our one date, on the street that day, angry at the hospital, or now.

She said it like it was a statement about the weather. "I love you."

It was my turn to look away, just as she knew I would. My breath was short, and my voice refused to cooperate and burned in my throat. For a split second I studied one of the saddles, the worn appearance of the horns and curled surfaces of the rosettes where the touch of human and horse had at first softened the leather but where the man had left it to stiffen and dry. The dust on this particular saddle had been brushed as she had passed, probably by one of the sleeves that were tied at her waist. The leather surface underneath had held a warm glow that promised romance and freedom, and you could almost feel the gathering of equine muscles as they reached out and grasped the rotation of the earth.

I looked closer at a small spot on the cantle and at a singular drop of blood that had landed there. Blood drops at a uniform volume of .05 milliliters and in a tiny ball. Upon striking a surface, the blood leaves a pattern that will be dependant on the type of surface it falls upon. Splatters. On the smooth leather of the saddle, the drop had remained relatively intact with only one scalloped droplet having escaped at eighty degrees and perpendicular in direction.

I'm sure the blast in the little room was deafening, but I didn't hear it.

EPILOGUE

I didn't go into work the next day, or the day after that, or even the week after that. I've been drinking a lot, not with a conscious effort but more as a pastime. It's a nicer place to drink, since Red Road Contracting finished up. I don't think I drove them off, but maybe I did. There's still a lot to do in the cabin; I think I was making them nervous.

The new deck is my favorite part. It's about as big as the house and goes out the back door toward the hills. There's an opening in the middle where they said I could plant a tree in the spring, but for now it's where I toss the empty beer cans. It's an easy shot from the lawn chair, which I placed against the log wall of the house, and my sheepskin coat keeps me warm enough. The cooler is right beside the chair, so I don't have to get up much. Sometimes, at night, the beer freezes, but I just wait for it to thaw the next morning.

Periodically, vehicles come up the driveway; some of them are official and some of them aren't. The DCI Suburban was one of the official ones, and they brought the Bullet back sans bullet holes. They left the keys on the counter, and she sits out there pawing the ground, waiting. I guess Ferg got a new truck. Vic came by once, but now she just calls and talks to the phone machine. I've developed a tactic for dealing with these drive-by visits. No matter what time of day it is or what I might be doing, whenever I hear somebody coming up the driveway, I just step off the deck and start walking toward the hills. In a couple of minutes, I can be in those hills. Sometimes I walk; sometimes I just pick out a rock and sit. Nobody stays very long, but I lose track of time out there, and sometimes I remember coming out when it's still light, only to look around and find that it's dark. Sometimes, it's the other way around, and I get to watch the sun come up.

People leave food, but nobody ever leaves beer so, every once in a while, I have to make the run into the outskirts of Durant to buy it at the Texaco station near the highway. I haven't shaved in a while, so the kid that works there doesn't know me, or pretends that he doesn't.

I have a friend that showed up after a few days. One morning when I woke up in the lawn chair, he was lying out at the end of the back pasture, just at the sage. He didn't make any move to come in closer but just sat out there all day watching me. He would circle around the house, only to return to the sage after a while. I didn't think he meant any harm; like me he just didn't choose to go anywhere else. The next trip into the Texaco station, I bought dog food and left it in a bowl at the edge of the deck, along with water. Every morning it was gone and, after a few days, he slept there, as long as I didn't move much, which was okay, because I wasn't moving much these days. He had lost a little weight since escaping from Vonnie's mudroom, and Vic mentioned in one of her telephone reports that the Game and Fish guys had had quite a rodeo when he ran off.

One day, Henry's truck came up the drive and, as I started my usual retreat to the back forty, the dog ambled along after me. When I sat on one of my favorite rocks, he came over and sat down not too far away, and we waited for Henry to leave the house together. I reached over and rubbed my hand across the dog's big head, and he looked up at me. He had sad eyes, and it was as if he had had enough, too. As I petted him, he leaned on my leg. He really was a big brute, with a shoulder spread as wide as the trunk of my body. The hair was curly on his back with all kinds of reddish swirls and swoops. It looked like a bad toupee.

Cady called, but I knew her schedule and would call back and leave vague messages with her secretary while she was either in the law library, taking depositions, or doing whatever lawyers do when their secretaries answer the phone. It was odd to think of my daughter with a secretary, so I just kind of thought of Patti with an *i* as a babysitter who talked with a funny, South Philadelphia accent.

Vic called at about five-thirty at the end of each day with a report of ongoing concerns. "Hello, shithead. This is the person who's doing your job for you as you lay out there and grow increasingly fat and stupid in your nest of depression and self-pity . . ." The messages always started that way.

"We had a drive-by egging on the middle school, which leads me to believe there may have been an accomplice . . ." I nodded. Sound detective work.

"Vandalism was reported at the old stockyard. Reporting person said someone had moved his irrigation system twice in the last month, and this time the irrigation wheel-line assembly was broken. The attending officer questioned reporting person as to what the fuck he was doing irrigating in November? Answer, came there none . . ." I nodded some more.

"There was an official protest made as to the language used by said attending officer that was deemed profane and inconsiderate of the station and age of the reporting person, shortly after the irrigation incident . . ." I shrugged. It was to be expected.

"The officer is currently available for any and all comment . . ." I bet.

"Caller requested an officer to go tell her neighbor to turn his radio down. Caller would not give her name, and said she did not know her neighbor's name. The attending officer did find a handsome, young dentist working on a car stereo in his Land Rover. It was NPR out of Montana, and the attending officer informed the dentist that he could go ahead and listen to whatever he damn well pleased as loud as he damn well pleased and to not pay any attention to the witch next door . . ." I knew Bessie Peterson, and this was far from over.

"Further complaints of noise were duly noted . . ." Um-hmm . . .

"Jim Keller returned from his hunting trip, and rumor has it he and the Mrs. are going to be going their separate ways. Personally, I think it's the best thing that could happen to Bryan."

I nodded.

"Department received a memo faxed over from the hospital asking for the formal release of Mr. George Malcolm Esper. Jesus . . . Malcolm . . . I'd try and run away, too. I signed it and got Ruby to fax it back over before the little fucker escaped again . . ."

There was a long pause before the next one and with a soft and melancholy quality that I had never heard from her before. "Attending officer thought about filing a missing persons bulletin for a sad, overweight, self-deprecating, yet strangely charming sheriff today. The officer thought it might be of interest to the missing person that said officer had turned down not one, but two high-paying, high-profile jobs because she guessed she'd just lost interest in being anywhere else . . ." My eyes welled up a bit, and I waited.

"Walt, you need to come back to work, you're not fit for anything else . . ." Another pause. "Ruby misses you, Ferg's bored, Lucian is about to irritate the shit out of all of us because I don't think he sees his position as being temporary, and Dorothy says she's ready to come out there and kick your ass but doesn't know if she should bring coleslaw?" There was another long pause.

"It's been almost two weeks, and that's long enough. I just thought that I should tell you that this is my last call because I'm starting to feel like an enabler . . . If you want to know what's going on in the kingdom, you're going to have to come out and fight a few dragons." Another pause. "Anyway . . . the attending officer misses you." She hung up, and my last contact with the outside world went dead.

Along with one of his food drops, Henry had left a message on the back of the manila envelope that contained the last photographs of Cody Pritchard. "There is lasagna in the refrigerator along with supplies to make sandwiches and a six-pack of canned iced tea." Fingered in the dust on the smooth surface of the piano lid were the words, PLAY ME. I ate the lasagna.

This morning a maroon van bounced up the driveway, and it was only when I got back and discovered there was a frozen box of turkey Hot Pockets, one ceremonial beer, and the Cheyenne Rifle of the Dead, that I remembered it was Thanksgiving. The rifle was lying across my recliner, looking much as it had when I had left it in the tack shed. I spent the rest of the morning trying not to look at it; but, by lunchtime, when I had come in from the deck to eat a Hot Pocket with the beer of temptation, I leaned against the counter and looked at the .45-70. A thought occurred to me, and I fished around in the pocket of my coat and pulled out one of Omar's cartridges. I walked over and picked up the rifle and lowered the falling block with the lever. Empty. I guess Lonnie didn't trust me, either. I placed the round in the breech and then pulled the lever back up. I know it was my imagination, but the rifle felt much heavier.

I took a moment to think about the Old Cheyenne and how revenge doesn't ever fit when there aren't any bad guys. It wasn't that revenge was a dish best served cold, it was that it was a dish best not served at all. I thought about what it was the Old Cheyenne really wanted; it wasn't hard to figure out. The dead just want the same thing as the living: understanding.

I thought about how the two women's situations were alike, and how different the two cultures' reactions were. When Melissa had met this crisis in her life, her family and friends had restored her, but when Vonnie had faced abuse, she had met silence and recrimination, and the violation done to her child's soul had been swept under the Turkish rugs. Granted, it could be said that it was the times and not the culture that had dictated these reactions, and I hoped that was true. I really did.

I walked through the open door and onto the deck with the rifle in my hands. The sun was headed off to the west, and I could barely make out its faint glow through the heavy, ironclad bottoms of the clouds. I watched as the first flakes began drifting down; they would pile up against the hills, and the familiar landmarks of the ranch would gently disappear.

The dog turned to look at me from the far side of the deck but, when he saw the rifle, he began to rise and growl. I wasn't quite sure what to do, so I just stood there. He moved off and settled over the edge, periodically raising his head to look at me again, register a disapproving growl, and disappear.

I crossed to the lawn chair and sat down with the buffalo rifle across my lap. I reached over and flipped open the top of the cooler to find nothing. I was out and, if I wanted another beer, I was going to have to make the run. I sat there and looked at the hills and the increasingly gloomy world. I looked down at the Sharps.

I thought about what Dena Many Camps had said when she had run her fingers over the owl feathers and had quickly unbraided her hair; that there are spirits that linger near this ghost weapon and that they can easily take away the souls of those still living for the enjoyment of their society. I hoped the Old Cheyenne had come and gotten Vonnie, taking her to the Camp of the Dead. She was damn fine company, and she deserved better than she had gotten in this world. I strained my eyes into the distance and saw her there with them, and she was laughing and pulling a wayward slip of butterscotch back with two fingers. I saw her there along with Lonnie's legs. Maybe half truths were all you got in this life.

When I looked back down, I saw that the dog was looking into the snow where I had been staring, and the wind narrowed his eyes until he looked back at me. Just as I had thought all along, he could see them too.

I listened to the Canada geese as they honked their way south. They only flew about thirty feet off the ground, and I could hear the whir of their wings as they passed overhead. Then the ceremonial Rainier I had drunk earlier overtook me, and I fell asleep.

I awoke to the rattling sound of somebody slamming a hated yet familiar vehicle door, and he entered through the open front one of the cabin. It sounded like he was setting things on the counter and in the refrigerator. He made a number of trips and, through the open kitchen window, the smell of turkey and dressing joined with the cold air of the late afternoon.

There was a minuscule break in the clouds, and the thin sliver became a deep red as the sun started to drop over the mountains. I pulled my hat even farther down as the dog looked over the scattering angels of snow that had collected on the deck and on me. He rested his head on the edge and looked at me with the expectation of retreat glowing in his dark eyes, but I wasn't moving. I was too tired. Chances were Henry would leave the food and go, but I have to say that I was growing irritated as he lingered in my kitchen and arranged things in preparation for the movable feast. I waited, but he didn't go away.

After a while, he stepped onto the deck from the back of the cabin, and the beast growled a low and resonant warning. "Wahampi . . ." Things got quiet again; evidently, the dog had a strong Sioux streak. I didn't move, in hopes that he would leave, but that hope faded and the lid on the cooler squealed as over 220 pounds sat on it. Damn Indians, you never could get rid of them on Thanksgiving.

I could hear more geese flying over as he popped the tops on two of the canned iced teas and handed me one. I didn't take it at first, but he just held it there against my hand until I did. The honking continued and, with the beat of their downdraft, it sounded like every goose in the high plains was leaving. "You know, Lonnie told me something about those geese . . ."

I waited awhile, but finally responded. "Yep?"

"You know how they always fly in that *V*?"

"Yeah?"

"And one side of the *V* is always longer?"

He waited forever, and there was nothing else I could do. "Why is that?"

"Because . . . there are more geese on one side than the other. Um-hmm, yes it is so . . ."